Ciel Pierlot

BLUEBIRD

ANGRY ROBOT

ANGRY ROBOT
An imprint of Watkins Media Ltd

Unit 11, Shepperton House
89-93 Shepperton Road
London N1 3DF
UK

angryrobotbooks.com
twitter.com/angryrobotbooks
It's a bird! It's a plane!

An Angry Robot paperback original, 2022

Cover by Tom Shone
Edited by Simon Spanton and Travis Tynan
Set in Meridien

ISBN 978 0 85766 966 7
Ebook ISBN 978 0 85766 967 4

Printed and bound in the United Kingdom by TJ Books Ltd.

9 8 7 6 5 4 3 2 1

MIX
Paper from
responsible sources
FSC® C013056
www.fsc.org

Dedicated to Determamfidd, whose incredible work inspired me to start writing again.

PROLOGUE
Fire and Frigate

Arson is easier to commit than people make it out to be.

Even in the winter rains the fire burns brighter than a star, the plumes of flame licking at the storm clouds overhead, smoke consuming what's left of the sky. The blaze is far away, back in the heart of the city, but the sounds of sirens are still faintly blaring, red lights flickering in the distance as first responders rush to the scene to salvage whatever they can. There will be nothing left for them to find.

Traxi made sure of it.

She stands on a landing pad at the edge of the city, rain soaking into her clothes as she stares up at the frigate moored in front of her. The hard drive hidden in her jacket burns a hole in her pocket. Adrenaline is still coursing through her veins, hotter than the fire behind her. Her shoulders tremble from the cold and the wet and the *thrill*.

"If you don't have money," the man standing on the gangplank tells her, "then beat it."

A tentative step closer puts her under the protection of the frigate's looming stern, keeping fresh torrents of rain off her. "Please. I don't take up much space, I promise. I can work on the journey to pay my passage off world."

He picks up a supply crate and dumps it inside the ship's hold. Is it her imagination or are the sirens getting closer? There's no time for negotiation, no time to dig up money from some cache she doesn't have. One errant minute will result in her head adorning the planet's newest spire.

She has nothing to give him. Her job just went up in flames, her home isn't safe, her family – she glances over her shoulder for a moment, hoping, pointlessly, that she won't be alone. But of course there's no one behind her. All she does have is one hard drive that will kill trillions of people if it's ever cracked open. She promised herself, when she lit that first brick of firestarter in her now-burning office, that she wasn't going to be that person anymore. Their blind, obedient little killer.

"Please," she says again, grinding her teeth. "Sir, just to the nearest port. I want to–"

"I don't have time for vagrants."

The rain roars louder than ever.

"Sir..." Is he what she thinks he is? One of the people she's looking for? It's a gamble, but what else could she call the past twenty-four hours of her life if *not* a gamble? She sticks her left arm out. "I'll show you mine if you show me yours."

He turns around and gives her a second look. Grunts. Puts down the crate he was about to carry in. He rolls his left sleeve to reveal pale blue skin and a small tattoo adorning his wrist. A little bird drawn in white ink, frozen mid-flight, hovering just over his pulse point.

He grabs her offered hand and yanks her sleeve back.

Cold rain drips onto her exposed wrist, her skin as blue as his but entirely blank.

He draws in a sharp breath. "You're a filthy liar."

"I'm a filthy *recruit*. I want to help – I want to stop them. I've seen what they can do, I know how they work. That makes me valuable, doesn't it?" She yanks her hand back. "And I'm now also someone who could blow your cover from here to atmo if you don't let me on your ship."

To her surprise, he laughs. It's a grunt of a chuckle, but a laugh all the same. "Consorting with one of my sort's just as likely to get you tossed in lock up with me. You've got guts, kid, I'll give you that. Welcome aboard, then. And I don't hold with that 'sir' nonsense. My name's Mohsin."

She shakes his hand, once, twice. "Thank you."

Her first steps aboard the frigate feel more solid than any ground she's stood upon before. The ship's engines are making the floors thrum with power, ready to leap into the skies in a moment's notice, ready to skate through the stars like she never has before. To leave everything behind. The good and the bad. Her sister and her job. All turning to a trail of stardust behind her.

What would it be like to be as free as this frigate ship?

"What's your name, then?" Mohsin asks once he's closed up the main hatch behind her.

She smiles for the first time in days. "I don't know yet."

CHAPTER ONE
Red Dock

"Twenty kydis says you can't hit that!" a patron yells over the raucous cheering.

Rig stands on top of a chair that's leaning precariously against the bar, gun in one hand, mug of she's-not-sure-what in the other.

The neon lights of Red Dock shine brightly through the haze. When Rig breathes in, her lungs are thick with a mix of crystal smoke and a colorful assortment of gases from the refineries built into the outer walls. In the packed atrium, the air presses in on the thousands of people milling about on this floor alone, to say nothing of the twelve other floors of the spaceport.

The dense shopping area is filled with the sounds of bargaining, gossiping, and drunken slurring, all in a cacophony of different languages beyond just Deit-Standard. Even from her stationary perch inside a publica, she can smell three different types of sweet pastry being fried up, one made with pickled Ascetic plums that have an almost sickly aroma.

Maybe she can bribe one of the many *ludicrously* drunk people around her into buying her one.

"You're on!" she cries in response to the challenge. "Prepare to eat your words and also my cute blue ass!"

The crowd cheers. Half of them are so far into their cups they don't even know what's going on. They cheer simply because everyone else is. The beauty of drunken solidarity.

Her accuser is a hulking Oriate with what must be twice the usual number of spikes growing out of his skin. He crosses his arms menacingly. "Your mouth is writing a check your gun can't cash!" he taunts. That's not even how that phrase goes; yeesh, what an idiot. "Do it with both eyes closed and then I'll pay you!"

Rig throws back her drink, tosses the mug over her shoulder – there's another gleeful cheer as it smashes into something – and aims her weapon. The target is a can on a shelf at the other end of the crowded publica. Its patrons part faster than the wind.

Rig lines up the shot.

Closes her eyes.

Her gun is steady in her hands, familiar, a good weight. All it takes is a gentle squeeze of the trigger and...

Crack!

The excited cries hit her ears before she opens her eyes and sees that her bullet has pierced the can.

"Hah!" She points a finger at her accuser. "Eat that, you bastard!"

A frown curdles on his face. He grabs someone's glass out of their hand and balances it on the top of his head, spreading his arms in triumph because he must surely think he's called her bluff now.

"Double or nothing!" he declares.

A murmur runs through the crowd and Rig pauses.

"You know that's risky, right? We're talking insides on the outside, blood, murder, death, deathy-ness... deathing?" she asks. "Just pay up already and admit I'm fabulous."

He laughs, clearly drunk off his ass. "You said you could hit *anything*! You a liar?"

Someone in the press of people yells, "Just pay up!"

"Come on!" he insists. "Do it!"

If she misses, she's doubtful anyone in Red Dock will want

her hide for it. This place isn't exactly known for tight security or a desire to obey the law. Besides, she's good at what she does. Or at least that's her usual brag. She double-checks her grip, makes sure that she's aiming steady, and scrunches up her face in concentration as she gauges how sober she is. Sober enough.

Alright then.

Let it never be said that she is a coward. Actually, many people *have* said that, but not today. She raises her gun again and takes as careful aim as she can manage.

Crack!

The can is blasted off the Oriate's head and the publica descends into a roar of cheering and mindless noise.

With a sour expression, the Oriate pulls out his link and opens up a kydis transfer. Rig's link is similarly mounted on her wrist, attached to her glove, and all it takes is push of a button to exchange the money.

Her link chimes as it goes through, and she tips an invisible hat at the Oriate. "Pleasure doing business with you."

He just glares. She'll take that as a compliment.

"Next round is on my good friend here!" she declares to the crowd before slipping off her makeshift throne and vanishing into the throng of people.

She slides into a stool on the far side of the bar, next to an older woman who's sipping a glass of something that smells like a swamp mixed with silverite fumes. At her signal, the bartender passes Rig another round of whatever it was she had been drinking previously. She'd ordered an ale, but she doesn't actually know her ales that well and she'd just pointed at the nearest tap without looking.

"You were *quite* loud," the old woman next to her says, sniffing disdainfully into her glass.

Rig winces. "Sorry, ma'am."

She gives Rig a long, stern glare before finally conceding, "But you are a good shot. What faction are you?"

"Er. Pyrite." *Formerly.*

"Hrm. Do you know why you call yourselves Pyrite?"

"...Cause of the god? Cause pyrite crystals spark fire? Cause shiny things are cool?"

"Because you're all fools digging for gold where there's only dirt." The woman gives her another hard look. "I'm from Ascetic. We could do with a shot like you, if you ever felt like joining up with a *proper* faction. You know, one that doesn't spend all its time in spires, mindlessly tinkering."

"Thank you for the offer, ma'am," Rig replies, because although she's got a blanket dislike of factions, this woman in particular hasn't done anything worthy of rudeness. "But although I can't defend Pyrite, tinkering as a whole can be quite respectable, if you do it with enough smart-assery. And I'm happy right where I am."

Which is nowhere in particular.

Plus she's got no desire to go back to any one of those three galaxy-conquering, warmongering, merry bands of bastards. Ascetic, Ossuary, and Pyrite. Lying bastards, terrifying bastards, and bastards out to get her. In that order. They've been cutting the galaxy up like a pie for ten thousand bloody years and she's much happier kicking them in the shins whenever the opportunity presents itself.

The bartender scooches over and takes away Rig's drink, instead passing her the tab. "Mohsin is ready for you, miss. Best not to make him wait."

"Thank you very much, good sir."

She transfers the proper amount of kydis, with a tip, before giving the old woman a casual salute. It's no crisp, militaristic, proper factioned salute, but it's good enough for a place like Red Dock.

The bartender jerks his thumb towards the back door.

Rig steps through and instantly finds herself in an elevator. She rockets up maybe five or six floors before stepping out.

This place has none of the clatter of the main publica, the

noise replaced by softer music and a low buzz of less rowdy conversation. Wall-to-wall carpeting, hovering chandeliers, and the sound of cards being shuffled for gambling addicts, all dimly lit with red light fixtures. There's a game of Ascetic roulette being played at a green velvet table to her left and a man setting up holo-pong to her right. A grin spreads across her face as her boots cross from the metal elevator floor to sink into the plush carpets like candyfloss.

She weaves her way through the fancy-shmancy super-secret back-upper room and takes a seat across from a man dressed in a brown leather duster.

"Heya, Mohsin," she says. "Good to see your ugly mug again."

He snorts in amusement. "I see you haven't changed a bit."

"I've gotten prettier."

He snaps his fingers at the bodyguard standing by his side. The guard is a Zazra, sporting the distinctive pointed ears and black facial markings of that species. Makes sense. She's seen Mohsin beat the crap out of enough people to know that he doesn't need *protection*. But Zazra have other specialties.

The Zazra man holds out one of his hands. How polite of him. "May I read you?"

She nods and tugs her sleeve back, sticking her arm out. "Yeah, go ahead."

Zazra hands are shaped the same as Rig's basic five-fingered set-up, but the skin on the backs of their palms is black as the stripes on their faces, rough and leathery, designed to protect their sensitive palms.

This Zazra places his palm gently on her wrist.

His eyes flutter closed. There's a soft brushing feeling in her mind as the Zazra uses his empathic abilities to read her emotions and see if she's here to stab them in the back. Or he wants to know if she's really as charming as she pretends. Six of one.

Damn those abilities are useful. All Rig gets from her Kashrini blood is blue skin and no hair. Not that she's anything less than proud of her species, but abilities like the Zazra have would be appreciated. Mohsin is half Kashrini as well, and he shares similar sentiments. There's a blue tint to his skin and he's got the purple eyes to show for it, but his blonde hair is all human. Makes it easier for him to get contacts sometimes. A lot of humans are too stuck up to deal with anyone who *isn't* human. In their minds, human equals faction. Faction equals good.

Yeah, *right*.

"She's clear," the Zazra says, pulling back and letting her fix her sleeve.

"Are you really surprised?" she asks with a smile. "We've known each other *how* long?"

Mohsin relaxes ever so slightly in his seat. "I didn't think so, but it never hurts to double check. Policy, and all. Drink?"

"You paying?" she asks. "If so, yes."

There's a decanter of Ascetic whiskey sitting on the table, and he pours out two small glasses, sliding one across the table to her. Not her favorite – too carbonated – but she'll drink it. Honestly, why does Ascetic carbonate nearly *everything*? Highly unnecessary, in her opinion.

Mohsin sets his glass down and licks the last of the gold liquid from his lips. "So what do you have for me?"

She produces a thumb drive from her pocket and slides it across the table towards him. "As promised. One stolen freighter filled with refugees. Those are the coordinates right there. Should be easy for you to send someone to escort them out of the Dead Zone and to a safe moon somewhere."

He snatches it up, holding it to the candle fixture on the table and getting a good look at it. With a wave of his hand, he dismisses the bodyguard, who goes back to lurking around their table and glaring at people who look like they might try and approach. "Are they safe?"

She nods. "Yeah. Last I checked in, anyways. Most of them are just refugees fleeing the war, but there's a couple of kids that ran from a factioned agriworld."

The Nightbirds, the group she and Mohsin work for, mostly work in people-moving. Getting refugees fleeing the ongoing war to safe planets. Helping former indentureds – like herself – smuggle themselves away from faction homeworlds and agriworlds. Hiding people from the law for as long as need be. When they're not moving folk from one end of the galaxy to the other, they're sabotaging every piece of faction tech they can get their hands on, stealing faction intel, breaking up faction bases. Just generally doing everything they can to slow the all-consuming, three-way war that so often puts their people – the Kashrini people – in the line of fire. Each member only has a handful of contacts so that if one of them gets caught they can't bring down the whole network – a set up that works just fine for Rig, who always has a good deal of fun pretending to conveniently forget things.

The thumb drive disappears into Mohsin's jacket pocket. "We can get some people to them as soon as possible. It should be secure, so long as we wait for any annoying patrols to calm down a bit first. If they've got kids with them, I don't want to try anything before we know we can get them out safely. How many of them were indentured?"

"All of 'em. Twenty-one. We got their tracker chips out before we moved 'em onto the freighter, but Ascetic is going to be *pissed* at us."

"It's not like we're taking more heat than normal here. *All* the factions are *always* pissed at us for freeing their indentured–"

"Or for sabotaging their supply trains," Rig breaks in. "Or stealing their weapons. Or for coding a virus that got into Pyrite ship systems and made every sound speaker play 'Rainbow Asteroid Party' on repeat."

He chuckles in a rare show of non-grumpiness.

"Hey, it was worth it. Anything to piss them off. Keep them distracted, keep them off their game." If a Pyrite ship spends one hour pulling their hair out and trying to fix their broken communication systems, that's one extra hour the Nightbirds have to evacuate a Kashrini settlement that's about to become a war zone. Rig leans back in her chair. "So what's my next job? You mentioned that I might actually get paid for this, and to be honest, I could seriously use the kydis."

Her ship isn't going to fix itself, after all. There are bad scrapes in the hull, the cannon is a bit roughed up, and the engines are running on nothing more than fumes and what little she can scrape out of the depleted fission chargers. The old girl has a couple more hops left in her, but unless Rig can fill her up soon, she's going to end up dead in the black. No power means no heat, no oxygen circulation – a combination that makes one very dead Rig.

Fortunately for her, Mohsin isn't the sort of person to leave her high and dry.

"I've got a job lined up for you," he tells her. "It's not quite the usual thing. Friend of a friend told me about it 'cause I mentioned you needed cash for ship upkeep. Crate full of merchandise needs to be shifted into Ascetic space."

While she doesn't like Ascetic, she has to admit that it's the enemy territory she's most comfortable in. She can get in easily, get out easily, and usually has a fun time while she's there. "Where *exactly* in Ascetic space?"

"Heart of it. The Ascetic homeworld itself."

"I know someone there. Haven't seen her in two months."

"So I've heard. I also heard this *friend* of yours," he says with a wink, "has hooked you up with a nice set of clearance codes to get onto the homeworld. Figured you'd be the best bet for this job."

"And this is… legit?"

"It's solid. I know lawful work isn't usually our cup of tea, but I heard your wallet was in a sad spot and thought you might make an exception for this." He gives her a lazy smile. "I know artifact reclamation is a side project you dabble in."

He's right. When Rig has time, she frequently hunts down the bits and pieces that factions have stolen from the Kashrini over the millennia. Jewels that were plucked from the necks of corpses, statues pulled from every place of worship they used to know, all the precious things from stories and legends. She figured that since she'd managed to steal her own research three years ago, then she'd make a pretty good thief.

She'd been right.

She'd gotten a taste of reclaiming things from Pyrite three years ago, and she's wanted more ever since. They tried to take everything from her, and they're trying to take everything from the Kashrini. Stopping them, even in small ways like this, is an indescribable satisfaction.

"Where am I picking up the goods?" she asks.

"I can have one of my guys drop the crate off in your ship right now, if you want. I'll assume you've changed the damn passcodes again?"

"You know me so well. Give me the info on who I'm taking this to, and I'll give you the new codes."

Mohsin has his link attached to his wrist, the small flash of metal almost hidden in the leather of his gloves. He presses it and a small holographic field pops up, displaying a series of coordinates and what looks to be a letter of introduction. "Transfer done." He taps a key, and her own link vibrates. "No deadline, but don't take too long or else he might get skittish and find someone else. You know how these types can be."

"I'm not green around the ears, Mohsin."

"It's why I save all the best jobs for you."

"*Aw*. You really do care."

"You're one of the best I know. You've proved that time and again over the years. It's less caring and more... practicality?" He shrugs. "What can I say, you're good at getting the job done."

How sweet. "Do we need anything from Ascetic space that I can get while I'm there? You know me, I like to linger on that giant garden they call a homeworld."

"Not that I–" Blood drains from his face as he stares at a

point over Rig's shoulder. His hand automatically reaches into his jacket, wrapping around the pistol he has holstered under his shoulder. Not drawing, just waiting. "Ah shit."

Rig freezes. "Are we blown?"

"Yeah, and not in the fun way." He lowers his hand. "Turn around, but slowly. Anyone you know?"

With a forced casual air, as if she's only getting a look at the bar's menu, she tilts her head at just the right angle to get a glimpse of the unwanted guests.

Two humans are loitering at the edge of the bar, armored and armed. Bounty hunters? No, they're too – for lack of a better word – *clean* looking. Clean and *shiny* armor at that; they're not worried about standing out. Her eyes narrow as she scans them, looking for a symbol. A flaming gear is emblazoned on their chest plates.

Shit.

"Pyrite," she hisses under her breath.

Rig is longing to leap out of her seat, ready to draw her weapons and shoot when Mohsin gives her a stern look. It as good as glues her back to her chair.

He shakes his head. "Don't."

"Mohsin, if they're after us–"

"Are they? And for the sake of the gods don't draw attention to yourself. They might pass us by if we stay seated and careful," he mutters.

"I wasn't followed, okay?"

"I didn't say you–" He curses under his breath. "How would you know if you were followed *anyway*? The whole point of someone successfully following you would be *stealth*. You wouldn't have noticed."

"Weren't you *just* the one telling me all about how great at my job I am?"

"Yeah, when it benefited me to say it, sure!"

"Well yelling at me isn't going to help any, now, is it?"

"*Neither* is yelling at *me*!"

"Okay then!"

"Okay!"

Their whispered shouts cut off as the music in the chattering bar slowly wells down. They weren't the only ones to notice that Pyrite showed up. Funny how faction soldiers can really kill the mood.

She knows that if she can get behind some good cover, she can probably outshoot them. Pyrite armor has weak spots, and she knows them all. The real question is how much back up they've brought. Dealing with thugs is a whole different numbers game than dealing with one of the *factions*. Factions have *armies*. For all they know, Pyrite forces could have the entirety of Red Dock surrounded by now. She tries to run through scenarios in her head – how many can she take out, how does she best run from them, what's the fastest way back to her ship?

"You shoot now, and you'll get a hundred civilians caught in the crossfire," Mohsin sternly reminds her. He jerks his head towards his Zazra bodyguard and says, "Give them the standard welcome greeting and see if you can find out who or what they're here for. I'm getting her out of here before bullets start flying."

"Good luck," the Zazra replies before striding over towards the two enemies, drawing their attention.

The waiting is the worst part. Rig doesn't turn around to look at the Pyrite soldiers again, she doesn't want to attract their attention, so she just has to sit here. Like a stump. While Mohsin watches discreetly over her shoulder until his Zazra bodyguard has done a sufficiently good job of distracting the targets. She wants to sit perfectly still, but even that would be a tell, so she casually sips at her drink. The alcohol sours on her tongue.

Her mind unhelpfully dredges up memories of Pyrite torture instruments, and she has to kick the thought away before it makes her sick.

After an eternity, Mohsin slowly stands up, his posture

forcefully relaxed. "I'm going to go ask my bodyguard what the trouble is," he tells her, each word calm and deliberate. "Wait forty seconds after I leave before you head to the bar. Tell the bartender that I'm ordering a crystal shot and she'll get you out of here."

"Got it," she replies, her hand so tight around her glass that one twitch of her fingers would shatter it into dust.

He leaves.

She counts down the seconds, resisting the urge to turn her head around and see what's going on. Mohsin will be fine. The guy practically runs this place, he's carved out a business for himself here over the years. Half the usual punters that come through here know who he is and would whip out a gun in his defense. There's nothing unusual about him stopping a couple of Pyrites who've wandered into his bar.

She tries to tell herself that this is going to be fine.

Finally the allotted time passes. She grabs her glass and stands up, holding her head low so that her face isn't easily visible.

She heads to the bar, making sure she doesn't move like she's in a hurry, that she keeps her steps nice and even. She doesn't want to attract attention by appearing as though she's running. She only glances over her shoulder once. It looks like the Zazra and Mohsin have successfully drawn the soldiers' gaze towards a security monitor on the wall, as if they're actually trying to help them. Knowing Mohsin, the monitor doesn't actually work – or if it does, it's rigged.

The woman tending bar gives her a smile as she steps up. "Anything I can do for you?"

"Yeah." Rig sets the empty glass down on the counter and hopes that this works. "I need a crystal shot for Mohsin."

"Sure thing."

With a professional smile, the woman steps aside to let Rig behind the bar. She presses a button hidden on the underside of the countertop and a hidden hatch on the floor slides open, revealing a ladder.

"Thank you," Rig tells the bartender, slipping a few kydis into the woman's hand. "For your troubles."

Then she jumps down onto the ladder.

The hatch above her head is closed again and her world is plunged into darkness.

Only after her eyes adjust can she see the dim light fixtures built into the sides of the vertical tunnel. Her footsteps on the ladder rungs echo in the metal corridor as she descends, keeping her eyes firmly on her hands to avoid slipping. She doesn't know how long this tunnel is or where it leads, and if she falls she very well could die. Still, better a fall to her death than the slow tortures Pyrite will come up with. They have no moral boundaries, no scruples when it comes to violence, and no shortage of fancy devices to play around with.

She knows better than anyone what they're capable of.

All their overclocked guns, clever bombs, doomsday buttons – she had a hand in all of them at some point or another.

Relief floods through her when her feet finally hit solid ground and she can step off the ladder. Short-lived relief, however. She's not out of the asteroid field yet.

Noise and lights flicker in from ventilation grates set into the floor. This tunnel must be in the airways. She pries open one of the panels to let herself pass through, putting the sheet of metal back in place once she's crossed through into a separate ventilation shaft.

She's pretty sure she's nearing the starboard lifts; all she has to do is keeping heading in that direction and then she can start making her way down towards her ship.

The noise of people talking and moving about fades as she moves through a more cramped section of air vent. Good news for her. It'll be better to drop down from the ceiling in a relatively deserted part of the spacedock than land on top of some poor folk who didn't sign up to have a random Kashrini woman hit their faces with her boots.

She reaches down and starts prying open the grate beneath her feet. It's stubborn, but she gets it all the way off, shifting it to the side and looking down to make sure the area below is clear.

She drops down.

She lands in the middle of a quiet section of the spacedock. Only a few people are milling about; they quickly look the other way and pretend as though they don't see her spontaneously appearing in their midst. In a place like Red Dock, most just want to mind their own business and ignore what isn't either profitable or hilarious.

The elevators are nearby, and she gets on the next one heading to the lower levels.

Every second she's in the elevator is a second at which she's convinced those Pyrite soldiers are going to jam its controls and it's going to stop and she's going to be trapped in this because it's such an obvious kill box – she takes a deep breath.

She hits level five with her palm on one of her guns, the cold grip of the semi-auto pistol pressed so tightly into her hand that it'll leave a pattern imprinted on her skin.

No one's here – not for her, at least. It's packed to the next galaxy and back, of course, just with tourists and criminals and the standard bunch of ne'er-do-wells. No sign of the two soldiers from Mohsin's bar, and as she scans the throngs of people, she can't see anyone else wearing unusually clean armor or the Pyrite symbol.

Her heart pounds.

As she walks through the crowded atrium again, she does another check of her body language – still relaxed, still inconspicuous. She tugs her headscarf up, just a little bit. Enough to make it difficult to get a closer look at her face, but not so much that she looks like she's actively trying to hide her appearance. It's an art form, one that she is usually better at. She pinches herself. Freaking out isn't going to help her. What *will* help is keeping her cool and staying focused.

All she needs to do is get to her ship without incident. Then she's in the clear.

Pyrite has sent people after her before, she reminds herself. They've never managed to stay on her tail for very long. She's got a dozen friends with safe houses and hidey holes scattered across the galaxy. They'll never pin her down and they'll never take her back. She can make it.

Color flashes in the corner of her eyes, the red and blue of Pyrite's symbol.

She freezes in her steps, her hand a moment away from drawing her weapon, cursing herself for letting them get so close–

Click.

A rifle is pointed at her head.

"You are under arrest."

Even her lungs seem to stop moving. Her eyes dart to the man pointing a weapon at her and she can see the shiny red armor underneath a civilian coat. They're hiding in the crowd; of course she didn't notice. Why couldn't she use her brain for one minute and realize that's what they'd be doing? It's what she'd do, after all. After so long chasing her, she should have expected that they'd pick up on a few of her tricks. Half her usual kit would take civilians out in a burst of fire, and she refuses to drag a bunch of innocent people in her mess. All she's really got are her guns.

What can she do?

Two thoughts filter to the surface. Firstly, that they are going to take her alive. If she's dead, she can't give them the research – *her* research – that they want. And second, that there are more than just this one.

"I understand," she tells the soldier.

Deep breath in.

She flashes her left arm up and wraps it around his wrist,

digging into the soft spots between his armor until she hears something *snap* and the gun drops. Her right hand goes for one of her guns. She spins on the balls of her feet, pushing the man to his knees and yanking his arm back until the slightest movement by him would cause it to dislocate.

She puts her gun to the back of his head.

"Shoot me, and your friend dies!" she calls out. They're listening. She knows they are. "I'm not messing around!"

A scream goes out through the atrium and people begin to panic.

"Stand down," a new voice says.

Three more Pyrite soldiers emerge from the crowd, weapons in hand and aimed straight at her. The crowd scatters like a school of fish facing a shark, but there's nowhere to go. The atrium isn't designed for mass evacuation. There's no flashing sign marked 'exit.' The crowd parts away from the confrontation, sure enough, but they can't get far.

One of the Pyrite soldiers reaches out and snatches a civilian.

Fuck.

He holds the woman in one arm, and with the other puts a pistol to her temple. "Release our comrade and stand down. Or else we'll kill her. You're opposed to civilian casualties, are you not? We were told you no longer have the... *taste* for that sort of thing."

Rig's hand is shaking.

The civilian woman opens her mouth. Rig braces for her scream, but instead the only sound that comes out is a calm:

"I suggest you release me."

Rig blinks.

The Pyrite soldiers glance down at the woman, their helmeted faces reflecting her dispassionate features. The roar of the crowd quiets. Everything seems to fade away as if the galaxy is focusing on the unfamiliar woman. Does she not know what sort of things Pyrite will *do*?

The woman – a Zazra, like Mohsin's bodyguard – looks

down at the arm across her neck with apathetic disdain. "I *won't* ask again."

She glances between the soldiers, one eyebrow arched in a silent question. Their blank helmets turn to look at one another and Rig can only imagine that the confusion on their faces is a mirror of her own.

When none of them reply, the Zazra lets out an exasperated sigh.

"Fine."

She moves.

Her body is almost a blur as she grabs the soldier's arm, drops to one knee, and throws the large man over her body like a sack of feathers. His back smacks against the ground with the sort of bone deep *crack* that would have made Rig wince if she weren't staring, slack-jawed, as the woman brings her boot down on the man's helmet. There's a metallic groan of the helmet giving way and then a wet squelch that makes Rig gag.

The Zazra turns to the other two soldiers.

One shoots – she's already dodged before he pulls the trigger. She twists around his gun to grab the barrel and then uses it to yank the soldier towards her, letting him fall into her fist. The chest plating caves into his solar plexus with a sickening crunch beneath her hands. She spins around, using the body she's holding to block the rain of bullets that the last soldier unleashes upon her, and then she tosses the corpse onto the remaining soldier.

He throws his dead comrade to the side – just in time to get a spinning kick to the head.

The man goes down.

Blood as red as his armor splatters the ground beneath his shattered helmet.

Fuck, Rig thinks, and then again for good measure, *holy fuck*.

The Zazra woman bends down to pick up a black duffel bag that she must have dropped when the Pyrite grabbed her.

Smears of blood dot the silvery gauntlets she's wearing. The red shines as she moves her hands.

"Well?" she asks Rig.

Rig tries to make her mouth cooperate. "Uh."

She sighs, bends down to pick up one of the dead soldiers' guns, and then shoots the man that Rig has pinned.

Rig feels strangely detached from her own body. She lets the corpse fall without taking her eyes off the woman. Who *is* she… how did she… Rig has never seen *anyone* face Pyrite – or any factioned soldiers, for that matter – and come out without a scratch, let alone take out four of them without breaking a sweat.

A siren screams through Red Dock.

"Damn it." The Zazra spins around, holding up one hand in a loose fist.

Bright red lights start to flash as a monotone voice comes through the speakers, demanding they cease and desist. Another squad of Pyrite soldiers is pushing through the atrium, weapons raised and ready to fire as soon as they clear the crowd. Rig's eyes dart to the walkways overhead and counts another team shooting grappling hooks into the steel beams overhead, preparing to jump down.

The Zazra slings her bag over her shoulder. "They sent for backup. Why are those bastards after you, anyways?"

"That's a long story," Rig replies, wide eyes staring at the approaching Pyrite soldiers. They need to run. She's screaming at her legs to move, but she can't quite manage anything more than a tremble. "Really long."

"I see."

The Zazra slides her feet into a low crouch, one armored hand brushing against the floor like an animal preparing to pounce. She's not going to – she *is*.

Although Rig doesn't know if this woman *can* fight off dozens of Pyrite soldiers, she also would really prefer not to find out. The Zazra can do what she wants with her life, but if Rig doesn't get the fuck out, *now*, she's going to die. Or, more likely, be tortured until she sings to Pyrite's tune and *then* die.

In a burst of desperation, she grabs a handful of the woman's shirt and tugs her away from the rapidly approaching enemies.

"*Run!*" she yells. "I have a ship – we can make it!"

For a moment she thinks the woman is going to protest, and then she's running after Rig.

They crash through the atrium, Rig with far less dignity than her strange new associate. Bullets crack past them as the Pyrites open fire – one tears through Rig's shirt, and another cuts a hole in her headscarf. At least it isn't her *ear*. She jumps a crate and then turns down a corridor, crashing into the wall in her haste. Her palms slap against the metal before she's off again, her heart beating wildly against her rib cage.

"Left!" she calls out to the Zazra, who's already a number of feet ahead of her.

They skid left down a smaller corridor.

"I hope you have a plan!" the Zazra yells over her shoulder as they book it down the corridor, dodging bullets from a group of Pyrite soldiers chasing after them.

"Plan? I'm running for my life! What part of that says 'plan'?"

"You dared three Pyrite soldiers to face you and you *didn't* have a plan?"

"The extent of my plan was to hit them with Panache and Pizzazz!"

"This isn't the time for theatrics!"

"No – my guns!"

"You *named* your guns Panache and Pizzazz?"

"Yeah, what did you name your guns?"

"I don't have guns!"

"Well that sounds like a mistake–" Rig ducks a bullet as they turn another corner, "–considering the circumstances!"

Rig slams to a stop in front of the right set of doors and throws them open to reveal a small hangar bay. She slides in first and then slams the doors behind them.

Her ship sits in front of them, and behind it, a vacuum-guard field paints a glowing blue tint over the star-filled blackness of space. Normally she'd love to stop and admire the pretty picture her bucket of bolts makes. Instead, she dashes up the gangplank with the sounds of Pyrite bullets shooting the door down on her heels.

A blast of fire – grenade – takes down the hangar bay doors.

Rig almost fumbles, slamming her hand onto the lock and punching in the code just as the soldiers step over the ruined doors, their limbs dragging lines through the debris and smoke-filled air.

Shwoosh.

Rig has never been so relieved to hear the sound of her ship's hatch sliding open.

"Get in!"

She and the Zazra leap through one after the other, and then she's able to shut the hatch behind them. With a touch to the wall-mounted security panel, a glowing holographic panel springs up at her fingertips. The floors rumble as a blast rocks the ship – the Pyrite soldiers have opened fire.

She almost trips over an unexpected crate. Mohsin must have come through and had his people bring the merchandise on board before everything went to shit.

Adrenaline and panic send tremors down her fingers.

She redirects all the power to the shields. Just in time. The next few blasts fire off and the ship groans under the strain.

Collisions send Rig stumbling into walls as she runs through her ship towards the bridge. She built near every feature of those shields, and while she knows that they'll save her life, she also knows that they won't last forever. They won't be safe until she can get away from Red Dock and enter luminalspace.

"Can you shoot a cannon?" she calls out to the Zazra.

She slides into the pilot's seat, slamming her palm down on the controls – a *shwish* as the lock scans her fingerprints and powers up the ship's basic systems for her. Panels and screens flicker to life on the console.

The Zazra woman is right behind her, jumping down beneath the main cabin and into the co-pilot's seat where she can access the ship's cannons, her head just a bit below Rig's feet. A quick series of punched in commands from Rig gives the Zazra control of the weapons and overrides the main system lock.

"Hard light or particle?" the Zazra asks as she straps herself in and grabs the controls.

"You've shot a particle cannon–" Nope, ask questions *after* they're out of here. "Never mind! They're hard light."

The next burst of bullets comes for them as the Zazra quickly spins the lower mounted cannon around and opens fire. Rig glances at the rear-view holographic screen and watches as the Pyrite forces scatter.

Some of them throw up hard light energy shields for cover, kneeling down behind the walls of light and continuing their assault on the ship.

Neither her pistols nor her ship's guns can do much about those, other than trying to bash them down. Her bullets are made of hard light too. Hard light can't penetrate hard light.

Fingers moving fast as light, Rig flips off the brakes, pulls the gangplank up, and engages the subluminal engines. Her ship comes alive with a roar of power, the engines singing with the promise of freedom and survival. With another blast of fire from the Pyrite soldiers, a quick glance at the holo screens shows more soldiers pouring out of seemingly nowhere. How many of these bastards did they send after her? She picks up the pace, flipping on the artificial gravity and powering up the luminalspace bubble generator. A red warning light goes off in the corner of her vision. Shields down to fifty percent.

Rig switches on the lower repulsors and then the ground falls out from under them as they lift off, hovering above the hangar bay floor.

Her engines whip up a dangerous wind, pushing at the soldiers that are too close to the ship. A hum runs through every inch of the vessel, making her bones resonate – the thrum of her ship preparing to activate the warp bubble, which will propel the ship in to luminalspace at her signal.

The Zazra hisses in annoyance. "Pyrite dreadnaught."

Fear makes Rig's breath crawl back into her lungs.

A massive ship drags itself into view outside the hangar bay forcefield. Massive, elegantly sleek in that stupid way Pyrite design favors, and along the prow is the flaming gear sigil of that faction, painted larger than the entirety of Rig's ship.

"If they shoot, they'll hit the station. All we need to do is dodge their mooring cables and make sure their fighters can't pin us down. Easy-peasy." Rig's under attack, she's being shot at, and she's grinning. "Strap in."

"I'm *already*–"

Rig punches it.

Rig puts her ship into a steep nosedive, hurtling underneath the belly of the Pyrite dreadnought, hoping to move fast enough to avoid getting caught by mooring hooks. It won't buy her much time, not with those damn clever targeting systems Pyrite has. A dark cloud is released from the ship's belly above their heads. Rig's monitors freak out. The cloud gains clarity as it approaches. It's maybe fifty fighter ships, all screaming towards her, guns blazing.

"Oh, lovely," the Zazra grumbles, even as she spins the cannon around to fire on the Pyrite ship, their shots quickly absorbed by its shields. "Any bright ideas?"

"Just the one bright idea," Rig says. Her hand grabs hold

of the luminalspace ignition. "We run. Clear us a path!"

There's just enough time for the Zazra to blow up one of the fighters – *good* aim. It leaves them a pinhole of a space to fly through, almost nothing at all, but Rig is *very* good at what she does. She aims her ship towards the gap.

And yanks on the lever.

CHAPTER TWO
A Peculiar Cactus

Reality blurs.

The stars in the viewport pop out of sight, every part of the ship, including Rig, shaking from the initial acceleration. Red Dock vanishes behind them. The Pyrite dreadnaught vanishes behind them. Everything just... falls away. The starlight flashing through the bridge smooths out into the blank, white light of the luminalspace tunnel. The engines stabilize as well, the rocking becoming a peaceful hum instead of a rough trembling. The warp bubble cheerfully vibrates as it wraps around her ship, creating the protective layer necessary to travel through a luminalspace tunnel without being torn apart by the crazy physics of the faster-than-light zone.

A sigh drags its way out of Rig's lungs as her body sags into her seat.

Wait, no, hold on.

She spins her chair around, draws Panache, and aims the gun at the Zazra. "Alright, who are you? I'm guessing not Pyrite?"

"Pyrite?" The Zazra spits on the ground. "Don't insult me."

Even though the question had been one Rig needed to ask for paranoia's sake, she's not surprised. The Zazra doesn't really fit the bill for Pyrite.

Pyrite is, was, and always will be the faction of industry. Their domain is technology, and just about everyone Rig knew from her days stuck under their thumb was shuffled off into research, engineering, or some form of development. By contrast, Ascetic prefers the spiritual. Being a theologist there is a perfectly acceptable career, whereas in Pyrite you'd just get laughed at and handed a screwdriver. That said, Ascetic is just as vicious as Pyrite, only they justify their actions with the claim that they're 'helping the galaxy heal as a collective whole' and 'reclaiming injured worlds' and 'look at us, we're so innocent, all we wanna do is garden and wax philosophical, now stand down and let us take over or we'll kill you.'

Ossuary is… kind of a mystery, if Rig's being honest. So little information about the faction leaves its territory, and even on her infrequent dips into their space, no one ever is willing to talk about, well, *anything* really. The common joke – always told away from any potential Ossuary ears – is that it's called Ossuary not after the god they worship but because the place is so silent and dark it may as well be a crypt itself.

She's not sure which the Zazra is, but, given that few people leave Ossuary – or leave *alive* – she's willing to bet Ascetic.

"Still haven't told me who you are, and also what the fuck all that was about?"

The Zazra, apparently uncaring about the gun to her face, simply crosses her arms, drawing attention to the strange, lightweight armor that shimmers over every inch of her arms and hands. Interesting. Rig has never known a Zazra who felt comfortable having something cover their palms, given that it would completely cut off their empathic senses. "I should ask you the same thing. *Your* actions got me involved in all this, not *mine*."

"You beat the shit out of three of them."

"Killed, I believe. And it was four."

"Pretty sure that's worse?"

"Regardless," the Zazra continues, ignoring the point about murder, "I am grateful that, despite dragging me into this, you also provided me safe passage off Red Dock."

Rig had a snarky comment she was going to make, but

now it dies on her tongue. "Sure. You're welcome. Although I can't say how *safe* our exit was. You didn't get injured, did you?" She can't *see* any injury, but those gauntlets could have seriously banged up the woman's knuckles, and she knows how sensitive Zazra are about their hands. "I have a medkit on board, but it's nothing major so if you're badly hurt we'll need to find a medcenter or a hospital or something."

"No, I'm fine, thank you." The Zazra clears her throat. "Is the gun necessary?"

"I don't even know you, and you murdered people like two minutes ago," Rig reminds her.

"That was *your* mess. I merely finished it, and may I point out that I'm stuck with a complete stranger, on a ship I can't pilot, heading to an unknown destination."

"Oh, right. I've set course for the Ascetic homeworld. We should get there in about eleven hours. Unfortunately," Rig explains as she checks the fuel readout and sees that there's no way her ship could hop out of luminalspace and still have enough juice to generate another warp bubble afterwards, "I don't have enough fuel to drop you off somewhere along the way. Only have enough for the one jump. Free passage though – I won't ask you for a single kydis once we get to where we're going, I just can't stop. I didn't mean to steal you away from your own ship. I have a friend who could–"

"No need. I don't have a ship. I *said* I can't fly."

"How'd you get to Red Dock, then?"

"Passage on a cargo freighter."

"What were you doing there? Are you a bounty hunter or something? Skills like that, you could make a killing. Literally."

The Zazra gives her a glare, but it's not that impressive. Rig doesn't even flinch. "You're rather nosy, aren't you?"

Perks of being on the run for a long-ass time. Her nosiness has increased substantially in the past three years, making her... nosier? Possessed of greater nose? "Yeah, sorry about that. So. Bounty hunter? Lawman? Ex-military?"

"I suppose bounty hunter is close enough," the Zazra concedes, "as I *am* looking for something."

"Some*thing*," Rig asks, a tiny warning sign flashing in the back of her mind, "or some*one*?"

"Some*thing*."

Safe, then. She relaxes and holsters Panache. "So, where you headed? I know a couple people on the Ascetic homeworld, I could try and hook you up with a free ride in payment for stealing you away. Only seems fair."

The Zazra stares blankly at her. For a moment, her green eyes might as well be a void. "I... I don't know. I didn't have a destination in mind."

Weird, but she's used to ferrying passengers who have no real destination in mind. Refugees just looking to get away from the Dead Zone Conflict, or indentureds making a break for it, she's smuggled 'em all. People looking to get *away* rather than go *to*. The only problem, really, is that her usual companions tend to be from a similar walk of life as her, and some random bounty hunter doesn't fit that pattern. She'll have to sleep with one eye open. Or not sleep at all.

She steps out of the bridge and gestures for the Zazra to follow her.

She heads into the main room, picks up the heavy crate that Mohsin dropped off earlier, and hauls it into the cargo bay on the starboard side of her ship. It's more of a nice cupboard than anything else. "Cargo bay is here, it's small." She steps about two paces backwards and gestures to the main room around her. "My bunk is above this room, galley's built into the wall, and there's a bathroom and stuff on the port side."

The Zazra surveys the ship, pacing around the area.

"There's, uh," Rig clears her throat to stop the Zazra from poking at a panel on the wall. "There's another bunk over port side as well if you want to nap. Bit dirty, but it's got a cot, so. Better than nothing, right?"

"I've slept on worse," the Zazra says, and then clarifies, "A cot is welcome."

"Riiiiight." Rig furrows her brow. "Not picky, I guess."

The Zazra wanders through the common area, her armored fingertips dragging softly across the backs of the bolted-down sofa. "What's its name?"

"*Bluebird*. She's gorgeous, isn't she?"

"Yes," the woman says, and to Rig's surprise it isn't the least sarcastic. Something in her eyes has softened at the name. Does she have a fondness for birds or something? "She is. I assume you're Ascetic?"

The question physically pushes Rig away. She hardly fits the Ascetic stereotype. It's not like she spends her days meditating and growing flowers and sticking her fingers in her ears to ignore all her problems. And if part of her does fit that stereotype, she wants to know what part, exactly, so she can kick it to the curb. "Excuse me?"

"This is a *Verd-3000* twin engine schooner. Ascetic made. You're heading to the Ascetic homeworld. Are you intending on contacting the Ascetic authorities? Pyrite doesn't have authority on Red Dock and they certainly don't have the authority to deal with Ascetic citizens."

Contacting the authorities. *Suuuuure.*

"I have no intention of contacting *any* authorities. Now or ever. I don't like them and they don't like me; and I bet they wouldn't like some random bounty hunter capable of killing four factioned soldiers without proper authorization just hanging around, now would they?"

The woman's lips purse. "Perhaps not."

"Figured you weren't exactly on the lawful side."

"I *am*."

But the murder and the bounty hunting – and she'd just *said* that she wouldn't get along with the Ascetic authorities. Maybe she's a lot more devout than she appears. "Don't tell me you're some faction-loving goody-two-shoes?"

The sour expression on the woman's face curdles. "I have proper reverence for my faction. As should you."

"Well... fine. I mean it's not fine, but... whatever, we're going to be stuck together for hours and I don't want to argue with someone who could probably kick my ass from one end of the fucking galaxy to the other. Space dust under the hull, bygones be bygones, all that." She clears her throat and then awkwardly sticks out her hand. "I, uh... I don't know your name, but, I'm Rig. Nice to meet you, I guess."

Instead of shaking her hand like she'd been expecting, the woman gives her a small bow, inclining her head ever so slightly. Rig had meant the gesture to be one of transparency – if she wanted to take off her armor and shake Rig's hand plainly, she could read Rig's emotions. If *Rig* were a Zazra empath, she'd want to use every trick she had to make sure that the stranger she'd just hitched a ride with wasn't harboring any ill will.

"Nice to make your acquaintance," the woman says, all stiff politeness and formal courtesy. "I'm Ginka. You have an interesting name. Nouns are common enough names in Ossuary, but not in Pyrite or Ascetic."

"I could say the same to you. At least I'm not named after a tree... I mean, well, not that the ginka tree is an *ugly* tree, it's got all those pretty gold leaves, and aren't they shaped like stars, or something..."

Ginka places her duffle bag down on the sofa. Rig knows an exit when she sees one, so she heads back to the bridge to figure out what the fuck she's going to do next. The sudden appearance of Ginka is the easier problem to deal with. Passenger, short term, nothing Rig can't handle. No, the real problem, as per fucking always, is Pyrite.

They've found her.

She supposes it was too foolish of her to hope that they wouldn't catch up to her again. No one, not even her, can outrun one of the three factions forever. They're simply too big, their reach too long, and the neutral zones between factioned space get smaller and smaller every year, warships pressing against the empty pockets in the galaxy as though trying to squeeze the life out of it, walls closing in, crushing her...

Her hand tightens around the throttle lever as she gets her rapid breathing back under control.

At least while she's traveling in a luminalspace tunnel Pyrite can't track her. Not even their advanced technology has managed to lock onto one ship out of billions, traveling through one tunnel out of quadrillions. Hopefully, heading straight to the Ascetic homeworld will be enough of a surprising destination to shake them off her trail for a little bit and give her a break to plan her next move. It's stupid to imagine it could work out, given who she is, but part of her wishes she could stay on the Ascetic homeworld forever, stay with the one person she loves unconditionally...

It *is* a stupid thought. Eventually Ascetic would catch on to her presence there and then they'd toss her out – no one likes a thief and no faction wants a Nightbird in their midst. While in the neutral zones the Nightbirds have some respect for standing up to the factions, among faction spaces they're only known for being Trouble. Not to mention the fact that even if Ascetic would be fine with her sticking around, she doesn't want to live under another faction ever again. She wouldn't be able to handle it. The confinement, the rules, the similarities to Pyrite. The fact that, inevitably, she'd be found out and forced back into her old job, this time with different trappings for a different master.

She's done making weapons.

Under Pyrite, she had grown up in poverty. Once they'd found out she was smart, they'd brought her in to work in one of their prized spires of industry, and forced her to turn her research into weapons of war. Then they had turned around to smile at her and tell her that they were going to use those weapons against the Kashrini – wouldn't that be wonderful? Wouldn't it be fine for her, because she was so *different* from the rest of her species, so *special*, so *smart*, and they'd just be getting rid of those *other* Kashrini that didn't have use.

Three things made her of use in Pyrite's eyes. Three things that made her *better than*. Firstly, that she was clever in the specific, technologically inclined way that fits in neatly with Pyrite's values. Secondly, that she could be manipulated through threat of poverty and promise of reward into doing whatever they asked of her, no matter how morally repugnant. And thirdly, that she had no important family to back her up or strong ties to powerful people, and could be, if necessary, disposed of with little fuss.

For a faction that prides itself in being logical and smart and advanced, their measures of worth are subjective, arbitrary bullshit.

She can feel invisible hands scratching at her brain again, reaching through her skull to clutch at her mind, clawing down to grab at her guns.

"I'm safe in *Bluebird*," she mutters, too quietly for Ginka to hear. "I'm safe."

For now.

She pulls up the call screen and plugs in Mohsin's number. It takes a moment to connect as the signal bounces between dozens of communications satellites floating through various luminalspace tunnels between her and him, and then a somewhat fuzzy image of his face fills the screen.

"Heya," she says, waving to cover that she's shaking from nerves. "I got out."

He sighs in relief. "Thank fucking – after the alarms started going off, I thought for sure you were gonna… well. You're alive."

"Takes more than a couple Pyrite goons to send me to the afterlife."

"I'll drink to that." He gives a tense laugh. "You dropped their tail okay? They're not still hanging off you?"

Paranoia makes her do a quick double check. Nothing is

showing up on her scanners. Of course she's in the clear, it's not like they'd be able to track her in luminalspace. Not unless they've bugged her ship – and *nobody* bugs her ship without her noticing. Communications satellites work in the mess of luminalspace tunnels because they're constantly sending out a signal yelling 'Hey, we're here! Use us!', but her ship doesn't do anything like that. Just to make sure, she runs a sweep of her system, turning to the side for a moment to tap out a command for a full ship scan. Nothing pops up. She's still safe.

"Not as far as I can tell," she reports. "They'll try, but unless you told them anything, they'll have no idea where I'm headed. Besides, they'll probably waste a whole bunch of time regrouping and re-strategizing before trying anything else."

"Not to point out the obvious, but they must have found you on Red Dock somehow. There's no way they'll have a hunch about where you're headed, is there?"

"I didn't leave a trail, and Pyrite doesn't do 'gut feelings' or anything."

"For a tech-loving society, they're a pretty dumb bunch, huh? Figure out how they tracked you to Red Dock? I put the metaphorical screws to a couple of my people and no one said anything to anyone about you coming to meet me."

"No." Which does worry her. She has guesses, not answers, and she likes being sure about things. "They could have caught me on camera while I there, maybe, sent a message out – Nearest Pyrite patrol ship could probably have gotten to Red Dock in the short time I was there. Red Dock isn't a small spaceport. Plenty of snitches, I'm sure."

He slowly nods along. "Possible, very possible. Some good news though. No one snitched on that refugee ship you helped with. I got confirmation that three minutes ago they landed on Pahena – that tiny little moon just outside the Dead Zone."

She breathes a sigh of relief. Figuring out how to steal the ship had taken a solid month of planning, and it had been difficult to make sure the refugees all managed to pile onboard without drawing attention from the authorities. "Glad to hear it. Should I call you when I get to Ascetic?"

"Best not. Listen, if you're still alive, that's probably all I should know. It doesn't matter that Pyrite was after you, not me. They still had the guts to come to my spacedock, and we've gotta play it safe for a bit. The less I know about what you're doing, the better. Make sure you're real careful the next time you call – I don't want them tracking the signal."

Justified offense rears its ugly head. "I've scrambled this call under twelve different codes and routed it through another three different planetary spacedocks to make sure it can't be traced. I have been doing this for a *while*, thank you very much."

"Fine, fine. My bad."

There's a slight rustle of movement as Ginka comes to stand behind the co-pilot's seat, lingering just close enough to let Rig see her. Rig gets the distinct impression that Ginka is a ghost – silent, creepy, and vaguely ominous. All she needs is to be transparent.

He raises an eyebrow at Ginka. "Who's your friend?"

"Uh." Rig pauses as she tries to figure out something to say that doesn't make her sound like an idiot who got suckered into letting a bounty hunter onboard her ship.

Ginka helpfully steps in. "I assisted Rig in deterring the Pyrite forces."

"Gotcha. Thanks for taking care of this idiot," Mohsin says.

"How sweet. I'm blushing," Rig flatly replies. "Thanks for letting me know you're still alive and all, and take care of yourself, okay?"

He signs off with a parting, "Stars' favor to you, too."

As soon as the call drops, Ginka asks, "Who is he?"

"Friend of mine. He's a…"

"A *criminal*, I'm assuming."

Yes, but she didn't need to say it so derisively. Mohsin is one of the best sorts Rig knows. "He's a good man. And there's nothing *wrong* with being a criminal."

Ginka frowns in clear confusion. "Yes, there is."

She gives the Zazra a smile. What a cute, naive little statement. "You'll learn."

"Hm."

"You're a prickly one, aren't you?" she says with a snicker. Ginka turns on her heels and walks out. Rig can't help but laugh outright at the stiff petulance of it. "Alright, Cactus."

"Excuse me?"

"Cactus. Cause you're prickly."

"What?" Ginka deflates, shoulders and mouth drooping ever so slightly as she blinks at Rig in surprise. "You're... *naming* me?"

"It's a nickname. Do you not have nicknames in bounty hunter school?"

"I, that is–"

"While I stand by my creative genius, if you've got a better idea, I'm always open to suggestions–"

"No." She folds her gauntleted hands stiffly behind her back. "Cactus is much better than what they called me there. And I'm perfectly happy saving the name Ginka for special occasions."

Special occasions?

What a strange woman.

INTERLUDE
The Shard of God

A young woman stands in front of a shard of crystal. It stands tall, looming over her, almost as high as the ceiling. It's a jagged thing, made of sharp edges, and it shines with a ghostly light, catching a rainbow of colors inside it. Beneath it is its reflection, sitting on a glassy pool, undisturbed in the dark chamber.

She is Ghoul X-74. Ghoul, to denote her rank as the lowest level of Operative in Windshadow Secret Police. The rest is to specify *her*. In theory she has a name, although she doesn't know what it is, and even if she did it is irrelevant by comparison.

This is the first time she has had enough security clearance to see the shard herself.

A whisper of fabric over stone.

She is no longer alone.

A man comes to stand next to her.

She gasps and drops to one knee, keeping her head bowed and focused on the floor, not daring to look her organization's leader in the eye. "Lord Umbra! Forgive me, I did not notice your approach. My eyes were not sharp enough. I shall do better next time."

"Had to see it for yourself?" he asks, his cool voice whispering over the ground like a fog.

"I was... curious," X-74 says.

"Were you now?"

"I apologize for doubting." She chances a glance up at him. "I simply…"

He gives her a knowing look and gestures for her to stand. "I give you this story so that you may have the truth and see with eyes unclouded. Ten thousand years ago," he begins, his words echoing through the chamber, a familiar story that has been written into X-74's bones. Into the bones of every member of their faction. "A star fell into the galaxy. It was a dying world, burning out its life as a comet, destined to die, shattered into a thousand pieces throughout the cosmos. Three great deities had guided it safely through the stars for an untold age, but their strength waned. The end was coming for them. However, they were powerful and wise, and not all of them willing to die."

X-74 nods. She knows this. She is not ignorant, and she was raised properly. "Pyrite, Ascetic, and Ossuary. The old ones."

"Of those three mighty gods, only one survived the star's fall. They went on to have children who contain the true blood of the gods in their veins. The just rulers of this galaxy, descended from immortals. It is this line of children who will eventually rise up to secure their destiny, throw off the shackles of false pretenders and take their place on the throne of the gods." He gestures to the shard in front of them. "The question of which one survived has torn the galaxy apart."

"But we know the truth, don't we? This shard of the star – it's proof, isn't it?"

"Yes. It is not wrong to seek reassurance of our superiority. We of Ossuary know the *truth*. It was Ossuary who survived, and it was Ossuary who propagated the line of lords and gifted their descendants with long life. And we know this because our mighty lord, our king, our Tenus, is their direct descendant. He will rule for one thousand years before passing into the next world."

And as Windshadow, they defend and protect that superiority, their greatness, everything the shard in front of her represents.

Umbra turns, the white fur of his cloak dragging over the marble floor. "I hope you truly understand the significance of what it is we do. We do not falter. We do not bend. We serve Ossuary to the death. Never forget that."

With a final flash of white fur, he vanishes.

X-74 looks up at the shard.

All her life, she has known that she is not one of the blessed lines, the families that are lucky enough to have Ossuary's blood running in their veins. She is only barely Ossuary, and she knows that when their hour of glory arrives, she will benefit little from it. That's alright. It is enough to know that she is on the right side of this war, and she is honored to fight and die for the glory of Ossuary.

The shard is proof. They're right. She fists her hands into the fabric of her pants, digging in to ground herself as she tries to comprehend what their faction's inevitable victory over Pyrite and Ascetic will look like.

CHAPTER THREE
Ascetic Homeworld

Rig sits plopped down in the cargo hold with the doors wide open so that she can keep a close eye on the main room, choosing a spot in the corner so Ginka would have a hard time seeing her. She doesn't much like being spied on.

Her experience with taking on passengers is, admittedly, limited. Mostly she only transports refugees, cramming as many people as possible into her ship and running as fast as possible to the nearest safe planet or moon or spacedock. Sometimes there's a bit of a kerfuffle about food or room, but usually it's pleasant and she gets to have a wide variety of interesting conversations about planets that she's never set foot on.

Ginka's different.

The Zazra had spent the first ten hours of the eleven-hour trip dead asleep. So dead asleep that Rig did, at one point, check to make sure she was still breathing. Which, yeah okay, it's nice that she kept out of Rig's hair. Not that Rig *has* any hair, but she digresses. The silence was weird, but welcome. Now Ginka is still silent, but up and about and really, *really* distracting.

She's not even *doing* anything in particular. She's just... wandering around the ship.

Right now, Rig can see her through the open doors as she ambles through the small circle of common space. She picks up a box of instant coffee and examines it, giving it a sniff before putting it back down in exactly the same place she found it. A piece of paper pinned to the galley hull is given close examination, as though the doodle is of some great significance. She looks over the boxes of protein packs and vacuum-sealed food only briefly. There's a loose couple of nuts and bolts lying about the counter and she paws through them, her fingers surprisingly elegant despite the heavy-looking armor she's still wearing. Which... seriously, is she incapable of relaxing?

Rig tries to ignore her and gets back to the task at hand.

Her left pant leg is rolled up to her knee, exposing a lot more of her chalky blue skin than she usually prefers. Her right hand holds a janky, homemade tattoo gun.

Even though they're currently hidden – and *always* hidden under her clothes – there's a mess of tiny white dots on both her thighs. She's on to her knees now, and with luck she'll be working down to her calves in the next year. When she'd started out three years ago, she'd used tally marks. Then those had been too big and she'd been running out of space, so she moved to dots.

The tattoo gun *whirrs* as she carefully makes twenty-one dots on her left knee.

Twenty-one refugees on that ship she pulled out of the Dead Zone. Twenty-one people Mohsin is picking up and taking to somewhere safe.

It's not pride or arrogance. She doesn't want anyone else to see them. It's just, it's... her hand almost slips on the final dot. The marker of the final life she saved today. She can't count the number of people whose deaths she's responsible for. It's literally impossible. Working as a weapons developer under Pyrite meant that she never knew where exactly her work would end up once it left the testing stages in her lab. So, she can't count how many her weapons killed, but she *can* count how many people she's saved now.

When she's done, her knee is a blotchy purple mess of blue skin, red tenderness, and fresh white ink.

Rig rolls her pant leg back down, and shifts to work on her bike.

The thing is a sleek black beauty with neon pink racing stripes along the sides, and normally she loves tending to it like it's her precious child. The drag flaps need a bit of adjusting today. And she could use a nice, familiar task while she waits to arrive on the Ascetic homeworld.

There's a loud *clank* that makes her ears wince.

She glares at the source of the noise to see that Ginka's sorting through the tool box in the kitchen. Oh for–

Rig lowers her screwdriver and leans backward for proper yelling, "Need anything, Cactus? I'm glad you're finally conscious, but uh, you're kinda making me twitchy. There're lasers in that box."

Ginka taps a finger against something just out of Rig's sight and asks, "Is this you?"

There are no pictures of Rig taped up in the galley, which means it can only be one other person. "No," she says stiffly. "That's Daara. My twin sister." She tries to fake a laugh. "She's the pretty one."

Rig doesn't like looking at the photo much, but she keeps it up anyway. Every day she tries to make herself look different from her sister. Tattoos. Rough clothes. Plain face. Maybe it's horrible to say it, but one of the things she likes about not being able to see her sister anymore is that she no longer feels like the chipped cup in an otherwise matching pair.

Another tap against the photo. "Is she wealthy?"

"Huh?"

"The jewelry."

"Oh. No, no, we really weren't – she was just fond of fancy headscarf pins and the like. All of 'em are plastic."

"Hm. What is she then, if not wealthy?"

"A juggler," she drawls sarcastically. It's certainly a more entertaining story than admitting Daara was a laborer on a construction crew. And she doesn't want Ginka to judge her sister, even if it is from a distance. "She was also a sword swallower and a hologram jester."

Ginka nods. Apparently, insincerity goes over her head. "You keep referring to her in the past tense. Is she dead?"

"What – no!" Rig fumbles with her screwdriver, almost scraping her hover bike's sleek paint job. A curse tumbles out of her lips after it. Recovering, she sticks it in a socket and starts prying open a plate on the chassis. "She's not *dead* – she's... on the Pyrite homeworld. Look, does it *matter*?"

"If you separated, then–"

Rig's hand slips and she gives the plate a harder yank than she'd intended to, ripping it off her bike, the rough edges scraping her fingers. "Shut up about her! It *doesn't* matter, okay?"

Ginka drops her hand away from the photo. "...My apologies."

Tension makes her movements jerky and clumsy as she shoves her hand into the guts of her bike and starts picking at wires. There's a cut on her ring finger from the plate and she shoves it between her lips to soothe the pain, iron bitter on her tongue and her tight jaw making an imprint of teeth on her skin.

It doesn't matter. Daara had decided to stay behind, to stay in Pyrite, and that had been the end of that. Only it isn't, not really. It feels *unfinished*. Like a conversation between her and Daara that had been abruptly cut off.

"Is that a Yzra *Striker*?"

Rig jumps because Ginka's voice is a lot closer than she'd expected. She hadn't even heard the woman approach. When she lowers her hand, she sees that Ginka is standing right next to her. She sighs. Best move on, she supposes. No need to hold a grudge just because Ginka poked at a bruise.

"Yeah. It's one of the older models. I fished it out of a dump," she admits, "but when I cleaned her up she turned out a lot nicer than the newest piece of crap they put on the market. You... like bikes?"

Ginka takes an almost excited couple of steps closer to the bike. Her pupils, normally thin slits, blow wide and round until the black has almost completely swallowed up her irises. It's... kinda cute. Like a small and fluffy animal. "I had a – someone I know used to read a lot of pilfered bike magazines. I'm not exactly a good flyer, but I liked watching him read."

She scooches over and pats the section of metal next to her. "Pull up a bit of cargo-bay-floor and take a look, if you like."

"Ah." Ginka leans in and then holds out her hand to Rig. "May I?"

There's something in the way her eyes can't meet Rig's directly, the bunch of her shoulders, a little bit of red in her cheeks – she's sheepish. Well, what d'you know.

She obliges and hands over the screwdriver, flipping it around so that Ginka can grab it by the handle. "Knock yourself out."

Slowly, carefully, Ginka's metal-covered fingers almost stroking the machinery, she tightens the loose screws that are preventing the drag flaps from opening all the way. There's a practiced ease to her motions that speaks of previous mechanical work, but she hesitates in all the standard parts of a bike. Does she have experience working with ships or something?

Now Rig's doing it – she's analyzing Ginka in the same way that Ginka was digging around *Bluebird*.

"So, Cactus," Rig starts, watching her rub a smear of engine grease across her cheek. "Were you always a bounty hunter?"

"No."

"What were you before that?" She pauses to look at the deft way Ginka is pulling on the bike's internal wires. "Were you some kind of scavenger?"

Ginka exchanges the screwdriver for a weldstylus. "Are *you*?"

"Am I what?"

"A scavenger."

"I prefer to think of myself as a reclaimer."

"And what are you reclaiming today?"

"On the Ascetic homeworld? I honestly don't know. My contact there is legit, so nothing too sketchy – and if it's going to a homeworld then it's unlikely to be anything really *bad*. Hey, *you're* not Ascetic, are you?"

"No."

Well that's *that* theory ruined, although it makes sense. Ginka neither looks nor acts like an Ascetic. Of all the three factions, Rig hates Ascetic the least, partly due to the fact that they've got a larger streak of pacifism than the other two. Or they're better at pretending they're pacifists, that is. None of the factions are anything other than warmongering bastards. Perhaps she only likes Ascetic for the one person she cares about living under their rule.

But the pacifist image doesn't fit with Ginka. Also, although Rig hates to generalize, not a lot of Zazra are under Ascetic rule. Zazra are from Zi'li, and that moon was originally colonized by Pyrite, and then Ossuary, but the place has had naught to do with Ascetic.

Pointedly, Ginka clears her throat and changes the subject. "Have you ever been to the Ascetic homeworld before?"

"I've been a few times," Rig replies.

Many times, actually. Far more often than she should. By all rights, she has no reason besides work to set foot on that planet, given how dangerous core faction worlds can be for someone with a Nightbird tattoo on their wrist. Anywhere like that is a place she tends to avoid worse than a black hole. It's simply that the Ascetic homeworld has one thing in its favor, despite the law enforcement, the colonialism, the bigotry, and the general snobbishness.

Rig's eyes glaze over as she watches Ginka work.

So far, it's been smooth sailing on their way to the planet's surface. They'll be docking in the homeworld's capital city, not that it means much. All the faction home worlds have been built up and built up and built up to the point where almost the entire planet is itself one massive city. The Ascetic homeworld is a green planet, not due to the land itself, but due to the giant floating gardens that cover its skyline and the green glass they use to build their fanciest, highest-up buildings. It's pretty to look at, but after a while all Rig can see are the people who died building it.

She pauses and glances at Ginka, who's silently parted lips seem to be stuck forming an answer. "Have *you* ever been there?"

"Once," Ginka says.

"Did you like it?"

"I... did not see enough of it to say."

Rig snorts. "That's a diplomatic way of saying 'no.'"

"It wasn't a *diplomatic* trip." Ginka caresses the bike's steering. "Did you name this one too?"

"Chickadee."

"Are you... *fond* of bird names?"

"It's, um... the reason I named it that is because the chickadee–" She coughs. "The family of bird that the chickadee is from is called the tit family."

Ginka leans her head against the bike. "That is *terrible*." It's said without any actual malice, and so Rig will take it as the compliment it's truly meant to be. "How long till we touch down on the homeworld?"

A ship-wide alert goes off.

"I guess, now?" Rig says, standing up and dusting her pants off. "Back off the bike while I land us."

Ginka nods, already grabbing the protective cover and beginning to fix it back into place. "I'll go get ready."

"Really hoping you clean up nice. That shirt has bloodstains on it."

"Just fly your ship."

When Rig reaches the bridge, she pulls them out of luminalspace and takes the controls for herself, guiding *Bluebird* towards one of the many docking ports that she can see in the distance.

A message from the homeworld port authority comes through her ship's speakers. *"Please provide identification."*

Rig considers her various fake identities to find the best one for the task. Anything she's ever used to sneak into Pyrite space has to be tossed out. Even the slightest blip on their radar could get them descending down upon her.

She pulls up an older ID file. "This is uh, Anaris Ish'lana piloting *Verd*-3000 designated '*Meteor Maiden*.' I'm here for a meeting with a Mr. Iris?"

"Clearance codes?"

She plugs in the long string of numbers and sends it off. "They're all yours."

"...Access granted. Please proceed to docking bay R-3."

"Thank you kindly."

Within no time at all they've cleared through the stratosphere and she pulls them up to circle around one of the main city's spaceports. There's a bit of air traffic, so she switches the ship into neutral while waiting for the spaceport's go ahead to land. A groan of protest rumbles out of *Bluebird*'s engines.

She hops out of her seat, giving her limbs a good stretch.

The uneven hum of her ship has returned to its usual bumping as she walks over to the hole-in-the-wall guest bunk to tell Ginka that they're gonna be landing in a minute.

"We're here, Cactus! If you want a view of the gorgeous skyline, now's your–"

She should have knocked.

Ginka is sitting on the bed, still fully dressed and armored, paused in the middle of sticking a syringe needle into an unmarked bottle filled with something clear and shimmering. Her head jerks up at Rig's entrance, expression flickering through surprise, to annoyance, to embarrassment.

Rig clears her throat. "Hey."

A very awkward silence stretches between them.

"That, uh," she says, gesturing at the bottle, "that looks an awful lot like liquid shinedust."

It's like the doors shut behind Ginka's eyes. She directs her flat stare away from Rig. "Think whatever you like. I don't care about your opinion of me."

With a practiced hand, Ginka draws five milliliters into the syringe. She covers the bottle, putting it back into her black duffel bag, and then returns to the syringe. An armored finger gives the glass a tap. Then she stabs the needle into her thigh. Straight through the fabric of her pants. As she presses her thumb down on the plunger and the drug hits her bloodstream, she leans back, sighing in sheer relief, her eyelids flickering closed.

"Ready?" Rig asks once Ginka's removed the needle.

Ginka stiffly nods, avoiding looking her in the eye.

"Look, I'm really not going to judge," she promises. Sure, her kneejerk reaction is negative, but there's no reason for her to get all preachy from her non-existent moral high ground. "I get it. Stuff can be... hard sometimes. And it can be hard to deal with it."

Damn, she might have turned to substance abuse at some point too, after everything she did under Pyrite. If she hadn't had Mohsin around in the beginning to kick her in the ass and point her at a job and tell her to work instead of moping like an overdramatic playwright – his words, not hers. At least now she now knows why Ginka was on Red Dock. It's probably the easiest place in the galaxy to get any number of mind-altering concoctions.

Ginka rubs her thigh, still not looking at her, and quietly says, "It's not quite like that. It's... it's complicated."

"Stuff usually is."

"Hm."

Rig heads back to the bridge with Ginka following her like a shadow, and then lands *Bluebird* in one of the spaceport's more cramped and out-of-sight docking bays.

The ship gives out a metallic groan and a hiss of air as it touches down.

Everything gets powered down with a *whhhrrrr-grck*.

Yeah... that's not the noise it should be making. Rig needs fuel. Badly. She had better get paid within seconds of meeting up with this Iris guy because right now her ship isn't going to be up for a stern chase. Ascetic is usually safe from Pyrite, but Nightbirds aren't welcome in any type of factioned space to begin with.

She smooths her hand over the dashboard. "You'll be fixed up in no time. I promise I'll take care of you."

Ginka is standing still as a statue by the entry hatch, her plain black bag clutched in her hands and her eyes staring blankly out into the docking bay. She doesn't really move even when Rig approaches her.

"Hey," Rig says slowly, "you okay?"

Ginka blinks and the stiffness vanishes. "Fine. You should go meet up with your client."

"...Right."

Once everything's smoothed out and they've got a couple of the spaceport guys mooring their ship down, Rig applies a set of hover fixtures to the crate and carefully escorts it out of *Bluebird*, letting it drift alongside her at waist height. If she doesn't know what's in it, she's not going to jostle it more than she has to. Sometimes things explode.

"Who's your buyer?" Ginka asks.

"Some owner of some shop. I've got coordinates and a letter of introduction right here," Rig replies, patting the pocket of her leather vest even though in actuality the letter is in her link and there's no need for a paper copy of it. Paper is expensive, she can't afford that shit all the time. Only librarians can reliably get their hands on paper.

The Ascetic homeworld really is beautiful, she thinks when

they get out of the spaceport after paying the ludicrous docking fee. A clear blue sky surrounds them, puffy white clouds lazily floating through it without even the slightest threat of rain. Two of the homeworld's six moons are faintly visible against the sunlight. Given how high up the spaceport is, they are treated to the sight of green-glass buildings, massive skyscrapers dipped in shimmering green, and everywhere there are open pavilions filled with growing things. Flowers, trees, all sorts of plants Rig never grew up knowing how to name. They cover the roofs of buildings, they hang from walkways. Entire floating gardens drift through the city, held up on hover platforms that stay a good hundred meters above the sky traffic lanes.

Above the spaceport entrance is a holomosaic, depicting the so-told founding of the homeworld. It shows the planet being plucked out of the cosmos by the emerald hand of Ascetic themself, and from it, the aura of Ascetic spreading to the surrounding star systems in faux bas relief. As people pass under the mosaic, some of them glance up and raise their fist to their forehead to show respect.

She leans against a concrete wall while she waits for a taxi to show up, taking in the sights and the sounds of the city, and above all else the faint smell of flowers that has mixed in with the dirty pollution smells that all city planets have.

"It's so warm," Ginka remarks, tilting her face up to the sky.

Years on a ship, docks, and distant moons will do that to a person. Rig remembers her first few months spent in space, where her skin longed for the warmth of a sun. She's gotten used to it, but it's still a treat to be in air like this. It makes her bones feel melty, lazy, like she could just lean over and take a nap right here.

All the factions have their tricks, their little ways to make their enemies misunderstand them. That's Ascetic's. The lure of complacency. The benevolent mosaic of Ascetic seems to smile down and a row of soldiers in green armor march into the spaceport under it. Such beautiful armor, too. White crystal plating in smooth, elegant lines covering up bottle-green nanomesh bodysuits. A flower hiding its thorns.

A group of security guards pass by. Rig tugs her headscarf down a few centimeters to cover a slice of her face and shuffles to the side to hide the crate from view. They don't give either her or Ginka so much as a passing glance. Phew.

"So," she says awkwardly. "Do you have any plans for the homeworld? I don't know if this is where you want to part ways or…"

Ginka doesn't look at her, instead looking out at the skyline. "Why not?"

An uncertain frown works its way onto Rig's face despite her efforts to seem cool about this whole thing. "Well then… thanks for the save on Red Dock. It was really nice to meet you, Ginka."

"You as well," Ginka replies.

She sticks her hand out. "Good luck with whatever it is you're looking for. Stars' favor to you."

"May your eyesight never fade." As per last time she'd offered a handshake, Ginka simply bows.

An odd parting phrase. Rig's awkward hand ends up waving a goodbye as she strides off, leaving the Zazra behind to seek her own fortunes. Time to meet her contact and get some money and then get some fuel at last.

It's a one-hour taxi flight from the spaceport to the industrial section of the homeworld's undercity, where the shop Rig needs to deliver to is located.

Both the Ascetic homeworld and the Pyrite homeworld are city planets, the entire surface one big honkin' megalopolis. It's a natural side effect of so many people having moved and lived there over the course of thousands of years. And with each little industrial boom each faction goes through, another few stories of height are added to the cities. She doesn't know what the Ossuary homeworld is like, though. Probably the same, considering relative population sizes.

The Ascetic capital city is filled with towers and floating gardens and wide-open shopping districts. If she had to put a word to the place, she'd pick 'circular.' Pyrite tastes favor complex whorls and spiral patterns; but somewhere in the annals of history, some Ascetic architect had decided that The Hot Thing in design was circles. Concentric rings of overlapping tiles on the paved streets, towers domed at the top with round windows, the gardens viewed from above appearing to be infinite trefoils of greenery. Even the old fashioned, gear-wound clocktower that marks the very center of the city has circles instead of arrows on its hands and all the numbers on it are curved. The effect of it all is undeniably pretty, although, when the taxi makes sharp turns, she tends to get a bit dizzy if she looks down. Down in the lower levels the sunlight is patchier, supplemented with neon light fixtures and glowing holograms of trees that imitate the sky gardens. Instead of the constant blanket of flowers everywhere, she starts seeing fungus gardens, teeming with bioluminescent mushrooms and brightly colored algae.

They pull to a stop maybe three hundred levels down from the upper city. Rig has to do a bit of careful finagling to get the crate out of the taxi without bumping it on the doors, or on herself. She tosses an extra couple of kydis chips to the driver to get the woman to wait while she does the drop.

It's dark down here. The glowing fungi and dirty streetlamps give the place a sickly pallor. The glass skyscrapers are replaced by beaten up metal buildings, the polished stone floors replaced by uneven concrete. Cigarette smoke mixes with the slimy fungi smells. A woman with a torn jacket bumps into Rig, shoves her hands in her pockets with a glare, and stomps past. That seems to be the general sentiment in the lower levels, upon further examination. There are more hastily erected lean-tos and temporary shelters here than she'd expect from a homeworld, and from the distinct lack of anyone official looking, it's clear that the city above doesn't much care what happens down here – so long as it doesn't leave here. Keep the unseemly out of sight – an Ascetic motto.

A young boy lurks against a shop corner, his hood tugged up as he eyes the people that walk past. Oh-*hoh*. Rig knows *that* look from a mile away.

The boy is about to push himself into the street towards a woman carrying a purse when Rig hustles up the sidewalk, grabs his hand, and tugs him back against the shop wall.

"Hey, what are you–"

She yanks him back towards her before he can get away and chides, "You're about to make a dumb mistake, kiddo."

He glares at her, trying to tug his arm out of her grip and failing spectacularly. "What would *you* know?"

"Did you see that woman's shoes?"

"…yeah. So?"

"Their soles were worn out to the edge of the galaxy and back. Next time you're picking a mark, look at their shoes. It's always the shoes that give rich people away. They like to be comfy, see? Don't steal from those that got nothing, got it? That's rule number one. Nod if you get that."

He nods.

"Good. Do better next time." With a sigh, she lets go of him and fishes around in her pocket for a handful of kydis. A few chips isn't enough for even a fraction of the fuel she needs, anyway. "Here," she says, slapping them into his palm. "Oh, and next time, make sure there's no one paying you too much attention. Your posture screams suspicious. If I were a cop, you'd be fucked. Now scram."

He gives her a confused look before apparently deciding to accept his burst of good fortune and runs off with his cash.

She watches him dart through the narrowing street past a group of people huddling around a lamppost. Tents have been squeezed into the cracks between buildings, and people are squeezed into the tents, and as she watches, the boy slips into a tent to tug on a woman's threadbare skirts. She bends down to pick him up with too-skinny arms. His mother, perhaps?

Something in Rig's chest twists. She might be better off than them, but at least that boy still has his mother.

The refugees that she stole a ship for and smuggled out of the edges of the Dead Zone could very well end up in a tent city just like this one, on some other planet in factioned space. She and Mohsin always try to send people to the little spacestations and colony moons that are relatively untouched by the factions, not the massive industrial worlds that were conquered thousands of years ago. But even with their best efforts, sometimes refugees have no choice but to go to the faction homeworlds, to the places where the war won't reach them. Making the decision that Rig would never make for herself: safety at the cost of freedom.

Her hands shoved in her pockets, she turns away from the refugees and crosses the street, keeping a watchful eye out for any members of the Military Police that might be in the area.

The shop she's looking for is just up ahead, a tiny hole-in-the-wall sort of place.

She has to duck her head to get under the low door. There's a busted-up hologram catalogue fixed to the wall and a countertop in front of stacks upon stacks of boxes and crates. She taps the rusty little service bell sitting on the counter.

"Coming!" a dusty voice calls out.

A shifting of boxes later, the proprietor steps out. He's a tall, weedy Trant – a four-armed species with grey skin. He adjusts his spectacles and peers down at her. One of his hands starts signing his words out as he says, "Can I help you?"

"Looking for a Mr. Iris?"

He gives her a twitchy sort of smile, his signing hand flexing. "You've found him."

"Oh, cool. I'm Rig, Mohsin sent a message ahead that I'd be coming. I've got a letter on my link…"

"Ah, no need, I received his earlier note. Crate?"

She hefts it onto the counter. "And payment?"

With three of his four hands, he deactivates the hover mechanism and hefts the box up onto his shoulders. His fourth hand keeps spelling out his words. Maybe he doesn't know she doesn't speak Trant sign language, or maybe it's just a force of habit. "Come on behind the counter. There's a bag of unmarked kydis here for you."

She hops over the counter while he pushes boxes around. There's a weird musty smell in the back of the shop, like dust, if it were possible for dust to get wet while still being bone dry. The same smell lingers on a cloth pouch filled with a fistful of ten-thousand-kydis chips. Ah, the sweet smell of cold hard cash. She picks up the pouch and breathes in deep – and then promptly sneezes.

She flicks a strange feather-covered object hanging from the ceiling and watches as the shards of stone hanging from it glint in the light. "Can I ask, who are all those people in the undercity?"

"Refugees, mostly. The Divian Moon city was unlucky enough to discover that a bunch of their mountains had valuable aradium ore in them last week. They were attacked not a day later. Two hours. Five hundred thousand dead, and the rest…" His third hand gestures to the door and the streets outside. "They're lucky they had a ship fast enough to flee."

Divian Moon? That's well past the Ossuary-Ascetic border. The war pushes further and further every year. Proving the superiority of your own faction's god is a damn effective drug when it comes to motivating people to march off to battle. "Who did it?"

"Ossuary. They never even gave those folks a chance to fight. They simply came and…"

He trails off with a shudder, casting a fearful glance to one of the many odd objects sticking out from between the crates. This one is a dented black shoulder pauldron, weathered with age in a way that suggests it's made of non-ferranealed metal. Must be from the Battle of Eighth Sun, about three hundred years before Rig's time, but she knows the look of older materials pretty well and she knows how much that armor sucked during that battle. Too fragile, favoring light weight over sturdiness. Mr. Iris's gaze flickers to the sigil emblazoned on the pauldron. The all-seeing eye of Ossuary. The many golden rings of it draw her in, a swirling optical illusion that hypnotizes her into staring longer and harder than she would otherwise.

She snaps herself out of it and looks back to Mr. Iris. "That's rough."

"Mm. Ascetic and Pyrite are terrible, make no mistake, but Ossuary…"

"Pyrite's worse," she automatically replies. She presses her lips into a tight, thin smile. "I guess we'll agree to disagree."

With a multi-shouldered shrug, Mr. Iris abandons the issue. He retrieves a crowbar and cracks open the crate. A dust cloud poofs up as the lid slides off.

Inside is all manner of curiosities, so named, presumably, because it makes her so curious that she shamelessly leans on one of Mr. Iris's lower shoulders to peer over the lid and get a better look at the sparkling treasure within.

Maybe a dozen items of varying sizes and shapes are packed into the crate, nestled in protective layers of wrapping, like chocolate gems during the Ascetic Summer Festival. One by one, Mr. Iris removes the antiques, laying them out on a square of fabric next to one of his elbows. Each is given special consideration, examined from multiple angles, *tsk*-ed and *hmm*-ed at as he turns them over.

She stares in wonder at an intricately carved wooden puzzlebox, no bigger than her thumbnail and detailed enough to necessitate Mr. Iris's smallest magnifying glass. There's a scroll made from flat reeds slotted together, covered in sharp lettering, the ink a suspicious brown color. A necklace made of diamonds that makes her head feel foggy when she looks at it. Some sort of flute that's cast in silver and bronze, emeralds resting on the keys like buttons.

When he removes a threadbare handkerchief, she realizes it's a miracle half of this survived however many transfers and luminalspace jumps it took to get here. Some of it, the jewels and such, would be fine, but there's a bottle of ink that she knows is on its last legs.

By the time Mr. Iris removes the final object from the box, her mind is so glazed over in wonderment that the shining orb almost slips past her gaze.

Almost.

She blinks. Stares. "That's Kashrini."

"I beg your pardon?"

She pushes past him, her fingers gently gripping the cool glass sphere. It's a glass orb, hand-blown going by the slight inconsistencies in shape, and inside is the most beautiful crystal statuette. Two figures cut from some sort of white stone are wrapped in an embrace, their arms raised above their heads. Where their hands meet, a ring forms, and atop that circle rests a shimmering red-orange firestone.

"I know this! I tried to steal it eighteen months ago. Would've gotten away with it too if it weren't for Pyrite turning up at the last minute." Her smile is older than herself. Old as the first time she was blessed enough to hear the myth. "That's Dare of the Spire and his lover, Shen."

"I haven't heard the name."

"I suppose you wouldn't have. It's Kashrini history. It was my favorite story when I was a kid. Still is. Dare was a folk hero, from the old days. Before the Kashrini were subjugated by Pyrite, a tower called Agaraan Spire was the heart of our planet. It was–" She hesitates. "Well, we're not actually sure what it was. It's been so long, and it was probably a lot of things. A religious center, a historical building. Somewhere for us to worship the gods we've forgotten, we think. A center of commerce maybe? It was a symbol. Or it's become a symbol."

Her people barely know what it actually was. What it's *become* is far more important. At a certain point, the truth and the story blend together into a tangle that's impossible to decipher. And in the end, when almost everything the Kashrini had has been taken from them, does that difference matter? If the story inspires, is that more important?

"Once Pyrite invaded," Rig continues, "They occupied the Spire and used it as the base of their operations. They subjugated all of our planet from that Spire, ruining our history, corrupting our legends and turning them to their purposes. Dare burned it down over five thousand years ago, so all we have left are these sorts of relics."

Just as she can't undo what she did under Pyrite, her people can't get back the entirety of what they lost. What they *can* do is try with every damn breath in their bodies to stop Pyrite from taking anything else. Triaging a wound instead of tending to scars.

She realizes she hasn't blinked for a while and does that before her eyes start to tear up. Wouldn't want to cry on the polished glass. "Is this important to you or–? I'll buy it?"

She'll be taking it regardless of his answer, but parting on good terms is also important.

"No, no," he replies, "I don't need it. It's yours."

She does a double take. "Seriously?"

"It's Kashrini, not Trant. I have less claim to it than you do." His coughs make Rig want to cough in sympathy. "Hold on a tick. I think I have something somewhere in here."

He shuffles around again, his four arms creaking as he opens cupboards and rattles in drawers. Eventually, Rig *does* cough, but it's more due to the clouds of dust he's kicking up. When he emerges from his disaster zone, he's wielding a nanosilk-lined bag. From experience, she knows a bag like that will protect even the most fragile of artifacts.

"Ah-hah." His hands slowly wrap up the glass ball in the fabric. "Won't scratch it at all."

"You are a godsdamned treasure."

His lighthearted laugh deteriorates into another bout of coughing. "Thank you very kindly."

"Stars' favor, Mr. Iris!" she calls back, sauntering out the door.

Two of his hands cheerfully wave her goodbye as she leaves.

The glass ball doesn't weigh much as she carefully cradles it in her arms on her way back out to the waiting taxi.

She's spent a significant chunk of time over the past three years recovering things that have been lost to the Kashrini. Out of all the myths and legends her people have, the tales of Dare of the Spire and Shen are the greatest treasure of them all. It's more than just the story of her people – in her mind, it has always been *her* story.

It's a shock to have found it, and in such good condition, too, considering the material. Glass is one of the rarer materials for her to deal with, although the crystal inside is more common, if only barely. Most materials that are degradable, easily broken, or valuable aren't usually found in Kashrini art nowadays. Stone and bone are her better friends. That's not to say that Kashrini didn't *use* those materials – the orb in her hands is clear proof otherwise. It's simply that their planet was invaded by Pyrite so long ago that most of their culture has been erased from the annals of history, and physical items are easier to destroy than tales.

The beautiful sights of the upper city are grey in Rig's eyes on the taxi ride back to the spaceport.

Factions. All the same, really. They can dress themselves up in as many tricks as they want; but in the end, they're no different from one another. The galaxy was better off without them, in her mind, although it's impossible to go back to what must have been better days, ten thousand years ago.

She casts a dirty look up at the beautiful mosaic when she reenters the spaceport.

"Here," she says, slipping the taxi driver more money as she exits the vehicle. "Best for everyone if you forget all about me."

She gives her a nod and tucks the kydis into her pocket. "I never saw you in the first place."

Good fellow.

She keeps her head down and her pace even to avoid any unwanted attention as she walks back into her hangar bay, only to see Ginka sitting on *Bluebird*'s gangplank.

"Hey?" she asks tentatively, coming to stand in front of Ginka. "I thought you'd have left by now. Are you okay?"

That black duffel bag is still clasped in Ginka's hands as she looks up, her green eyes strangely flat and unreadable and also undeniably tired. She rises to her feet and says, like she's reading a report, "*Bluebird* has been refueled."

"Sorry?"

"I spoke with a member of the port authority," Ginka informs her, "and I was able to make arrangements to refuel your ship. One of the fission chargers had blown out and I had that replaced as well. The shield generators were also restored. There were no additional repairs necessary that either I or the spaceport staff could detect."

Nope, Rig still doesn't have any damn clue what's going on. "I, I don't... Ginka, you shouldn't have. Seriously, you shouldn't have. I don't have the money to pay for this; I can't end up in debt to anyone here."

"No debt," she replies quickly. "I handled it."

She *paid* for all that? What the fuck? *How* the fuck? If Ginka's secretly a rich motherfucker, then what was she doing hitching rides to Red Dock? Seriously, the woman owns *one* bag of stuff. How could she afford to refuel and fix *Bluebird*? What the fuck sort of high class, fast working bounty hunter *is* she, because that's the only source of revenue Rig's brain can come up with right now.

"Where did you get the money?"

"That's irrelevant," Ginka instantly replies.

"O-kaaaaay." Bounty hunter business. Gotta be. Or selling drugs? So long as they don't end up with a murder investigation looming over them, Rig's willing to let it slide. There's a lot she's willing to let slide for a fueled and fixed ship. And if it does come back to bite them in the ass, at least she'll have a ship capable of making a quick getaway. "Why did you come back though? I thought you were looking for something?"

Ginka opens her mouth. Then closes it. Then admits, "I don't know where to find what I'm looking for. Or have any leads at all, really."

"Not a clue, huh?"

"No. And... and I don't have anywhere else to go."

Rig gently rests her hand on Ginka's shoulder and smiles. "Sounds to me like you're in need of a reclaimer. Come on, Cactus. Let me show you around the Ascetic homeworld while I do my thing, and then we can talk business. If you can pay for fuel and repairs, you can afford my fees."

CHAPTER FOUR
The Librarian

Even though Ginka has done Rig a couple of very nice favors, what with the ship and the Red Dock assistance, there are still some things that Rig thinks might be best to keep on the downlow for right now. Until she knows Ginka better, at least, or figures out what do to about what her new tagalong is trying to locate.

"I'm gonna be gone for a bit," she says, leading Ginka through the bustling, sunlit streets on the outskirts of her final destination. "I'll figure out lodging and stuff. No offense, but I'm not letting you sleep on my ship alone, and I'm not going to be staying the night on *Bluebird*. Don't worry, there are a *ton* of fancy hotels around here."

Ginka's keeping pace behind, slowing down a bit the longer they walk. Not a fan of the growing crowds, maybe? "Oh... that's fine."

"Of course it's fine. Here, just ahead. There's this really nice café that I'll drop you at. It's got a bunch of pay-by-the-hour netspace terminals, so you can do some research about whatever weird thing it is you're looking for. Sound good?"

"...Hm."

Despite Ginka's lack of enthusiasm, Rig's bouncing up and down as they stroll through the more luxurious sections of the capital. Skyscrapers, hanging gardens, all of it glistening under the bright blue sky. Massive towers and compounds surround this extensive section, like a tiny, protected valley. And up ahead, past the last few rows of upscale shops and cafés, are a series of white marble and green glass buildings. Silver wire domes and the tips of lush conservatories peek over the shop roofs.

One of the Ascetic homeworld's Historical Centers.

Every homeworld has them. Preserving the records of their glorious and probably falsified pasts is one of the things that Ascetic, Pyrite, and Ossuary all hold close to their hearts. Even though she dislikes the factions, she too has old stories in her bones. She doesn't know a single person who *isn't* like that. The Kashrini have storytellers to pass along their peoples' tales. She knows, for example, that Undarians tell their history through long and complex pantomimes, and that Oriates used to hold coming of age competitions to determine if a child was ready to learn their old legends. The three factions, however, write everything down and store it away in great libraries, hoarding the knowledge like platinum bars.

She might not love the principle behind them, but she can't deny she loves the libraries themselves.

"Here we are, Cactus." She comes to a stop in front of a cute little café. Ascetic doesn't really *do* signs, so there's a unique ornament of a glass star hanging over the entrance in lieu of one. "Your stop. If you've got the kind of money to refuel my ship, then you can eat your heart out. And then probably eat someone else's heart out if you're still peckish."

"…Mm."

"Cactus?"

When she turns around, Ginka's eyelids are dropping, her usual stiff neck now sagging down. Ginka blinks hard and deliberately as though trying to use her eyelids to punch her eyeballs back into full functionality.

"Hey, you alright?"

Another forceful blink. "Fine."

"…Are you falling asleep on me, Cactus?"

Ginka shakes her head and it sort of flops around instead of neatly going side to side. "No."

"Okay, *well*, if you're *so* awake, then where am I dropping you off?"

"Um." Ginka's jaw cracks open into a yawn. She looks briefly panicked and slaps her hands over her mouth. "I'm awake," she quickly denies.

"...Uh-huh." Rig looks her up and down.

On a whim, she reaches out to poke Ginka's cheek. Ginka swats her hand away like she would a lazy fly, but it's *so* uncoordinated and she sways on her feet as she does so, nearly toppling over.

"I *told* you I'm awaaaaa–" Ginka's own words are betrayed by a second yawn.

Rig snickers. "*Awww.* Does the big mean cactus need her nap time?"

It's probably meant to be a glare, but the look Ginka gives her is more of a bleary-eyed squint. "*No.*"

She can't help wondering if Ginka has some kind of sleep issues as well as... well, as well as all her *other* issues. First, she'd slept for an unreasonably long amount of time on the trip here, and now she's passing out standing up. Does she have some kind of chronic exhaustion problem or something? Or is it a side effect of whatever drug she was taking earlier today?

Yeesh. She glances over at the café. There's really no way she can just dump Ginka at a table and hope that a cup of coffee will fix it, is there? The Ascetic homeworld relentlessly cracks down on anything *unsightly*, like homelessness. A lone Zazra wearing dirty and slightly bloodstained clothing passed out on a table in a café is exactly the sort of thing that results in someone calling in a complaint and then Ginka getting dragged off somewhere. Or Ginka killing a bunch of police a skip and a hop away from the Historical Center. Not great options.

Godsdamn it. She's too nice.

"Ugh." She turns back and offers Ginka a hand. "Come on. I know a place where you can nap."

Ginka looks down at the offered hand and then ignores it, continuing to slowly stagger after Rig, swaying with each step.

"You're *so* sleepy," Rig says with a grin.

"'m not sleepy," she mumbles. "I'm deadly."

"What are you gonna do? Snore at me?" Her lungs shake with repressed laughter.

Ginka gives her another failure-glare.

She leads Ginka down the street and towards the looming gate at the end of a pavilion – one of the few entrances to the Historical Center and the assorted libraries and living complexes within its great boundaries. Marble walls greet them, pillars etched with abstract images of flowers and vines, fat green gems sitting atop the stone.

A wavering hard light energy field connects the pillars, protecting the solid metal gate behind it. Enough power running through it to shock anyone stupid if they tried to push past it. Rig knows from experience that it's a field she couldn't bring down without at least a few hours and equipment she doesn't have on hand.

"Rig," Ginka says slowly, staring owlishly at the solemn, masked guards posted by the gate as though they'll shoot her on sight. Which, given how important Historical Centers are, probably isn't a *wrong* assumption to make. "Can we... be here?"

"Yeah, we can."

"Can I... nap here?"

"Sure. I wouldn't recommend napping *right* here though. Concrete can leave you with one hell of a crick in the neck in the morning."

She takes another jaunty step towards the gate.

The two guards move forward.

There's more of them, hiding or patrolling somewhere. Not a lot though. No one's *really* going to attack the Historical

Center. Destroying all that history? Over ten millennia's worth of artifacts and books and stories? It's unthinkable. Even during wars, libraries and knowledge centers are spared. So long as they're factioned, that is. The three factions and the vast majority of the galaxy that falls under their rule would never do such a thing to their history, and yet what's left of Kashrini history is scattered to the winds. So Rig has to be her own librarian for her own people.

"State your name and intent," one of the guards demands.

Military Police guys in the city? Objectively terrifying. But these guards? They work for the library, and that's the one part of Ascetic space that's safe for Rig.

She keeps her hands at her sides, smiling politely at them. "Please inform First Assistant Librarian June that her favorite person is here to see her."

The guard murmurs the request into his earpiece.

The seconds drag on and Rig's grin just grows.

After a moment, a staticky and incomprehensible confirmation comes through. The guard nods to his fellow, stands back, and deactivates the energy field, allowing the metal gates to grind open.

"Thank you kindly," Rig says with a smile as they let her and Ginka pass.

The two of them pass through with ease and climb up the low, wide steps that greet visitors to the Center.

The Historical Center is massive, and it is only one of many on the Ascetic homeworld. Sweeping pavilions lead up to sprawling libraries, museums, and theaters. A statue of Ascetic themself looms above them, casting a long shadow across an ornate and well-trimmed garden. The god is cut of emerald glass. They're depicted as they always are, a naked figure with skin marbled like tree bark, their face lowered and blank, their hands held regally above their head. A large white gem hovers between their cupped hands, slowly rotating and sending rainbow fractals scattering across the statue.

While Rig cannot see the temple devoted to the god, she knows it must be here somewhere, in the very heart of the Historical Center. No other place in the capital city would do, really. In all her visits here, she has never cared to see the main temple where Ascetic is worshiped, or where the High Shamans hold court, or any of the other important places. They're far enough away that they're not a danger to her. They only interest her in the vaguest sense – in that they are indeed *places* and that they must be avoided.

The only important place she cares to visit is one relatively small archival library.

"This way," she tells Ginka, leading her through the lush gardens and statues and making sure she doesn't pass out and plant face first into a decorative pond.

Past the visiting worshipers, past the librarians taking a lunch break, past the honored historians who sit in peaceful contemplation of the landscapes devoted to Ascetic – blah blah. Rig didn't care for that factioned shit when she was under Pyrite and she doesn't care for it now. She turns her nose up as she passes.

Another series of low steps lead up the archival library. The building is glass, although they cannot see through it, and one wall is built into a concrete tower, the peak of which is overflowing with greenery. From that tower, a waterfall flows. It sparkles like diamonds, running over the top of the library and then over the side into a nearby garden's reflection pool.

Rig types a code into the key panel attached to the library's door. There's a *click* of a lock, and then a *swoosh* as the doors open.

She sweeps her hand towards the doors. "Welcome to the best library there is, Cactus."

Despite having been in this particular library numerous times before, it never fails to take Rig's breath away.

As with all places of history and lore, there is a solemn, reverent hush in the building's halls. Not to say that it's dead quiet, not at all. There's a constant susurrus of noise, whispered debates between academics, the sound of pages – actual paper pages, whole books full of them – being turned, artifacts being shuffled around. Feet dragging over thick carpets. The rustle of heavy surcoats and the clattering of keys.

And the air – thick with the smell of dust and old things, but not repulsive. Homely. Comforting.

Most of the people in here are casual scholars. Every tenth desk perhaps, holds a true librarian, noticeable by the patterned surcoats they wear and the chatelaines of keys and code cards hanging from their belts.

When Rig turns around, she sees Ginka still standing in the doorway, gaping. "Come on," she says with a light laugh. "Haven't you ever seen a library before?"

"No," Ginka whispers. She pauses to yawn again. "I've never been inside – not one like this. We aren't allowed."

"Well we're allowed *here*."

Ginka chews on her lower lip. "Are you *really* friends with a *First Assistant Librarian*? How does someone like that even associate with someone like you? Er – not to be rude. But you *said* you didn't want any contact with the authorities, and a librarian is about as high up the chain of importance as you can get without being in the army or actually leading a faction. You're a Pyrite criminal."

Rig knows what she is.

And so does June.

They walk through the entrance halls and into a larger atrium. High, bottle-green glass ceilings greet them above and rich musky carpeting ushers them in underneath their feet. Upper levels and balconies wrap around the room, turning the inside into a maze of shelves and archives and desks. The light that pours in is flickering and wavy, contorted by the water that runs over the top of the building, and every dancing ray of sunshine bounces off the emeralds and diamonds positioned around the room, catching the dust motes in the air and turning them into gold flakes.

In the center of the atrium is a grey-haired librarian surrounded by a group of young children.

Ginka comes to a sudden halt at the sight, although it might be the sleepiness as well, because she sways a bit and ends up slouched against a pillar. Oh well. Not like they have a deadline. Rig stops as well and lingers.

Words flit towards them on a lazy breeze.

"I give you this story," the librarian is saying, voice low and steady, yet filling the room with ease and catching the ears of every child around him, "so that you may know the costs of duty and how best to pay them. This is the tale of a Devoted Thorn, and the trials she undertook to save the Shaman of the Body, twenty-seventh of that title. This Thorn was small of stature, and she could never defeat her comrades in battle. But strength alone is never the key to victory."

The story is one Rig is vaguely aware of.

Ascetic propaganda, mostly, glorifying the bloody machinations of one of Ascetic's heroes, a member of the Devoted Thorn ranks – bodyguards to the High Shamans. When Windshadow appeared, Ascetic and Pyrite had to come up with an answer to them. Pyrite bulked up their intelligence organization and created the Crimson Butchers, a front-line combat unit – Rig is pretty sure Mohsin used to be a member, actually, although she's never asked. Ascetic's response had been slightly more defensive, their military police forces growing, and they'd created the elite ranks of the Devoted Thorns to protect the important targets that a Windshadow assassin might be tempted to take out.

Not that either response has been particularly effective. Arms races never work. They're just a black hole, devouring the innocent bystanders in this never-ending war.

"…and thus she set her cunning trap," the librarian is saying, "Despite the doubt of her fellows, her enemies began to stumble towards the temple doors, and that is when her final blow was dealt!"

The children gasp, and there's a slight hitch in Ginka's breath.

"That," she insists, "is *not* what happened."

Rig shifts the bag containing the glass orb from her hands to tie it around her belt and let it hang against her hip. "Oh? You know a different version?"

"The *correct* version," Ginka replies, wrinkling her nose at the librarian, even though the man is too far away and too engrossed in talking to the group of kids to either hear or see them.

"Hah. Yeah, sure you do."

"Excuse me?"

There's a surprising amount of outrage in Ginka's voice. Enough to give Rig pause for a moment before saying, slowly and a little in disbelief that she has to explain this to someone who works outside of the factions like her, "I mean, they're *all* the correct version. They're all fake, too."

Ginka's brow contorts itself into a deep-set, confused frown, but before she can reply–

"Rig!"

A woman comes running down the hall, her slippers muffled on the carpeting, and Rig exhales. She exhales for the first time in a long time.

June.

It's been over a month since Rig's seen her, but it isn't until this moment, as June hurries toward her – skirts gathered in her hands, belt of keys clattering, curly brown hair bouncing about her shoulders – that Rig realizes a month is way, *way* too long.

Like Mohsin, June is part Kashrini, only it's barely noticeable, and she's human enough to allow her to be a librarian. She is the most beautiful woman Rig has ever laid eyes on. Each time she sees her, her beauty appears to have only grown. No one else in the galaxy is as stunning as she is, from the slightly blue glow behind her brown skin to the deep-purple-tinted richness of her dark eyes to her soft pink lips that are currently spread into a wide, joyous smile. All for Rig.

Without really being aware of it, she breaks into a run as well. She and June collide halfway. As they always have.

Forever meeting in the middle.

And then June is warm and heavy in her arms, and Rig's kissing those pink lips and smelling that spicy perfume June always wears.

It might be years or seconds, but they do pull apart. Just a little.

June gives her arm a playful swat. "And *when* exactly was the last time you called me? A simple 'I'm not dead' would have sufficed."

"Sorry," Rig says, undoubtedly grinning like an idiot. "I was going to call after I got the refugees out of the Dead Zone, but then I found out I was coming here anyways for a job, and stuff got... crazy."

"And are you going to introduce me to your friend, or shall I?"

Sheepishly, Rig turns around to point at Ginka, who's still slumped against the pillar. "Ginka, this is June. She's a First Assistant Librarian here, and she's my... uh, well, she's my girlfriend. June, this is Ginka. We ran into each other on Red Dock and due to a series of, uh, bullets, she ended up hitching a ride to the Ascetic homeworld with me. I'm showing her around, for the time being."

Ginka awkwardly shuffles over when Rig makes an inviting gesture.

"It's good to meet you, Ginka," June says, holding out a hand.

Ginka ignores the offer of a handshake and bows to June. It's more of a half-body flop, and Rig's actually pretty impressed that she manages to straighten up once she's done. "It's a pleasure to meet you too, honored librarian."

"Aren't you formal?" June withdraws her hand and smiles the warmest of her polite smiles. "Although I am touched – albeit not literally – by your trust."

"Huh?"

"…Unless you *are* interested in using your empathic abilities on me? I'm perfectly open to the idea. I've not met a Zazra before, I admit, but I've read six different treatises on personal and professional Zazra customs when dealing with other species. So please, don't feel as though you need eschew your comfort on my behalf."

Shrinking away like a wilting leaf, Ginka clasps her hands behind her back as though she's worried June might reach out and bite them. "I don't, I'm not really–"

"She likes wearing those fancy gloves," Rig explains, tossing Ginka the easy out she so clearly needs.

"Oh." June raises an eyebrow. "You don't take them off?"

"No, not really," Ginka says in a voice so quiet it's practically a squeak.

Desperate to change the subject, Rig steps back and gestures to the nanosilk bag hanging from her belt. "I almost forgot – *this.*"

Suddenly the businessy, librarian side of June comes out in full force, as it always does when she's confronted with something old and rare. She pries the glass orb out of the bag, bending down to look until her nose is almost brushing the glass, all casual elegance in the curve of her neck and the gentle fall of her curly hair.

"How intriguing." There's a twinkle in her eye as she straightens back up and turns on her heels, beckoning for them to follow. "Let's continue this back in my office."

Rig easily trails after June, like a puppy on her heels.

"I–" Ginka clears her throat. "I can leave if…"

That's sweet, but it's not necessary. "Eh," Rig replies with a shrug. "You helped me get this thing all the way, even though I didn't know it was anything special until recently. You can take a look if you want. Besides, all the really nice sofas are in this direction."

It seems as though she's not the only puppy here, because after a moment of apparent deliberation, Ginka traipses after them.

June tends to have that effect.

No one else in the library so much as blinks at them as they pass, despite Rig and Ginka's appearance. June leads them down a winding series of halls into the heart of the library. As First Assistant Librarian, she's second in command of this entire building, and thus has the second nicest office space.

Her office is much larger than just another cubicle. It's sectioned off by a set of towering double doors that lead into a sprawling space, wallpapered with bookshelves and hidden doors and stasis-locked cabinets that promise strange artifacts inside. In the center is one of the largest desks Rig's ever seen, half of it covered in papers and a fancy computer terminal setup. A bit of happiness wells up in her when she sees that June's still got the mini-freezer stashed under her desk. Rig gave that to her. June tends to forget to eat while she's working so Rig had figured that easier access to food would help.

June clears off some space, laying down a protective blanket to cover over half the desk so she can set the glass ball down. There's a neat, practiced pace to June's motions as she gets out her kit.

In the back of the office, Ginka has decided to lurk by the door like a bouncer at a club.

"Must be, what," Rig asks, "a couple thousand years old?"

"There's only one way to find out." June snaps on a pair of gloves. She pushes the nanosilk to the side and scans the surface of the orb with a handheld tool. "Glass dates to about five thousand years old and handmade, going by the imperfections in the surface. That's evidence of breathite stone particles, right there; see that bubble? Only found on the former Kashraa. I can't get a good read on the crystal sculpture inside however;

someone must have restored this, and the stasis field residue is
throwing off my scanners."

Good thing about the stasis fields though. Rig's not sure it
would have survived all this time if someone, a long time ago,
hadn't decided it was worth preserving.

June draws in a short breath. "This crystal is *incredible*. I
think that's an *actual* firestone, not a more common magnian
opal. It's hard to believe that this has lasted so long."

"I'm glad it did."

"As am I. It's stunning. So," she asks, swapping to a
magnifying glass and inspecting the statuette inside, "what *is*
this?"

"Sure." Rig plops down into a chair and resists the urge to
put her feet up on June's desk. She explains, "It's an image of
the two figures who destroyed Agaraan Spire."

A perplexed frown twists on Ginka's lip. "*What* Spire?"

"Agaraan," June explains. "Although you wouldn't have
known the name. To non-Kashrini, you would only ever have
known it as one of the major spires on the Pyrite homeworld,
formerly known as Kashraa." She grabs the smallest
magnifying glass Rig's ever seen and takes another look. "This
is a *fantastic* example of the xandi style typical of that period.
See the maker's mark on the base? Undoubtedly done using a
micro-chisel instead of a laser. There isn't the depth typical of
a laser…"

Ginka's eyes close for a second, and then she almost falls
over her own feet as June descends into more and more
detailed analysis. "You said there were sofas?" she asks.

"I sure did."

"There's a lounge two buildings over." June gestures to the
right. "And you're welcome to look around, but please don't
go lower than the third level," she adds. She taps her palm
against the chatelaine hanging from her belt, jingling the keys
and cards and magnifying glasses hanging from it. "If you
don't have the proper clearance our security measures will

activate the moment you try. You... won't enjoy the security measures."

Ginka gives her a short bow that almost sends her toppling feet over ass. "You have my word."

"See ya in a bit," Rig says.

Once the door shuts behind Ginka, she leans against the table with a sigh, careful not to mess up June's precise set up of tools.

"...I really do hope she doesn't get lost and try to go past the third level," June frets. "Our newest ball lightning project has just been brought up from the twelfth level to the fourth and it's not exactly pleasant to get caught by."

"I didn't think those projects were your sort of thing?"

"They're not, but I've been chatting with a Fifth Assistant who was involved. You know me; I try to keep a finger in every pie that's inside this library."

In Rig's opinion, that'd be Ginka's fault if she's dumb enough to disregard the warning. But it is June's library, and thus she knows that June considers herself to be held accountable for everything that happens inside it, no matter what. Everything, that is, aside from Rig's actions. That was the accord they struck up so long ago, when they barely knew each other.

Two and a half years ago, Rig had been looking for a solid information broker. All her contacts pointed her towards one woman. June. At first, she'd thought that an Ascetic was a bullshit info broker – but a librarian? That had tickled Rig's interest. June is brilliant at what she does. As many librarians are, she's a hub of information, every rumor in the galaxy floating through her ears, and a walking encyclopedia of history.

One of the scanners beeps and June hastily scrambles to read it.

"Oh!" She enthusiastically shows Rig the screen. "Five thousand, three hundred and twenty-nine years old. More or less. There is, of course, a slight margin for error."

"Damn. It must have been carved only just after the Spire was destroyed and mythologized." Such a pretty thing, even without the historical significance. She brushes a fingertip against the cool crystal. "Can I take it with me? I'll keep all the protective stuff, I promise."

"That depends."

"Oh?" She wriggles her non-existent eyebrows. "Got any kinky conditions for me?"

"Can I please take some more detailed scans for our archives?" June's hands are twitching towards her instruments. "Just a quick holographic image of the surface? A particle analysis, maybe?"

Rig snickers and then sticks out her tongue. "You love tech more than me."

"Is that... is that really what you think?"

"No, I–" Her jaw uselessly flaps about for a moment while she tries to make words happen. "I didn't mean it like that."

With that usual fluid grace, June abandons her scanners and sits down on the desk next to her. She leans her shoulder against Rig's, a soft hand seeking hers. "I *do* love you, you know. I just get... caught up in everything. Tech is constant and predictable, and I *appreciate* that, yes. I also love that you're *not* like that. So there's no need to worry about whether or not I'm replacing you with my admittedly marvelous new holo-imager."

"Oh. Good. Right." Rig presses a quick kiss to June's cheek and laughs. "For a second there I thought you were gonna say that you want to make a hologram clone of me."

"I would not do that," June says slowly, like she'd been mentally writing that idea down and now has to scratch the thought out and throw away the pen. "Because that would be unethical."

"Not to mention unromantic."

"That too. And I *am* aiming for romantic, you know."

This kiss is slower. They have time now – and isn't that such a rare luxury. Rig can blast around the galaxy all she wants, but when she's always moving around she's not staying in one place and enjoying it. She leans into her love and bites her soft lips, tangles her hands into June's curls, and just enjoys the warmth and the sweetness and–

"Hey hey," she says with a grin, coming to a sudden realization. "When you said earlier that you try to keep a finger in everything in this library, does that include me?"

June bursts out laughing. "That's a *terrible* pick-up line."

"Well, is it working?"

That's when June's computer beeps.

"You have *got* to be kidding me." Reluctantly, June pulls away and hops off the desk to reach for the monitor.

"Better reassure your boss?" Rig asks with a laugh. "Let him know that you aren't blowing off work to fool around with some random ex-factioned Kashrini criminal?"

"Yes, but in my defense, this hypothetical random ex-factioned Kashrini criminal has a very nice ass."

Aw. June thinks she has a nice ass; that's the sweetest thing. Rig reaches over to give her a light smack on her ass when she leans over to check the monitor.

June giggles. "*Hey.* I'm *trying* to work."

"And *I'm* trying to distract you. Is that even anything important?"

With an annoyed sigh, June pushes the screen away. "No, it's not. Just more rubbish about this damn book we're having delivered in a few days. It's not even my department, but I keep getting blasted with messages about it."

Rig is then the one getting very *very* distracted as June pulls off her key belt, drops it onto the desk, and starts yanking off her surcoat.

"It's all *proper packaging* this and *wrong couriers* that," she continues. The surcoat falls to the ground and she begins unlacing the white dress she wears underneath it. "Honestly, just because I'm second in command here doesn't mean that it's my job to micromanage this. I *analyze* it, yes, but the actual logistics of getting it here should be sent to Transport and Security, not *me*. One of these days I'm going to get sick and miss work and this place will fall apart and my boss will *finally* realize that I am holding this place together with string and tape."

The dress is tugged off, revealing a whole lot of tantalizingly bare skin. The pink outline of her bra is visible under her thin chemise.

Rig just stares. "Are you *seriously* stripping and ranting at the same time?"

A faint blush spreads over June's cheeks. "I'm being efficient?"

"Oooh, *efficient*, how sexy."

There's a smile on June's lips that matches her own. "If you'd rather I *stop*…"

"No no, I'm getting into this idea of efficiency." She wiggles her brow suggestively. "Gonna do me good and fast?"

"I believe it would be 'do you *well*.'"

"Oh my gods, did you really just correct my grammar right now? You are *such* a librarian."

June places her hands on the sides of Rig's thighs. Her curls tumble down her shoulders as she leans in, smile in her eyes and a lascivious grin on her lips. A pang of lust shoots through Rig. "Yes, I *did*. And here I thought you were a fan of the sexy librarian stereotype?"

"Big fan," she says quickly, struggling to make her tongue function. "Big, big fan."

Her hands move over June's, undoing the buckle of her belt and letting the whole thing – guns and all – drop onto the desk. She tangles her fingers in June's curls, bringing her closer–

June's computer beeps again.

"Oh come *on*!" Rig glares at the thing. "Can I shoot it? *Please*?"

"No shooting technology." June pulls away again – gods

damn it – and checks the computer, frowning at it in annoyance as she reads the screen. That frown shifts into confusion. "Security's calling me?"

She shifts the alert to her link and opens the channel. Voice only, cause… well. Partially undressed.

"This is First Assistant Librarian June Rivera, how may I–"

"Pardon the interruption, but there's someone currently being detained at the gates. She does not have proper clearance on their person, however she claims to be associated with a Kashrini that does have such clearance to enter. She's requesting to speak with said associate."

Oh for fucks sake. Rig groans and pinches the bridge of her nose. "Ginka, you *dumbass*." Then to June, she says, "I'll go spring her if you write me a note?"

June nods. "Someone will be along shortly. Please hold your position."

There's a quick affirmative from the guards and then the call cuts out with a pinch of static.

"One second," June says, plucking a blank key card from a drawer and quickly sticking it in the computer to burn a clearance code onto it. A moment later, the card spits out and she hands it over. "Give her this. It should let her wander about any of the non-restricted zones without hassle."

"Thanks, babe." She leans in to quickly steal a kiss. "Don't get dressed while I'm gone."

June snorts in amusement. "I wouldn't dream of it. Go free your friend."

Friend seems a bit strong. She'd personally go for 'weird associate' if she had to pick. "I'll be right back."

She snatches up the key card and steps out of June's office with an annoyed cloud hovering over her.

The cloud keeps hovering all the way out of June's library. Of all the inconvenient fucking times for Ginka to do something stupid and get herself caught by security… Why did she have to intrude on Rig's *convenient fucking* time? Her feet splash through the decorative fountains, scaring the shit out of some poor jewel colored fish and one seriously offended bird, as she takes the straightest possible line towards the front gates.

Two guards are watching this side of the gates, but there's no Ginka in sight as Rig approaches.

She flashes them her ID card. "I got a call that my friend was waiting for me?" She jerks her head towards the closed gates. "Did you kick her out? That's just rude."

One of the guards runs the card through a small scanner and then nods at his associate.

There's a *whirr* as the energy field on the other side of the gates deactivates and the thick metal starts to slide open as Rig makes her way down the shallow stairs.

"Seriously, Cactus," she says once she makes it past the final step, "why did…"

Ginka's not here.

Shit. Paranoia and panic scream through her mind and she reaches for her guns because either something's happened to Ginka and the guards didn't help, or something's about to happen to her – but her guns are gone, left behind on June's desk. She's unarmed. She's *unarmed*. How could she have been so stupid–

"Hello, Traxi," a calm voice says.

She whirls her head around to the right fast enough for something in her neck to crack.

A human woman is standing there, pale haired and wearing glasses, cool as anything. She's wearing a dull grey coat and a blank, practiced smile.

And everything about her, from her posture to the flash of sickly blue under her coat *screams* Pyrite.

"Thank you for coming quietly," the woman says in a blank voice.

The Center guards are in on this or they just don't care. No help from them. And apparently a thousand neurons in Rig's brain are all firing at full speed in a thousand different directions because what comes out of her mouth is:

"Yeah," she remarks flatly, "as my girlfriend can attest to, 'coming quietly' isn't really my thing."

The woman ignores her and simply nods to someone – *someone standing right behind Rig, oh fuck–*

Something heavy and blunt slams into the back of her head when she tries to turn around.

Pain bursts through her temples.

Darkness descends.

INTERLUDE
Sparrow and Ghoul

Ghoul X-74 runs down the dark corridor.

Thirteen paces, control panel – she has to get the bulkhead doors open. She throws her body to the ground to avoid the enemy bullets whizzing over her head and rolls up into a low crouch, grabbing the nearest opponent by the front of his shirt, pulling him down and slitting his throat with her blade. More shots; she turns and blocks them with the corpse then throws the body at the next attacker.

She snaps up, planting a spinning kick into the enemy's head while they're distracted, grabs their gun, shoots the control panel.

Sparks burst in front of her eyes as the security mechanism goes down.

With a heavy groan and the screech of metal, the bulkhead doors begin to slide open – only a few inches, but X-74 has always been slim, and she can slip through the small cracks that the larger opponents she's up against can't.

She draws a second knife from her belt and throws it with unwavering accuracy at an enemy preparing to shoot her. The blade buries itself in their forehead and she twists through the open doors.

Two minutes and thirteen seconds to find and assassinate her target before the mark is on an escape pod, off the ship, and into safety.

An eternity, in her eyes.

She jumps up, grabbing onto the edge of a ventilation shaft and–

Ding.

The lights turn back on.

X-74 drops to the floor as the training complex is illuminated and the bots deactivate. A holo projection automatically pops up to display her score – an incomplete mark – before being dismissed by the Controller overseeing today's practice.

The Controller steps into the room through a hidden door, an unfamiliar man walking behind him, and X-74 automatically bends into a low bow.

"That's enough for today," the Controller informs her, "I believe we have seen all we need to."

He turns and gestures to the person behind him. A man, about her age, with tawny skin and dark hair similar to hers. His eyes, however, are a pure, deep black. An auspicious feature, to have eyes the color of raven's feathers. A streak of pure silver cuts through his hair by his right ear – not a sign of age, but a side effect of the unique Windshadow link he wears as an earpiece.

"This is Sparrow-Seven," the Controller says.

Sparrow – the first rank of Handlers, and superior to X-74. They're both the lowest on the ladder, but all Handlers are technically superior to Operatives. Another glance and she can see a small, soft, brown feather hanging from a strand of his hair, to denote his rank.

She bows to the Sparrow, as well. "A pleasure to meet you."

"The pleasure is all mine. I'm sorry for interrupting your training," he replies, smoothly, elegantly, and genuinely. As a Handler, he can mostly do what he likes in dictating an Operative's movements. He doesn't need to apologize for anything. And yet he does. "But it was stunning to watch you work. You're very impressive."

"I... Thank you. I am unworthy of such a compliment."

He opens his mouth to say something, but the Controller cuts him off. "X-74, as you may or may not be aware, you are a contender for fast-tracked promotion. As such, despite your low rank, we've seen fit to assign you a permanent Handler. Namely, Sparrow-Seven, should the two of you work well in the field. Both of you are to report to my office in one hour for your first assignment."

With a sharp nod, the Controller turns and leaves.

X-74 gives the Sparrow a far deeper, more respectful bow. "I'm honored for the chance to work under you. Please take care of me."

"Likewise," he replies, and then there's a faint bit of a smile on his lips, unexpected but not unappreciated. "Now that he's gone, could you run through the gauntlet again? You were doing something rather interesting with your knife and I'd love to get a closer look."

"Oh, oh of course." She's not quite sure what else to say. "It wasn't anything special, I assure you. I stick to the standardized moves."

He shrugs, casually, and then remarks, "There are always ways to improve upon the standardized, right? I'm sure someone as skilled as you has invented a few original tricks here and there."

No, she hasn't. She's pretty certain she isn't *supposed* to, either. And for that matter, she's also pretty certain that he isn't supposed to be *asking* her about it as though it's a *good* thing.

But she finds herself running the gauntlet again, regardless.

CHAPTER FIVE
Pyrite Intelligence

Rig wakes up and then instantly regrets it.

There's a pounding ache in her temples, and her vision is all fuzzy for the first few moments after she manages to crack her eyelids open. A light somewhere is flickering on and off in time with the beat of her pulse as it runs tight along the expanse of her skull. She feels vaguely dizzy and a bit like she's going to be sick.

"I'm glad to see you're awake," says a familiar voice.

She opens her eyes further. It's that woman again – the one from outside the Historical Center. Only this time the coat is gone, revealing the blue and grey uniform of not just Pyrite, but specifically *Pyrite Intelligence*.

That snaps her awake with a burst of fear and she jerks backwards–

She's tied down.

She's stuck in a chair, hands bound together and fixed to the table in front of her by a hard-light clasp. As she pulls and pulls against the restraints all she manages to do is bruise her wrists. No way she can brute-force her way out of it, even though all her instincts are telling her to try. Her feet aren't bound, though, so maybe she could stand? She shifts slightly, grounding her feet–

A rough hand claps down on her shoulder, slamming her back down into the chair. She darts her eyes up and sees a man decked out in the same uniform, a gun resting at his hip. Another glance around the room shows a number of other strangers dressed in identical terrifying uniforms.

The woman, sitting across the table from her, smiles. "Don't worry. We have no intentions of hurting you and I think we'd all prefer it if you didn't force our hand."

Rig would *love* to shoot her... only she's unarmed. She doesn't have her guns.

Oh, thank the gods.

She *doesn't have her guns*.

Pyrite Intelligence has *her*, but they don't have what they *really* want. The smallest smidgeon of confidence returns to her.

Pyrite Intelligence is a pervasive monster, ever the threat, ever prepared to stomp down the streets and arrest some poor bastard on trumped-up charges. Unlicensed inventions or stolen machinery – whatever is most convenient. It could be worse, she supposes. They could be the secretive spooks Ossuary uses to enforce their rule – Windshadow, they're called. They're invincible, which is almost comforting; because in contrast, she's tricked Pyrite Intelligence once before, hasn't she? She left once, didn't she? Surely, she hopes, she can do it again.

She takes stock of the room she's in, searching for something that she could use or that would give her a hint of her location. It's a cramped room, dimly lit and dingy. Neon papers deck the walls, year old film posters dotted in with an eclectic assortment of advertisements. Shinedust smoke hovers in the air, foul and thick, obscuring her vision like a fog.

"I apologize for the manner in which we brought you here, Traxi, but–"

"Rig," she replies, automatically. "My name is Rig. Do I get the honor of your name?"

"I am Special Agent Fen, of Pyrite Intelligence, as I'm sure you can guess." Nothing about the woman's posture changes, but Rig gets the distinct impression that a box on the 'how many things Rig is allowed to know before she's executed' list just got checked.

She sniffs and tugs at her wrists again. "So what'd you offer Ascetic for this?"

"I beg your pardon?" Fen replies, her face a smooth, practiced blank.

"You wouldn't have kidnapped me if you didn't have the okay to be here. Sure, they're probably not my biggest fan, but odds would have been that they would be far more interested in a Pyrite incursion than one ex-factioned vagabond. So... What did you give them? Pyrite's not going to be announcing a formal alliance with those – oh, what did we call them? – 'nature-worshiping morons'?"

Not even a flinch. Damn it, Rig's main combat skill is pissing people off. Without it, she's fucked.

"Ascetic can be understanding at times, when we share common interests," Fen says unhelpfully. Common interests like what? Being anti-Rig? "We were rather hoping that you could follow that example. You're better than they are."

"Why, 'cause I was born under Pyrite?" Rig snorts. "If you want to appeal to my sense of faction pride, I don't have one."

A pitying look comes over Fen's face. A fake one, but it's a good effort. "I'm sorry. It's a sad fate, to serve no great cause, to have nothing more important than yourself to rally behind. No code of honor. I had heard you'd fallen into thievery, but I didn't want to believe it. You had such promise."

Condescension? Really? When Rig was twelve, she was the first and only Kashrini student in her weapons development unit. People have been talking down to her for as long as she can remember. She'll let Fen keep trying that one if it makes the agent feel better.

"Just get to the point," she demands, giving another futile tug on the handcuffs. "I have a date tonight."

Is it already tonight? Or is it the next day? How long has she been out?

Fen smiles that fake smile. "We would appreciate it if you would return the nanomite weapon plans you stole from us."

"First," she corrects, "they weren't actually *weapon* plans. They were *schematics,* and *you lot* decided that they would be absolutely fantastic as a way to mow people down." And she's spent every single fucking day since she left trying to somehow help the people who have been displaced because one of her bombs fell on their city or who were ripped from their homes by Pyrite soldiers armed with her weapons. "Second, bit of a conundrum, isn't it? Can I steal something if I was the one who invented it? I'd use the word 'reclaim' instead of 'steal.' Third – No."

A cautious incline of Fen's head. "Those plans don't belong to you, either. They were sold before you deserted us three years ago. We are simply attempting to retrieve stolen property and return it to the proper buyers."

Buyers?

Rig didn't know about any buyers. Either Pyrite is trying to sell them to a neutral third party, or, even more perplexingly, to one of the other two factions – an idea she struggles to wrap her head around. While she knows that sometimes there's hidden cooperation between two of the factions, that's usually in relation to hunting down those aforementioned third parties, the sort of people that, like Rig and the rest of the Nightbirds, are undisputedly anti-faction. Selling a whole-ass superweapon to a different faction doesn't make sense. It must be some kind of set up, surely. Have Ascetic and Ossuary tear each other down and then swoop in later to clean up the remains of both?

She has to stop her mind before it spins in circles. There's nothing she can do about it right now and it doesn't change the fact that nobody is getting their greedy little hands on her schematics.

She changes tactics. "How do you know I haven't destroyed them?"

"Oh, Rig," Fen says with a knowing sigh, "of course you

haven't. You can insult us all you like, but you're *proud* of the work you did in the First Spire of Military Innovation, aren't you?"

Rig gapes at the woman. *Proud?*

Her stomach churns, images of what her work accomplished rising unwanted to the forefront of her mind. The initial nanomite tests... clinical and distant when she'd hand over the prototypes and ideas, but then a few days later she'd see the notes show up on her desk from whoever was lucky – or unlucky – enough to work with her.

Couldn't locate the neck accurately enough to sever it in one application, they'd tell her. *Two were incinerated by miscalculated energy input*, they'd say. *Have a look at the chemical composition of the ash those people left behind and do let us know how we can intentionally replicate the result*, they'd say, because gods only know we need more fucked up ways to kill around here.

Bile burns at the back of her throat. Deep breaths of the smoke-filled air only make things worse. It's thick and oppressive and her flailing memories turn the staleness into the stench of formaldehyde. Once, she'd visited the mortuary and watched as a medic dissected the victim of her failed bio-targeting nanomites. They were supposed to sever the enemy Oriate's arteries. Instead, when the medic opened the woman's body up, the soup the nanomites had turned her internal organs into had poured out. Pink, chunky gore had splattered onto the floor and splattered onto the medic and splattered onto Rig's shoes.

Rig clenches her hands into fists.

"The only thing I'm *proud of* is burning that cursed place to the ground," she snarls, and then, for good measure, spits in Fen's face.

Fen doesn't flinch. "That's enough immaturity, don't you think?"

"Get fucked."

Then, to her horror, Fen reaches out and lays her hands gently over Rig's cuffed ones. "There's no need to be so defensive. We aren't here to hurt you. We're trying to make the galaxy a safer place. Isn't that what you want as well? Our weapon schematics could ensure peace and stability–"

"*My* schematics," she repeats, seething. She tries to tug her hands away and the hard light clasp only hums under the strain. "They were built by *me*, built based on *my* DNA – they're *mine*."

Fen smiles. "Now *there's* that pride."

"Shut *up*!"

"Who made you so ashamed? Don't try to fight what you feel. You deserve to be proud of what you've achieved. Rig, you're the only one who can invent all the incredible things you've built. You're cavorting around the galaxy right now, and I know that even misguided as you are, you're trying to do the right thing. We can help you be part of something greater. You're special; you know you are. You're the only one who can help remove the threats to our galaxy."

"Threats? You people are the threat, and if you think I'll help you kill every Kashrini in the galaxy then you're insane."

That smile fades into a slightly sad expression. "You must not have understood us properly in the heat of the moment back then. We would never wipe out *all* your people. That's in direct opposition to what we *really* want. We need to protect ourselves *and* our Kashrini citizens from dangerous radicals–"

"Nightbirds?" Rig says. She doubts there are other dangerous Kashrini radicals out there besides her and Mohsin's group. "The ones messing with your supply lines to the front? Sabotaging your warships? Freeing your *indentureds*?"

Fen doesn't see the connection that Rig is sarcastically waving in front of her face. "Exactly. I'm glad you've heard of the threat they pose."

Rig's shoulders relax slightly. Fen's good, but she's not nearly as well informed as she thinks she is. "You know, you're not half bad at this. It's too bad for you that you're three years too late."

"Excuse me?"

"Check my wrist."

A slight push of Fen's thumb slides Rig's glove up enough to reveal the small tattoo of a white bird resting against her pulse.

Fen's mouth does a series of painful contortions before settling into a blank straight line. "Oh, Rig," she says with a disappointed sigh. "You're better than this. I'd really been hoping you knew that."

"I'm better than *you*," Rig snaps. "It took you three whole years to pin me down while I was running around as part of your so-called radical threat. Kinda pathetic, don't you think?"

"Please listen to me. You need to return the schematics and come back to Pyrite so we can hand them over to the proper buyers, and this can all just blow over for you. We are patient. Our buyers are *not*. I've been given a good deal of leeway in what methods I may use to bring you back into the fold, but you are leaving me with precious few options."

At that, Fen finally removes her hands from Rig's and reaches into her breast pocket. She removes something shimmering, places it down on the table with a neat *click* and then slides it towards Rig.

A big, blingy, plastic headscarf pin twinkles innocuously in the light.

Rig stares at it until her eyes start to water. The last time she saw something like that, it was tucked behind Daara's ear. When she speaks, she can't manage anything louder than a whispered, "Where did you get that?"

That creepy smile of Fen's returns. "Why don't you come back to our headquarters, and we can discuss the pin there?"

"Tell me where you got it!"

The lights turn off.

What the fuck kind of intimidating tactic–

"Perimeter team, check in!" Fen demands. There's the rough scrape of metal as her chair slides back. "Secure the room, lock down the target…"

This isn't part of their plan. But if not, then who – the mysterious buyers? Another interested party? Not the Ascetic Military Police; there's no way. Rig's heart skips a beat. This isn't their plan. Which makes this an opportunity for her.

She leaps to her feet, hands still bound to the table, one foot snaking behind the chair leg to kick it out–

Light appears in the room.

Everything gets very fast all at once.

A black clad figure stands behind a guard, a formless, featureless mask covering their face and ears, and Rig knows that hair–

Sickly, gold, electric light crackles like a sheath around Ginka's gauntlets as it throws her suddenly-here figure into relief, having appeared out of nowhere quicker than a star winking out. She's gripping one of the guards' heads, and Rig can smell burning flesh and hear the man scream as the electricity that's blooming around Ginka's hand fries the man's brain.

Rig should be trying to escape but she can't move. It's not terror that's freezing her to the spot, she's not afraid of Ginka in the way she should be. Instead, she's fascinated.

It's like the fight against the soldiers on Red Dock but ramped up by whatever strange light Ginka's gauntlets are producing, and the old weapons developer in Rig is entranced.

Ginka moves with the grace of a lithe predator. A flick of her hand sends the dead man tumbling to the ground, and then she springs. That gold light forms into two blades, one gripped in either hand, that slip through the last two guards' weapons with ease. Their guns fall to the ground in multiple pieces. She pounces on one guard, slits the woman's throat, and then leaps off the falling corpse to stab both blades through the last one's head.

A bullet blurs past Ginka's ear. The gold blades shatter like glass.

She forms a knife and throws it at the table like a dart. Rig yelps as it narrowly misses cutting her hands off.

The blade buries into the metal table straight through the

hard light clipping her hands in place. Easy as a hot knife through butter.

But hard light can't cut through hard light like that–

Another crack of a gun rips the thought from her mind, and instinctively she kicks her chair towards the last guard, making the man stumble and fall over, and then she punches him across the face, the metal around her wrists rattling.

Ginka moves faster than Rig can see to grab Fen up by the front of her shirt, throwing the agent onto the table and tossing her gun to the side.

A hum of machinery.

The lights turn back on.

"Cactus?" Rig asks, trembling a little.

"June requested my assistance once you disappeared. Sorry for the delay," Ginka says calmly, the mask making her words almost emotionless. "There were a series of patrols outside that I had to take care of first."

Rig turns to Fen, whose face is partly smooshed into the table like a dough ball. She grabs the fallen gun and aims it between Fen's eyes.

"Alright asshole." She peels her lips back and bares her teeth at Fen, the emotion twisted with worry and annoyance. With her free hand, she plucks the pin from the table and shoves it at Fen's face. "Tell me where you got this."

Fen only glares.

Ginka's armored fingers grip Fen's hair, yanking her head up. "You're in charge here, aren't you?"

Fen doesn't respond, but it doesn't seem like there's a need for it. Ginka does some sort of wrenching movement to the woman's arm – there's a crack of bone. Rig gags and Fen screams through clenched teeth.

"Now you're going to answer all my associate's questions," Ginka says calmly.

Fen spits at them. "I should have known you'd play dirty. There's no honor left in you."

"Oh shut up about my honor," Rig snaps. "The pin. *Now*."

"You're a fool if you think you can stand against us," Fen replies, hissing each word out as though they are poison and she wants to see Rig die a slow and painful death. "Neither of you will be alive for much longer if you continue to defy the will of Pyrite. I hope you're happy with your little rebellion."

"The pin! Tell me!"

With a defiant glare in her eyes, Fen opens her lips, flicking her tongue against one of her back teeth. The pressure forces the tooth to pop out and she crushes it between her teeth like it's nothing more than candy.

"No, no, no!"

Without any idea how to stop it, Rig tries to throw herself across the table, but it's no use.

A minute later, Fen is unconscious. Soon to be dead.

Ginka lets the woman's corpse drop. Damn it all – they barely got anything out of her, and she was a special agent, she would have known everything important...

Rig slams her fist down on the table. "Fucking cheater!"

"We need to leave," Ginka says. "This location isn't safe and there's little to be gained from the corpses."

The pin is cold between her fingers. Tiny fabricated c-stones – a knockoff of the more expensive coralite – are studded around faux-silverite wires. The metal is the exact same color as the white ink of her tattoo. It's so fake, so silly, so... so *Daara*.

"Rig," Ginka insists. "We need to go."

She forces her limbs to move.

Gun at her side, pin tucked into her vest pocket, she runs. They dash out the room, Rig close on Ginka's heels but unable to fully keep pace with her.

Ginka does not take her through the main hallway they burst into; instead she's led through a hidden side door and down a flight of stairs that spits them out into the chill air of an alley next to the dilapidated building. How did Ginka even find that passage? Surely she hadn't had that long to go looking around. How long was Rig out for?

Shouting cuts through the night. In the distance, the clamor of more armed soldiers rushing towards their location grows louder and louder.

How long have they got? Ten seconds, maybe?

Ginka kicks a tall bin over and there's Chickadee in all her glory, not a scratch on the bright pink stripes and sleek black paint – Rig has never regretted those stripes in the two years she's had her bike, but she has to admit they're a tad distinctive. Not ideal for evading Pyrite Intelligence agents.

In her slight defense, she's usually not doing that while riding her bike; *Bluebird,* by comparison, is perfectly unremarkable.

"June gave me the temporary key code for your bike. We didn't know if official library transports would be tracked or not."

"Is she alright?"

"Worried, but fine. Seems as though PI wasn't willing to step foot inside another faction's library." Ginka reaches into a compartment hidden in the chassis and tosses something heavy at Rig. "Here."

Rig's gun belt drops into her open hands, Panache and Pizzazz shining in the neon lights of the city around them.

She considers her two guns. "You fly, I shoot any suicidal fucks that come after us?"

"Only if you want us to crash." Ginka holds out her hand and it occurs to Rig that she's asking to borrow a gun. "I'm not a half bad shot."

Rig ignores her. She slides the belt over her hips and buckles it with one hand before tossing Fen's stolen gun to Ginka. "Take that instead. My guns stay with me."

She hops onto Chickadee and slides forward to allow Ginka to awkwardly perch behind her. Rig's link syncs up with the bike's system and unlocks it, letting it roar to life as she shamelessly gives the engine a good rev.

"They're back here!" someone yells.

An agent is standing at the entrance to the alley way – the only entrance and exit. He reaches for a gun.

Rig's a faster draw then him. She's a faster draw than Ginka.

Panache's muzzle is smoking in her hand before the agent can finish signaling for backup. With a *thud* the body hits the ground, and then Rig is holstering her gun and blasting out of the alley at full burn, speeding over the corpse blocking the way.

Pyrite Intelligence isn't bad, she'll give them that.

Three skiffs stationed along the main road. Those are blocking the main way out. Couple more agents on foot – easy enough.

Rig leans down low over the steering as Ginka shoots.

Three bullets – three skiff drivers.

Another burst of speed and Rig sends Chickadee slipping through a gap between two skiffs down the street. Once they're clear, she pulls into a sharp turn, hurtling down an alley. She can feel the bike shift as Ginka moves to aim and then can hear the crack of her gun going off as Ginka downs a pursuer.

Bright shop lights and neon signs flash past her eyes, blinding her with nighttime darkness one moment and some pulsating hologram of a weirdly fish-shaped logo the next. They nearly run over a group of teenagers; the indignant yells follow them as they hurtle down the street, the noise swiftly lost to the roar of the wind. Behind them is the telltale screech of Pyrite flic gas engines.

A shot whizzes over her head. Another crack of a bullet from Ginka and then Rig is spinning them into heavy traffic, dodging between skiffs. Should slow Pyrite's larger vehicles down for a bit.

One hand on the steering, Rig holds up her wrist and activates her link.

The flickering holo projection of June pops up from her link.

"Rig?" she says, her jaw gaping open. "You're okay! Ginka found you?"

"Yeah! But it's bad – it's Pyrite Intelligence!" Rig yells against the wind. "They ambushed me, I don't know if *Bluebird* is safe or not, I don't know how many of them are here…"

June holds up a finger and turns to something out of the projector's view. A truck narrowly misses Rig. "*Bluebird* likely isn't safe right now. Return to my place. They wouldn't dare step foot in a library – not unless they're suicidal. I'm calling the MPs. They'll be told not to interfere with you while I alert them to the presence of PI in the city."

"PI probably has the okay to be here."

"I have a friend in the MPs. He'll make sure at least one squad is conveniently uninformed."

"You are a godsdamned miracle–"

"Flatter me once you're safe."

June's image vanishes in a flash of light as the projection cuts out.

A sign explodes above Rig's head as PI bullets fly past. She tosses her head, shaking sparks off her headscarf.

She aims the bike towards a series of tunnel intersections and reaches into a pouch on her belt.

It's a good thing she has so much experience flying using only one hand, or else she would have crashed by now. She also has flown her bike with her toes, but hopefully it won't come to that. Her free hand passes a flash pellet back to Ginka.

"Can your fancy armor magic overcharge this?"

There's a pause while Ginka takes it and then she says, with an echo of some sort of sadistic joy, "Yes."

Rig swerves towards the tunnels.

Behind her, she can feel Ginka throw the pellet, and then blinding bright light explodes behind them.

It's like a star imploding at her back.

A handful of heartbeats before the light fades, Rig throws Chickadee into the nearest tunnel and hopes. And prays. If her prayers are filled with swearing, then well, at least whatever Kashrini gods are still out there will know her sentiment is genuine.

As soon as she's in the tunnel, she yanks the bike around, pulls them into a tiny service corridor, and switches off the engine.

The noise of skiffs rushing past can be as loud as it damn well pleases, but she and Ginka need to be deathly silent for PI's vehicles to pass them by. She can hear their distinctive engines pass by their hiding spot. Not safe yet though. They'll still be looking. They'll never stop looking for her.

"This is our chance," Ginka whispers.

"Yeah. We just need to wait a few more minutes and then we're home free."

"What? No. I mean this is our chance to follow them."

This isn't just Ginka having a few screws loose; all screws have been forcefully removed from her person and the memory of screws has been wiped from her brain. "Are you kidding me? We're gonna get caught. We're gonna get *killed*."

"We're not going to get killed. Agent Fen likely oversaw their operation here, and PI doesn't tend to split leadership on missions. Although they'll have a central leader back at their headquarters, their forces here will be scattered. They'll be running around like a headless jaggire searching for us. We pick one of their vehicles, tail it, and eventually it'll head back to their base. We can clean it out and get the information we need."

"You're insane."

"I'm opportunistic. This is a chance; I'm going to take it. Didn't you want to know about that pin?"

The pin burns in her pocket.

She kicks her bike back to life. "Yeah. I do."

It takes only a minute for the PI skiffs to roar past their hiding place. Rig abandons her last two functioning brain cells and follows them.

CHAPTER SIX
A Social Faux Pin

PI is heading towards the city's Industrial Sector.

Fucking great.

Warehouses, heavy machinery, dark rooms full of metal crates and chains and other things that go clank. Rig's favorite place to be sneaking around in. Not creepy at all.

She still thinks this is kinda a lot stupid. But Ginka's right. She *needs* to know if that pin was Daara's or if it was just a wild shot in the dark from PI, or if... There are way too many 'if's here and the way they scratch at her mind is driving her mad.

One of the skiffs skids to a stop, the group inside jumping out and heading into a nearby building complex. The rest of the skiffs peel off and head back towards the city proper, likely to resume the search. As much as Rig still thinks this is a mad idea, she has to appreciate the irony of it. The one place they'd never look for her is on their front doorstep.

She spots an out-of-the-way rooftop nearby and parks her bike there.

Rig presses a button on her link.

The stealth generator around Chickadee kicks to life. It's reminiscent of a sheet of water falling over the surface, wavering under the night sky and hiding it from view.

Then they're scoping out the building.

"No guards," Ginka says, crouched on the edge of the rooftop as Rig's very own seething gargoyle. "Two side entrances – look where they've parked extra skiffs."

"They've got permission from Ascetic to be here, remember? We have no idea if they can just call in local reinforcements. As much as I love the idea of storming the front entrance, guns blazing, we'd likely get flattened in a second and then I'll never find out anything. How quiet can you be?"

Ginka just laughs. The sound is flat through the mask, more of a sudden cough than anything else, but still distinctively a laugh.

"Right," Rig mutters. "Forgot you're a freaking ghost or something."

Somehow Ginka manages to cast an imposing shadow even in the darkness of night, the lights of the city around her making her seem a thousand kilometers taller than she actually is. Part of Rig, the stupid part of herself that's never content, never happy with who she is, wishes that she had that ability. Sure, she has charm, and she's cultivated her charisma into a weapon, but when she needs to make someone shut up she has to sass them until they can't think of a reply. She has a feeling Ginka could do it in half a second with a glare.

What Rig *is* good at, though, is scaling down the side of a building.

In no time at all, her boots are thudding down onto the right warehouse level, and then she's darting across the space, hiding behind shipping crates and parked skiffs as she makes her way towards the building.

"I've got the west entrance," Ginka whispers. "You take the east."

Then she disappears, as though melting into the shadows around them. There one moment and gone the next.

Rig gets the distinct feeling that she's going to have to put up with a lot of that.

A ways away from the east door, she stops behind a crate filled with potted plants and checks her entry. Two guards –

not that well armed, but they've got that distinctive fuck-off look that nasty fighters have. One of them puts his fingers against his ear and nods before saying something into the link.

They haven't noticed her yet. Good; it'll make her job easier.

She flips a gun into her hand, and with the other she retrieves a small compact from her belt. It fits into her palm. She opens it, positioning the mirror at just the right angle to see around the corner of the crate.

Peek shooting – it's one of the most dangerous parts of a firefight, but the most viscerally satisfying when she gets it right. In essence, it's peeking quickly out from behind cover to find out where the enemies are, and then popping out for only a second to get a quick shot in. The key to winning is knowing where the baddies are and getting the quickest but most accurate of glances. Rig has found that the best way to do it better than everyone else is to avoid needing that initial peek.

There's no such thing as cheating in a gunfight and there's no such thing as cheating against Pyrite.

She looks into the mirror and burns the two goons' position into her mind.

She shuffles enough for the edge of her shoulder to be just barely exposed. Then she props Pizzazz up over her shoulder, aims, and fires two quick shots.

Two sharp cracks and both guys fall.

There's a click as she snaps the mirror shut, and then she's running over to their fallen bodies. Sticky, rust-smelling blood has started to pool around the corpses; she tries to ignore it and just not breathe too deeply.

Another shot from Pizzazz blows open the lock on the door.

She slips through, guns at the ready.

The inside of the warehouse is a mess of winding corridors, weapons parts, supply crates, all sorts of things needed for a long term stay on this planet. It looks as though PI was either planning on this being a longer operation or they've got some other nefarious plan in the works.

Technically speaking, all the three factions are at war with each other. They've all been at war for ten thousand years. Never really stopped. Can't prove that your god is the bestest god ever if you give up, after all. But it has, over the course of history, occasionally occurred to each faction at some point or another that if they're going to keep tabs on each other, they might as well know where their enemy's secret spies are. So if Ascetic gets word of a PI hideout on their home planet, then, well isn't it better for all involved to let PI keep using that base? Ascetic can keep an eye on them, and if they blew up the place and tried to kick PI out, then chances are PI would simply come back in short order. And then Ascetic would have to find them all over again.

It's just common sense, in Rig's opinion. Although she hates that the factions occasionally have some.

This place isn't heavily staffed. She slides past one guard – quickly taken care of with two bullets – but she doesn't see more than the odd maintenance bot as she makes her way to the center of the warehouse. It's a good thing that the place is empty, and logically she knows that it's not inherently suspicious, but still. Weirds her out. If she had hair, it'd be standing on end right now.

The center – dead center; she's good at navigation – is what looks like some sort of communications room. It's a chamber littered with high-powered computer terminals, signal amplifiers, and, as she discovers as she paws over a holo field filled to the brim with lines of text, obscure clearance codes. If PI has hauled in some tech like this, they must have been expecting to need to transfer a really large data file...

Of course.

Overconfident bastards. Thought it would be easy to get the schematics from her, did they? Vicious satisfaction wells up within her and she has to push the feeling down. Pyrite'll *never* get back what she took.

"Anything?"

"FUCK!"

"Calm down, honestly," Ginka says, leaning against the wall where she has suddenly and mysteriously appeared. Her mask is still on, so Rig can't tell for sure, but something in her voice suggests a diabolical grin. Cactus *indeed*. "Your eyesight needs sharpening if I can sneak up on you like this."

Rig points a rude finger at her. "Is that how you do your work? Kill people via giving them heart attacks?"

A thoughtful tilt to her head. "I've never tried it. Maybe it'll be funny. So, anything?"

It takes another minute for Rig to still her rapidly pounding heart. "No. Just all this equipment. You were right, with all their forces out looking for me, this place is pretty deserted. I counted a grand total of three guards, and their security systems are basically nonexistent."

Something a bit like a hum floats through Ginka's mask. "Strange. I removed the squad that we saw arrive, but they weren't exactly the fighters of the bunch."

"You think that they're coming back?"

"It's certainly possible."

"How much time have we got?"

"How would I know?"

Can't assume too much time, then. Can't do much here either. But this is a damn information treasure trove, and there has got to be something buried in here. Rig reaches into a pocket lining her vest and retrieves a slim infowafer. It gets plugged into the fattest, fanciest, high powered-est computer terminal in this place. A press of a few buttons later, and it's hacking into the system and has helpfully pulled up a glowing holographic input panel for her to type on.

She slides into a chair and gets to work.

It shouldn't be a surprise that their systems are barebones at best, and yet she still feels some sort of shock. No, maybe it's not shock. Disappointment perhaps. All that's here is pretty much what she should have expected – tech to send the plans back to Pyrite or to the organization's mysterious buyers. No nice maps or movement records. No shiny file politely marked as 'Our Evil Agenda.'

She groans as she goes through the scrubbed systems. "It's all a mess."

Ginka leans over her shoulder. As is the case with many things Ginka does, it's an action that probably isn't meant to be intimidating but comes across that way, regardless. "Try communication records. If we can call whoever they last spoke to, we could trace the signal and work backwards from there."

Rig lines up the call, sets up the trace, and dials.

It only takes a moment for the call to connect. The screen flickers to life. A pinch of static; it's a very long-distance call, after all. And then the screen is swiftly filled with the image of a Pyrite Intelligence agent.

It's a man – human, probably a few years shy of middle aged. A gnarled scar on the right side of his face, copper hair, and a strong jaw. That jaw drops open the tiniest bit when he sees Rig.

She revels in that moment of shock.

"I take it," the man says as he recovers, "that Agent Fen is dead?"

"Yup." She leans back in her chair, crosses her arms, and plops her boots down on the terminal. "I didn't like her demands and then she killed herself before we could get anything from her. How rude."

"Shame," he replies curtly. "Pleasure to make your acquaintance then. I am Agent Janus."

"I don't particularly care. Fen mentioned being allocated a number of methods to bring me in. I need to know what she meant. Tell me about the pin."

He exchanges a look with someone off screen and then gives a signal. "You have sixty seconds."

Black consumes the screen.

Did he drop the call? When she checks, the trace is still going, narrowing down to somewhere in Pyrite space.

A moment later the screen glows back to life, displaying a dimly lit room and a woman tied to a chair.

Her heart skips a beat.

Her eyes drink in the first sight of Daara that she's had in three years.

Her twin sister has always been identical to her, but now her blue skin is pale from lack of sunlight, sharper lines under her purple eyes, her bones more visible than they should be. PI has stuffed her into some stark, pale red and blue uniform, placed a number tag on her chest, and worst of all, they've stripped her of her headscarf. As though they tried to tear away everything Kashrini about her. Rig sits tense in her chair, her hand pressed against the screen as though she could just reach out and...

This is wrong. It's all wrong. Daara is supposed to be safe. Daara stayed behind while Rig fled because Daara is loyal to Pyrite, Daara has nothing to do with any of this, Daara wanted to stay. She loved Pyrite. That was why Rig let her sister stay; because she loved Pyrite and because, surely, it's pointless to attack someone who is loyal and uninvolved and who didn't do anything wrong.

Her lips move but she cannot give voice to Daara's name.

Daara's bared head tilts up and her beautiful eyes widen. "Traxi?" she gasps.

Rig.

"Yeah," she replies anyway. Pins prick at her eyes and her vision blurs. "It's me. Daara, it's me, I'm going to save you, I promise, I'll get you out of there–"

Daara shakes her head furiously. Fear or panic or something else. Rig can't tell. She's been apart from her sister for too long. "No. You can't – you can't fight PI, you can't fight Pyrite, it's impossible."

"I can't let you just–"

"Don't do that stupid thing you do! For once, just do the sensible thing – *Please*, if you just give them what they want then they'll let me go, and then... then *we can both go home again.*"

"I'm going to save you," she repeats. "I promise. I'm coming for you, Daara, I'll–"

The screen goes black.

Janus's smirking face reappears. "I trust you understand our position?"

"I…" Think, what can she do to save Daara now? She has to lie – bullshit her way into more time to come up with some plan. "I understand. I don't have the schematics on me. I split them up and scattered them when I deserted. Give me some time and I can get them to you, just please don't hurt Daara."

Janus raises an eyebrow, and she gets the feeling that he's laughing at her. "How generous do you think we are?"

"How stupid do you think *I* am? As if I'd ever keep the parts in one place."

This time he does laugh, a short, barking laugh. "You *are* as arrogant as claimed. We'll be keeping an eye on you. You have one week. Don't bother trying to find us when your time is up. *We'll* find *you*."

Static.

The feed has cut.

"Trace failed," Ginka reports in a blank voice. "They scrambled the call and didn't give us enough time to–"

Rig slams her fist into the terminal. "Damn it, I *know*!"

They must have known that there was a trace. That wasn't even a full sixty seconds with her sister. They lied about that too. Pyrite always lies.

"We need to leave," Ginka insists. "PI forces are likely about to converge on this building, and we have to be out of their sight before they arrive. Run now, think later."

I'll save her, Rig thinks, numb as her boots thud through the warehouse after Ginka.

I will.

INTERLUDE
The First Fall

Spirit X-74 is enjoying her new promotion as she runs through the halls of Gundapura Palace, her feet silent against the marble floors. Not that it matters. Her pursuers are loud enough for three of her.

A shot cracks above her head. She twists and slides across the stone, letting the bullet pass over her, grabbing a needle from her thigh holster as she reaches the corner of the hall. A soldier is hot on her heels, gun raised, taking aim again. Damn Pyrite soldiers – they still can't shoot for shit. Corner, pivot, a flick of her wrist sends the needle from her fingertips into the soldier's left eye.

There's a meaty *thunk*-squish as the six-centimeter needle buries itself seven centimeters deep into the man's head.

She skids around the corner. A knife flashes towards her neck as she straightens – another guard, this one smarter than the last. This one knows not to bring a gun to a knife fight, at least. Her palm darts out, grabs his wrist and pushes the strike the smallest bit to the side, making space for her to step inside his guard, create a knife, and shove the blade into his heart. Another tug of her wrist lets him fall to the side off her weapon, avoiding the bloody body hitting her and weighing her down.

The communicator buzzes in her ear, *"Fifty-two seconds until the skiff leaves. X-74, you need to move."*

"Understood," she replies, taking off down the next set of corridors that lead to the landing platform.

Red tripwires crisscross above the floors – she leaps over them easily, her feet hitting the walls as she darts from surface to surface, dancing through the traps.

The voice belongs to Thrush-Seven, her Handler. This is the first mission they've run together. They've been partnered for only a month – a month filled with more training than sleeping – and both have been promoted once to allow them to take missions as a team, instead of working with a larger group as most in Windshadow tend to. Ghoul to Spirit. Sparrow to Thrush. One more set of promotions is left – her to Phantom, and him to Raven – and that boost in rank will let them go on the highest priority missions.

The two of them could be the organization's most successful test so far. Most partnered teams fail within a few years, cohesion between the two members usually not strong enough, and, frankly, the fewer number of people on higher ranked missions usually increases failure anyways.

They just need glowing records to get promoted and prove that they were worth the effort their masters put into them.

X-74 dispatches the next set of guards easily.

Snakes her fingers around the first one's wrist, grabs the woman's gun and rips it from her. Uses the weapon to shoot and kill the other three before slamming the woman's head into her knee, breaking her nose and driving the shards of bone into her skull. Bleed out or brain trauma; either way, the woman's dead. And if by some miracle she lives, well, it doesn't matter. She can't see X-74's face, and Windshadow makes no secret about their operations here.

"Turn right."

She turns, fast stride never faltering. "Locked door up ahead."

"Hacking it now. You have less than ten seconds until the target leaves."

Another crack of a bullet from behind her, but there's no time to deal with it and she's on a straight path towards the door.

Pain blossoms in her left thigh. She's hit. She can run through it.

Starlight streams in through the growing crack in the door up ahead, patches of night sky shining through, and behind the doors she can see the landing pad. And her target, one leg already inside a skiff, the engines rearing to go.

"I'm not going to make it!"

As she slips between the crack in the doors, there's a roar of an engine. The target's skiff pulls away. Guards descend.

"*Six meters from the platform. Seven. Jump!*"

"But–"

"*Now!*"

She pushes past the guards, her heart pounding, absently making and throwing a knife towards one of the attackers just to get them out of the damn way. Her eyes track the skiff as it gets further – her foot hits the edge of the platform and she *leaps…*

X-74 wakes up in the medbay.

The heady hum of medication thrums in her veins, dulling the pain she knows must be there, making her limbs heavy and stiff. As her vision gains clarity, she can see thin tubes leading into her arms, prickling uncomfortably where the needles are attached to her wrist. A monitor is clipped to one of her fingers. Her palms tingle from the contact and the painkillers pumping through her veins. Her neck is made of lead, but she moves it anyway, turning to stare at the person sitting by her bedside.

"Oh," Thrush-Seven whispers. He nervously looks over her, checking the machines she's hooked up to, as though making sure she's not convulsing or otherwise worse off for having woken. "You're awake."

"I'm sorry."

"Don't be." With a sigh, he presses his eyes tightly shut. She can see his hands tightly gripping each other in his lap, his knuckles white. "I am the one who should apologize. The mission failure rests on my shoulders, but more than that I... I'm responsible for your injuries. The call to pursue the target was mine."

"It's my job to follow your orders. I should have been faster."

"You had been shot in the leg. I shouldn't have *given* the order. I should have told you to retreat, we could have regrouped and tried again – X-74, you could have *died*." For some reason this seems to be of great importance to him. It is her job to die for Windshadow. If anything, it would be a worse blow for the organization for *him* to die, given that Handlers are less disposable than Operatives. "I made the wrong decision, you tried to protest, and I ignored you – that is unacceptable."

Why does he care? "It was your call to make. Not mine. I'm sure that if I hadn't allowed myself to become injured, I would have been able to follow your orders. I'll do better work for you next time, I promise."

He stares down at his hands. "We've been pulled from the field for the next two months. Training and recuperation."

"I'm sorry."

"Please, don't apologize. I think... I think we need to change how we... this isn't working. Our performance is faltering."

Of course. She should have been anticipating this, honestly. Partnered teams so rarely work out, after all. They can't always be the exception to the rule. "I understand. I'm sure you'll do better without me dragging you down."

"No – I'd like to continue working as your partner. If you'll let me."

"Let you? It's not my call to make."

That pensive look again. "That... might be what's not

working. What... what do you want to be different? Regarding our dynamic, that is."

She opens her mouth and then snaps her jaw tightly shut. What needs fixing is obvious. Her skills have to be improved, she has to get better at following his orders, his role is to guide her. That's just how it is. But that's not what she *wants*; "I want you to listen to me."

Shit. She shouldn't have said that...

Thrush-Seven nods, a sincere and intense glow to his dark eyes. Instantly accepts that. He didn't even think it through. That... that doesn't make sense. He has no obligation to do so. "Of course. I should have, on our mission. There is insight you have in the field that I don't, given my relegation to the back lines and our respective specialties."

"You could join me," she suggests, her voice wavering. He'd said, when they first met, that there are always ways to improve upon the standardized, right? Surely she won't get in trouble for suggesting this, right? "In the field. If you want more information and insight."

"I could?" His tight expression lights up at that, as though she's truly told him something he's never heard before – an idea so ludicrous he simply can't believe it. Handlers are cleverer than Operatives. That's just how it is. "I could. I'm a good shot, I can try to keep up, I'd have a better understanding of your skills, and I could react more accurately from the field. Assuming, of course, that you're alright having me stand at your side. My combat skills aren't on the same level as yours."

"It, it sounds like a nice idea."

A warm smile creeps onto his lips, and it shocks her how much that changes him. He bows his head slightly, his hair falling like water and the thrush feather brushing his collarbone. "Yes. It does."

"You still want to be my Handler, then?"

He holds out his hand. "I'd rather be *partners*."

Improve upon the standardized, she reminds herself. She chews on her lower lip and finds herself returning that small smile of his. She doesn't shake his hand. "Partners."

CHAPTER SEVEN
Panache and Pizzazz

Either June's friend comes through, or PI has a limit on which sections of the city they're allowed to enter. Whichever reason, once Rig turns Chickadee towards the Historical Center, she notices that she can't see any more PI skiffs.

Even still, she doesn't chance going through the front gates. She zips around to the far back of the Center, where the residential buildings are – librarians, after all, aren't allowed to leave their libraries, so every library comes with its own set of apartment buildings.

Everything seems so much quieter when she finally pulls her bike to a stop in front of the back gate.

Ginka jumps off, Rig kills the ignition on her bike, and then June is dashing down the gate's stairs, the light globes adorning the gates bathing her in velvety yellow halo. She slides to a stop before her slippered feet can cross the final stair that marks the border between the Historical Center and everything that lies outside.

She ushers them in through the gates with nervous hand gestures. "Are you alright?"

"Peachy. All clear once we entered this district," Rig informs her, gravitating towards the warmth of June. "I think we're safe, for now. Not sure when *Bluebird* will be okay to go back to though. If they fuck with my ship…"

She trails off when June lays a comforting hand on her shoulder, tugging her close into an embrace.

"I need an explanation," Ginka snaps.

"You were *there–*"

"Not about what Pyrite is doing." She pinches her mask and the flat black suddenly turns into a soft piece of fabric – is that nanomesh? With a rough jerk, she rips it from her face, her pupils slitted with anger. Her rage is a flickering thing, icy one moment and molten hot the next, and it makes Rig take a step back in fear. She jabs a finger at June. "You *deceived* me. You told me to help her, and I trusted you because you're a damn librarian; but you tricked me into saving a fucking *ex-factioned deserter.*"

Rig stiffens. "You knew I wasn't in their good graces."

"There is a galaxy of difference between being a criminal and being a deserter, and you both *know* it."

June steps forward and puts herself between Rig and Ginka. "That's enough."

"You lied to me–"

"I omitted an irrelevant detail. The two are not the same."

"She's committed treason–"

"Against a faction that I am not a part of and even if I were, it wouldn't matter to me. Now," June adds, taking a deep breath and leveling Ginka with a stare that makes most people hang their heads and tuck their shirts in, "you saved my love from PI, so I'm willing to overlook this. Stay the night and cool your head. We can discuss things rationally in the morning when nerves are less frayed."

There's a tense moment of silence.

Ginka's back is straight as a sword and her eyes twice as steely. "Let me make one thing clear. The only reason I'm not going to report you both to whatever nearest authority I can find is because the faction you betrayed was *Pyrite,* and not *Ossuary.*"

She turns sharply on her heels towards the gates.

Shit…

"Wait–" Rig reaches out before lowering her hand, out of some silly fear that Ginka will bite or something. "Please. I need your help. I can't fight like you can."

"No."

"You're Ossuary – don't you want to kick PI's face in?"

"I can do that just fine on my own."

"I'll…" She swallows painfully and offers, "I'll owe you a favor. If you help me. Come on, please; you get a free favor from someone who knows every port of trade like the back of her hand, and you'll get to do all that factioned crap of proving Ossuary's better than Pyrite and, and… I *need* your help."

All she can see is the silhouette of Ginka's back.

"*Please*. You *said* you needed a reclaimer."

"I need to think," Ginka mutters.

Before she can take the last step back outside the Center, June retrieves a key card from her chatelaine and tosses it at her. Quick as a felidae, her hand snaps up to pluck the card from the air.

"That will get you back in," June explains, still sounding a touch cold. "If you change your mind. But you had best change it quickly because the credentials expire in twenty-four hours."

"Hn."

And then Ginka disappears into the night, card in hand.

Once the gates close behind her, June sniffs, turning her nose up. "She's…"

"Prickly?" Rig suggests weakly.

June steers Chickadee into the skiff lockbar next to the apartment tower's entrance, Rig trailing behind, her feet shuffling against the smooth stone paving of the Center.

"To say the *least*," June says, aggressively punching in a lock code. "I don't see why you need her."

"June… you weren't there. You didn't see what she… I'm a good fighter, okay, and I know it – I can beat up guys in bar fights and shoot a fallen eyelash off someone's cheek at fifty paces, but I can't... I can't do what she can do. Fuck, I don't know anyone who can. *Maybe* Mohsin, but Nightbirds aren't... For all our fucking around with the war, we're not soldiers."

A bit of fiddling with the dozen pieces of security apparatus hanging from June's chatelaine gets the apartment door to unlock and slide open, a wave of warm air hitting them and washing away the nighttime chill. Given the late hour, there's no sound but the soft hum of a heater and their footsteps as they quickly head towards the elevator.

"All I'm saying," June continues as they rocket up towards the top floor, "is that she doesn't seem worth it."

"She had these... this *tech*." That gold light flashes through Rig's memories, and she finds that same burst of awe reappearing in her chest from the memory. No, more than just awe – *jealousy* as well. "It was like hard light, but it couldn't have been; it could cut straight through hard light without any trouble. Until now, I thought the only thing that can do that is helltech."

"Helltech? The term is familiar, I simply can't quite recall..."

"Hard electric light technology. But she *couldn't* have been using helltech. It requires massive generators, and even if she were carting those around somehow, if it was helltech, she'd be dead."

"Dead?"

"Helltech is toxic."

June winces. "Even so. You're good enough with a gun to fend off PI without her."

Without really noticing she's doing it, she reaches her hand into her pocket to clutch at the headscarf pin. The plastic is the same temperature as her skin by now, her thumb running over the fake c-stones enough times for her to memorize every scratch on its surface. Was it really Daara's? Did PI simply grab something that they knew was close enough to what her sister wears, knowing that it would hit Rig all the same? Or did they rip it from Daara's scarf once they'd stripped her and thrown her in chains?

Her teeth toy with a crack on her lower lip until she's ripped off a loose piece of skin that gets stuck in her gums when she tries to spit it out. "It's not just about fending PI off."

"What do you mean?"

"They…"

A knot has formed in the base of her throat, cutting air off from her lungs and choking her attempts to speak.

The elevator *dings.*

June steps into the hallway and gently tugs Rig towards the door. "Come in. It's a very late hour and I imagine that eating something would do you a world of good."

Too much adrenaline and panic is whirling away inside her for that to be a good idea right now. She hastily shakes her head.

"At least drink something then."

The apartment door opens and then she finds herself being guided towards June's kitchen.

The kitchen is a small galley, a little table and a set of well-sat-in chairs pushed into a corner nook and a pot of flowers hanging over it, occasionally dropping loose petals onto the table like confetti. Rig takes the seat that is hers, the one tucked most deeply into the corner, because June is always getting up in the middle of meals to fuss with something or other and likes not having to wriggle past the table to do so.

Like the vast majority of Ascetic people, June has always been a firm believer that there is no ill in the galaxy that can't be improved by chocolate. Within minutes, a steaming cup of cocoa is pushed into Rig's hands and June is sitting across from her.

She lays her hands atop Rigs, curling their fingers around the warm mug. "Breathing is important as well, love."

Only then does Rig notice she's been holding her breath.

She lets it out. In, out. Purposeful. This is her body, and she can control it. It will not fail her. The thrum of adrenaline is fading from her system, working its way out at a glacial pace, threatening to abandon her all at once and send her crashing to the ground. June's snug grip is the only thing keeping her hands from shaking.

"You don't have to tell me anything," June says.

She can do this thing where she makes her voice smooth and soft and quiet, and to Rig it sounds like molten chocolate, comforting and bolstering. As much as their relationship started around Rig telling her stories of her adventures beyond the Ascetic homeworld, she has always thought that June is the best storyteller she's ever heard. A story voice like that is a gift and a curse, as a librarian. Being too good at one's job is always a mixed blessing under faction rule. As Rig well knows.

"They have Daara." It's a whisper. A confession. June is ever so talented at coaxing them from her lips, and she loves her for it.

June sighs, her shoulders sagging. "I see. Did you..."

"Yeah, I saw her. She wasn't hurt but... she didn't look good. Like they'd been keeping her there for years."

"Did they take her into custody right after you deserted?"

"I don't know. Maybe. Maybe they were waiting. June, they mentioned buyers – who would they be selling to?" A thousand questions pour forth from her mind. "If they've had Daara all this time, what have they done to her? If I'd gone back for her, could I have saved her? There must have been something I could have–"

June nudges the cocoa closer to her. "Drink. The past is immutable and there's no point agonizing over hypotheticals."

Rich chocolate coats her tongue when she takes a sip, warmth spreading down her throat to sit low in her stomach – a stomach that rather pointedly takes a moment to remind her that she hasn't eaten in almost twenty-four hours. Not that she could hold down anything solid with the anxiety rolling away inside her guts, but she can and does gulp down the full mug of cocoa as fast as she can without making herself sick.

The empty cup clicks back down on the table and June takes her hands again.

"They want the schematics." This Rig says even quieter. A stupid, paranoid part of her brain is whispering at her, telling her that the walls have ears, even though she knows June's apartment is the safest place in the galaxy, right next to *Bluebird*. "They want my nanomites and I can't... I can't." Tears claw their way out of Rig's eyes. Her lungs don't seem to work right anymore. "They won't give up, June. They never stop. Even if I can save Daara I can't stop them from following us again. I ran – I ran but it didn't work. Why can I never leave that godsforsaken faction behind?"

June sighs, deep and slow, her shoulders sinking with the grace of mist settling on the ground. "I don't know. I'm not certain – we can figure this out. Surely. Where did you hide the hard drive?"

The sob trapped in Rig's throat comes out as a hiccupy, delirious giggle. "I didn't."

"Huh?"

"I *destroyed* the hard drive."

June sucks in a sharp breath. "You destroyed... but, but that was *groundbreaking* science. All that knowledge..."

Such a *librarian* thing to say. Another messy giggle shakes a tear out of her eye. "The hard drive is gone. The schematics aren't."

She reaches behind her back. Her palms wrap around the grips of her guns. The faint *click* of the magnets on her belt being released. The weight of the guns shifting from her hips to her hands.

Panache and Pizzazz glint as she sets them down on the table.

"Love?" June cocks her head. "If you want a place to put your guns, you know there's a spot in the bedroom for–"

"Pick one up," Rig whispers.

"Pardon?"

"Pick one up and try to shoot it."

With a thoughtful frown, June picks up Panache, albeit with an aura of great skepticism. She raises the gun, points it at the wall, and pulls the trigger.

Nothing happens.

She tries again and still nothing.

"What do you actually know about my research?" Rig asks, staring down at her hands.

"You were one of Pyrite's foremost experts on nanotech, specifically working under their weapons development program. The nanomites you invented are bio targeting, designed to read genetic code and activate upon discovering the correct genome sequence," June lists off. "Not precisely my area of expertise, I confess, but I do understand the basics."

"My guns are biolocked," Rig admits, taking the guns back and returning them to her belt. "The nanomites... They were based on my DNA. I kept the schematics and placed them in Panache and Pizzazz. They're in the grip. A scanner is set up inside the gun's frame, it lets the nanomites scan the genetic material of whoever's currently holding them. Unless it's my relatively-fresh DNA, they won't allow anyone to so much as remove them from the magnetic holster on my belt, let alone actually shoot them."

June pauses, her hand rising to cup her chin, one finger tapping against her lips. "PI wouldn't be after you for mere safety locks."

"Pyrite *does* have other nanotech experts. I like to think they don't have any as good as me, but they do exist and I worked with them for years, June. These nanomites – it wasn't an idea I should have pursued, and I can't say I didn't know what it'd lead to, because I think I did, deep down. It just... it seemed less important than the discovery itself." She draws in a rattling breath that jars her lungs. "The nanomites, when uncontained, enter the target's body through the skin, make their way into the cells, and attack the DNA. Kills the host slowly. Painfully. They can be released like a gas. No fighting back until it's too late, no resistance. Doesn't waste the crops of an agriworld or the machines of industry planets. Clean. Neat."

Exactly the sort of thing Pyrite prefers.

She licks her lips, tongue running over chapped skin, and continues, "They can't get to the nanomites without my DNA to unlock it; but if they do… they planned to bastardize them, strip them down and repurpose them until the genetic marker isn't specifically *my* DNA. It'd be *Kashrini* DNA. They'd–" Bile burns in her throat, and she pushes it down. "They'd kill all of us. Nightbirds, the indentured, me–" Her eyes flicker up to the purple behind June's eyes. "*You.*"

"Oh, Rig…"

That voice almost breaks her heart. "Please don't hate me."

"What, no, of course I don't hate you." June takes her hands again, squeezing tight enough for her pulse to beat in Rig's bones. "I, of all people, understand that need. The need to *know*, to discover. I know how it can block out everything else and I could never hate you for that."

Right. Librarian. "I thought… I know you want to stay safe. Here. In this library. But if Pyrite releases the nanomites, not even here will be safe. Not for you."

"Not for you, either."

"…No."

"Then that makes us even. Besides, that hypothetical situation will never become a reality. If you're the only one that can unlock those plans, I know you'd *never* do it."

"I'm *not*," she whispers. "I'm not the only one, don't you see? It's *my* DNA. Which means *Daara* can unlock them, too."

June blanches. "Do you think she'd…"

"Do it?" Tears claw their way out of Rig's eyes. Her lungs don't seem to work right anymore. "I don't know. She's always been so *loyal*, even though Pyrite's never done shit for her, and she refused to come with me when I left; I barely understood her three years ago. I... I honestly have *no idea* what she'd do now."

If she'd cared more, if she'd tried harder, if instead of standing back and letting Daara go her separate way she'd held on twice as hard – maybe then she'd have a clue as to where her sister will draw the line in the sand.

But no. She hadn't cared enough.

June chews on her fingernail as she thinks. "Is there anything we can do?"

"Kinda hoping you'd have an answer there."

"I could spend a decade studying and I'd still never know as much as you do about nanomites. And we haven't got a decade. I think at this point the best thing we can do is get some sleep. Unless there's anything that needs to be done right this second, you can sleep on it first. Plan in the morning."

She lets June gently prod her out of the kitchen and into bed. Exhaustion claims her before she can pull on a night shift.

CHAPTER EIGHT
To Find a Compass

A thin line of light streams in through Rig's eyes.

Flaky specks are crusted around the corners of her eyes and her veins seems to be filled with concrete instead of blood. Uncountable aches fill her body. In the few minutes it takes for her to fully wake up, she is more one massive bruise than she is a person. Then she blinks, rubs the sleep from her eyes, pushes the nightmares to the back of her mind, and pulls herself into a person-adjacent form.

Her hands reassure herself of her own existence. Fingers running over the smooth expanse of her bald head, the tiny, raised bumps of the dot tattoos on her thighs, prodding carefully at a tender sore spot on her hip, and then lingering on the scar across her lower belly where she removed Pyrite's chip almost three years ago.

She had sat in the hull of an unregistered frigate as it fled the Pyrite homeworld. A scanner propped up by her side to guide her, a scalpel in her hand, two shots of whiskey in her system. Balled the end of her scarf up and bit down as she cut. Mohsin had taken pity on her afterwards – he's a good sort, if gruff – and had helped her trembling fingers stitch the wound.

The chip was a small thing. A centimeter in length, and a tenth of that in width. Blood-stained. Smooth. Capable of transmitting her location to Pyrite from twenty star systems away with pinpoint accuracy.

It had sat heavy in her palm until she chucked it out into space behind her.

Soft sheets slide against her skin as she sits up. She's not in space anymore. She's here. Here on the Ascetic homeworld. The scars and the tattoos are *hers*, all the ways in which she reclaims her body from Pyrite.

June is curled up in bed with her. She's not alone.

Rig buries her head against June's back, pressing her eyes tightly shut until stars bloom in the backs of her eyelids.

She doesn't want to be awake. As much as she might like to think otherwise at times, June's apartment isn't actually bubbled off from the rest of the galaxy. Time ticks on, even here. It isn't possible to curl up under the bedsheets, cover herself in the warmth and the darkness, and pretend as though Daara's fine and no one's hunting her and the monster under the bed will go away when the lights turn on.

Years and years ago, when she was a child and when her mother still lived, she and Daara would hide in their mother's closet. All of them were indentured; they lived in one of the matchbox apartments near Pyrite's Thirteenth Industrial Complex, and, as such, their mother's closet was tiny and bare. But there had been one big, velvety, lexur-fur coat, given to her by her mother, and Rig and Daara would snuggle up under it, claiming a sleeve each and falling asleep against each other.

At the time, Rig had found it the coziest thing in the galaxy. When she'd gotten older, she'd hated the memory, the tangibility of their poverty, part of a larger insidious hatred of Pyrite that had crept up on her as she saw more and more of their faction.

Now she wants nothing more than to crawl back into that closet and fall asleep.

June snores.

She smiles between June's shoulder blades and sits up – reluctantly; But she's upright, and that's something, at least.

She gently brushes a knuckle against June's cheek. Her love

is fast asleep. Chestnut curls halo around her on the pillow in a tangled mess, her nightshirt falling off one shoulder, the fabric pattern of her pillow imprinted on half her face. Her mouth hangs open ever so slightly, and a bit of hair is stuck on her lip. The most beautiful woman Rig has ever seen.

Gently, not wanting to wake her, she tucks the stray lock of hair back and presses a kiss to her forehead.

Then she throws on clothes. For about a year now, she's kept a few spare sets of things here – shirts, underwear, a toothbrush. Occasionally, she'll return to find that June 'just happens' to have acquired an additional pair of house slippers or more washcloths. Her babe is not particularly subtle.

She stumbles out of the bedroom. One of them has to make coffee, and as she's awake it looks like it's gonna have to be her.

Unlike the hectic panic of last night, a hushed calm lingers in the rooms of June's apartment. The meticulously organized and cleaned kitchen has a stillness to it that Rig slowly peels away as she goes through the motions of making a pot of coffee.

She drags her hands down her face as she waits for the water to boil. She needs to figure out what the fuck she's doing.

Step one: Find Daara.

Step two: Save Daara.

Easier said than done. If Daara's anywhere, she'd be in the Pyrite Intelligence Headquarters, and nobody knows where *that* is.

As much as she became acquainted with Pyrite's darker side during her last few weeks under that faction, they never reveal PI's secrets to anyone without the highest clearance. No matter how useful Rig's research was to them, they would never give that clearance to a Kashrini. Only humans are so lucky. That's how every faction is. Humans first, all other species second. Occasionally hand out neat postings to those other species, like her own respectable job under Pyrite, but never allow anyone who isn't human a taste of real power. Call it fair. Kill anyone who says otherwise.

Okay. Step zero-point-one: Find PI's hidden headquarters.

She stares at the slowly boiling kettle and mutters, "I'm gonna need a compass."

It's been a long time since Rig's needed to hire a compass, and all her usual contacts wouldn't be applicable here. She's had to track down people and artifacts before, but not tricksy faction intelligence organizations. June's associates in that profession wouldn't be helpful, for the same reason. When Rig can't find an artifact or other physical object herself, June's more legitimate side of things comes in. Rarely does June have reason to hire a compass beyond her assistance in Rig's line of work.

With a sigh, she sinks down into a chair and pulls out her link.

The call goes through and she finds herself being glared at by a hologram of Mohsin's face.

"Heya–"

"It's two in the fucking morning," he grumbles. "I fucking hate you; this better be *fucking* good."

Sure, she knows that if he *actually* hated her, he wouldn't have picked up the call in the first place. Even still, she can't help feeling wounded in a way she normally wouldn't. Pyrite always rips the scabs off her old wounds.

"I need a compass," she repeats, trying to sound apologetic. "It's–" She takes a deep breath. She can do this. Keep it simple. "It's Pyrite Intelligence. They've got my sister. I need to find their headquarters."

Mohsin's jaw falls open and a cascade of curse words pours out.

"Yeah, yeah, I know," she says with a wince. "It's not a good idea, it's dangerous–"

"I can't help."

She freezes. Her fingers tighten around the link. "Oh."

"It's not…" He runs a hand through his hair and scratches his neck. "Rig," he says, serious and stern, "this isn't what we do. There are compasses in the Nightbirds, we know there are, but if I pointed you at one, they'd get a PI shaped target on their heads, and we're not cut out to deal with that. Straight up, we're just *not*. I'd be sentencing one of us to death by telling 'em to help you."

Right. Of course. Reasonable. She tries to keep her face straight, not to show the way her heart sinks. "I get it," she quickly reassures him. "I'm sorry for asking."

He sighs. "Listen. I'm not your boss; we're not like that. Not gonna get mad at you for putting family first. I'll have a couple other people take over for you while you're gone – not as *good* as you, but they'll manage. Go do what you gotta do."

"Thanks." She forces her lips to press together into what's supposed to be a smile. "See ya."

He signs off and she's left staring at her link in her hands.

The kettle whistles.

The sudden noise makes her jump to her feet, scrambling to take the kettle off the heat and start making coffee, dropping everything at least twice as she does so.

The doorbell rings.

Rig's fingers do something weird and spasm-y and she almost drops her mug.

Should she answer? She's allowed in the Historical Center, sure, but librarians having romantic relations is sort of frowned upon, and if that's June's colleague or something, she doesn't want to get her girlfriend in trouble. But it could be…

She opens the front door.

"You promised me a favor," Ginka says. She's standing still as a menacing statue in the doorway, shoulders squared and jaw tense.

Relief and surprise mix in Rig, and all she can do is gawk like a moron. "You came back."

"I have nowhere else to go," Ginka admits, quietly. "And

I'm going to need that favor sooner rather than later if I agree to this scheme of yours. I have conditions. I will not kill certain Ossuary agents. I will not commit seditious activities against Ossuary. I will not enter Ossuary space." Her eyes glance down at her armored hands for a moment so brief that Rig nearly misses it. Damn, would it kill her to let someone else see her emotions? "If we capture a PI agent, I demand to question them before we kill them."

She wants to what now? Rig's kinda figured that her faction loyalty runs deep, going by her outburst last night, but she didn't think it extended into... well, into *torture*. Because make no mistake, it's clear that Ginka's talking about torture. That deadly serious look on her face can mean nothing else. Rig doesn't condone torture – she *really* doesn't – but if it'll help get Daara back, she thinks she'll be able to turn a blind eye. She's done it before, after all. Under Pyrite. And getting her sister back is a far greater cause than anything Pyrite's ever made her do.

"O...kay," Rig acquiesces. "I can play by those rules."

Ginka nods, a sharp jerk of her head. "Good."

"Do you... want to come in?"

"I, ah... Yes?"

"Right."

She steels herself. A bit of awkwardness is nothing compared to whatever horrors PI could be subjecting Daara to. It doesn't matter if Ginka is abrasive or occasionally terrifying; she's also extremely useful, and Rig would be even more of an idiot than she normally is if she balks under some tense conversation.

As soon as they've stepped into the apartment, Ginka's nose twitches. "Do I smell coffee?"

"Uh, yeah–"

She finds herself promptly nudged out of the way as Ginka beelines straight to the coffee.

Then she watches with growing horror as Ginka pours the coffee grounds into a mug and starts fishing packets of things out of her pockets, ripping them open with her teeth and adding a series of suspicious white powders to the coffee. Seriously? Is Ginka *seriously* going to... In *June's apartment*? That's just rude.

Some foul stench is coming from the mug of what's basically sludge, and Rig scrunches her face up. Ginka takes another sip, and her jaw moves in a way that can only mean she's chewing it. Good gods.

"Do–" Rig tries to avoid equating that... *that* with the inviting mug of normal coffee she'd poured herself earlier. "Do you need a doctor?"

"For what?"

"I feel like that's going to give you a heart attack."

Ginka stares into the black sludge. "If I am fated to construct the means of my own demise, then isn't this the kindest of weapons?"

"...That's too philosophical for eight in the morning."

The kitchen door slides open and a bedraggled June shuffles in.

June stops dead in her tracks. Her face is partially covered by her curls, and her eyes are bleary and narrowed into tired, annoyed slits that glare at Ginka. "Hm. So you came back. Have you made your decision, then?"

"Er, yes," Ginka says, and then adds, "Honored Librarian. Please forgive my earlier misconduct."

With a wave of her hand, June dismisses the matter and continues to shuffle her way towards the coffee. She gives the pot a sniff and turns it around before pouring a cup. "Where did all the grounds go? Did you just make a really weak pot?" She takes a deep sip and then sighs, content and slightly more awake than before. "Ah, no. This is the good stuff."

Rig casts a surreptitious glance at Ginka's mug. "I wouldn't make you the weak stuff, I promise."

"So," June says, now that she resembles a person. "Living room?"

"Sorry?"

"I can't exactly fit three people at my kitchen table, and I think that there are probably some things we need to discuss."

Ah. Right. Because every aspect of Rig's precarious life is falling apart around her.

She ends up sitting on June's sofa; tucked into one corner, her legs folded under her, her torso sinking into the plush cushions. June settles next to her, close enough to touch if she wants, but far enough to give her space. Ginka stands, rigid as a piece of metal, arms behind her back, as though she teleported here from a military parade ground.

"I'm a bit uncertain about the details, I admit," Ginka begins, "so I will make a few assumptions. Correct me if I'm wrong." She clears her throat. "You deserted Pyrite three years ago."

Rig nods. "Yes."

"Now Pyrite is attempting to bring you back into the fold."

"Me and my schematics, but yes."

"And they're torturing your twin sister to do it."

She flinches, her back pressing into the sofa hard enough to imprint the fabric pattern into her skin. "Yeah, thanks for that pleasant reminder, Cactus. Exactly the sort of cheerful shit I wanna hear this early in the morning."

"I'm simply trying to clarify the picture." She begins to pace back and forth, a frown contorting her features, tugging on her dark Zazra facial markings. "Pyrite wants schematics. Schematics..." Her green eyes focus on something only she can see. "Are those *weapon* schematics?"

When Rig opens her mouth, it's to give a 'yes.' Only there's something a little *too* curious in Ginka's voice, and so by the time a word makes it out of her lips, she lies, "I'm sure Pyrite tries to turn everything into a weapon. But no, I didn't design one for them."

Fortunately, Ginka's too busy staring off into space to notice the curious glance June shoots Rig.

"I suppose Pyrite has a great number of weapons being

developed at any given time," Ginka mutters under her breath. "Your non-weapon schematics – can we use them as bait?"

"No," she lies again. "They were destroyed. I just told Agent Janus I could get them to buy time."

Ginka arches an eyebrow. Whatever. She can deal with the suspicion. It's not like she hasn't been expecting it. "...Very well. I'll proceed with that in mind. That does unfortunately eliminate my first idea, which was to use those plans to draw out PI and loosen their hold on your sister. This will complicate things."

Fine. Rig's life is already complicated. "I need to find Daara first," she says, summarizing what she'd thought of earlier. "Get in touch with the right compass and figure out where PI's headquarters are."

June nods thoughtfully. "Yes, that makes sense. It's not as though PI helpfully labels these things on any map."

"I got in touch with Mohsin, but there's–" Rig hesitates. "He didn't help."

"PI operates out of a constantly moving spacestation."

Her mind skips a beat. "What?"

"A spacestation," Ginka repeats. Casually. As if that's not probably one of Pyrite's best-kept secrets. "It's near impossible to track. The frequency at which they change systems is unknown, although it appears to be about once a fortnight. Even during that period, the station hardly remains in the same place within a system, and they rarely get close enough to fall into a planet's orbit."

"How the fuck do you even *know* that?"

"I have... encountered PI before. In my line of work, we occasionally... bump heads."

"What, have people hired you to whack PI agents before or something?"

"PI has a great number of enemies, many of whom are wealthy, well connected, and able to get their hands on all sorts of information. And," Ginka adds, "I already have a person in mind. I've worked with this compass in the past. He's trustworthy, good at his job, and based on the edge of Pyrite space, which I imagine means he'll be in the best position to help us find a spacestation that is *also* in Pyrite space."

So long as this compass can get the job done and so long as this concession keeps Ginka on board, fine. Rig crosses her arms. "If your guy even *looks* at us funny, we're going to revisit this discussion."

A tight nod. "Understood."

June gives Rig a faint smile. "Go get your guns, love. As much as I enjoy having you here, there's not much time to waste. I'll arrange an escort to *Bluebird* while you get ready. My friend in the military police can make sure that the spaceport is clear when you arrive and that you won't be bothered leaving."

"Sounds good. Break, then; we'll all get our shit together and head out."

"I'll pack some things for you. Food and such."

"You can cook? Since when?"

"I'm well versed in the art of heating up pre-packaged and freeze-dried foods. I simply make sure to get my hands on the upmarket versions."

"That sounds about right. You pamper me too much."

"Someone has to."

Rig draws in a deep breath as she heads back to the bedroom where she left her kit. She's not a thing that needs caring for, she's not a burden. She knows June didn't mean it like that, of course she didn't; it's just difficult not to bristle at something someone else would have meant as an insult. Too much time spent in the company of her fellow uncouth scoundrels, half of whom have been brainwashed into the faction mentality that claims people like her are a waste of space. No matter how frequently she tries to return to June, she is always aware that she stays away too long.

There are no further tremors in her hands as she gets her

things together. She straps her belt on, the pouches of her kit resting against her hip, a comforting and familiar weight. Wire in her single fingerless glove, spooled next to her link. A tiny knife brushing her ribcage, taped to her skin under her shirt, the handle just touching the wire of her bra. Panache and Pizzazz in their place of honor, magnetically holstered to her belt against her lower back.

A flash of pink.

Her eyes catch the color on her way out – one of June's handkerchiefs left lying about on the dresser.

The soft musk of her perfume still lingers on it. Rig gently picks it up, folds it into a neat rectangle, and tucks it into the breast pocket of her vest. As close to her heart as she can manage. A line of pink peeps out in the semblance of a kiss.

There are whispers when she returns to the living room.

Her ears catch the sound of her name. It's not the best idea. It's not even a good idea. Still, she can't help lingering at the door and listening in.

"–if you hurt her," June is saying, "I will hunt you down and ensure that you are gift wrapped and handed to my associate in the zoology department. They've just discovered a new species of felidae, you know. Twice the height of most humans, canines longer than my handspan, and used to roaming the perilous jungles of Darent, so I imagine that they'd find someone as small as you easy prey."

A beat of silence. Damn, Rig loves her girlfriend.

"We have an understanding then," Ginka stiffly replies. "I have no intention of hurting her. May Ossuary blind me if I break my word."

It's comforting to know that Rig has someone on her side who will throw attackers into a pit of people-eating animals should the occasion call for it. Her hand reaches for the door panel, a smile on her lips, and then–

"Do you love her?" Ginka asks.

No hesitation. "With all my heart."

"If she asked, would you leave with her?"

Her hand freezes. She can no more open the door than she can sprout wings and fly.

And June's not saying anything. Why is she not saying anything?

"I don't... That is..."

June's voice is hesitant and stilted and there are long pauses in between her attempted sentences. Each pause is a second Rig's heart doesn't beat. There's the quiet rustle of fabric and she can practically see June shifting from one foot to another. One of her nervous ticks, and how can Rig know her that well and still not know what she's going to say?

"It's, it's more complicated than that," she finally says. "I have to look at this logically, for her sake. I am... safe. A library provides political protection and security that she can take advantage of and that I can—" She coughs and instead continues, "I'm safe and she leads a very unsafe life and I... I need to be safe. Here. For her."

Right. Of course. Rig swallows painfully. That's very practical. June is practical. She's always known that. This is not a surprise. This *shouldn't* be a surprise.

"And besides," June quickly adds, "she would never ask."

Rig stumbles.

The toe of her boot smacks into the wall.

Shit – they probably heard that. She opens the door as fast as she possibly can to hide her eavesdropping.

"Ready?" she asks with a fake smile. "It's a long way to Pyrite space."

Ginka barely glances over at June – who seems to have shrunk in on herself – before replying, "I always am."

There is silence between the three of them as they leave the apartment complex.

Chickadee is waiting where Rig left it, untouched and spotless. A squad of MPs is lingering outside the gate, as well, led by someone that gives June a pleasant nod and smile.

And when Rig kisses June by the gates, on the final step of the Historical Center's boundaries, she can almost pretend as though she never heard that conversation at all.

INTERLUDE
Bird's Eye View

Spirit X-74 dispatches the last of the bodies, dragging the guard's corpse into a dark corner of the bell tower. A press of her fingers to each guards' pulse confirms that all of them are dead except one. Pity. Her blade must not have gone deep enough. The man is bleeding out, but it's best to ensure these things. She snaps his neck.

"Area's clear," she says as she returns to Thrush-Seven's side.

"Good work. We have five minutes."

Parts click together with quiet *shhhh-kllks* as Seven assembles a sniper rifle and sets it up on the low ledge of the bell tower overlooking the city. Light shines off the high-powered scope before he covers it with a non-reflective lens. All the better to go unseen.

The link he wears as an earpiece activates. A tiny hard light screen forms to cover his right eye, syncing up with the digital enhancers built into the scope. Although she's never worn one of those Handler links, she can imagine the breadth of information it's delivering to him at the moment. Running through the math of the shot – and he's already a better shot than her even without the tech.

There's something so elegant about the way he handles the rifle, his fingers running over each part, cataloging them, making minute adjustments to the gun's positioning. Everything just so.

He stares down the sight and makes one last change before leaning out of the way. "Care to look?" he asks.

Tentatively, she approaches the rifle, kneeling next to him. The gun is positioned on a stand, so there's nothing she can *really* do to mess up the sight line, but she's still cautious of destroying his work with a stray nudge of her hand.

Down the glass lenses and digital enhancers of the scope, she can see the form her target takes, outlined in red from the advanced sensors.

"Who is he?" she asks. Appearance and location. That's all she was told. Only enough about them to ensure a clean death. Seven had been informed that the target had been caught contacting suspicious persons, and he had told her in turn; but even then, their Controller knows more than they ever will. Still, she's curious. "He doesn't look like an enemy operative."

"He's not. He's one of the Nightbirds – Pyrite's biggest problem, outside of us and Ascetic. Seems like their group is pushing into Ossuary space now. He contacted a mercenary band we've had our eye on for some time." He gestures to the bodies in the corner of the tower. "*Those* mercenaries."

Taking two enemies out with one job. She approves.

She peers through the scope again, struggling to figure out where to put her hands to avoid messing it up. "How do I...?"

"Here." His voice is a low whisper against her ear as he takes one of her gloved hands and places it over the stock. "Like this."

Seven's hand ghosts over hers, shifting her grip on the rifle. She shivers despite the midday sun. Cold air whips around the tower they've been holed up in, spending hours staking out the area, waiting for the perfect shot.

"It's funny," she muses, "how small everything seems from up here."

Laughter ghosts on his reply, "I do like getting a bird's eye view of everything."

"Oh gods." She snickers against the stock, trying very hard to keep still and not throw off the shot. "You're *terrible*."

"Should I take that as a compliment?"

"Absolutely."

There's the echo of an unwelcome sound.

Her head snaps up, away from the scope. "Footsteps."

Seven is instantly on alert, drawing his gun and turning to face the stairwell door. Targeting crosshairs appear on the screen of his link, fixing in on the noise, the vibrations of the building – everything. She only wishes she could have that much information at her fingertips.

"Three hostiles," he reports. "X-74, you should–"

Gunfire bursts down the door.

Plans have changed. X-74 abandons the sniper rifle, darting to her Handler's side as she forms a dagger.

These enemies are rebels, just like their targets. Heretics. No one defies Ossuary's rule. It's a rehearsed line in her head, a thought that she fills her mind with as she flips her knife around in the palm of her hand. She throws the knife at the enemy's knee as Seven lines up a shot. The man screams, clutching his knee as he falls to the ground. There's the *crack* of a gun going off as Seven shoots the man in the heard before he can hit the ground.

Then she's flipping out of the way to avoid a punch to the face. Seven gets another shot off, but it's close quarters; guns are of limited use here, and the bullet only hits the second target in the arm.

She engages the second target, but the third is...

A knife whizzes towards her face, her body coils to dodge – too slow.

Blood splatters her face.

What? She wipes blood from her eyes. Seven's hand is in front of her head, the knife caught in his flesh, straight through his palm, and he's bleeding. Everything goes red as he cries out in pain, dropping to his knees and curling over his injured hand.

"Seven!"

His attacker dies with a slit throat and a gurgle, and then she's darting towards the last of the attackers, carving a path across his torso, shoving him to the ground and plunging her dagger into his eye. Again and again. Blood splatters. Ensure the kill – ensure his death, ensure the kill, the bastard–

"Stop!" Seven orders in a hard tone that brokers no disagreement. "X-74, *stop*."

Shaking hands discard her blade in the corpse. She drops to her Handler's side, scrambling for the supply bag they brought with them, digging through it until she finds the medkit.

"I can fix this," she tells him, opening the kit up and staring unthinkingly at the supplies within. "Tell me what I'm doing."

He gives her instructions through teeth gritted against the pain.

Remove the knife. Clean the injury. Contact gel. Compression bandages. It'll heal, but...

"I'm sorry. I'm wasting your time – we're running up against the deadline," he tells her as she ties the bandages off. "You need to make the shot or else the target will escape."

"But I, I'm not certified for this–"

"As if some damn formal certification matters. There are no other options." He stares down at his mangled right hand. "I can't shoot."

Right. Okay. No other options.

She kneels next to the rifle, double checks to make sure it hasn't been jostled during their confrontation. Just like in training. She's done that before. She can do this. Her thumb flicks off the connection between the scope and Seven's link, and the red outline of the target fades into view before her eye. The crosshair is aimed at the figure's head.

"Take three deep breaths."

X-74 doesn't nod, but she does make a slight hum of acknowledgement in the back of her throat.

"After you exhale on that third breath, that one to three second pause is when you want to shoot. Remember, this isn't semi auto, so you can and should hold the trigger down even after you feel the shot go off. Follow through the action. Have you accounted for everything? Distance, wind, planet rotation?"

"Yes," she replies.

"Ten seconds till you lose the window of opportunity." She focuses on the sound of his voice, letting that drown out the part of her mind that's still panicking. His uninjured hand rests on her shoulder, steadying her. "On my count. Three. Two. One–"

She shoots.

CHAPTER NINE
Tides and Tales

A series of polishing cloths lie next to Rig's elbow as she shines the glass ball's surface, cleaning off nonexistent dust, working for the sake of having something to do. The two figures inside it seem to smile back up at her, even though the minimalist carvings on their faces don't indicate any particular expression. Her thumb has been rubbing at an invisible speck in front of Dare's crystal face for what feels like forever.

She glances back over her shoulder.

Nothing new on the bridge. No alert that they've arrived in Pyrite space yet.

It hasn't been twelve hours yet, she reminds herself. Just under twelve hours. Close to that. Almost that? Maybe it *has* actually been twelve hours and *Bluebird*'s autopilot hasn't turned off and–

She glances back at the bridge again.

Nope. Still in luminalspace, still fine, still condemned to the black pit of waiting.

When she turns back to the orb, Dare's blank and sort-of-smiling face is there to greet her. Of all the stories about him, of all the tales of his greatness, why aren't there any stories about him having a sibling? Why did he have to be an only child? Why couldn't there be some memorable escapade where his sibling – a sister, perhaps – fell into the evil clutches of a Pyrite asshole or some such similar bastard and Dare had to take his intrepid crew and rescue her…

But there's no story like that. No hint of what Rig should be doing.

She takes another peek at the bridge.

"You're going to snap your neck," Ginka remarks.

She's been bustling around in the kitchen for some time now, and a medley of fantastic aromas are beginning to waft through *Bluebird*'s main room – which also doubles as the galaxy's tiniest galley kitchen. Most things on the ship are two or three different things at the same time. The average schooner is not burdened with an overabundance of floor space, and *Bluebird* is no exception.

Rig tries and fails to muster an impressive dirty look. "Forgive me for being a tad bit stressed over here, Cactus."

There's a *clink* as Ginka places two bowls down on the table and slides one towards Rig. "Eat. It'll help."

"This is packaged protein?" she asks, holding up a forkful of mush.

"I used what I found in the galley. Nothing new."

It smells spicy. Like peppers or taleen chili paste. Rig thought she ran out of those sorts of non-perishables months ago. She takes a tentative bite and then swoons. Holy shit. It's… it's good. It's packaged protein and it's *good*. There's nothing that can be done for the texture, but there's a complex flavor to it: spicy and sweet at the same time, and Rig can feel her tongue start to burn from the heat in the best possible way.

"How did you accomplish this magic?" she asks, in between shoveling food into her mouth.

Ginka shrugs. She twirls her fork around elegantly before digging in with slightly more dignity than Rig. "You had spices on board already."

"That's *it*? Just… spices? I've tried, but all I get is a burning hot mess."

"Just spices."

"Who taught you how to cook?"

That is apparently not the right question to ask. Ginka stills in that way she does, like something inside her is going cold. "Someone used to spending long periods of time in transit," she eventually replies. "He taught me how to cook during a journey to Tsuni, once. Many years ago. We spent a whole month aboard ship and, well, the standard packaged flavors can get really dull. I never managed to get as good as him, though."

"Huh." Rig takes another bite, melting inside as the flavor rolls over her tongue. Guess three years in space isn't quite enough for her cooking skills to develop. How long has Ginka spent hopping around the galaxy? Five years? Ten? "Can you teach me?"

"I don't know," Ginka says. A thoughtful frown tugs her face to the side. "I'm sorry, but... it doesn't feel like something that's mine to give away. Or not wholly mine, at least. It's... it's *his*, too."

Ah, so that's how it is. It's not just a thing she does, it's a memory as well. Rig can understand. Her life is made up of different bits of different people and stories, stitched together until they form something that resembles a complete person. Pieces of memory and myth poured inside the shell of her body. Not that she doesn't think of herself as being, well, herself. She is the master of her own body, her own form in this galaxy, and she'll fight anyone who says otherwise. Those bits and pieces are her. All the way through. She chose them to take with her.

There's a *beep* and a lurch of the ship and–

She does actually crack her neck this time as she whirls around in her seat to stare at the bridge.

"We're out of luminalspace." She swallows, the echo of spice fading already to the bland taste of agitation. The bowl of deliciousness gets shoved aside to clear off the tiny hologram projector built into the table; again, like everything on the ship, the table is two different things. Three, if being her workbench also counts. "Call your compass."

Ginka pushes her bowl aside and hooks her link up.

The call goes through after a moment. A glowing screen is projected, floating an inch above the table, and Rig turns it so that both she and Ginka can see the screen. And so that *both* of them are in the picture. She'd rather this compass know from the start that he's dealing with her, not just Ginka. This is her sister they're dealing with, after all. She might let Ginka take the helm when it makes sense, but it's *her* show.

"Hello," the man on the other end of the screen says. He's human, a series of colorful tattoos covering his neck. "How can I... Oh. It's *you*."

Ginka smirks. "Triton. It's good to lay eyes on you again."

Rig knows that name. A year ago, she'd attempted to hire him to locate a set of ancient Kashrini headscarf pins, but his prices had been so ludicrous that she'd turned him down without looking into his reputation more. Unless something has seriously changed, he's out of their price range. She still can't afford him. If Ginka's not carting around millions of kydis, they're flat out of luck. She's willing to bankrupt herself to get Daara back, but no compass worth their salt would take an IOU. Unlike Ginka, she doesn't think she could pay him with a favor, either.

"If it isn't my favorite monster under the bed. I'd say I'm happy to lay eyes on you, too, but we both know that'd be at least a little bit of a lie," Triton says with a faint smile. He does something out of screen to a computer terminal and there's a *shwoosh* of a door sliding shut. "I'm private enough to talk business, assuming that's your reason for calling."

"Do I call for other reasons?" Ginka asks.

"You might want to meet up for a nice cup of tea. Miracles can happen."

With Ginka, no fucking way. "We're here for business," Rig confirms, leaning a little closer to the screen. "We're trying to find the headquarters of a certain organization. An... intelligence organization. Faction organization. If that's not something you'd be willing to fuck with, we understand, but I'd appreciate it if you'd tell us up front."

It's only barely noticeable when his eyes widen for a split second. He slowly turns his gaze to Ginka and gives her a once over. "I thought we had an understanding..."

Ginka glares at him. "It's Pyrite Intelligence."

"Oh. Pyrite, huh?" He glances between the two of them, "Which of you is the client?"

"I am," Rig says.

At the same time Ginka says, "But it's going on *my* tab."

Triton sighs and sinks into his chair until it seems like the chair is going to consume him. "Can't I work for a paying client, for once?" he grumbles. Holy fucking – is Ginka getting this for *free*? "I mean, I'll do it, obviously, but mark me down as distinctly unchuffed. So, Pyrite Intelligence. That's a tough engine to overheat. Doable, but again... unchuffed. I'm sending you the details of a party that a friend of mine is hosting two days from now. A number of people will be in attendance, including myself and a Pyrite Intelligence agent. I'm going to need you to steal his link for me."

"Easily done," Rig replies. Early days of her career had seen her pickpocketing like a pro. From there, she'd moved on to higher levels of theft while still keeping her deft touch at sleight of hand and all the tools of the trade.

Ginka gives her a look.

"What?" Rig gestures to her entire body, "Thief, remember?"

"Fine. My skills in that area are likely less well developed. Triton, can you send us a dossier on this agent?"

He's typing down something out of their sight. "Yeah, I'll send it over as soon as I can. Here I am, hacking into my friend's guest list. For you. I hope you appreciate how much I suffer."

"Greatly," Ginka drawls.

Triton just rolls his eyes as he types away. A few moments later, Ginka's link buzzes, signaling that the information has been sent and received as promised. At least this guy seems good for his word. In Rig's experience compasses tend to be trustworthy, but they're still criminals, and not all people respect the idea of honor amongst thieves. Frankly, given that he's not getting paid for this, Rig almost couldn't blame him if he chose to screw them over or just straight up tell them to fuck off.

"That's what I have to get you to Tides. I'll send the dossier once I get it." Triton gives them a sarcastic two-fingered salute. "See you shortly, my dear monster. And stars' favor to you both."

The call flickers out and the holo screen vanishes back into nothing.

Rig scarfs down the last few bites of her dinner before it gets cold. Not that cold protein is the worst thing she's ever eaten. "So," she says slowly, trying to figure out a way to word this question that doesn't make it an accusation. "Triton."

"Yes?"

"He's uh… working for free? For you?"

"Yes."

"So… is he your dealer, or are you blackmailing him, or sleeping with him, or what?"

Ginka chokes on her food, her eyes bugging out as she gasps for air around the lungful of spicy hot protein.

"Is that a yes?"

"No!" Ginka insists, "I am not sleeping with him! I'm, I would never!"

"Such stringent denial–"

"*No.*"

"Eh. He's not bad looking, on a purely aesthetic level. I wouldn't have judged you if you were sleeping with him."

Now they're finished with dinner, Rig gets up and clears away their plates. She still has that itch under her skin, that anxious need to do something with her hands. *Bluebird* isn't big enough to store much of a water tank, so the dishes are cleaned with an ultrasonic cleaner, disintegrating the layers of dirt and protein remnants on the surface. Same as how the shower works. Or anything that would usually require water. All water is reserved for drinking and occasionally flicking at Ginka to annoy her.

Gods, she always loves taking water showers back in June's apartment. Standing under the warm water for as long as she can, usually until June joins her – which she does only partially to conserve water. Rig scours her hands clean, and for one brief moment lets the memory of June's perfume fill her mind. The memory of safety and love and gods she misses it.

"Meeting at a party, huh?" She takes a look at the spice containers that Ginka left out and memorizes which ones were used. "Does Triton often do that?"

"He never works out of the same place twice. I've met him in spaceport publicas and palace halls. According to the info he sent, this party is being hosted by Madhumita Moor. She's fourth in line to inherit a seat on Pyrite's Council and is currently ruling as Governor of Tides. It's the third moon orbiting Mazu. A massive trading hub. Very... affluent."

Rig bends down to put the dishes away and narrowly avoids banging her head. "You can just say rich as fuck."

"Then yes, it's rich as fuck."

"So how are we going to fit in at a fancy party?"

Ginka pauses and it occurs to Rig that perhaps she actually hadn't considered that little problem until now. "I suppose if we plot course to Tides as soon as possible we could arrive the day before the party and go shopping for appropriate attire? Triton has been kind enough to provide invitations for us under generic and discreet aliases, but we should be careful not to draw any unnecessary attention to us. Governess Moor is not a woman we want to cross."

An infiltration type of situation, then. Sounds fun. Any excuse to get dolled up and pretend to be richer than she actually is. "Can you get through an evening without stabbing someone or scaring a rich bastard shitless?"

"You have so little faith in me."

"I think I have exactly the appropriate amount of faith in you, given what I've seen so far."

"Then you haven't seen enough of me."

"Hey now," she replies, trying to force a laugh out, "I'm a taken woman."

Ginka opens her mouth to respond and then closes it with an annoyed glare. Good call. There's no sass fest that Rig can't win. Grumbling all the while, Ginka turns back to her link and makes a big show of being way more invested in the data Triton sent than she probably actually is.

After making sure the kitchen is spic and span, Rig nips onto the bridge for a moment to change their luminalspace course to Tides.

If they have good luck and smooth sailing, they should arrive on the moon in four hours. Plenty of time to pick up some fancy outfits and make sure that her nails are buffed and her shoes are shined. Or whatever it is rich people do. She never meshed well with high society, not even when she was still under Pyrite. Not that she hadn't been invited to do so. Her bosses had been eager to take her to parties and show off their One Kashrini Who Made The Cut, because if she can come this far Then You Can Too.

Hopefully her desertion wiped the smirks off their smug faces. Not their poster Kashrini anymore, is she?

When she steps back into the common room, Ginka is returning from the tiny spare room, carrying something in her hand.

"Cactus?"

Ginka sits down primly at the table, waits for Rig to sit across from her, and then sets the item on the table. It's the same vial that Rig's seen before – the one with what looks to be liquid shinedust in it.

"As I said, I'm going to need that favor sooner rather than later." She taps the vial with one armored finger and the sound rings through the common room. The liquid ripples and shimmers in the light. "This," she explains tersely, "is Grace. As far as I'm aware, PI doesn't have access to it, but there have been rumors that they know what it is and are working to develop it. If you ever see it, hear a whisper about it – I need it."

This is both a very easy and very *shitty* favor to ask for. "I'm not a drug dealer."

"That's the favor I'm asking for. Take it or leave it."

Rig stews in her own moral stewiness for a minute, staring at the vial of Grace and wondering just how much this is worth to her. "Fine, I'll get it for you if I can," she decides, and then adds, because it's important and she's feeling that petty need to flip the conversation at Ginka, "But you're going to have to answer one question for me."

"…Very well. Ask it."

"Your gauntlets," she says, gesturing to the shiny metal covering Ginka's arms. "The light they produce. It's capable of cutting through hard light, but it can't be helltech, obviously, and I've never seen anything like it–"

"It *is* helltech."

It's a good thing Rig's no longer eating, because if she was, she'd choke and die. "Excuse me? You–" Her jaw falls to the floor and she can't tell if she's scared, angry, or some combination of the above. "But that's… You actually brought helltech onto *my fucking ship* and didn't tell me and – you're going to *kill us both* if you activate those things!"

She scoffs. "Don't be absurd."

"Helltech generation produces toxic byproducts, Cactus, you should fucking know that if you're wandering around with those damn death traps around your arms!" She recalls the fight against Fen and blanches. "Oh gods, I breathed that stuff in earlier, didn't I – Am I gonna die?"

"Rig," Ginka snaps. "Calm down. *You* are *not* going to die from my helltech." She curls her fingers into a fist and then relaxes them, her gaze softening into something more somber as she looks at the movement of her hand. "Those that designed these knew that the toxic byproduct was the one thing preventing helltech from being utilized as weapons. So that was the first thing they countered." She snaps her hand into a fist again. "There aren't any toxins being released into the air; you have nothing to worry about."

A sigh of relief sags Rig's shoulders even as her mind is still processing everything she's just heard.

"How did they do it?" she ends up asking. She's a nanotech expert, not a helltech expert, but that doesn't mean such a scientific conundrum doesn't tickle her curiosity. "And if they could change the generation process so that there's no toxic byproduct–" which they *must* have done, because how else would they stop the release of toxins? "– then why wouldn't–"

Ginka shoots her a glare. "I'm *not* a scientist."

Right. Damn. A more optimistic thought drifts through her mind and she latches on to it. "Well, if we make it out of this alive, and with Daara alive, could you take me to meet these magic techies?"

"Trust me," she replies, almost sardonically, "you *don't* want to meet them."

The pin that PI stole from Daara still rests in Rig's pocket. She runs her fingers over the smooth plastic, her eyes glazing over as she looks at Ginka's helltech gauntlets, trying to figure out how they work.

Without really thinking about it, she blurts out, "Did they hurt you?"

Ginka snaps upright as though a chiropractor just punched her spine back into place. All the blood drains from her face and she's so bad at hiding her emotions that it's painful. "They... No, that's – why would you ask such a thing?"

"At a guess, your gauntlets are probably experimental. If they were more mainstream, I'd have heard about them before," Rig explains, trying to keep her voice even because Ginka looks like a spooked animal ready to make a run for it. "Also it's fucking *helltech*. That stuff's made of danger. It wouldn't surprise me if it hurt to put those on the first time. And I know that scientists – *factioned* scientists – are often willing to ignore a whole lot of other people's pain when they're gnawing at an interesting experiment."

"No," Ginka replies. It's not at all convincing. "No, you're wrong, you've got it all wrong; they weren't–" She snatches up the bottle of Grace and leaps out of her seat as though her chair was electrocuted. "You have no idea what you're talking about. You told me it wasn't tactful to ask about what Pyrite's doing to Daara – don't ask *me* about my helltech. Eat your own words and get some damn tact yourself. Now I'm going to get some sleep and I suggest you *don't* disturb me."

She stalks towards the spare bedroom, storm clouds practically radiating off her.

"Hey," Rig adds softly, before Ginka can disappear, "I'm sorry."

Ginka stumbles but doesn't stop.

Eerie silence settles over the ship, and eventually Rig puts the glass orb of Dare and Shen back into its protective clothing wrapping and shuffles back into the bridge. She closes her eyes and tries not to think about what Pyrite's doing to Daara, despite the snarl of Ginka's words echoing in her ears.

Four hours to go till Tides. Almost there.

CHAPTER TEN
Party Planning

Their landing on Tides is blissfully uneventful.

Triton, despite Ginka calling him an elusive wanderer of a man, apparently has a lot of pull with the higher ups – the higher ups of most planets, given how Ginka describes him. He's gotten them clearance codes, official aliases, the whole works. Rig's honestly pretty impressed. It gets them past the system patrols, the local police patrols, and even the official Pyrite port authorities when they finally touch down. That part she lets Ginka do, making sure that she wears one of her bulkier headscarves to cover her face and stays out of their way during the tense two-minute conversation.

After they land, they split up with plans to meet for dinner later.

Ginka goes shopping, Rig goes on the far less fun venture of renting a luxury skiff. They simply *have* to show up in style, after all.

Tides, as a whole, is lovely in a way that should make any decent spacefarer slightly suspicious and keep a close eye on anyone around them. In places like Red Dock, one has to watch their pockets. Places like Tides, on the other hand, make Rig feel the need to watch out for police, for the loyalists, for just about everyone and everything, really.

The planet is an ode to Pyrite and the faction's influences. It itches at her.

In the capital city of Marina, where they'd landed, Rig is instantly greeted by the curvy lines and gaudy colors of Pyrite architecture. Spires that jut high above the ground, winding skifftrain lines between buildings, covered glass walkways crisscrossing every level of the city, and the skiffs are things of pure beauty. Under Pyrite, technology is never hidden, so long as it works perfectly. Pipes, wires, and engines, all on display. All cogs of the giant machine. Here, massive wheels are built into the city, churning away a steady froth of water, white droplets misting the lower levels, coating the sides of concrete buildings in an iridescent shimmer. A hundred floors down, Rig imagines it must seem like rain. The wheels grind away and build up electricity – for on the blue moons of Mazu, almost all the energy comes from the water, and Tides is the undisputed queen of them all.

Farther towards the outskirts of the city, the water will shine with lanterns, and the streets will be twisting, intricate things that lead to villas and private museums, luxury spires of invention. And farther away, far enough to be *out* of the way, the water will be murky with pollution, the air will be heavier with smoke, and the iridescent shine of the buildings will be from oils and liquid gases.

Securing a skiff for tomorrow night is easy. Paying for it – now that will be a challenge. Rig's shuffled a few fake credit accounts around to buy herself some time, but when that time is up she'll need to beg some kydis off either Ginka or Triton. Both seem to possess shocking levels of secret riches, so hopefully that won't be a problem.

That night, she and Ginka grab dinner from a street vendor, a bag of clothing tucked under Ginka's arm and a bill for a skiff rental in Rig's pocket.

The lower cities on Pyrite planets are always rife with ordered chaos.

Upper cities are neat, well-run machines. Lower cities are where all of that is made possible. Around Rig are currently a thousand people pushing past, yelling at vendors and hawking goods, all surrounded by blinking neon signs that are the stars above their heads, fending off the darkness of night more efficiently than any moon.

A group of passing Hassha catch Rig's attention. The species is known for being able to see in the dark and handle hot objects with their bare hands – even white-hot metal won't burn them. In Pyrite cities, they're usually encouraged to work in industrial divisions, working night shifts in massive forges. This group is probably off to relieve the day crew and get to work for the night.

For a brief moment, Rig's jealous.

Hassha and their fire-touch. Zazra and their empathic skills. Oriates with their armored skin. Trants and their four-armed dexterity. So many useful abilities; and yes, they're taken advantage of by the factions. That sucks, objectively. But they still have those talents. Kashrini? They've got nothing. They can't do anything more than humans can.

It's a stupid jealously, really. Rig pushes it down and follows Ginka through the market, ignoring the Hassha.

Ginka seems to revel in the street food, biting into meat so spicy it's turned an aggressive shade of red, a shy sort of enthusiasm to her demeanor as she picks out buns stuffed with pickled vegetables in every shade of the rainbow, her eyes doing that wide-pupiled thing when she tastes the unexpected sweetness of snow apples. It's the enthusiasm of one who might have travelled the galaxy, but never stopped for a moment to *be* in the galaxy.

Rig's got a skewer of spicy grilled fish and river reeds; but as she chews on it, all she can taste is the bitterness of Pyrite's smog. A home she has long since turned her back on... It's the taste of her old life, her tiny apartment in the slums of the Pyrite homeworld, her workshop in the Spire. The quick and easy dinners her mother would leave on the stove for her and Daara when they got back from school.

It's ash on her tongue.

"Here," she says, leading Ginka off the main street.

The two of them squeeze into a corner and perch on rickety chairs near a table that's been sandwiched between two food stands. A mere meter away is the crush of people, the bustle of it all so great that it allows her and Ginka privacy.

Ginka chugs a bowl of curry and then points at a sign behind her shoulder, "What's that?"

"It's… a recruitment office?" Weird question to ask. "No one there's going to be looking for us, so there's no reason to worry or anything."

"Recruiting for what?"

"…The army?"

Ginka pauses, a meat bun hovering in front of her wide-open mouth. "What are they doing that for?"

"To… to get soldiers? Does Ossuary… do they *not* do that?"

The bun vanishes in two neat chomps. "Why would they? If you're suited for the army, then you're told to join the army."

"Wait, so Ossuary just *tells* you to be a soldier? I mean… Okay, sure Pyrite'll sometimes say the war is getting 'worse'," here she uses air quotes, "and they'll have a 'minimal draft' but that always ends in like a year or less once their forces are at whatever magic number Pyrite's determined is ideal for the current situation."

"What an odd way of doing things. Under Ossuary, your occupation is usually determined at birth. Species, family history, medical exams – it all contributes to where you're placed." Ginka shrugs like what she's just said *isn't* really creepy. "Sometimes those initial decisions are reconsidered later on and you're put somewhere else, but usually it's accurate."

"So you don't have any choice at all? No free will?"

"And is Pyrite a bastion of free will?"

At least Rig had been the one to decide to enter her Spire. Although, she realizes with a jolt of surprise, maybe she hadn't been, really. If Pyrite hadn't carefully designed things so that

Kashrini are largely stuck in poverty, then her mother wouldn't have died and she wouldn't have been facing destitution. If she hadn't needed money, she might not have considered setting her sights on such a prestigious Spire. If she hadn't been told for years by her teachers that she had an obligation to use her clever mind to become a weapons developer, she might have turned her talents elsewhere.

"No," she slowly admits to Ginka. "No, I guess it's not.'

She puts her skewer of fish down and leans back in her chair, staring up at the levels of city above them and the light mist from the water wheels that's dusting this level of the city.

"I cannot believe I'm the one to say this," Ginka points out, "but you may want to lighten up. Otherwise the stress of being caught and killed by Pyrite will kill you before Pyrite gets the chance."

Rig shovels the rest of her skewer into her mouth and forces herself to choke it down. "There we go. Problem solved; you're no longer pushed into the role of resident optimist."

"I wouldn't say I'm optimistic or pessimistic," Ginka counters. She pauses making her point to stuff an entire bun into her mouth and then somehow manages to speak without spitting or choking. "I'm simply realistic. It's not my fault the galaxy so often disappoints."

"I suppose that's one way of looking at things. A depressing one, though."

Ginka ignores that completely and instead holds out her link. "I received a file from Triton earlier today. It's the details regarding the PI agent that will be present at Governess Moor's party."

Finally. "Anything juicy?"

"I don't know, I was waiting to rendezvous with you before I opened it."

"How polite." Rig props her head up on her hand, using her now cleaned skewer to pick her teeth. "Show us then. Let's see who we're dealing with."

A holo screen pops up above Ginka's link. It's mostly text – walls of information that seem to be predominantly covered by angry black redacted boxes. Triton might be the best compass in the galaxy, but he clearly isn't the greatest hacker. It's not a surprise really. While the two skill sets overlap, they're both their own respective specialties. Ginka flicks through the pages of the dossier until she comes to a profile that includes a picture.

"Shit," Rig says at exactly the same time as Ginka says: "Fuck."

The smarmy face of Agent Janus stares up at them.

His holographic face slowly rotates around on the screen, letting him smirk at them from every possible angle until Rig has the strong urge to smash Ginka's link.

"Okay, what are the chances," she asks, "that this is all a coincidence?"

"Absolutely none."

"Right, okay then, so we're fucked." There are only two real options she can think of, and neither of them bode well. "Either Triton is at this party because Janus is, or Janus is at this party because Triton is. You've worked with Triton before, what are the chances that they're working together to stab us in the back?"

Ginka pokes at a platter of aggressively orange curry with a spoon, a thoughtful frown furrowing her brow and pinching the Zazra stripes that adorn her forehead. "Slim to none, actually. Triton is a former Ossuary librarian, so–"

Rig almost swallows her skewer. "Say what?"

Ossuary librarian – Rig's mind spins in circles, a gear thrown out of sync with its fellows. It's practically unheard of for librarians to abandon their library. It's just not a thing. It doesn't happen. It's as silly as saying 'let's make a planet rotate backwards' or 'let's make the Pyrite Council embrace individuality.' And from Ossuary? That place is an information blackout and they're known for having almost no deserters or turncoats.

None that live for longer than a week, that is.

"You heard me," Ginka confirms. "He deserted Ossuary a number of years ago but cut a deal with Windshadow to secure his own life. So while I'm certain that he would sell us out in an instant to *them*, he wouldn't to PI."

"Does everyone under Ossuary's rule just do whatever Windshadow says?"

"Yes."

"Lovely. The clarity of dictatorship." As much as Rig hates PI and is scared shitless of them, she's really glad that the intelligence organization they're dealing with *isn't* Windshadow. She's heard enough rumors about them to know that if she gets even a whiff of a hint of a clue that they're in the same system as her, she should grab her bags and run. "Well, at least we can be certain that Triton isn't going to stab us in the back."

One certainty in this apparent disaster.

"I wish this were an Ascetic ball." Ginka takes a bite of her curry and chews on her spoon. "Their habit of wearing masks for the entire evening makes it easy to blend in. Pity Pyrite doesn't appreciate that particular brand of mystique. I suppose if it's *Janus*, and he knows your face, then our infiltration plan will have to change."

"Nah, it won't."

"He's *seen your face*."

"Yeah, but he's *human*. I'll just wear different clothes, put on a different headscarf, and use makeup to make my face look different. He'll never know."

"I'm still doubting this plan. It's risky."

"How many times have you been mistaken for some other Zazra?"

"…I no longer doubt your plan."

"And you have everything ready to go?" June asks.

Rig's link is propped against the wall of *Bluebird*'s tiny washroom, generating a hologram that's happily humming away and showing June. Pallets of powders in varying shades of blue are spread out across the sink, brushes lying about, lipstick tubes worn down to waxy stubs. Rig has contoured her cheekbones, done a distracting smoky eye, and made her nose look far smaller than it actually is. *She* barely recognizes herself. Janus won't stand a chance.

"Yep," she replies, doing up the buttons on her shirt. "It should be simple enough. He might be a decent agent, but there's no way that he'll catch me doing a lift on him if Ginka's running interference or keeping an eye out for any guards that might be watching too closely. I've stolen a dozen links before; this won't be all that different."

There's a careful hum as June thinks it through. It's a damn shame that she can't be here right now, that she's bound to her library more thoroughly than the moon Tides is bound to the planet Mazu beneath it. Nothing could make Rig feel more confident about this job than having her love at her side. June wants to be safe, doesn't she? Wants Rig to be safe with her? Wouldn't they both be safer if they were together, surely, because there's nothing in the galaxy that could stop Rig if she's fighting to protect June...

She gives her shirt a particularly rough tug to straighten it out and tugs those thoughts from her head at the same time.

"Governess Moor will be a different factor. Have you considered her?" June asks.

"There are about five thousand rumors about her floating around the netspace – I looked her up. Not sure what's real or not, and since I'm stuck using a Pyrite netspace connection right now, I'm dealing with their stupid censorship as well."

"I've done some research," June remarks, her chin resting against her hand and a tiny frown pestering her otherwise calm expression. "Madhumita Moor is not a woman to be crossed. She once had an Ascetic diplomat beheaded after he spoke to a Pyrite librarian on the planet. Just to make a point that he couldn't steal any of their knowledge without punishment.

After she took the man's head, she took the heads of everyone else in his diplomatic convoy. She left one of them alive, but not before branding the poor person with the flaming gear of Pyrite."

Branding. Lovely. "That seems like bad manners."

"It caused a bit of a stir. Would you like to see our file on the incident? It includes a number of images of–"

"Ew, gross, *no*. I don't want to see a bunch of headless corpses *or* a Pyrite brand right now, thanks. Babe, don't take this the wrong way, but sometimes you're *nasty*. And not in the fun sense of the word."

"Sorry. Our database doesn't have much else on her that's *solid*. It's predominantly rumors and disreputable gossip magazines." June's typing away at a keyboard as she talks, mouth tugged to the side in concentration. "There's not a lot we can retrieve from Pyrite space, after all. We also have nothing on this Triton person."

She adjusts the holster that'll secure her guns to her lower back. "If he's associated with Windshadow, you wouldn't have jack about shit in your archives. And don't worry too much about Moor. We're not going to fuck with her. Just… one of her guests."

"Are you aware that if you die I'm going to have to avenge your death?"

"That does sound troublesome."

"It does. You see, I had this wonderful book on thirty-ninth century Ascetic history delivered only yesterday, and I really need to write up a thesis on that."

"Those are some excellent priorities," Rig says with a laugh.

"The Shaman of the Mind themself awarded our library special commendation for acquiring the book," June insists, struggling to keep a straight face. "It cost over two hundred thousand kydis to deliver."

"I see that these are dire circumstances."

"I'll be very put out if I have to break my vows and travel

halfway across the galaxy to avenge your death. And then, of course, after that I would be on the run from Governess Moor's successor, and that would put a serious damper on my planned reading list, I have to say."

Rig blows the screen a kiss. "I'd best not die then."

Finishing touches to her outfit go on. Gold cufflinks. A dark blue necktie, secured with a faux firestone.

June looks up from her keyboard and makes an appreciative hum, grinning at her. "Well, *hello*. I do love you in a suit."

"Want to see my shoes?"

"Oh, *yes*."

Rig plops one foot on the counter so that June can see before straightening up. "I thought I'd go for a subtle look."

June snickers. "*Extremely* subtle."

She takes the pink handkerchief she stole from June out of her usual leather vest and tucks it into the pocket of her suit. She's wearing a bright pink and navy three-piece ensemble, sharply tailored for maximum comfort and to let the jacket conceal her guns at the small of her back. Various parts of her kit are tucked away into the suit as well. This, at least, she didn't have to buy here. This suit has been lingering in the back of her closet for a while now, kept in reserve and tailored perfectly to fit her needs for both fashion and fighting prowess.

She might be broke, but she knows when to invest money in a nice suit.

And, well, it makes her ass look good.

Priorities.

"I look so snazzy."

"You always look snazzy."

"Flatterer." It occurs to Rig that now that she's dressed to kill, she should hang up the call. They have a deadline to meet. A party to infiltrate. She can't spend forever talking to June in the protective confines of *Bluebird*'s bathroom. From the creeping fall of June's expressions, she can see that it occurred to her as well. So she goes with the important bits. "I love you," she says again. "So much. I'll call again once we've got a location from Ginka's compass friend."

June presses a lingering kiss to her fingertips and then gently touches the screen. "I love you too. Do be careful."

"I always try."

There's a static blip as June hangs up the call.

Time to go to work.

Rig steps out of the bathroom, walks about two steps – *Bluebird* is a lovely ship, but she is not built for size – and then knocks on the door to Ginka's room slash the storage space.

Less than a heartbeat later, Ginka slides open the door and stares at Rig with tired eyes. Did she just wake up from *another* nap? To absolutely no one's surprise, she's dressed in all black. Short, tight black dress with long sleeves that… those are gloves. Sleeve-gloves. Okay. And look, under the dress are black tights and black boots. Who the fuck even sells such a boringly weird dress?

Rig gives her a look. "Part of the fun in dressing up revolves around not looking like a dominatrix that doesn't have real person skin."

"I have skin," Ginka grumbles.

"That's exactly what someone who doesn't have skin would say. Also – and I'm not trying to judge you or pressure you here, just pointing out the obvious – it would probably help to have your hands uncovered. Who knows how many people here are going to be our hidden enemies. A simple handshake could really help us out when it comes to finding those who are trying to kill us."

"I know what I'm doing." Ginka stares back at her and then looks down. "Are, are those…"

Rig strikes a pose, doing a little tap dance against the metal floors. "Pink sparkle shoes. Oh *yeah.*"

"Can I pretend I don't know you?"

"You have *no* taste."

"Black blends in. Those are going to make you stand out. That's just... that's illogical."

"Ah, but you see, that's the genius of it. If I look like I'm trying to stand out, then no one will suspect me of being there to commit a crime, because surely someone as bedazzled in pink as I am would *never* dress this way if I intended to commit said crime. It's reverse psychology. Advanced stuff, I know."

"That's not how it works."

Rig just laughs, and neither of them acknowledge that Ginka never answered the bit about not wearing gloves. It's odd, and definitely more than a little bit paranoid, but Rig decides not to pry. As far as she knows, the wearing gloves thing isn't a Zazra tradition, although obviously she's not a Zazra and therefore can't say if there are certain groups that prescribe to the Ginka's Gloves theory of empathy or not.

Instead, she saunters out of the ship and down the gangplank, letting Ginka traipse after her. "Come on, Cactus. I got us a luxury skiff. We're gonna be so fancy."

"I would hope so, as that was literally your only job yesterday. We *needed* a skiff," Ginka reminds her as they meander their way out of the spaceport. "For events like these, they're practically as necessary as an invitation. Remember, even the slightest hint that we don't belong will be pounced upon."

"I'll be fine. I blend in well."

Ginka just raises a scathing eyebrow.

"I'm a people person," Rig explains. Unlike Ginka, who she suspects will stand out simply due to a distinct lack of social skills. Standing out due to charisma isn't a problem if the play is to charm a target. She's lifted valuables from people before, and the entire time she did it she was smiling and chatting at them, and they never suspected a thing. "Listen, if you keep looking stiff and awkward, that's going to stand out more than any clothing. You need to... oh, I don't know; it's all about body language, isn't it? Posture and such."

As arranged, the skiff is waiting for them, hovering on one

of the spaceport's landing platforms. It's got a bot pilot, a small control unit built into the steering designed to confirm their reservation, fly them there safely, and then return.

"All I'll say in response," Ginka adds as she takes a prim seat next to Rig, "is that if your methods get us killed, I will hunt you down in the afterlife."

"You believe in an afterlife?"

"Of course. I won't be given a seat of honor in it, not considering what I am, but I will still be able to bask in the glory of Ossuary themself when I die. Even if I fail them in life, I can serve them in death." Every single word is spoken with a completely straight face. "All those loyal to Ossuary know this."

"Sounds like a shit afterlife…" she mutters under her breath.

"Doesn't Pyrite believe the same?"

"Firstly, I don't believe what Pyrite believes. Secondly, not… not really. The general opinion seems to be that we're all tiny little bits of Pyrite themself, and when we die, we lose our individual nature and return to Pyrite. Cause, you know, if you can't be a mindless cog in the machine when you're alive, then you sure as shit don't get a choice about it in death."

"Hm."

Outside the windows the city flashes by.

Spires peter out into smaller buildings as they get to the outskirts of the city. All of Tides is built above the endless sea of the moon, and here the hovering platforms are more spread out to let bits of the ocean peep through. Some platforms are turned into forests or gardens – all meticulously tended, of course. Ascetic prefers to let nature grow on its own, claiming that the spirit of Ascetic themself guides the shape of all flora, but that is not so with Pyrite. Giant trees grown into twisting shapes, vines engineered to be brightly blue and red. All of it winds around massive metal sculptures, abstract and beyond Rig's comprehension. She's never been an artist in that respect.

Daara always had more of an eye for that sort of thing, working in construction as she did. A talent for seeing and shaping beauty out of thin air, exemplified best in the shimmering and glittery way in which she preferred to style herself. This is the sort of place that she would find beautiful beyond compare, and for a moment the desire to have Daara here is so keen and overwhelming that it hurts.

Finally the skiff slows down in front of the largest manor that Rig's seen on this planet.

Churning water wheels flank it on both sides, giving it the impression of floating on a cloud of mist that blends into the glistening, pale-blue metal of the building. Bright lights decorate almost every inch of the place, shining spotlights onto the elaborate metal carvings that work their way up the sides, illuminating the trailing runway that leads up to the entry pavilion, and moving in front of it all are the headlights of luxury skiffs dropping off passengers.

"Hey, listen," Rig says as the skiff pulls into the runway lane. "I don't know for sure what you meant by 'considering what you are.' I can't imagine anything good. You should know that the important thing isn't 'what' you are, but 'who' you are. What you do. How you act. And that's entirely up to you. Not Ossuary."

Ginka doesn't so much as look at her. "Who I am," she replies, each word deliberate, "has *always* been up to Ossuary."

"Fuck that. You're not under their heel now. You *never* have to be under *anyone's* heel."

"You're remarkably naive for a thief."

And proud of it. "Naivety is always a better choice than pessimism."

"Oh look," Ginka says with absolutely no subtlety. Not even an attempt was made. "We're here."

This conversation isn't over, but Rig'll allow it to be postponed.

Surprisingly warm night air greets them as they step out of the skiff, a welcome change from the stuffy skiff air as it lightly ruffles Rig's clothes. Sure enough, when she looks around there's a series of air heaters disguised as statues scattered around the open courtyard. Such a waste of power for a few minutes of warmth. Have the people here never heard of scarves?

A short man in uniform takes their invitations from her as they head up the path. The stepping-stones beneath her feet are made of delicate metal, each circle tempered at different heats to bring out patterns of color in the iron blends.

"Welcome," the uniformed man says with a bow, before passing on their invitations to another butler standing at attention in front of the doors.

Towering double doors loom in front of them. Wire has been inlaid on them, twisted into the forms of two leonine automatons, fang enhancers frozen in a snarl to scare away unwanted visitors.

The doors slide silently open, and then Rig is staring into the heart of a ballroom, dazzled by the sudden onslaught of color and song. Bright lights shine on a high glass ceiling and a colorful swirl of dancers, rich voiceless music floating through the whole kaleidoscopic affair. She feels microscopic in comparison. A small, scared voice in the back of her mind wants to run. She wraps her fist around that voice and shoves away. This will be her playing field, she will bend the party to her uses even if at first it spits her out.

The doorman hands their invitations off to a third butler who opens the envelope and announces, "Madime Trishi Ana of the Twenty Seventh Spire of Aeronautics, and escort!"

"Which of us is the escort?" Rig whispers as she and Ginka descend into the throng of this place.

Ginka shrugs. "Me, I suppose. Since you claim to be more of a people person."

"'Claimed'? Psh, I was stating a *fact*."

"Whatever you say. But don't forget your promise to me."

"Promise?"

"Once you've gotten what you want from Janus, he's *mine*." A determined smirk cuts across her lips. "I need to question a PI agent and he's so kindly stumbled into my path."

She flinches at the ice in Ginka's voice. "I haven't forgotten. As long as you can wring some information about Daara out of him before you wring his neck, I won't stop you." Trying to shake off the malice Ginka's radiating, she gestures to the ballroom in front of them. "Shall we?"

INTERLUDE
The Dance

Elegant strains of music float up through the layers of concrete and steel beams, a soft melody that tugs this way and that like a gentle summer breeze or water lapping at the edge of a fountain.

Although Spirit X-74 is high up, standing on the roof of a tower, the winds that should rip at her have smoothed out as though lulled by the music of the ball down below. It's a grand masquerade, lively enough that even the assassination she'd carried out only a half hour ago has yet to dampen the guests' spirits. Part of that, she suspects, is that many here in Ossuary space are so accustomed to the fact that Windshadow comes and goes as they will.

"I've sent confirmation to our Controller," Thrush-Seven informs her. He touches his eye-piece link and powers it down to all but its base functions. "We have to wait perhaps twenty minutes or so for a skiff to arrive as it's been determined that perimeter containment is a higher priority than our extraction. A few of the Ascetic infiltrators might have escaped."

She stares out at the city, a circuit board of blinking lights against a midnight sky. "There are worse places to wait."

"True enough. And it wasn't even that difficult a mission."

"It was all over so quickly. I memorized twenty different terms of address for *nothing*. Er," she quickly corrects herself, "I know that proper respect to those above our station is important. Showing we know where we are in the social hierarchy is key. I wouldn't disgrace Ossuary in such a way."

"Don't worry," Thrush-Seven says with a smile, "I kinda agree with you. And hey, at least it wasn't a dinner event. All those damn rules about which utensils to be used when."

It had already been difficult enough ensuring that her suit jacket covered the helltech manipulators strapped to her forearms, she can't imagine having to navigate those and be expected to daintily use silver cutlery at the same time. "I think I would have stabbed our target with a fork."

He laughs, smothering the undignified chuckle with the back of his hand. "If it gets the job done, anything goes."

Seeing him laugh like that never fails to bring a small smile to her lips. "I still can't believe that they spent a whole three days teaching us how to dance and then we didn't even *need* to. Not that I would have minded, but still. It was sort of anticlimactic, wasn't it?"

"I–" He gives her a look that she can't decipher, for the life of her. "I didn't think... did you *want* to dance?"

"No... I mean, well, yes, maybe. I don't know. It looked... fun?"

"Well," he says, shifting from one foot to the other before holding out his hand, a faint flush high on his cheeks, "I don't see why we couldn't right now. We can still hear the music, and we have the time."

She glances down at her hands, double checking to make certain that her gloves are still on before she tentatively rests her hand in his. Even through the heavy fabric she can feel the warmth of his hand, and some long-buried voice in the back of her mind whispers that she could feel so much more if she just took her gloves *off* – she crushes the voice. Nothing good shall come of listening to it. Her partnership with Thrush-Seven is worth more than giving in to some stupid curiosity.

It takes them a bit of fumbling to remember what they're supposed to be doing – the lessons had been extensive, yes, but also very fast, and they've had a bit of an eventful evening. One of his hands rests on her waist and she rests one of hers on his shoulder, and she manages not to crush his feet when she steps closer.

"How is this somehow more difficult than it was when we had a Controller breathing down our necks?" she asks after narrowly avoiding stumbling backwards.

"I suppose it's because no one's here to correct us when we slip up."

When he spins her in a slow circle, she finds that the movement is easier than it should be, considering that she's still wearing the spindly heels her disguise had required. After so long practicing dancing wearing nothing more cumbersome than the standard Windshadow uniform, doing the same while dressed in silks and jewels feels oddly restrictive. And yet at the same time, she can see the necessity. Seven twirls her around again, the balls of her feet spinning on the concrete roof, and the jewels dangling from her neck spin with her, as much a part of the dance as the two of them.

Then her necklace gets tangled in Seven's thrush feather.

"Damn it," he mutters, pulling the feather out of his hair and extracting it from the mess of beads and chains around her neck. A broken hair pin hangs from the tip of the feather's glassy white shaft, snapped in two from the strain. "I can't even dance properly, and now this – I look ridiculous."

"Not at all. May I?"

"Go ahead."

X-74 reaches up to her ear and removes the clip-on earring that she'd been wearing. It's a simple glass bead, shimmering turquoise with flecks of deep emerald hiding under the surface. A hollow line runs down the core. Should be the right diameter, give or take. She takes the feather and runs the shaft through the center of the bead, giving it a solid twist and shove to make sure that it's jammed tightly in there before she clips it into Seven's hair.

"There," she says, her face oddly warm. "The color suits you."

He gives her a sweeping formal bow, reminiscent of one of the many over-the-top greetings they'd had to learn over the past week, and he does it with just enough sarcasm to make her laugh. "I give you my thanks." And then, more sincerely, "It's beautiful."

When they resume the dance, she finds that the steps come far more easily.

CHAPTER ELEVEN
Special Agent Janus

"Synchronizing our links in three, two, one–" Red lights flash on both Rig and Ginka's links. Rig tucks hers into a hidden pocket in her headscarf, and she can see Ginka use some sort of sticky pad thing to attach hers to her skin, her hair covering the device where it sits behind her pointed ear. "Alright then, Cactus. We're good to go. You go right, I go left, call out Janus when you see him."

Ginka's reply comes through with an echo from the link. "Understood. Don't get caught, *Madime*."

"I could say the same to you, *escort*," she replies with a laugh. They're standing off the ballroom in a smaller alcove, but she tries to make sure her voice isn't too loud anyway. "That all-black dress of yours certainly looks dominatrixy enough to fit the title."

Ginka opens her mouth and then snaps it shut, instead choosing to roll her eyes so hard that they might fall out of her skull. "We *do* have a mission to get to, don't we? It needs to be done before the evening is up and if I stand here listening to your quips the entire time we'll lose our window of opportunity."

"Not a fan of quips?"

"Not a fan of *yours*."

"Ouch." She claps Ginka on the shoulder and *gods*, that woman is a solid wall of muscle, despite being tiny. If she didn't know better, she'd say Ginka's biceps are made of metal. If she flexes, that tight dress will tear open. Actually, that could make for a pretty good distraction if they need it during the course of the evening. "I'll try not to be too offended," she says. "Good luck."

"Keep your eyes open."

They split in the most forcibly casual way possible – Ginka makes to go grab a flute of champagne from a passing server and Rig turns to put on a show of admiring the metalwork hanging from the wall before wandering off.

It *is* actually beautiful metalwork, in her defense. Elegant wire sculptures built into the walls, curling like bronzed snakes around columns and arching into twisting, abstract shapes that hang from the ceiling along with the hovering chandeliers. Metalwork isn't her specialty, but she's relatively certain that they've used specific chemical dyes to stain the iron different colors, replicating all shades of the rainbow.

If she had two unsupervised minutes with a plasma saw, she could rob this place *blind*.

As much as she hates Pyrite, she has to admit that their artistry is technically lovely. Shame that it's tainted for her now. She's seen Daara work long hours on little sleep installing such things, laboring to the point where the metal would cut into her calloused hands and not even the strongest soap could get the smell of oils and greases out of her skin. Seen too many warships engraved with the same whorls and spiral patterns.

Disconnecting every horror she's seen Pyrite commit from every bit of beauty they can produce makes her temples pound from frustration. And yet she still tries. Maybe it's a sliver of faction loyalty, lodged deep in her subconscious. Maybe it's something left to tie her to Daara. Maybe it's because if she constantly thinks the worst of everything and everyone associated with Pyrite, it'd make the galaxy too small and too dark, and that's not a place she wants to live in.

And if everything and everyone associated with Pyrite is

terrible, then what about the other factions? What does that make Ossuary and Ascetic? What does that make Daara? What does that make *June*?

What does that make everybody, really? Who can claim to be completely unaffected by the factions and to have not affected them in turn? Rig knows her own mistakes, knows how she's helped the war machine of Pyrite, and she can't deny them. But even those who fight against the factions from day one – they're not untouched by them either. Nothing in this galaxy can be. She's here on Tides to defy Pyrite and save Daara, but she bought food yesterday from someone who will in turn pay tithes to Pyrite, and thus her kydis will end up in the hands of the people she claims to fight. Is there some ideal level of disconnection from the factions and their crimes that a regular person can reach?

She wanders out of the main ballroom and down a side hall, passing people parading about in their fancy dress.

So far, no sign of Janus.

A snatch of noise wafts into her ears as she passes a door that's been left slightly ajar. Her natural snooping instincts kick in and she stops, leaning against the wall as casually as she can, peering through the crack to see who's inside.

A woman sits upon a luxurious chair, dressed in the sharpest of red and blue suits. Stern lines cut through the woman's already imperious features. In her hands is a sword, less ceremonial and more functional, the tip of the scabbard resting against the floor between her legs and her hands folded atop the pommel. She's not alone – two men in guard uniforms stand in front of her and another woman in a blue dress is perched on a fainting couch, a gun holstered at her shoulder.

"I want another perimeter sweep," the woman with the sword demands. "Double time, Lieutenant."

One of the guards salutes. "Of course, Governess."

Oh shit, *that's* Moor? Rig takes a closer look. Something

shines atop the Governess's suit, and then Rig has to suppress an angry gasp.

A Kashrini pendant is hanging from the Governess's neck. It's silver, metal inlaid with curving white gemstones, and while she can't place a name to it, she'd know that style of design work anywhere. She almost snickers after the initial rage passes. It's actually a diadem, but Moor apparently doesn't know shit and has misidentified it as a pendant. What an idiot.

"I checked the guest list as you asked," the woman in the blue dress says. "Your suspicions were correct – Nine additional invitations have been issued within the past forty-eight hours."

Nine? One for Rig, one for Ginka, yes, but that still leaves seven newbies unaccounted for.

"Something's wrong here," Moor snarls, "and I intend to find out what. Once Triton has finished his work for me, I want him moved to my bunker."

"Yes, Governess."

One of the guards turns towards the door and Rig quickly moves as far away as she can without looking suspicious. She pretends to be very engrossed in the metalwork on the walls, hoping the guard won't notice. His footsteps move away from the door. She lets out a sigh of relief when they head in the opposite direction of her.

"Ginka," she whispers, putting her finger to her link to open the channel. "I stumbled across the Governess. She's got a hunch something's up with this party."

"*We're already playing it safe,*" Ginka replies. "*There's little else we can do.*"

"Yeah… about that. I'm also going to steal the Governess's necklace tonight. Just a heads up."

"*What?*" That's more of an angry hiss than anything else. "*Are you actually insane? We cannot attract that kind of attention and there's no damn reason for you to do this. Don't you fucking dare.*"

She's gonna dare. Once an opportunity presents itself. "Let me do my job and you do yours. I won't get caught."

"*Rig–*"

She cuts off the link channel.

"Deep in thought, miss?"

Something cracks in her neck as she whips her head around. "Huh?"

The speaker is… they're Kashrini. A young man, dressed in a servant's uniform, midnight blue skin exposed. No headscarf. Not allowed here, maybe? They didn't take his from him, did they? Rip it off his head like… The image of Daara without her headscarf rises to her mind and she has to shove it down. Work now. Once she saves Daara, she'll buy her sister all the loveliest scarves in the galaxy.

Not a drop spills from the tray of drinks the servant is carrying as he bows to her. "Forgive me for startling you, miss. I was merely wondering if I could offer assistance."

"Oh. Oh, no, thank you." She randomly points to the metalwork in front of her. "I, uh… I was just admiring the art."

"Of course. Governess Moor spared no expense in decorating her home here."

No kidding. "And I imagine she wants everyone to know that."

"Ah, yes." Interesting. The man doesn't look the least bit scandalized. She's proud of that. It's no wonder a fellow Kashrini wouldn't be so deeply entrenched in the servile mindset that some faction loyalists can have. "Her tastes do favor the extravagant." His purple eyes – so similar to her own – dart to the tray in his hands and he holds it out. "Champagne, miss?"

Miss. He's calling her 'miss.' She debates if keeping her cover is worth being rude to him, before reluctantly correcting him, "It's *ma'am*. Not *miss*. Don't be the broken cog in the machine. Many will not be as lenient as I am."

He flushes. "My apologies. Ma'am."

"And I don't need any champagne. But thank you for offering. If you don't mind me asking, how long have you been working for Moor?"

He checks the link on his wrist. "Eight hours."

"Seriously? Do you work for a catering company or something?"

"Something similar, yes. But I doubt my work would interest a Madime."

"You'd be surprised," she tells him, trying to shake off the feeling lingering in the back of her head. "I make it a point to speak to everyone, high or low. After all, I'm Kashrini just like you. I didn't come from much more than I imagine you did, you know. It helps me rule my spire better."

"How open minded of you. Is that your reason for being here tonight? To speak with the high and the low?"

"Work and pleasure. That's probably the case for most people here."

"I imagine so, yes. Do you enjoy your job?"

Now what would a Madime say to that? "Yes, although it *is* a lot of work. Delegating is trickier than people assume."

A pause flitters between them as a passing guest steps close enough to hear them, and her fellow Kashrini almost glares at the party-goer before his eyes fade back into showing nothing at all. Is he, too, looking to be uninterrupted? Or does he simply not care for the guests here? She can't really blame him either way. Such excessive opulence and grandeur does little to endear her to the people here.

"Just so," he says when they have privacy again. "If I may ask an… informal question? One Kashrini to another?"

If her ears were physically capable of pricking up, that's what they'd be doing. "Go ahead."

"You're a Madime, you probably know all the people here tonight, don't you? I've heard rumors that a compass is going to be here." She almost chokes on her own spit. He continues, voice lowering even further, "A compass named Triton."

"Triton, huh?" She forces it to come out as bland as oatmeal. "Sounds sort of familiar. What do you want with them?"

"My associates and I are looking to locate someone," he tells her easily, so open, so unsuspicious...

First, he gets her form of address wrong, then he admits to trying to contact a compass, and *then* tells her that he's not alone? It appears as though she and Ginka are not the only people sneaking around at this event. Only, unlike the two of them, he's complete garbage at keeping his cover intact.

"I'm really not sure," she says, smiling at him. "But I can go ask around, if that would help?"

His shoulders sag ever so slightly in relief. "Thank you. That would be... much appreciated."

"No worries."

She gives him a final forced smile before walking back towards the main ballroom, keeping her steps measured and even. This party is really getting interesting, and damn it, there was already enough *interesting* in it for her liking. There is such a thing as *too* interesting, and it's called a heart attack.

A beep chimes against her ear.

"What is it?" she asked as soon as she adjusts the link to send her voice to Ginka.

"Target spotted. He's sneaking down a side corridor."

"Not suspicious at all."

"It looks like he's calling someone – I can see him holding something up that might be a link."

"How kind of him to show me exactly where my mark is."

"What's our play?"

"I'll, uh... I'll try and dance with him."

"Can you even dance?"

"Passably. And there are so many other mediocre dancers spinning around in circles right in front of us, so even if I fail, I won't stand out."

Besides, it's easier to lift things from someone when you can go with their own movements. Makes it harder for them to feel the departure of their stuff. That's a lot tricker when they're standing still.

"*Fine. But if he starts to suspect anything, anything at all, retreat and let me try. I'll watch your back.*"

"Copy that."

Rig scans the room. There's a bunch of elevated areas around the massive dance floor, some covered with sculptures, some with buffet tables, and one with a damn fountain. A number of tall doors are set around the room and in between them are small alcoves, ostentatious ornaments, and corridors leading towards the other – probably off-limits – sections of the palace.

"*Turn twenty degrees to the left. Straight ahead. The entrance is behind the statue of the leaping tyth cat.*"

She pivots, finds the corridor and statue in question, and strides straight ahead.

Things get a little quieter once she passes the statue, something about the curvature of the ceiling affecting the sound reverberation – or something like that. Quiet enough that if she puts her back against the corner and doesn't make a sound, she can pick out the faint sounds of Janus talking to someone.

"–more time," he's saying, in a rushed tone.

The voice that responds is so very distant that she has to hold her breath to hear it. There's a staticky lilt to it as well, so Ginka was right about him calling someone on his link.

"*I've been...*" She's only getting every other word, but she thinks the voice is male. Possibly. Maybe. "*...leniency will not last. I've given you... tracking codes for X-74 as well as... Quite the risk you've taken.*"

"None of them are on my level, even if they *do* figure out I'm here," Janus brags. He doesn't sound as confident as he had when she'd chatted with him on the Ascetic homeworld. "I promise, you won't regret this."

"*Overconfidence will...*"

"It's not overconfidence. X-74 can kill all of them with her hands tied behind her back. I've lured the others here for convenient clean up – you're *welcome*, by the way – and then I can get what I need once they're dead."

"*…results… Sooner rather than later.*"

"I've already got the sister. She's the best bait for those schematics, now that I've managed to track down the developer. Come on. You *know* that this is the best chance any of us have gotten in years."

An icy chill runs down Rig's spine and makes her shudder. The smug way he says that sets her blood on fire, that gloating pride of having got Daara in his clutches, the way he's tossing that information around to – to what? Buy himself time? Is he talking to his boss? Got in trouble with PI higher ups for not instantly dragging her in?

"*…a few more tries. Further failure will not…*"

"You won't be disappointed, Lord Umbra," Janus promises. "I'll get you the plans before you know it. And my link?"

"*…if you follow through. If not…*"

"I understand."

Silence. The call must have ended.

Okay… she has to calm down and think. Easier said than done. Pyrite doesn't usually use titles like 'lord,' and if that *was* Janus's boss, then why did Janus have to explicitly *say* that he had Daara? Surely his boss would already know? And who's X-74? Who are the *other* people that Janus has lured here – is it Triton? Why would Janus be trying to kill Triton?

There are so many variables – *too* many – and she can't stand it, her brain whirling around in circles trying to figure it out.

Janus's footsteps draw near.

Shit – act casual.

She darts out from behind the statue and snags a glass of champagne from a passing server before wandering back towards the corridor just as – hopefully – Janus will be leaving. If not, she's going to look really awkward trying to bump into someone who's not there.

Janus walks out.

She very purposefully bumps into him.

Champagne spills onto the floor as she jerks back just in time to avoid getting any on her suit or on his.

"Oh gods!" She shoves the glass onto the statue plinth and makes a show of embarrassment. She tilts her voice just a pitch deeper. "I'm so sorry, do forgive me. I can't believe I was so clumsy."

"Don't worry about it." He adjusts the lapels of his dark suit and gives her a roguish grin that's probably tailored to make people swoon. "I'm lucky to bump into a pretty lady like yourself. I'm Darian Janus. Pleasure to make your acquaintance."

He offers his hand, a pleased twinkle in his eyes when she shakes it. She rests her fingers just against his wrist, trying to see if she can lift his link, but the telltale feel of metal isn't there. How annoyingly clever. He's not wearing it on his wrist. And another interesting realization – he actually used his real name. Didn't even throw a fake title on there or anything as an explanation for his presence here tonight.

"I'm Madime Ana," she replies, "Not going to give me your title, or do you enjoy making people guess?"

"While I'm sure that would be a fun side benefit, I have no title whatsoever. I'm sure that must come as a shock for a Madime such as yourself, but it's true."

Running her eyes up and down his form serves multiple purposes. It makes him think she's taking another look at him now that she knows he's not titled. It might also make him think she's checking him out, should she take a flirting approach later. And, most importantly, it lets her scan him for places he might have hidden his link.

"I can hardly be scandalized by that, I suppose," she tells him. "After all, being Kashrini, you can imagine the more humble origins I have."

"Quite right." He bows to her, offering his arm. "Care to dance?"

Well if he's going to do the hard work for her, she won't protest. "I'd love to."

After offering a silent apology to June – who she hopes would approve, given the criminal circumstances – she takes his arm and lets him guide her onto the dance floor.

It takes her a minute to recognize the music. Regardless of what Ginka says, she does know how to dance. Tapping her hand against her thigh in time to the beat as they walk onto the floor helps her get a feel for the rhythm, and then Janus places one hand on her waist and takes her own with the other, leading her in a slow sort of dance that has enough twists and spins to let her slip her hands into his pockets, if need be.

"Tell me," she asks, "what's an untitled man like yourself doing here?"

With ease, he spins her around; she takes advantage of the movement and glances at his belt, only to be disappointed at seeing nothing more than a buckle. No link there, either.

"I'm here on someone else's invitation," he confesses. "As spectacular as this party is, I didn't originally intend on being here – I know," he adds with a laugh, "scandalous. Don't tell the Governess or she might have me shot for disrespecting her."

"Oh? What made you decide to attend?" She gives him her most winsome grin. "The lovely company?"

"Business, I'm afraid. Surely a woman like you knows that even the most lovely of parties can't escape shop talk."

Does she ever. She conjures up the memory of her old spire's Madime, a strict and pompous sort of man, and draws her next words from him. "Those of us in such positions have obligations too important to be placed on hold for an evening."

"We see eye to eye, Madime. I'm glad that being what you are has not interfered with making you into the most accomplished woman I see before me. You are a credit to the history of your institution, I am sure."

"Thank you. It's always good to hear such unbiased opinions from my fellow Pyrites."

Pride wells up within her at the confused furrow of his brow. Take that. He can't even figure out how he's being insulted.

The lights and colors of the ballroom spin past her as he twirls her in his arm, dipping her down for a vibrant beat in the song. Her pink shoes shine on the reflective dance floor, and for one moment everything seems to slow down as her eyes catch movement. His jacket flashes open just the tiniest of bits and there.

A link, clear as anything, tucked against the inside pocket of his jacket.

He pulls her back up from the dip and she goes with the motion, pushing herself up as well – just a little too much, a little too fast, and little too hard. As a result, she smacks against his chest. In that second of distraction, where his mind is probably focused on the fact that he banged into her, she snakes her hand into his pocket and takes the link. Her fingers flip it around, cradling it in her palm.

"I'm so sorry," she says, smoothing out his jacket and attempting to look flustered. As her fingers slip down his silk suit, she clips the link to the inside of her sleeve, hiding it against her wrist. "I'm all wrong-footed today, it seems. It's been a while since I danced, I didn't mean–"

"It's quite alright, think nothing of it. Clearly my eyes weren't sharp enough." The smile he gives her is a little flat. "What you said before, about being Kashrini…"

"Hm?"

"I haven't seen many of your kind at this party, but I'm sure that you would have paid more attention to the comings and goings of your fellows. I'm looking for someone. A Kashrini." As much as she desperately wishes otherwise, she doesn't think he's talking about that infiltrating servant. The galaxy doesn't have a habit of letting her off the hook like that. "She's a technician, lower class – probably skulking about somewhere.

I imagine she'd be quite noticeable. Arsonists aren't known for subtlety."

Pro: Her disguise is fucking fantastic.

Con: Literally everything else.

She pretends to scratch her head, opening up her link at the same time for Ginka. "An arsonist? At *this* event?"

"It's likely," he replies. "Although she could be elsewhere. She's been travelling in the company of a Zazra; have you seen one?"

"A Zazra? No, I don't believe so."

His hand tightens around hers and she's not sure he knows he's doing it. "I'm not surprised if you haven't seen her. She knows how to hide, but I *know* that *she's* here. Madime, if you see either of them, I must ask that you tell me at once. They're dangerous people, the Zazra especially so."

Over the link, Ginka swears, "*Shit.*"

An idea occurs to her. "Well," she says slowly, drawing the word out, "there was this *one* Kashrini."

Janus perks up. "Do tell."

"They're a servant – and they're suspiciously *awful* at it. I almost thought that they weren't a servant at all, except it seemed silly at the time to question the Governess's security. But if there *is* a dangerous Kashrini on the loose here tonight…"

He stops dancing, coming to a sudden and nearly disastrous halt – another dancing pair avoided colliding with them by inches.

"Where are they?" he demands.

She gestures in the vague direction of the fake-servant. "Oh, somewhere over there."

"Thank you for telling me, ma'am," he says. He bows sharply and quickly. "Enjoy the rest of your evening."

He dashes off as though rabid animals are on his heels.

"Damn straight I will," she mutters.

"*This is bad,*" Ginka's voice says. No kidding. "*Meet me in the alcove next to the buffet table.*"

She turns and weaves her way through the whirlwind of dancers to the edge of the room. The beat of the music seems to match the tempo of her pounding heart. Faster and faster and faster. PI might be tough, but they only have just one guy here tonight. Hopefully she's thrown him off her trail; and they've got the link, she's got the link, they're almost done with all this. Even stealing the diadem is still doable. Right?

The alcove is blessedly quiet, and Ginka's lurking form is a welcome sight.

"What the *fuck* was that?"

"Hello to you, too." Rig glances over her shoulder to check and see if anyone's followed her.

"Janus?"

"Can't see him. I think my lure worked."

"Good job coming up with that."

"Yeah… about that – I didn't come up with anything. I really *did* meet a weird Kashrini servant. He and some of his *friends* are looking for Triton. Seems as though we're not the only people infiltrating this party, Cactus, though we certainly seem to be doing the best job of it. Hopefully–" although she's not really all that hopeful, "–Janus and that fake servant will duke it out while we get what we need and run."

Ginka presses a finger to her lips, flattening out her frown, humming thoughtfully as she stares intently at thin air. "It may buy us some time. This is getting worse and worse; do *not* go through with your fool plan to steal from the Governess."

"But that's *my job*–"

"That doesn't matter right now," she snaps.

"You don't *get it*," Rig replies, trying to hold back her sparky anger. Just because Ginka's *right* about the timing of it all doesn't mean that the diadem isn't important. "That's *Kashrini* and she's wearing it like… like it's a fucking *trophy*," she hisses. "That's what Pyrite does, okay? They take and they take and they take, and if I don't stop them every chance I get then they *win*, and I can't–"

"Your sister or your job! Pick!"

Rig tenses, the sudden question kicking her in the gut. "I... It's not that simple."

Ginka draws herself up. "It *is*. I get that this is a difficult decision for you. Do you think that I've never had to pick between my work and someone I care–" She cuts herself off. "Make up your mind now, Rig, or else this operation is over and we figure something else out, because I refuse to work alongside someone who's going to abandon the mission at the drop of a hat."

She needs Ginka. She needs to find Daara. Deep breaths. Her mind spins in circles to try and rationalize the decision and spits out, "I can come back for Moor's stolen jewelry?"

"Good decision."

"Cactus... I'm sorry." The upbeat party music seems almost insulting. Doesn't it know what Moor has done? Doesn't it know what Pyrite does? "Pyrite's taken everything from my people. And I'm... I'm getting *tired* of Pyrite taking everything from *me* – my values, my ideas, my lines that I try to draw in the sand. Maybe you don't know what it's like to have Ossuary take you from *you*, but it feels fucking *awful*, okay?"

To her surprise, Ginka just laughs. It's short and sharp and it sounds like broken knives. "Trust me," she says bitterly, "I understand what it's like. So take it from someone who also knows: one day, you will have to choose – yourself or your faction. In your case it's your job or your sister, but there will be a choice, and if you don't make it, the galaxy will make it *for* you. You just chose your sister over your job. You *made* your choice. Stick with it."

"You're a fucking cynic," is all Rig can blurt out.

"So what?"

So it's depressing and horrible and defeatist. She sighs. "Whatever. You want to focus on the task at hand? Go for it. You're right; I pick my sister."

"Good." Ginka resumes her thoughtful expression. "The

question we need to be asking ourselves is why did Janus know that *I* would be here and yet be uncertain of *your* presence..."

"I don't know," Rig admits. "When I spoke with him on that call on Ascetic, you were wearing that weird mask, right? He couldn't have seen your face then."

"Where did I slip up?" Then she hisses, "*Triton*. He must have sold us out."

"You know him more than me."

"Damn it!" Ginka curses under her breath, tightening a gloved hand into a fist. "Why am I slipping up? I'm supposed to be *better* than this."

"Whoa – it's okay. Everyone makes mistakes." She pulls the link out of her sleeve and shows it off, letting the metal of it catch in the light. "Don't tell Triton just yet. Call him and figure out where we're supposed to meet him now that we've got it. If this is a setup, I'd like to be skedaddling before Janus gets our scent again."

"I share the sentiment – though not your word choice. I don't *skedaddle*."

Ginka pulls her link out. The call connects within an instant and she holds her link in the palm of her gloved hands so that Rig can hear and see his floating hologram image as well.

"Triton. I hope you're ready to deal with us." Which is both polite and also very threatening. As per Ginka's usual, it would seem.

"My favorite monster," Triton says in greeting. "I'm assuming from your call that you have my prize? That, or you're about to tell me everything's gone wrong and that I should flee into the night. I'm hoping for the former, but with you I can never tell."

"We have it," Rig tells him. "I lifted it from the guy. He shouldn't suspect a thing until he tries to use it to call his ride out of here. There's plenty of fancy clocks hanging on the wall, it's not like he needs to check the time every two seconds."

"Good, good. I'm in an office deep in the west wing. Pinging my location for you now – it should be easy enough to get to. I'll arrange things so that the guards and servants have cleared out. I imagine you don't want anyone trying to tell you that you're not allowed back here."

There's a buzz as the information goes through. Ginka nods sharply at the data package, all picture-perfect determination. "We're on our way."

The call cuts out.

Ginka stows her link with hands that shake in anger. "That lying bastard."

"Please don't beat the shit out of him until *after* we've gotten a location from him. If *I* have to put *my* job on the backburner, you can manage to put aside your vengeance quest or whatever too."

"I know how to get a job done."

It's up to her to hastily follow along as Ginka sets a quick pace towards the west wing.

As promised, the hallways of the west wing go from being crowded with party guests, to sparsely populated with servants, to completely empty as Ginka drags Rig through the twists and turns towards Triton's office. No noise emanates from Ginka's footsteps and, in comparison, Rig's feel louder than a ship's engine. Her job requires the ability to walk softly, and she's no novice at the artform, but Ginka is deathly silent compared to the faint click of her pink shoes on the metal floor.

They come to a stop in a small deserted corridor, Ginka tapping out a code onto a wall mounted panel. A light flashes to confirm the code and part of the wall fades away to reveal a set of doors. A stealth cloak? Exactly like the one on Chickadee. She knew that Triton was good at his job just from his reputation, but that man really has superb taste if he uses the same tech as her.

Once she's been pushed through into the room, Ginka shuts the door behind them. This place is so filled with Pyrite spiraling furniture and faction memorabilia that it is clearly not

Triton's, not unless he's secretly been a die-hard Pyrite loyalist this entire time. Borrowed for the evening, probably. The man himself is lounging behind a wrought-iron desk, his feet up on the top and his hands busy fiddling with a series of holographic panels that are quickly dismissed with a flick of his wrist as soon as he sees them enter.

"Welcome to my place, dear monster," he says cheerfully.

Ginka doesn't return his levity. "Triton. We're on a bit of a tight schedule, so if you could get this done with, it would be greatly appreciated."

He sighs in disappointment. "Oh, alright. Link?"

Rig tosses it straight into Triton's hands.

"Excellent," he says with a grin.

"Get it open," she tells him, "and see if you can access the files inside."

He swings his feet off his desk and places the link down, pulling out a set of pliers and opening the back of the link up. "Am I looking for anything in particular?"

"If you can run a search on the name 'Daara,' that'd be fantastic. But honestly, I'll take whatever I can get."

Multiple color-coded wires are strewn about his desk, and he plucks out a green one to attach to the link's mechanical guts. The other end gets plugged into a computer terminal and he begins to assemble a spare parts abomination out of the link. She watches the swift movements of his fingers as he adds a converter here, a red-crypter there, messing with aspects of the link that she doesn't understand, which says less about her and more about how skilled at his job he is.

Lines of code start to appear on the computer's holo screen. Triton hums thoughtfully as he reads them. "Nothing in the files, I'm afraid. This link is practically empty save for evidence of a few erased calls, which maybe I could get at under usual circumstances, but they've even scrubbed the evidence of which communication satellites they bounced their call signal off. I couldn't access them even if I tried."

Damn.

"But you can still get me to PI's headquarters?"

"Should do." He explains, "Every PI link has to have a way of locating their headquarters, otherwise agents who have been undercover or otherwise out of contact with their organization can still return to wherever their headquarters happens to be that week. It's a piece of firmware buried deep into the circuits. I'm basically stealing that."

"Wouldn't there be some sort of safety protocol to prevent people like you from doing exactly what you're doing?" Rig asks.

"Oh, yes, but I'm *very* good at my job. It allows a one-time communication to the headquarters' systems. The agent connects it to a ship's computer, puts in the correct code that only they know, and the system sends the ship to the right destination. Which unfortunately means that what I'm stealing for you isn't going to last long. I can get the current one-time code, but it's going to move before the week is out, and if you can't get there in time, you're going to have to come back, and I'll do this all over again."

"That's fine. I don't plan to dawdle on the way."

"Got some big important reason why you're in such a rush?"

"Not any of your business."

Another series of beeps emanates from the link and Triton's face lights up in glee. He unplugs all the wires, disconnecting everything until there's just the link left. "Here you go," he says, holding it out. "All done. Good luck."

Rig closes her fingers around the link and–

As soon as it's back in her hands, Ginka darts forward, grabs Triton's shirt, and drags him to his feet.

Wires tumble off his desk and onto the floor as he coughs and sputters, her fist against his throat.

"Cactus, maybe don't choke him to death before he can talk–"

"Who else are you working for tonight? How *many*?" Ginka

demands, ignoring Rig in favor of spitting the question out at him. "Did you really think you could double cross us and I wouldn't see it?"

Triton's eyes are wide as dinner plates. "N-No one! I swear!"

"Lie to me again. I dare you. You know what I'm capable of."

"I'm not lying, I promise! I have no other clients tonight, I'm just here for you and to consult with the Governess, there's nothing else. I wouldn't double deal; you know me."

If Ginka doesn't stop, the man is going to die trying before he can spit out a single answer. Rig reaches out a hand and stops just short of laying it on Ginka's shoulder. "Hey. Let him breathe for a moment. He helped us out for free even if he might have sold us out. Don't repay the favor by actually killing him, okay?"

"*Favor*?" Ginka retorts, "You think he's doing this for us because he likes me? My people spared his life, working for free is him *returning* the favor. And," she adds, glaring at Triton, "I know exactly who you are – or did you think I had forgotten? You're a traitor who abandoned his library, and the only reason you're not dead is because you're valuable and were willing to compromise. But I should have known you have no loyalty to anyone – certainly not to Ossuary."

"I haven't sold you out!" Triton insists, trying to yank his shirt out of Ginka's unshakeable grip. "I wouldn't do that, no matter what you think of me. I didn't tell anyone you were coming, and I have no other clients."

Ginka drags him closer until his face is centimeters away from hers. "Then *why* does Special Agent Janus know I'm here?"

All the blood leaves Triton's face. "He... He knows *what*?"

"He knew I would be at this party tonight. Now, when I encountered him before, I took great care to ensure that he didn't see my face or hear my voice and now *suddenly* he knows that I'm going to be here. The only person who knew, besides

Rig, was *you*." Ginka bares her teeth at him as though they're fangs. "What's he offering you? Is the information you gave us even accurate? Which side are you *really* on?"

"I, I have *no idea* how he found out – I swear it!"

"Lie to me one more time–"

Oh for...

Rig steps in. "Cactus. I think he's telling the truth. Besides, we're wasting time. If we leave now – well, it's not like he knows where my ship is or what its name is. Can't sell information that he doesn't have."

Ginka keeps one eye on Triton as she snaps back, "What if he–"

There's a knock on the door.

"Well, well, well." A vicious snarl pulls at the corners of Ginka's mouth. "If it isn't your other clients. Did you know I've been looking to put the screws to a PI agent? Perhaps I'll make you watch so you'll know just what I'm going to do to you once I'm done with him."

"The–" Triton stumbles and stutters over the words, gaping at the door. "The stealth cloak – it... it would have reactivated."

Rig pauses. They'd gotten codes from Triton to enter, so whoever's outside *doesn't* have codes, which means they're *not* a client – they're knocking on an invisible door. She swallows a lump in her throat. That means the real question is if it's Janus or the Kashrini servant.

Another knock.

"D-Don't open it," he begs. "Let me go. *Please.*"

Kkrrrrrrrr–

He's shaking like a leaf in Ginka's iron clad grip. "They're hacking the lock."

The door slides open.

Someone steps into the room.

It's not Janus.

It's not the Kashrini servant either.

It's an unfamiliar human woman, tall and lithe and clad in

all black. A strange streak of white hair is running through the woman's blond curls, like a fake bit of hair that's been clipped over her right ear, next to an unusually shaped link.

The silver barrel of a gun shines in her hand as she points the weapon straight at Triton.

"Hello again, Triton." Her voice is deep and sharp. Her black eyes slide from Triton to Rig without even noticing Ginka. "And oh look, it seems as though you've brought me exactly who I was going to ask you to find. Two birds, one stone."

She turns the gun on Rig.

CHAPTER TWELVE
Birds and Monsters

One moment, Rig's about to be shot.

The next, Ginka's throwing a chair at the strange woman's head.

It smacks into her face at full speed. She falls, back arching as her head goes down, arm flying up. Her gun goes off with a *crack*, the bullet harmlessly hitting the ceiling.

Rig gapes. "Holy shit–"

Ginka bodily hauls Triton out from behind his desk, dropping him to his shaking knees and dragging him away from the downed woman. Unconscious? No – a weak and pained groan emanates from the woman's crumpled form.

"Back door?" Ginka demands.

Triton's trembling finger points to a corner of the room. "S-Servants' corridor."

"Go. Now."

Rig flips her guns back against their holster. Fire burns through the fast paced, panicked drum of her heart as she sprints after Ginka and Triton.

Another stealth cloak drops to reveal a small door built into a corner of the office. Triton throws it open, and then they're running out and into a deserted corridor, their footsteps echoing against the walls.

There are no sounds of pursuit from behind them, no crash of doors being broken down, no further gun shots. Doesn't mean they're safe or that the woman is out of the fight for good. In fact, when she considers how silent someone like Ginka can make herself be, it probably means the opposite.

Once, June had taken Rig to see a zoology project that a fellow librarian had been working on. A forest had been built into the library, full of birds and insects and all sorts of animals from all over the galaxy. A felidae had been released into the enclosure, and everywhere it walked, it brought silence with it. Birds stopped singing. Insects stopped chirping. Nothing beyond a tense, all pervasive silence.

The same silence that seems to sink in through the corridor right now. As though something in the wind is chasing them.

Triton is huffing and puffing. Not used to sprinting, is he? "There's... On the roof. Emergency skiff."

"Stairs?" Ginka demands.

"To our right."

They skid around a corner, Rig dragging her hand against a sculpture to steady herself as she turns. "Who in the fuck was *that*?"

"You tell me," Ginka snaps, spitting the question at Triton instead. "I *saw* her link; do you think I'm blind? You're dealing with a Handler and you didn't *tell* me?"

"I didn't know!"

"Bullshit," she hisses under her breath. "She *knew* you."

"I worked with her – I don't know, five years ago? Six? I thought she forgot me!" he quickly explains, the words tripping out of his mouth like a drunkard stumbling out of a publica. "She's Thrush-Eleven, or... or she *was*."

A pounding headache of frustration is beginning to crack through Rig's raging panic. "Enough, both of you! Why are we being chased by a bird?"

"Not a bird." Ginka slides to a stop, yanking open a door labeled with a red emergency sign. Beyond it is a series of crisscrossing staircases leading up into the very top of the mansion. "It's a rank. Thrush is the middle rank for a Windshadow Handler."

Ice seems to pour into Rig's veins. Windshadow. Holy fucking *gods*–

"Now both of you, *quiet*. They'll find us regardless, but you could at least try to keep quiet so that we don't attract other attention."

Rig stumbles up the first set of stairs, taking point as Ginka guards their rear. Sandwiched between them is Triton, being about as useful as a floppy noodle.

"How," she asks, "can they find us if we're being quiet?"

"You have a heartbeat, don't you?" Ginka replies, leaning over the railing to check the stairs below them as they ascend.

That's no small bucket of terrifying.

Because she absolutely doesn't want to think about that too much, she asks Triton, "How many floors to the roof?"

"Seven," he replies, "Then we'll be almost directly above the ballroom. I don't think there'll be any security up there, but – can you jack a skiff?"

"Yes," Rig and Ginka say at the exact same time.

At least one of them will be able to do it if the other is too busy fighting. That little bit of hope takes her up the next two flights of stairs, her lungs beginning to object to the impromptu workout.

She smacks a quivering Triton on the arm. "Come on. Toughen up. We're going to get out of this."

"I'm a librarian," he moans, "I'm not cut out for this."

June's a librarian as well, and Rig knows that if she were here instead, she'd have already taken charge of the situation like the born leader she is.

Ka-chnk.

That doesn't sound good.

Rig stops and looks over the edge of the stair rail, peering into the depths below them. Darkness sits on the bottom floor of the stairwell, and she's pretty sure that it was well lit when they entered. Red toned lights illuminate everything that she can see, but as she watches, the light fixtures on the second floor flicker.

Ka-chnk.

Another floor of lights goes out.

"They're sealing us in," Ginka says. She turns to the nearest door, spins – her foot smacks against the metal, kicking it open. "This is about to be a death trap. We'll get to the roof some other way."

The three of them hurry out the door, Rig tugging a stumbling and shell-shocked Triton along behind her. This hallway is exactly the same as the one a number of floors down, same red and blue lights, same shiny floors. Same lack of people. A *suspicious* lack of people. As far as she figured, Triton only cleared out the serving staff on his own floor to give them a clear shot to his office. This area shouldn't be deserted.

She pauses before turning around the next corner. "Ginka…"

"I *know*, damn it," Ginka curses under her breath a few times. "I don't know what to; strategy isn't *my* job."

"And it *is* mine? I'm not a tactician."

It doesn't seem like her words got through. Ginka's breathing hard, like she's about to start hyperventilating as she rants, "I don't know what to do, I don't… I'm not supposed to work alone, this is why I keep making stupid oversights and failing to see things that are dancing right in front of my eyes–"

"Hey, hey, calm down. We need you focused."

Quietly, painfully, Ginka confesses, "I'm not supposed to *be* alone."

Rig draws herself up as she hauls Triton forward. "Well, I've got some good news, Cactus. You're *not* alone. So get your shit together because I can only carry one deadweight around, *not* two."

"I… That is–" Every muscle in Ginka's body goes stiff. Her eyes focus on something around the corner. "Rig, I believe I found that friend of yours."

Rig shoves Triton behind her, keeping him firmly hidden behind the corner pillars as she steps out.

"Hello again," says that mysterious Kashrini servant.

He's standing at the end of the corridor, guarding the doors that must lead to one of the upper levels, that same unreadable flat look on his face. The servant's uniform is gone, revealing dark clothes and a strange contraption around his waist. A series of power packs, maybe? A generator? From the generator hangs a cable, and at the end of the cable is a cylinder that he grips in one hand like a weapon.

Never before has Rig been so glad to have her guns in her hands. "Heya," she replies, because that's only polite, isn't it...? And, oh gods she's being polite to someone who's probably an assassin – what the fuck is she doing? "You're terrifying."

"Thank you?"

"You're very welcome. Any chance you could just stand aside and let us run off?"

He flips the cylinder in his hand. "No."

Rig shoots him.

Gold flashes. The cylinder ignites a crackling beam of light that carves through the air and flicks her bullet to the side as though she'd done nothing more than toss a pebble at him. He twirls the sword – a golden blade; it's glowing and it's *solid* and...

Helltech.

Exactly like Ginka's.

The assassin seemingly drops the blade before grabbing it again, swinging it around on its cable like a whip. It's almost blinding, streaks of gold dragging across Rig's vision as she tries to keep track of the blade's movements; faster and faster it goes, switching between tight circles and wide arcs. It slashes against the floor and doesn't slow down. Deep molten gashes are carved into the stone floor with each pass of the blade.

Ginka takes a step forward. "Don't kill him."

"Wait, what–"

And then Ginka's dashing towards the killer helltech sword with reckless abandon.

Fuck this all with a rusty screwdriver.

In a move that goes against the shred of self-preservation instinct Rig has, she runs after Ginka, guns blazing.

The sword whips out.

A high keen of energy cutting through air is the only warning Rig gets before she's forced to drop to her knees, rolling forward and firing again, trying to pepper him with shots. He twists out of the way, pulling on the sword's cable and making it whistle past Rig's head on its way back to his hand.

Step one. Take out that sword.

In a flash of black, Ginka is suddenly right there, darting in front of Rig and drawing the assassin's attention. She can see a second of surprise on the man's face before he's pulling the sword back from her and sending it hurtling towards Ginka instead. She's about to call out a warning before Ginka disappears again.

What the...

Rig's eyes take a moment to catch up. Ginka didn't vanish, she simply moved faster than Rig could keep track of, her motions blurring into the motions of the sword as she spins and twists around the blade, weaving her way around the cable.

The surprise fades. Rig shakes the fog out of her head and takes advantage of how distracting Ginka is to get closer to the assassin. Close combat. Not ideal for guns. She flicks Panache behind her. There's a slight tug on her belt as the magnetic clip engages, holstering her gun for her. Her now free hand reaches into a pocket in her jacket and pulls out her slim blade.

She flips it in her hand, the flat edge against her forearm, and ducks into the assassin's range.

Cold steel slashes out. Her thumb presses a button on the hilt and an electric current runs through the blade.

The assassin notices her just before steel meets flesh and he drops low to the ground, rolling out of her range. Damn it – she pushes forward and then has to jump out of the way as the sword slices back towards her. His hands weave around the cable, drawing it back to him and then whirling it in a defensive circle around him to deflect her retaliatory burst of gunfire from Pizzazz.

Another screech of air. Rig drops to her knees as the sword cuts through the space where her torso just was. *Screech*, flash of light – she pushes herself to the side and the sword carves a line into the ground an inch away from her.

Rig's heart skips a terrified beat.

And then Ginka is leaping towards the assassin while his sword is occupied.

Ginka's fist slams into the ground, cratering it, shattering the marble into a hundred pieces in a blast of debris and sheer force. Holy fucking... Rig brings up a hand to shield her eyes, and she can see the assassin rush out of the swiftly dissipating cloud, trailing dust as he moves.

The sword is back in his hand and he flicks it towards the ground, shaking the dust off it.

Rig, in a moment of sheer stupidity, throws her knife at him, but he leans backwards far enough for it to streak past his nose, imbedding itself in the wall behind him with a solid *thunk*.

She runs after him again. In another burst of movement, Ginka's there before her, aiming a flying kick towards the assassin's head. He ducks – she goes hurtling past him, drops to the ground, pivots, strikes again, fist sinking into his solar plexus.

Rig shoots, and this time her bullet hits the distracted assassin, grazing his shoulder and drawing bright red blood.

Screech of air – *shit*...

She stumbles backwards to narrowly avoid death by sword-to-the-gut.

He recovers from the blow to his stomach, disengaging and flicking the blade towards Ginka again. Ginka's already moving to attack, dashing towards him with her hand raised; but he was prepared, and the sword is in his hand again...

It's close, too close, and Rig can do nothing but watch in slow motion as the sword cuts towards Ginka's head.

Ginka reaches up and catches it.

Gold energy arcs around her closed fist as she holds the glowing sword beam in place. The fabric of her gloves sizzles and starts to burn away but she doesn't so much as flinch.

The assassin's jaw falls open. His wide eyes locked on the blade caught in Ginka's grip. "That... that's im–"

Ginka yanks the sword out of his grasp and plants her knee into his gut. He collapses like a skiff with a broken engine, folding over himself as she lets him fall to the ground. Her hands reach for the cable, pressing where it connects to the generator at his waist, detaching it, the sword flickering out and dying.

"I know you said we shouldn't kill him," Rig says, out of breath as she staggers towards the two of them, "but he just tried to kill *us*. And he'll probably try again."

"I didn't take you for the murderous type."

"I'm not. But I'm not dying before I can get Daara back."

The assassin is staggering to his feet again and their argument cuts off.

Ginka grabs the man's shirt and flips him around, pushing him up against the wall. One hand pins his arms behind his back while the other reaches into his ear. Gross. She plucks out a tiny earpiece and crushes it between her fingers. Then she yanks down the collar of his shirt.

Something dark is inlaid under his skin on the back of his neck. Is that... Rig peers at the black smudge to get a closer look. Is that a tattoo?

"Hm," Ginka says thoughtfully. "D-39."

Why would a letter and number be tattooed on the back of his neck? Unless... Rig draws in a sharp breath. "Is that his *name*?"

The alarming implications of that seem utterly lost on Ginka. "As much as he knows his own name, yes." She turns back to the assassin and demands, "I'm guessing from your tech that you're not all that high ranking, are you? Inexperienced, too, or else you wouldn't have bothered to confront us before attacking. And if you had more experience, you wouldn't have almost blown your cover earlier when you spoke with Rig. Are you a Spirit? No, a Ghoul? Is this your first high ranking mission?"

He draws in a sharp breath of air and tries to crane his neck around, staring at Ginka incredulously. "How–"

"Don't bother asking, it was obvious. Now you're going to answer a few questions."

Since Ginka has it under control, Rig works her knife out of the wall where it's been stuck. The edge is nicked, but the electric current did a good job of cutting through the wall more than the wall cut through the metal. Triton peeks his head around the corner where they left him, his face drained of color but otherwise unharmed.

"Why are you here?" Ginka demands. "Your friend said you wanted Triton to find Rig – why? What is she to you? You wouldn't be contracted with PI, that's not how our lord plays things."

Our lord?

D-39, if that even is his name, just shakes his head. "I'll tell you nothing."

He gasps in pain as Ginka shoves him harder into the wall, his nose cracking into the metal, a trickle of blood rolling out of his nostrils. Rig winces.

"We just ran into your Thrush Handler," she continues, as though he'd never spoken. "An operation this size? And you're only a Ghoul? This isn't a standard team; this isn't the usual set up that would be sent to a place like Governess Moor's palace."

"How would *you* know? You're just her bodyguard–"

Gold light flares up around Ginka's hand, crackling like lightning, a storm contained in her fist. She punches the wall a hair's breadth away from D-39's head. Dust paints his paling face.

"Guess again," she hisses.

The helltech.

The helltech that's the same as D-39's helltech.

Without really noticing she's doing it, Rig's arm raises Pizzazz and aims the iron sights at Ginka's head.

"You're one of them." In her own ears her voice sounds strange and distant, fuzzy through the sinking realization that she's been travelling with one of the galaxy's most terrifying assassins and never knew it. "You're Windshadow."

Before she can say or do anything else, Ginka slams her fist into D-39's temple, the lightning dissipating an instant before the blow connects.

He falls to the floor in a slump once she lets him go, his eyelids shut as though he's only asleep instead of probably concussed.

"I thought you didn't want to kill him."

"I never said that. He needed to learn from this failure and the concussion should ensure that he doesn't remember what he said. He's only a *Ghoul*, after all."

Rig's surprised the only screaming she's doing is internal. "*Only* a Ghoul? *Only* a terrifying assassin? Is that *it*? How *silly* of me to overreact like this – *what in the fuck is going on here!*" Oh, there's the external screaming. Lovely. Her hand is shaking around Pizzazz's grip. "You're *Windshadow*, and Windshadow is apparently here to *kill me*. Has this whole thing been a setup? Did you get Triton to help us so that you could bring me here for your organization with a bow tied around my neck? Is the information he gave us even going to lead me to Daara, or just to another trap, huh? Are you going to pull some Pyrite bullshit on me and try to use her against me once we find her?"

Ginka raises her hands. The gesture makes Rig flinch in fear and she almost shoots – only Ginka is holding out her empty palms in the universal gesture of peace. "I didn't know they would be here. If I had–" Her mouth does a pained contortion.

"If I'd known they were here, I wouldn't have come. I promise you that."

"You aren't making a godsdamned lick of sense. And given that my life is on the line here, I'd really appreciate some fucking clarity."

Triton coughs at the end of the hall. "Your friend *is* Windshadow," he explains, "but as far as I know, she's never worked with a large group like this. It's not what she *does*. And I *really* had no idea that they'd be here tonight, I swear it; so it's not like I could have told her or anything. Now *please*, we have to get out of here before more of them show up and kill us all!"

Her eyes and Ginka's are still locked as Rig replies, "Run if you want to, then. They're after *me* apparently, not *you*."

"I'm *involved* now, that won't–"

Crunch.

Rig whips her head around.

Triton's body falls to the ground, half his head busted in like a smashed melon. Wide, bloodshot eyes stare unblinkingly up at her as though he's just an automaton that's had a cruel marionette master abandon him. The acrid stench of blood reaches her nose and he's dead, he's actually dead – that was fast.

That was really fast.

Which means... Which means they failed. They failed to keep him alive and now all they have is that one solitary code. One chance.

Gold light glints over his corpse.

It's a dark-haired man, standing over Triton's body with a strange baton in his hands, gold helltech light running through it and blood dripping off it onto the floor. When he straightens up it becomes clear that he's clad in the same dark gear as the Kashrini assassin.

"Target Tessera located," the new assassin says in a flat and emotionless tone. Probably not even talking to them. If he's the same as D-39, then he's got the same earpiece. "One additional hostile."

Gold helltech flaring up, Ginka takes point, creating a glowing knife in her hand.

The new assassin pauses for the slightest of seconds when he sees. "What–"

Ginka throws the knife at him. "Get behind me!"

"You're on *his side*!" Rig yells.

"He's trying to kill you; I'm not. Make a damn choice!"

It's a pretty easy spur of the moment decision to make when phrased like that. "I'm going to find another way up!"

There's a crackling noise of helltech crashing against helltech as she turns and bursts through the doors that D-39 had been standing in front of.

The doors slam open into the bright lights and cheerfully loud music of the main ballroom, and she has to skid to a stop because she's on a balcony, and about to slam headfirst into the thick metal railing. She slows enough so that the railing only lightly smacks into her waist. Her head tilts downwards and she's faced with a sudden, sharp fall onto the ballroom floor almost seven floors down. It's like a pit. A colorful, whirling pit.

She tilts her head up to see another balcony above, probably about thirty – forty? – meters up.

Well. That's one way to the roof.

There's a crash less than a foot away from them and she thinks that baton-guy just broke part of the wall. Dust kicks up, stinging her eyes and cutting against her cheeks. She ignores it.

She flicks open a tab on her glove, grabbing onto the wire that's wrapped around her wrist. A magnetic clip is floating about in one of her pockets and she wraps the end of the wire around that a few times to make sure that it'll stick.

"Cactus!"

She turns around and sees that Ginka has a problem. The new assassin is clearly better than D-39, pressing Ginka back with his baton, the length of metal glowing with helltech light, leaving streaks of gold through the air as he swings. Ginka's knives and needles and whatever the fuck else she's making flash as well, but she gets the distinct impression that Ginka is hesitant to really go on the offensive – probably doesn't want to kill another of her *friends*.

Ginka throws a needle that goes straight through the assassin's shoulder. It must hurt like a bitch, but he doesn't even stumble.

They need to get out of here.

Rig twirls her wrist, giving the magnet and the wire a good spin. Twirls her wrist faster, her arm, her shoulder, the magnet whirling around until it's a blur.

Then she throws it at the balcony above.

It spins around the railing and then the magnet latches on to the metal. It holds when she gives it a solid tug.

She reaches out her non-tethered hand. "Ginka! Grab on!"

Ginka plants a kick into the assassin's chest, sending him skidding backwards, and then she turns to Rig and her outstretched hand. She hesitates, looking down at her own gloved and gauntleted hands and then at Rig's.

Oh come *on*, Cactus, that's two layers of fabric; she can do it, Rig believes in her.

With a hiss and a flash, the golden baton streaks towards Ginka's head, and that's the decision made for her.

Ginka's hand grabs onto Rig's forearm. She only gets a flash of the assassin trying to run after them before she gives two quick yanks on the wire and it starts to spin back into its holster.

Wind screeches past her ears as she and Ginka fly upwards.

After a fleeting eternity, the wire runs out and her palm smacks into the upper railing, and it's then that she realizes that Ginka is the heaviest person in the galaxy, because *gods* she feels like her arm is about to be ripped out of her socket.

Fortunately, as soon as she has that thought, Ginka scurries up onto the balcony with the agility of a spider defying the laws of gravity.

After that weight is gone, it's easy for her to haul herself up as well – not as gracefully, sure, but getting the job done.

"Any chance no one noticed?" she asks tentatively, wincing as she rolls her shoulder out and detaches her wire from the railing, letting it *shhck* back into her glove. "Because if we have to deal with Governess Moor as well…"

Ginka ignores the question and yanks the doors open, running into the hall. "Let's get to the roof. Triton's corpse won't go unnoticed for long and I don't doubt there are more Windshadow agents here."

"Right… right, yeah, okay."

Get it together. She shakes her head with the hope that it'll be like smacking a computer screen to get it to sort its shit out.

Ginka kicks down two sets of doors before finding one that's hiding a tiny stairwell, and then they're climbing more godsdamned stairs. Plenty of adrenaline is still buzzing in Rig's system, and she barely even notices the strain in her thighs as she keeps pace with Ginka's strides that are only the slightest technicality short of a full out run.

"Why *are* they trying to kill me?" she asks again, counting the floors as they fly up the flights of stairs. "You're one of them, you must have *some* idea."

"I have many ideas, none of them good."

"Oh, *thanks* for *that*."

They hit the top of the stairs.

Ginka kicks the door open with her usual dramatic flair and then they're rushing out onto the rooftop.

Wind grasps at her clothes and nighttime seems to set the palace and the city in the distance aglow. Spotlights are projected up from the base of the mansion, shining pillars of light to ring the rooftop. Reflective lamps on the concrete to guide descending skiffs blaze beneath Rig's feet and stars wink faintly overhead, almost hidden by the light pollution.

At the far end of the rooftop is a large bunker-like building. The main transportation up from the lower floors, perhaps?

It certainly looks like a cross between an elevator and a skiff launch pad.

And there's a landing platform with a lone skiff in front of them.

Perfect.

Rig hops over to the skiff's side and then hops to it, cracking open a panel on the dashboard to access the main computer.

"Can you work any faster?"

"Cactus, just let me do my job. *You* can figure out what they want from me."

"I don't *know*, I *told* you – this isn't *usual*. None of them are wearing masks, even though once they'd shed their disguises they should have hidden their appearance; their team composition makes no sense for the location; the only people after you are PI, and Windshadow has never once worked for Pyrite..." Ginka snarls as she keeps ranting to herself, as though she's forgotten Rig's here entirely. "The schematics PI wants from you aren't even *the weapon plans* so why would Windshadow have any stake in this? It doesn't make *sense!*"

Her hands fumble with the wire she's pulling out. *The weapon plans?* She'd lied to Ginka about the schematics, told her they weren't designed as weapons. Or... not lied, really, but misdirected.

"That's enough running, don't you think?" a familiar voice calls out through the night.

Shit.

The woman from before is standing in the stairwell doorway. Thrush-Eleven.

Dried blood is smeared around her nose and mouth, but her cold and sharp expression is unchanged. She reaches a finger up to the side of her head and touches the strange link that's wrapped around her ear. With a spark and a hiss of energy, a gold hard light panel appears, hovering in front of her right eye like a targeting screen.

"I'd like to do some more running," Rig nervously blabs. By feel, not taking her eyes of the Thrush, she keeps reconnecting the skiff's wires. "It's not the funnest sort of cardio but it'll do in a pinch. Before I run off though, I'd really like you to tell me one little thing: what in the *fuck* do you want from me?"

There's a near silent shuffle of movement.

Her heart sinks down into her stomach and then deep down into her sparkling pink shoes as four other Windshadows clamber up onto the rooftop, appearing around her and Ginka in a threatening circle.

D-39 isn't one of them, but baton guy is. One carries a gauntlet that's bulky and coarse compared to Ginka's sleek weapons. Another sports a heavy shotgun with glowing helltech lines running down the metal. The fourth carries a golden spear. All the golden weapons are connected to cables that run into power packs, the same as D-39's sword. In the night, the helltech burns brighter.

"Traxi, code name Rig," Thrush-Eleven states. "You're coming with us."

"It's just Rig, actually."

"Rig then. You're still coming with us."

"Fuck no."

Thrush-Eleven simply raises her gun. "If you and your companion do not stand down, then we will take you by force."

Something hums.

It takes her a minute to realize that it's the sound of Ginka's helltech gauntlets powering up, amplified louder than usual. The Zazra's shoulders paint a furrowed line of tension as bright gold light bursts to life, running under the fabric of her dress and burning it away until there's nothing but the metallic shine of her gauntlets and the glow of her helltech, all the way from fingertip to collarbone.

She flexes her arms, the lines of light flare, and two long sword blades form in her palms.

"If you want Rig," she declares, "You'll have to go through me."

A surprised smile spreads across Thrush-Eleven's face, her long blonde hair billowing in the wind. "Oh? Don't tell me – you're on this unicorn hunt, too?"

"Unicorn hunt–" Ginka's eyes flit to Rig.

She shrugs. "Don't look at me, Cactus, I don't know what a fucking unicorn hunt is."

"But..." Her lips part in silent confusion. "You said they weren't weapons..."

"I knew Lord Umbra sent others like us," Thrush-Eleven continues, far more focused on Ginka now than on Rig. Which... great, but also what the *fuck*. And hold on, that *name*... "You transgressed as well, right? That's why you're not with a Handler, isn't it? I'm impressed. Really, I *am*. You got so far on your own. You must have been quite good before you were exiled." She laughs and the sound carries in the wind like poison gas. "That's not an insult; we're all exiles here, after all."

Ginka's pupils are slitted so thinly that her eyes are almost completely green, the black swallowed up into nothingness. "You're saying that *Rig* is the weapons developer our lord sent us after?"

"You didn't know?"

"I–"

Rig's free hand draws Panache, the other still working at the wiring. "Cactus..." she says slowly, because if Ginka's double-crossing her, then, well, she'll probably die, but she can get one good shot off first and she can make it stick if she's fast enough. "Pick your battles carefully, now."

Ginka's still staring at her in confusion. "I... I didn't know it was *you*."

"Join us!" Thrush-Eleven's smile is too toothy for it to be friendly. She lowers her gun and holds out her hand. "We all were sent out for the same objective. We all transgressed in some way or another. Me and the Operatives with me found each other a year back, decided to work together on this. If we bring her in, Lord Umbra will welcome all of us back into the fold with open arms. We share the rewards of her capture and her weapon plans."

The weight of Ginka's gaze burns Rig like fire.

"It's been a few years for you, hasn't it? Same as us," Thrush-Eleven continues. "You're beginning to show signs of wear. You didn't have a large supply of Grace on you when you were sent out, did you?" Ginka flinches and the smile on Thrush-Eleven's face grows. "I had a good number of vials on my person when I was sent away. I've been sharing them with my friends here – I can share some with you as well. You won't last and we all know it, not by yourself, not with limited Grace."

The beat of Rig's heart is fast enough to be a constant buzzing in her chest, straining her ribcage and strangling her lungs.

Her finger ghosts over Panache's trigger.

Ginka swallows, her throat bobbing, her eyes wide.

"Sorry," she says, pressing her eyes closed and turning her back to Rig. "But no. It's as you say – I *am* on this unicorn hunt, as well. Only I'm playing by different rules and for different stakes." She straightens up. "So I'll say it again. You want *her*, you go through *me*."

What – but *why*?

Different rules and different stakes – what does that even mean? And Rig really hopes this isn't a going-from-the-frying-pan-into-the-fire sort of situation. But at this point, she thinks she has to take the help she can get. Beggars, choosers, all that. No good choices, and she's the one that has to make them.

"What?" Thrush-Eleven takes a half step backwards. "But you *brought* us here. The signal we received, the message telling us to come here – that was you!"

"I don't know what message you were sent, but it *really* wasn't me."

"I see," Thrush-Eleven says, dragging the two words out into an entire paragraph. "Pity."

Rig raises Panache, Ginka's swords twitch, the Windshadow assassins ready their weapons…

A thousand lights on the rooftop flare to life.

There's a loud slide of metal on metal, spotlights pointing straight at their standoff, nearly blinding Rig even as she squints.

Behind them, the bunker elevator opens to reveal a line of heavily armed Pyrite soldiers.

They're aiming wicked looking rifles at not only Rig, but the rest of the assassins as well, their red and blue armor muted and bloody looking. White light emanates from the torches affixed to their guns, the beams sweeping across the rooftop with blinding accusation.

The soldiers fan out, spreading enough that Rig can see again.

A new figure is standing in front of them, haloed by soldiers. Governess Moor. Her heels click on the rooftop as she takes a step forward, sword still in her grasp, fury tugging her mouth down.

"We're dead," Rig mutters.

"I," the woman declares, commanding voice booming across the rooftop as she places the tip of her sheathed blade on the ground with another click and rests her hands atop it with all the dramatic pomp of throwing down a gauntlet, "am Madhumita Moor, Governess of Tides. You are trespassing in my system, on my moon, and in my palace. You have damaged my home, you have broken my peace, and your actions have resulted in the death of a close friend of mine. Surrender now and perhaps I will grant you the mercy of a swift execution!"

Such a commanding tone makes Rig feel as though she ought to bow, or grovel, or something else subservient. She doesn't. "Governess, please, me and my friend had nothing to do with this or with Triton's death." She brandishes Panache at Thrush-Seven. "It was *them*!"

Come on, *come on*, why can't Rig get this engine started just a little bit faster…

Moor turns her nose up. "Hm. Not satisfying enough. Restrain them!"

Crack!

But the guards didn't fire. And if Rig didn't fire either then–

She turns to see the barrel of Thrush-Eleven's gun ever so slightly smoking.

Governess Moor falls.

Oh *shit–*

Beneath Rig's fingers, the two wires she'd been fumbling with finally connect. The skiff's engines hum to life.

She glances back at Moor's body, at the Kashrini jewelry on her neck. Does she have time? Could she make it, could she reach it before the Windshadow agents kill her, could she have both her job *and* her sister? She twitches towards it, fingers yearning to take it back–

Light glints off a gun barrel. She'd die first. And then Daara doesn't have a chance.

"Cactus!" she yells as half the soldiers rush to Moor's body and the other half hesitate as though waiting for orders that will never come and the Windshadow assassins dash across the roof. "Get *in!*"

Ginka leaps into the skiff a second after Rig.

They blast off the roof and into the night, spotlights at their backs and the sounds of gunshots below, and the Kashrini jewelry lost to her.

INTERLUDE
The Others

Spirit X-74 and Thrush-Seven are not often called in for clean-up missions; but it does, on occasion, happen.

No matter how infallible the galaxy believes Windshadow to be, those in the field are still people, and still susceptible to error – a lesson X-74 has learned before. So occasionally a rookie breaks their cover, a vital piece of intel gets overlooked, a target taken out before an exit strategy has been secured. It's rare, but it happens.

X-74 slits the last enemy's throat with a golden knife that shatters as soon as the body hits the ground.

She grabs the man's sleeve and pushes it back to reveal a bird tattoo on his wrist. Of *course*. What a pain. These Nightbirds are getting too close to Windshadow territory every year, even though it seems they're trying to keep to Pyrite space.

Her blood-soaked boots squish when she walks back to where Thrush-Seven is hacking into a wall-mounted console, erasing all evidence of their presence here. They'd been dispatched to clean up the mess caused by a team of six. Of those six, none remain. X-74 steps over more corpses than just those of the enemy as she returns to her Handler's side.

"There's a scrub team on the way," he tells her. A hard light screen hovers over his eye, the tiny reticule it displays moving about and contracting as it focuses on different aspects of the wall console's projected holographic screen. His link connecting him to the console, to its system, to the netspace as a whole. "Five minutes out. I'm redirecting skifftrains around this part of the city so that our transport can get in without difficulty." He sighs. "I *really* dislike clean-up work."

"Why do you think we got sent out here, anyway?"

"Because we botched that assassination on Kanin," he reluctantly admits. "And then there was the info retrieval job from our contact in the Praetor System..."

The Nightbirds have been forcing Pyrite's hold to weaken in the Praetor System. Good for Ossuary. In *theory*. "Those birds ran circles around us and ended up stealing our supplies as well as Pyrite's. Our eyes weren't sharp enough to catch them. I remember."

"Did you know that Pyrite bombed Dash Moon?"

"Seriously?"

"Fifty Kashrini settlements there. I imagine that Pyrite assumed one Nightbird spoils the bunch... or something like that." Seven huffs. "It's stupid, if you ask me. Pyrite doesn't seem to realize that a solid third of their population *is* Kashrini. The Nightbirds are making them panic, but if they keep indiscriminately bombing port towns, they're going to wipe out a large chunk of the workers that keep their gears running."

"Spectacular for us, isn't it?"

"Exactly."

She stares down at her bloody boots. "And yet we still managed to fuck it up."

Tensions are rising in the Praetor System now, and even though she knows the war has been shifting in that direction for some time, she can't help but feel as though their failure weakened Ossuary control in the region, in the long run. This clean-up mission clearly indicates that their superiors believe the same.

She and Seven have just been... not out of sync, but making a series of dumb mistakes. Every time it seems as though Seven is at risk, she fumbles, gets frazzled, tries to help him at the expense of the mission, even though she *knows* that the mission comes above all else.

"It could be worse, you know. This is only the second time this year," she reminds him, pulling out a handkerchief to wipe blood off her gloves and the bulky, wireframe helltech manipulators on her arms. "This could be our *permanent* job."

He shudders. "Please, don't even joke about that."

The wall she leans against is cold and somewhat damp from rain – at least wet weather doesn't impact the effectiveness of helltech. "I don't see why you hate it so much. It's certainly easier work than some of the other things we've done."

"I..." He glances over his shoulder to see the bodies littering the ground. "I don't like to see the mistakes. *Technically* this team was ready and *technically* their skills complemented each other, but if someone had looked more closely they'd have seen the cracks." He waves a hand at one of the dead Operatives. "Someone should have seen that she had an angry streak, and someone should have seen that *he*–" he gestures to a different body, "–wasn't well adept at maintaining a cover story, and it's... Something working well on paper just isn't good enough."

She *does* have to agree, although she shies away from criticizing whoever made the decision. A Controller must... must have just received wrong information, that's all.

"Doing things by the book is overrated," Seven mutters.

"Doing things by the book partnered me with you," she points out, "so perhaps there's some merit in it."

A tiny smile flicks across his lips. "True."

"And you're one of the very few Handlers in the field. Most don't have such a close eye on missions. You're... you're better. *Much* better."

He's visibly taken aback by that quiet admission. "Oh. I... Thank you. That means a lot, coming from you."

Why? She's no one special. She's about to ask why, and then...

Someone groans in pain.

She forms a knife in her hand at the same time Seven draws his gun, both whirling to face the source of the noise.

It's not an enemy.

It's one of their own, a Ghoul that they'd assumed dead.

In their defense, it hadn't been an unfair assumption to make – the man's dripping with his own blood, body riddled with bullet holes. Yet still, he lives. He doesn't seem to notice them at all, even as X-74 approaches with morbid curiosity. All he does is claw his way towards the corpse lying next to him. Half the dead man's neck is missing.

The Ghoul's whispering something, the words a rasp and a near silent breath.

"Wei," X-74 can hear him say as she gets closer.

He reaches for the dead man, entire body shaking, hand not quite able to bridge the gap, fingers nearly skimming the dead man's cheek. The corpse is an Operative, she realizes. A Ghoul as well.

It's a sob this time, and she can see tears running through the blood and dirt on his cheeks, "Wei…"

"Seven!" X-74 calls out in a panic, blanching and stumbling back from the dying Ghoul. "Seven, he, he's saying a name – I think he knows his teammate's *name*."

Seven jerks away from the console panel to stare at her. "*What?*"

Handlers, of course, are allowed to have their own names when they are children, and then when they become fully fledged agents, they are assigned a proper number. Operatives never get a name. They're born with one, usually, because children don't just spring into existence out of stardust, but they never know it. They don't need to. That's what X-74 knows, has been told her whole life. She doesn't need a name.

So how did this Ghoul find his? What possessed him to tell his… his friend? His partner? She doesn't even know what to think anymore. The dying Ghoul finally manages to rest his hand against the – against *Wei's* cheek. A gentle caress that makes X-74 feel ill inside, her guts twisted into knots. It's horrible, watching this. She's a macabre voyeur to something that shouldn't exist. But she can't bring herself to look away.

Seven appears silently at her side.

"The dead Ghoul's name is Wei," X-74 says softly. "I... I don't know how they know."

"I suppose they must have stolen his file, or one of his superiors did and told him," Seven guesses, just as quietly as her.

Blood drips drown the dying man's chin as he manages to get to one knee, leaning over Wei's corpse.

"We... we stole it," he whispers between choked mouthfuls of blood, finally noticing that he's not alone. "Stole it from our Controller. Lord Umbra, he... he must have seen us. He sent us here to, to fail. No way we could have–" he coughs as though trying to throw up his lung, "–could have succeeded. We transgressed. Got punished. Fair."

X-74 opens her mouth to protest that Lord Umbra wouldn't do that. Wouldn't toss away valuable agents just for one transgression...

But he would, wouldn't he? She rubs her arm, suddenly colder than before. If it were to protect Windshadow, Lord Umbra would do anything. Even beyond that, he is not a forgiving man.

"What's your name?" Seven asks, kneeling down next to the man. X-74 can't speak at all. "Or did you find only his?"

"...Erian."

"You know you're dying, Erian."

Erian spits out a red laugh. "...Noticed that, yeah."

"A skiff will be here in ten minutes. It could have the medical aid you need to survive." There's an oddly sympathetic softness in Seven's eyes as he talks. As though he understands. But how could he? He's a Handler; he's *always* known his name. "But you've transgressed. If Lord Umbra's aware of that as you say he is, you'll just be sent on another suicide mission, or forced out on a unicorn hunt to make amends. Or he'd do worse. And either way, Wei's gone. What would you like us to do?"

Erian's head hangs low, neck bowed. "Can you... can you make it painless?"

X-74 sucks in a sharp breath.

"If that's what you want." Seven raises his gun. "Close your eyes."

"I'd rather..." Erian gazes at Wei's face, as though all that matters in the entire galaxy are the man's bloodless features, "rather not."

"Of course."

"Seven..." she says hesitantly, trailing off as her thoughts fail to solidify into words.

Seven places the barrel of his gun against the back of Erian's head. "It's his choice. I won't take that from him."

Erian still does not close his eyes, but she does, unable to watch as Seven pulls the trigger.

There's the gunshot.

Then the sound of Erian's body slumping over Wei's.

She opens her eyes again. Those knotting worms return to her stomach, and she tells herself it's just because she's due for a dose of Grace shortly.

"It *isn't* fair," Seven mutters after a moment of silence.

"What isn't?"

"That I know my name but you don't know yours."

"Don't say that," she automatically replies. "It's just how it is. Don't – if you transgress like that, then you'll..."

"I know. I... I'm sorry."

She almost reaches for his hand before she stops herself. "Come on. I'll remove their helltech generators while you finish scrubbing the systems. We'll... We'll get the job done. That's what we do. Transgressions or not, our fellows won't die in vain."

"Umbra already ensured they did, didn't he?" Seven whispers, but it's so quiet that she thinks she might have imagined it.

Either way, no one else is out here to catch his words. Just her. And although reporting infractions is organization policy, she'll never reveal any of the more controversial aspects of him. She'll keep his secrets to the grave, and although she knows that it's wishful thinking, she likes to imagine that perhaps he might feel the same way.

CHAPTER THIRTEEN
A Hellish Explanation

Rig panics all the way back to *Bluebird*, sirens and alarms going off through the entire city of Marina. Fortunately for her, one small skiff marked with Governess Moor's identification stamp is completely ignored as she hurtles the vehicle towards the spaceport. She keeps her tongue firmly in her mouth the whole time. They can't afford to be arguing during a getaway. Or at least, that's what she tells herself. Part of her silence is due to the fact that she's pretty terrified of Ginka right now.

After abandoning the skiff to a very confused looking member of the port authority, she practically runs through the spaceport back to her ship, Ginka on her heels.

"Get in," she says once she opens up *Bluebird* and rushes up the gangplank. "We'll talk once I get us away from this damn moon."

Ginka just nods as she stumbles onto the gangplank.

Is she sick? Whatever – it can wait, just like everything else. They need to rocket out of here.

Rig hops into the pilot's seat and cycles the engines. She doesn't wait for clearance from ground control before blasting off and putting as much air between her and the city below as possible. *Bluebird*'s engines roar, her hand gripping the throttle tight enough to break it, heading out of atmo at full burn. The acceleration slams her back into her seat. As soon as they're through, she puts them into luminalspace towards one of the emptier systems near the Ascetic-Pyrite border.

"Alright, Cactus," she says once they're safe. When she stands up, she's hyper aware of the weight of her guns at her waist. "Time for some damn answers."

She turns to see Ginka collapse against a wall.

"Seriously, Cactus? You took a nap *right* before going to this thing, there's no way you need more sleep–" She pauses. "You okay?"

Sweat shines on Ginka's forehead, and underneath the dark Zazra facial markings her skin has taken on a sickly pallor. She sways on her feet as she tries to stand properly, planting her hands on the wall to keep herself upright. The usual slits of her pupils are oddly wide, and not in that sorta-cute way that happens when she's excited about something – it's an unfocused, glazed-over wide.

"I'm–" Ginka pushes herself forward with a drunken sort of stumble. "I'm fine. I… I just–"

She turns green and bolts towards the bathroom.

By the time Rig follows her, she's greeted by the disgusting sounds of Ginka throwing up the contents of her stomach into the toilet. Nausea, sweating – withdrawal?

She crouches next to the Zazra with a sigh. When she tries to pull Ginka's hair away, she gets her hand slapped, so instead she settles for rubbing what she hopes are soothing circles into Ginka's back.

"There you go. Better out than in," she says softly, and then wrinkles her nose as Ginka throws up again.

She sits with Ginka until the woman stops convulsing, her chest no longer heaving even without anything in her stomach to throw up, and then keeps sitting there until her breathing is somewhat back to normal.

The phrase 'like staring at a stranger' keeps floating through Rig's mind. But it isn't, and that's what makes it uncomfortable. It's still Ginka, even now that she knows the truth. Curled up on the bathroom floor like this, there is no part of Ginka that seems even the least bit intimidating, and it's challenging for

Rig to connect this woman with the woman who kills with ease and may or may not be out to kill *her*.

By the time Ginka is done retching, she's shaking like a ship hit with solar flares, sweat plastering stray hairs to her forehead.

"I'm fine," she insists. It comes out as a croak.

Rolling up the sleeves of her jacket, Rig slides one arm around Ginka's waist and helps her to her feet, spare hand grabbing a bucket from under the sink.

Underneath her hand, Ginka's torso feels like solid muscle stretched too tightly over nothing more than bone. She can count Ginka's ribs with ease. Tightening the belt a little is common among people living outside the factions – she's been there herself, on occasion – but this doesn't feel like that. Logically, she knew Ginka wasn't exactly in the best of states, physically, given the Grace and everything. Feeling it is a different thing entirely.

It takes a lot of small, slow steps to get Ginka to the spare cot, and once Rig's managed it, she places the bucket beside it and finds herself going through the motions of trying to tuck Ginka into bed.

"Don't." Ginka protests. "My bag... I need Grace."

Without thinking about it, Rig digs through Ginka's bag and fishes out the vial of clear liquid and the syringe stored next to it. She's about to draw a dose of it before she pauses, staring at the sickly and unsteady person before her and realizing that she's sitting far enough away to dodge a punch.

"Will this make you better?" she asks casually.

Ginka nods.

"Then no." She leans back to avoid the flimsy swipe Ginka aims at her. The Zazra is way too out of it to be a real threat right now, and that, of all things, is the first dose of real confidence that she's had since things went to shit this evening. "I'll give you your precious Grace once you've given me the answers I need. Fair is fair."

Her conviction wavers a little at the utterly heartbroken and pained look that pales Ginka's already waxy pallor, but she doesn't relent.

"Fine," Ginka mutters. "Ask your questions."

There's approximately five bajillion burning questions tumbling around in Rig's head right now, but she has to pick one, so she asks, "Are you still Windshadow? The stuff those other agents implied made it sound like the lot of you had been excommunicated or something."

"I am. I might be... I'm not... I'm still one of them," Ginka replies, stuttering through the words as though she's not sure what she's saying anymore. "I am a Phantom rank Operative."

"Phantom? What does that..."

"There are three Operative ranks. Ghoul, Spirit, and Phantom. Above Operatives are Handlers, with three similar ranks – Sparrow, Thrush, and Raven. Then there are Controllers, but they almost never leave our headquarters and are more of an information hub to ensure that missions are being run smoothly."

"Who's in charge of it all?" There's always a bigger boss, that's the one thing that seems to be a universal constant. "There was mention of some Under guy – or Umber? Something with a U."

A name she'd heard before...

"Lord Umbra. He manages our organization on behalf of Ossuary's immortal King Tenus."

Every word out of Ginka's lips has a rehearsed sort of air. No one outside of Ossuary really believes that their king is immortal, and 'managing' Windshadow seems far too light a term to be applied to such an organization. No one with an army of elite spies and assassins – no one with that sort of power – ever simply *manages* it.

"Riiiiight. Carry on."

"Three years ago, I... I transgressed. Or, well, I'd been transgressing for some time before then, but that was when

Lord Umbra found out. For agents that are still useful but in need of a lesson in loyalty, Umbra prefers to utilize what we call a unicorn hunt."

"That's a dumb name. Unicorns don't exist. If I'm your unicorn hunt, I'm pretty sure *I* exist."

Oh gods, she feels sicker than Ginka looks just thinking that. They really *are* after her. If they're after her, are they going to go after Daara, too? In some fucked up twist of fate, is PI's capture of Daara keeping her safe from Windshadow?

"Well, it's not that we're chasing something that doesn't exist, just something... rare. Hard to find. Umbra would never send agents, even ones that have transgressed, after an impossible target. That would be a... a *waste.*"

Sure he wouldn't. Sounds like a great way to get rid of people that have become a problem, and she's not dumb enough to think that this Umbra guy doesn't sound exactly like the sort of bastard that would send his own people out on suicide missions and the like. Also, where *did* she hear that name...

There's a brief pause as Ginka lurches over the side of the bed to throw up into the bucket.

"I know where I've heard that name before," she realizes while Ginka's puking her guts out. "That's the man Janus was talking to at the party. He mentioned luring people to the party so they'd get taken out – I think he must have tricked the other Windshadow people to come there. Told them Triton was gonna be there or something so that he'd round them up into one place and get them out of the way. Umbra certainly seems like the type to clean up problems like that. Which means..." Oh *damn it*, this just got way worse. "Windshadow are the buyers. PI mentioned that they'd already sold the plans – sold them before I left Pyrite. And if you were sent out three years ago..."

Ginka wipes her mouth with the back of her hand. "We were told to track down a missing Pyrite weapon that we'd purchased. I didn't connect it with *your* weapon earlier but...

the timelines match. And if anyone would develop a weapon that targets Kashrini, it'd be another Kashrini."

"That wasn't my intent," Rig snaps. "I didn't *want* it to be a weapon, I wasn't... I didn't think–" She chews on her lip and quietly admits, "I just wanted to see if I could do it. I didn't really think about what Pyrite would do."

"Why would I judge you for believing in your superiors?"

Guess Ginka's not one to talk. Rig shakes her head, unsubtly changing the subject. "Why would Umbra want a weapon like that? Nightbirds don't really go after Ossuary like we go after Pyrite."

"Probably a double cross. Claim to help Pyrite eliminate their problem and then turn around to use it on them at the earliest opportunity. It's exactly what we'd do to ensure our faction's glory."

"Why didn't you go with them, then? Back there – you could have taken me out, no problem. You certainly seem devoted enough."

"Like I said. Different–"

"Different stakes and all that, yeah, I remember. They're trying to get back into this Umbra guy's good graces, right? What are *your* stakes?"

"I... the nature of my transgression was more... I'm not doing this for *myself*, Rig." She stares down at her gloved hands. "You're doing this for Daara. I'm doing this..." It's the faintest of whispers, barely audible over the hum of the ship, but Rig can clearly hear her say, "I had a partner."

"A partner? As in..."

"My Handler. Most of the time Operatives are sent out in larger groups, sometimes with more than one Handler, but the roster changes depending on the circumstances. Partnered teams, where you're permanently assigned to one Handler – they're rare. They don't usually work out. You spend too much time working with just the one person, and often conflicts arise or emotions become an issue, or a dozen other problems.

I suppose my partner and I... I suppose we failed in that regard as well."

The familiar pain in Ginka's voice twists in Rig's heart. "You miss them."

"More than anything."

"They're your 'different stakes.'"

"...Yes."

"Huh. Okay." She frowns and considers the situation. "Are you going to kill me?"

"No."

"And are you still going to follow through on that favor for a favor deal and help me save Daara?"

"Yes."

"And the favor you want isn't me handing you the plans?"

"No. I... I really *do* require Grace. I *need* it. I need the time, I need to find a way out of my... my *punishment*."

"Right."

"You're not worried that I'll betray you?"

A corner of Rig's mouth twitches upwards. "See, Cactus, here's the thing. You're *really* useful to me. I think your company is semi-decent and you're fantastic in a fight and you know all this crap about PI and Windshadow. If you're going to help me get Daara back, then that's the important bit, isn't it? I'd like to not die after I save her, but that's a secondary sort of issue. Because the crux of the matter is, you don't know where the schematics are. So if you betray me? You *still* won't have what your Lord Umbra wants."

And if Daara gets saved first, then even *if* Ginka manages to figure out that the schematics are hidden in Panache and Pizzazz... Well, it'll be useless to her, because the only two people who can get to them will be safe from Windshadow and PI by then.

She gently tosses the vial and syringe onto Ginka's lap. "Here."

Ginka scrambles to grab the Grace, uncapping the syringe with her teeth.

Only a thin layer of the clear shimmering liquid remains in the vial and the scant five mil that Ginka draws into the syringe seems to cut the remaining liquid by a disturbingly large percent. She methodically taps the syringe then plunges the needle into her thigh, straight through the fabric of her pants, and lets out a relieved sigh as the drug makes its way into her system.

"You've only got a few doses of that left," Rig comments, staring at the vial.

"I know. I have perhaps two or three fights left in me."

"Two *fights*? What does it *do*, exactly? Thrush-Eleven knew about it. Seemed to imply she had some of it, too. You said you needed it 'cause you needed *time*."

Ginka turns the vial over in her hands. "You were right, earlier."

"I'm right often; you're gonna need to be more specific."

"Helltech produces a toxic byproduct called adrenomycin during the generation process. Windshadow technicians didn't *remove* those toxins, they simply... redirected them. You saw the generator packs the Operatives were wearing. Each one also connects to a veinport. The toxins are contained, pressurized so that they go from gaseous to liquid form, and then are released into the bloodstream." She holds up the bottle of Grace. "This neutralizes them."

Rig gapes at the horror of it all, the cruelty of it – the *stupidity* of it, for fucks *sake*...

"What kind of ineffective, unscientific, poorly conceived *bullshittery* is that?" she demands. "If it can be turned into a liquid and bonds with blood then just carry a bag of blood around in that damn generator pack and dump the shit in there. Or some kind of blood-filled protective casing around it, like a gel pack, or... I mean, if *size* is an issue and you don't want to be carting around a box of blood, double up on those damn connector cables and fill one of 'em with blood, and I guess if just opening up a container of toxic blood is an issue, some kind of vacuum-sealed drainage system – I'm just spitballing here, seriously, someone should have thought of *something* here!"

Ginka blinks owlishly at her.

"Oh, right," she realizes. "It's not about figuring out the problem, it's about *control*. Got an Operative up to some unsanctioned hijinks? Just cut 'em off from Grace and boom, solve your problem."

"Er, well, there *does* need to be a clear punishment for–"

"Do *not* make excuses for them, Cactus, I swear to gods. Why are you even wearing those? Take them off!"

Ginka recoils as Rig instinctively reaches out, pressing her back against the wall and clutching her gauntleted arms to her chest. "No! Don't *touch* me – don't touch them!"

Shit, forgot about the touching thing.

"I'm sorry. I didn't mean… If you want to wear death gloves, that's your choice, I guess." She pinches the bridge of her nose until it makes her eyes kinda hurt. "You people control your Handlers like that, too, or only the Operatives? I didn't see Thrush-Eleven sporting any helltech, just that fancy link."

That pained expression returns. Huh. She didn't seem all that broken up about getting *poisoned* by her boss. No wonder Umbra's using her former Handler – her partner – to control her. She must really care about them.

"A Handler's link isn't *just* a link. It causes that patch of white hair for a reason; it's attached to the skull. It lets them see better than a hawk on a clear day, hear things better than even a sensitive felidae's ears. They can access the netspace at will, connect with systems with ease that even experienced hackers don't have – it's a constant stream of information. If you're suddenly cut off from that…" She winces. "It's like being rendered deaf, dumb, and blind."

Lovely. "Did that ever happen to your Handler?"

"…Yes. Once, only for a brief while after a mission went bad. I don't want to talk about it."

Ginka pukes again, but it sounds like it's just bile this time.

"Do you think Janus knew they were there?" Rig wonders aloud as images of all the Windshadow agents swim in her thoughts. "And for that matter, does he suspect that we're not actually retrieving the plans? He knew *you* were there, after all, and he seems to know that we're working together."

"Surely he'd contact you in some way if he thought we were going after him. What use is having Daara as a hostage if he can't threaten you with her suffering?"

The images of Windshadow agents in her mind shift into Daara, bruised and battered, Janus looming over her. "Tact, Cactus, I am *begging* you," she replies through gritted teeth. "And I'm sure we'll find out. But we need to move fast. We're running out of time." She retrieves the stolen link from her pocket, turning it over in her fingers, inspecting it like she would an ancient Kashrini jewel. "We only have one shot at getting to their headquarters."

"We know where they are," Ginka says, mulling it over, "but we can't simply fly straight up to their spacestation and expect everything to go smoothly. They'll have patrols in whatever system they're in, security checks that we'll need to pass. A compass, even one such as Triton, can't fake those. If we can locate another PI agent, perhaps we can extract the information we'll need."

Pretty sure that's a polite way of saying 'torture.'

Of course, it *is* an option. Not one that Rig is particularly fond of, true enough, yet an option, nevertheless. They could stow away in a vessel bound for the spacestation, but that would limit their escape options, and she has no doubt that a prison break will be messy, at best. No, what they really need is some way to pass off *Bluebird* as a Pyrite ship. She just doesn't know *how*.

Ginka is still shaking a bit. "Are you... are you certain you don't mind me being involved in the planning? I would understand if you'd prefer, given the circumstances, to only have me involved during combat situations."

That might be reasonable; however…

Out of all the thing she's just figured out, the thing that she keeps coming back to is the fact that someone must have tattooed a damn serial number on the back of Ginka's neck and told her that was her name. Exactly like D-39.

Rig digs her fingers into her shirt right over the scar on her stomach where her tracker used to be. No one deserves to have that happen to them. *No one.*

"I'll answer that question if you answer me one of mine," she says.

"Very well."

"If you were given a serial number as your name, why do you call yourself 'Ginka'?"

An embarrassed flush cuts through the sick pallor of Ginka's cheeks. "I… I picked it. Six years ago – before I left. I wasn't supposed to and, well, a lot of things I did came back to kick me in the ass later, it seems."

Well now. Rig can feel a tiny smile tugging at the corner of her mouth. "Huh. It seems we have something in common."

"We *do*?"

"You think I keep correcting people about my name cause it's a codename or something? I was born Traxi. I left Pyrite. I changed it to Rig. I'm no more Traxi than you are whatever number they tattooed onto the back of your neck. We made ourselves, Cactus." She sighs and gets to her feet. "I'm not going to cut you out of this except for when you're needed to smack faces in. Drink some water at some point. Get some rest. Sleep on your side. Yell if you need anything."

She turns the light off, and she's pretty sure that Ginka's unconscious by the time she's stepped out.

A pervasive mist of emptiness lingers throughout *Bluebird* as she walks back into the main room. Feels as though their conversation drained all the energy out of her, leaving behind exhaustion, confusion, and an overwhelming sense of wrongness.

Due to the late hour, the electric lights throughout the ship are dimmed and soft. It's quiet, just the hum of the engines. With any luck, the silence and the time will help Ginka get a good night's sleep.

She was never able to take care of Daara like this. She should have. Maybe if she'd taken care of her more, things wouldn't have come to this. Maybe if she'd just been better at showing Daara affection, if she hadn't let her all-consuming work for Pyrite draw her and her sister apart, maybe then Daara would have left with her three years ago.

She sinks into the nearest chair, resting her head on the table.

When she closes her eyes, she can still see the smashed-in mess of Triton's head and hear the sound of his body hitting the ground. His skin turns blue, and his eyes turn into Daara's eyes, her sister's head cracked open. She bites down on her lip, her eyes snapping open.

In front of her, the glass orb shimmers in the soft light, making the firestone appear to glow, casting red fractals over the statuette inside. Dare of the Spire and his lover, Shen. She might not be anywhere near as great as Dare, but that doesn't stop her from needing her Shen just as much as he must have.

She removes her link, slots it into the table mounted projector, and calls June. It should be late afternoon on the Ascetic homeworld. Not a bad time. She doesn't want to wake up June unless she has to.

A panel appears, hovering above the tabletop as the call connects.

"Hello, my love," June says. She's in the middle of tying her hair back – must be appraising something or picking something up from one of the more mysterious sublevels of the library. "I'm glad to see that I won't need to avenge your death. How did it go?"

Rig tries to speak past the knot that's decided to pop up in her throat. "Oh, you know. We have the location, but the compass got killed, we almost got murdered by assassins and then by Governess Moor, and it turns out that Ginka is a Windshadow agent. And now we need some way of passing *Bluebird* off as a Pyrite ship so that we can sneak into the PI headquarters. I've had better days."

It's as though white paint has flooded through June's veins as she pales. "Oh shit. Ginka's... Ginka's Windshadow? Love, are you sure she's... if she hurts you I swear to every god that exists that I'll hunt her down and–"

"She won't. I don't think. She said she wouldn't and I don't... I don't think I really trust her, but I trust that I know what motivates her now. I don't know, am I being an idiot?"

"If you can't trust her, then I don't understand why you care enough to let her stay aboard your ship. It's a risk, and I doubt it's one you can afford right now."

It's difficult to explain why she's willing to take the risk. Earlier tonight she might have agreed with June, only after seeing Ginka miserable and sick and alone and, well, *pathetic,* she kind of can't *not* want to go out on a limb for her. "I... guess it is stupid, but... but I do care. A little. It seems like she needs *someone* to give a shit about her, and the only person that *does* care about her is gods-only-know how far away."

"You caring too much is going to get you killed one of these days," June points out.

Rig shifts awkwardly in her seat. "Me *not* caring is going to get other people killed."

June presses her beautiful brown eyes tightly shut. "I love you, but you need to learn when to give up on people. I understand going to the edge of the galaxy and back for Daara because she's your sister and you're under the pressure of familial obligation, but you barely know Ginka. Let someone *else* give a damn, for once in your life."

"But people *don't* always do that!" The great shame squeezes its way out of her throat, burning as it goes. "No one cared about my mother, you know – not even *me*. She was just gone, all the time, and one day she didn't come back from work; and I was sad, yeah, but I had never cared about her – really *cared* – and maybe if I had, she would have had something to come home to! I never cared enough about Daara. I made a half-assed effort to get her to run away with me and that was *it*. I should have done *more*."

Random people across the galaxy aren't Daara, and they'll never *be* Daara, but if she can just help them, just *care* about them, then maybe it'll help. Maybe it'll do *something*.

June's lips press into a cool and stern line. "If Daara had cared about *you*, she wouldn't have stayed. She decided that Pyrite was her home and that it mattered more than you did, and don't you dare act like that's your fault because you can't make that decision for someone else. I swear, I could *slap* Daara for what she did to you–"

"She didn't do anything to me–"

"She decided you didn't matter to her! You reached out and she pushed your hand away and threw her lot in with a faction that she *knew* didn't value either your life or hers."

"It's... hard," Rig murmurs reluctantly, "to give up your home like that. She had reason to stay."

"She had reason to *leave*."

Not really. "You aren't going to leave, either. That's what I mean – home is hard to break away from."

June recoils and – shit, that wasn't what Rig meant, that came out all wrong. "The circumstances are completely different – Daara was and *is* in danger under Pyrite rule. Whatever else I am, I am *safe*. And I assure you, I *do* care about you. I simply have to be rational about things. So *stop* turning things around just because you don't like that I've made an excellent and irrefutable point."

"I–" She gulps. "I'm sorry. I didn't mean it like that."

"Stop apologizing or I'll slap the 'sorry' out of you, too."

It's said so sharply and with such certainty that it does actually slap any and all coherent thought out of Rig's brain, and what her mouth ends up spitting out is, "That's kinky."

June blinks and then smothers an undignified laugh in her palm. "You're incorrigible, love." She drags her hand down her face. "Help Ginka if you wish. I'll trust in your judgement; just please, don't burn yourself up trying to help a damn Windshadow agent. You're already burning the candle at both ends trying to save Daara. Spread yourself any thinner and you'll disappear."

She lets out a deep sigh of relief. There's a difference between going with a gut instinct and having someone tell her that it's *okay* to go with that gut instinct. "Thank you. I just... Stuff's hard. Right now. With Daara captured and then everything else piled on top of that."

"Distract yourself. You said you need to get *Bluebird* to pass off as a Pyrite ship. How are you going to do that?"

"Uh." She tries to do as June says and switch her brain back into planning mode. "We need a transponder beacon," she realizes.

"A... a what?"

"It's... I suppose you could say that it's a device inside the ship that acts as a registry. It transmits a signal to the spacestation that reads as a Pyrite ship. Because they're near impossible to manufacture outside of Pyrite spires, they're considered to be just as a secure as anything else."

"Wouldn't they double that up with clearance codes?"

Rig laughs. "You're thinking like Ascetic would think. Old school fallbacks and all that. In Pyrite, everything is the latest tech. They're all so proud of what they can concoct that older methods are seen as beneath them. If we've got the right transponder, they wouldn't ask us for a clearance code because that would be 'implying that some ruffians could fake a Pyrite transponder.' Not that they'd think of it like that – it's not conscious. It's just how the culture works."

June lights up like the sun. "Clever. Use their mindset against them." She pauses, her mouth scrunching up adorably. "Question: why not just steal a ship?"

"If it's a working ship, we'd have to hijack it, and that takes a lot of time and a lot of prep if you want to do it without dying. An abandoned ship would have one, but if it's abandoned, chances are, it's broken. Any Pyrite stealth ship made in the last five or so years should have a useable one. Once I'm on board, I'll be able to locate it, strip it, and steal it. Er... I hope at least. Been a while since I was on a Pyrite-made ship. Let's just say I can do it; and then if I can't, we'll burn that bridge when we come to it."

"So how do you get our hands on one?"

"I steal it."

"I presumed as much, but how?"

"...That is the hole in my plan."

June tugs her mouth to the side, a habit of hers when she's deep in thought. "A transponder beacon..."

"Yeah."

"From a Pyrite stealth ship? As in... a ship that would have been designed to see combat?"

"Yep."

June winces. "I have an idea, but you're going to hate me for it."

CHAPTER FOURTEEN
The Dead Zone

Ten hours later, Rig pulls *Bluebird* out of luminalspace and into one of the last places in the galaxy she wants to be.

"You know," she says, her feet propped up on the terminal and a holo screen that's currently displaying a call with June on her left, "it's weirdly pretty out here. Horrible, of course, but... I don't know. There's a certain something to it. An appeal. I've gotten lost here before. It's – I don't think freeing is the word, given how precarious life here is but..."

June twirls a strand of her hair between her fingers. "With chaos comes opportunity?"

"Exactly."

"Describe it to me?"

Sending a recording of the ship's viewport to June would be easy, but it would be emptier. The life is in the story, and the telling of it.

"It's like an asteroid belt or the rings of a planet," she begins, staring at the space in front of her and trying to pick out the best of details to give to June. "Must look like one from a distance, too. Thousands – hundreds of thousands, maybe more – hunks of stuff floating around Hanera in rings. Occasionally, there's a break in the rings, probably from bombs or shockwaves over the years. When you get closer, the debris clears up. Some are rocks, pieces of the planet below that got blasted off – maybe thousands of years ago, maybe a few days ago. The planet shrapnel is deep, deep black, and it flashes green when *Bluebird*'s lights hit it. Some pieces are a sort of off-white mixed with soft pastels in every color you've ever seen light be – those must be from the moons they say Hanera once had. And some of it is from shipwrecks."

Dreams shine in June's eyes when she glances at her girlfriend. "What are the ships like?"

"To my right there's a torn-off engine. All that's left from the ship it would have been attached to are strings of wires, sort of reaching out like they're just waiting for their ship to return. It's big, too. Heavy looking, three-tiered ignition – must have been a dreadnaught. To my left I can see a lone bowsprit. It's old, too, really old; I have no idea what model it is. The tip of it curls into those whorls that Pyrite favors though, and by the size and design of it I'd guess that it would have been a luxury cruiser. Daara worked on building a figurehead for one of those once."

"It must have gotten caught out here. Blown off course perhaps?"

"Yeah, probably. There's so much interference out here that an older model ship could easily have gotten its nav systems scrambled worse than a M'rana finger trap."

"Is *Bluebird* alright?"

Lights wink cheerfully up at her when she gives her console a pat. "She's doing perfect. I wouldn't risk her out here if I didn't think she could handle it."

"And what about her pilot?"

"Huh?"

"Can *you* handle it out here?" June asks. The strand of hair she's playing with is getting tugged rather hard. "I know that this was my idea, but you didn't have to – you *don't* have to go through with it."

Wasn't as though Rig had any better ideas. They don't have time to play things safe, and they don't have time for her to sit on her ass and twiddle her thumbs while she comes up with the bestest, perfectest, prettiest plan ever. "I know I don't, babe. And I've been here before, remember? Sure, I've never been on any of the *planets* here, but I've made dozens of trips to the Zone over the past three years – mostly to break out any indentured Kashrini that Pyrite threw out here to aid in the war effort. What's that saying about old hats?"

"Hush and allow me to worry."

She grins. "Yes, ma'am, Miss Librarian, sir."

"*Really,* now," June says with a fond roll of her eyes. "I'm starting to get interference; your signal is going, but let me know when you've retrieved the transponder safely, alright?"

Rig presses two fingers to her lips and then touches the kiss to the screen. Static fizzles up as her fingers skim the intangible surface of the hologram screen. "I will. I love you."

"I love you too. *So* much."

With that, the call drops and leaves Rig alone on *Bluebird*'s bridge, a chill crawling under her skin that has nothing to do with the usual coldness of space.

"Where are we?"

Her heart enters luminalspace, promptly exiting her body through her ribs. "I swear to *fake fucking gods,* Cactus! You are going to *kill* me. Couldn't you knock or… I need to put a bell on you, that's what I need to do; I'm going to get a bell and put it on your shirt or something and every time you try to sneak up on me that stupid bell is going to ring and my risk of dying via heart palpitations will decrease by five thousand percent."

Ginka, leaning against the doorway, does not seem to care at all about anything Rig just said. Rude. After scaring her half to death, she could at least listen.

"Where the *fuck* are we?"

"Exactly where you think we are." She spreads her arms out before the viewport. "Welcome to the Dead Zone."

Ginka just stares.

"Oh," she adds, "and welcome back to the land of the living, by the way. Drink some water. Eat a food."

"*Why* are we in the godsforsaken Dead Zone?"

"We're going down to Hanera," she explains, pointing to the planet in the middle of the destroyed system.

Ginka blinks incredulously. "The *Throttle*? Why – because we can actually *breathe* there?"

"Among other reasons, but essentially, yes."

There are three planets remaining in the Dead Zone – Hanera, Sombri, and Duun. Every other planet has been blown up, and Sombri and Duun are far too dangerous for her to chance it, as both of them are filled with pockets of radiation that've poisoned large swathes of the atmosphere.

"You're insane."

"Charming. June and I came up with a brilliant plan while you were sleeping everything off. We're going to get a transponder beacon."

It's sort of surprising that Ginka doesn't ask what that is. But then again, perhaps Rig should have expected that. If she could pin *Bluebird*'s make and model at a glance, she clearly knows her way around ships.

"See," she continues, "we don't have the time to lure a Pyrite ship to us, and we don't have time to go to the center of Pyrite space and steal one. So we need to find a ship that's already *lost*. The Dead Zone is chock full of wrecked ships. I can trace the signal we're looking for and we can search to our hearts content until we get what we need."

"Yes," Ginka concedes, "but it is also full of scavengers, murderers, wild beasts, soldiers that were left behind and have gone mad – and a whole plethora of things that will explode if we so much as look at it wrong. Gods, we're lucky the last battle here ended earlier this year, or else we'd have been blown up by now. If we're *unlucky*, entire fleets of factioned ships will descend upon this system before we can safely get out of here."

It's hardly as though Rig wants to go for a picnic here. "We'll be in and out. Besides, Ossuary and Pyrite are busy duking it out in the Praetor System right now."

"That isn't exactly *far* from here."

"Yeah but... far *enough*, right? Also, I didn't see you coming up with any better ideas."

Annoyance and exasperation mix together in the pout on Ginka's lips. *"I,"* she says, each word slow and pointedly enunciated, "was unconscious. And furthermore, it isn't as though you came up with this idea either – June apparently did."

"She's good at that." Rig gets to her feet and meanders into the kitchen area. "Get comfy, we'll be landing soon. I also made coffee, by the way. In case you want to be disgusting."

She pours herself a fresh cup and watches in awe and horror as Ginka goes straight for the grinds and starts adding those suspicious powders. Idly, she pokes at the wrappers once they're empty.

Huh. Caffeine supplements, protein powder, multivitamins, and plain old sugar.

Suppose that makes sense, in hindsight.

She takes her mug and sits down at the table, sipping slowly at the unsweetened majesty of coffee more bitter than a PI agent's soul.

Ginka stirs her sludge and drains half her mug in one grateful sip – or munch? – before remarking, "I'm always surprised that a librarian such as June would be so cavalier towards your anti-faction activities."

She bristles and straightens up in her seat. "You better not be insulting her."

"No," Ginka quickly denies. "Of course not. It's simply... curious. If she's on board with everything you do, then why aren't you permanently living with her?"

"Thought you wouldn't support a librarian abetting lawbreakers."

"I don't, but my opinion is irrelevant in this matter. Don't dodge the question."

"It wouldn't be fair to June."

"She loves you and you love her. You should be together. I don't see how staying away is any fairer."

"It's complicated."

"It really isn't."

Guilt curls up in her chest as an old friend. No matter how many times she imagines remaining by June's side, the picture of it is always ruined by flames that consume and twist until it's swallowed up by the flaming gear of Pyrite. That's not something Ginka can understand. Ginka's loyal, devoted to Ossuary, and whatever friends and family she has are likely living happily under its banner. She was *Windshadow*, and while that doesn't mean she was treated *well*, it means that she was the one giving out the orders, doesn't it? Rig was always the one being kicked in the ass when she failed to follow an order in even the slightest way. Ginka's not split in half; she's not dragging around a steel cable that ties her to a faction she never wanted to serve.

It doesn't matter how far Rig runs or how long she stays away or how many connections to her old faction she tries to sever – Pyrite still has its claws in her. She'll die before she lets them sink their claws into June as well.

Shimmering hunks of metal float listlessly past the viewport as she turns her head towards the bridge. Is that all she is? A chunk of debris, drifting through space?

"June," she says at last, "deserves better than to be tied to me. She has a job and a home, and she's not in any danger of losing either. If I stay with her forever, I'd eventually be found out by the Ascetic MPs, no matter how well she'd try to hide me. I'd be a... a *thing*, needing to hide in her closet, needing to always dodge out of sight when someone comes looking too closely. If she wants to be with me, then she should be with *me*. Rig. Not Rig with a fucking asterisk attached. I couldn't do that to her."

Surprisingly gentle silence hovers between them.

"If you asked," Ginka eventually says, "I think she would leave with you."

One day she wants June to be sitting with her on *Bluebird*'s bridge, going out into the stars and traveling to every system they can reach. One day she wants to fix her ship up to the point where two people can comfortably live here, not just scattered about and shoved into corners as she and Ginka currently are. One day she wants to make a jump to luminalspace and not have the constant voice in the back of her mind reminding her that she needs to save enough fuel to make a jump back to June.

But it's just a dream.

Anger – hot, red, *bitter* anger – boils up inside her throat. "Don't try to lie to me, Cactus; don't you dare. I *know* she wouldn't, and so do you."

Ginka arches an eyebrow. "Ah, so you *were* listening in. I had wondered. Regardless–"

"She said *no,* and I *heard* her."

"You didn't see her face as she said it."

"No, no, don't pull that 'her mouth said no but her eyes said yes' shit on me. You don't even know her, you don't know her tells or her tics – *I* do. And I know that if she says she needs to be safe, then that's what she means. Why would she abandon a secure, pleasant life for someone like me?"

Someone prideful enough to never falter while doing the dirty work for Pyrite, so focused on what she could do that she ignored everything else. Someone cowardly enough to turn tail and run as soon as it threatened her personally. No matter what she does now, no matter how many people she helps as a Nightbird, she knows it doesn't erase how many people she hurt while making weapons for Pyrite.

"I know what people look like when they're kept from the one they love," Ginka vehemently insists. "You're not being forced away from her, you're not staying away because there are no other options, you have a *choice* – and you're choosing *wrong*."

Without thinking about it, Rig finds herself leaping to her feet, staring Ginka down. "Just because you *failed* at your fucked up job, got kicked out, and now can't see your *precious Handler* doesn't mean you know what I'm going through or what June should be doing with her own damn life!"

"I–" The wind has left Ginka's sails and she visibly deflates, taking a step backwards and sinking in on herself. "That is… I don't–"

Beeeeeeeeeeeeep.

That… is not a good sound. Rig can feel all her blood making a swift exodus from her face.

"What is that?" Ginka asks carefully.

"Heat sensors."

"What do you mean, heat sensors? We're in space. There is no heat."

"Ships give off heat."

"Ah."

They stare at each other.

Panic then slaps Rig across the cheek and she throws herself onto the bridge and into the pilot's seat, pulling up visual feeds and getting the radar to show something other than static… Shit, if there's static, it means that someone is trying to scramble *Bluebird*'s sensors. She drags her fingertips over the terminal screen and redirects every bit of power she can spare to the shields.

A warning light goes off.

With a flare of energy through the windshield and a screech from the sensors, a blast rocks the ship worse than if they'd crashed into an asteroid.

"Get to the guns, Cactus!" she orders.

Like the well-trained tool she is, Ginka obeys.

Shields are holding, although the hit took out a nasty chunk of their durability. She shifts the defenses around to concentrate the shields on the port side; that had to have been where the shot came from. The hit had been powerful too – a missile? Ship big enough for one of those – galleon or above.

She shakes the terminal screen and finally a hologram of

the rear visual feeds fizzles into existence. Something big is behind *Bluebird*'s port side. Another flicker of the screen. A *Leonine*-class warship...

"Pyrite ship," she spits out, following the word up with a dozen foul curses. "What are the chances they *didn't* follow us here from Tides?"

"Slim to none. How did they track us?"

"I don't know. They must have dropped out of luminalspace shortly after us, but... I don't know how they tracked us."

It's the only answer that makes sense, and yet she doesn't understand it. It's impossible to follow a ship in luminalspace due to the interference given off by warping space, not unless there's already a tracking device on board, and she knows that there's no such thing on *Bluebird*. She did an additional sweep for bugs after that earlier conversation with Ginka, too.

Paranoia hisses in the back of her mind – did she really remove her tracker all those years ago? Did they put more than one in her?

Of course not; she would have noticed by now. But still–

Another impact jolts through the ship, making her almost smack her head into the terminal.

Tracking thoughts later. Dodging thoughts now.

Instinct and memory kick in. She grabs onto the steering yoke and throws the ship into sharp nosedive. The Pyrite ship is close enough to tickle her, blasting past the viewport as she winds around a hunk of debris, its sleek and massive form consuming her vision – they need to get the fuck away from that. A hard light energy cannon glows in the warship's belly, and that's all the warning she gets before she has to pull off a fast barrel roll to evade the shot. It hits the debris around them instead and shrapnel from the explosion pelts *Bluebird*'s shields.

"Is there any way we can get out of this damn debris?" Ginka asks, thumbing the cannon controls.

"No, we stay in!" Rig double checks her automatic targeting array. Nothing but static. "All the interference from Hanera is stopping them from getting a lock on Bluebird. If we try to get out, they'll just lock on with heat-seeking bullshit missiles and blow us up in no time flat. Their ship is big as fuck, too, and with luck they'll have a worse time navigating this mess than me." Despite her best efforts to throw them off her, they keep right on her tail, even as she tries to thread the needle through a tiny gap in a piece of wreckage. The warship just blows the wreckage into bits.

In the seat below her, Ginka spins their cannons around to blow up a bit of moon rock near the warship, the shockwave shoving them off course for a moment.

Ginka hisses a curse. "They're trying to deploy mooring cables."

If those get a grip on *Bluebird*, they'll be fucked – unable to fly away or shoot back or even make a jump into a luminalspace tunnel.

Rig glances at Hanera, still slowly rotating in the viewport. She can do this. This is her ship, her home, her place of power, and she knows every inch of it from top to bottom. She can figure this out.

"Pyrite *Leonine*-class warship," she mutters, mostly to herself. "Agile, fast, armed to the teeth…" She frowns. "Shitty air filtration. Difficult to recalibrate."

Fuck up their systems and it'll take them forever to get it un-fucked.

"Call out where the debris is, Cactus," she says, shifting around in her seat so that one foot is on the dashboard. "I'm going to be flying blind for a minute."

"What!"

"I need both hands!"

She kicks her foot forward so that it's holding the steering yoke in place and turns upside down. Her head hangs off the edge of the chair.

Gods, the underside of the terminal is gross. She should really clean it.

"Debris at thirty-eight degrees!" Ginka yells.

She wiggles her foot and adjusts their course.

Gotta open up the engine exhaust vent. It'll wreak havoc on the engine filtration system, but that can be fixed later. She grabs the security override port pinlock and yanks it open, sticking her fingers into the circuits to find the connector between the terminal and the exhaust vents. It's slippery – a good hard pull tugs it free.

"Hundred and ten degrees!"

Another shift of her foot.

A blast to the left rocks *Bluebird* but there's not the hard impact of a straight-up hit.

Connect the redjack to the secondary filter, prevent any unwanted vacuum effects. An adjustment to the flare deployment…

She shoves the last wire into place and spins herself back upright, her head swimming for a moment at the sudden change in orientation. Her hand grabs onto the yoke as soon as her foot's gone, and she jerks the ship to the side to avoid a wrecked schooner.

Drawing in a deep breath, she taps out a comment to redirect the flares with one hand as she uses the other to keep steering *Bluebird* out of the warship's sights.

"I'm going to go for a full burn," she explains hastily. "Blast 'em with exhaust fission particles and throw all my flares at them at the same time – their ship's got open drag flaps. Fission particles get in through there and then they'll fuck up the air circulation. Flares will short out their sensors and then they'll be so busy figuring out how they're gonna breathe that they won't be able to keep up."

Light bursts in front of the viewport as they narrowly avoid another cannon shot hitting them, the shot streaking past them and smashing an asteroid instead.

"Do it then!"

Rig throws open the vents and blasts off.

The sheer power of letting her engines go at full burn rips through the ship.

It lasts less than a fraction of a second, the slightest explosion of starlight in her eyes, the quickest of jolts. The acceleration slams her back into her seat.

Pain cracks in her neck, blurring her vision for a moment, and by the time her eyes manage to refocus, she can hear Ginka cursing up a storm.

Hanera consumes the viewport – not because it's a large planet but because they are suddenly way too close. The blast punched them through atmo, toxic clouds sizzling as they touch the ship's shields, a gale shaking them to and fro more vigorously than even the shittiest of solar winds.

Her hands have a death grip on the controls, yanking as hard as she can to pull *Bluebird* up out of its collision course with the planet's surface. "Hold on!"

Every sensor on the console goes off, a veritable symphony of beeps and buzzes and flashing lights. Through the noxious green clouds, she can see the jagged shapes of the uncountable crashed ships that cover Hanera's surface. Towering dreadnaughts, half buried under dozens of other vessels. A ripped-up galleon, hanging in two parts from the extended wing of a warship.

Millenia of battles stain Hanera, so many ruins that no one remembers what used to be beneath them.

Ruins that are now coming up way faster than she'd prefer.

They need to slow down. She flicks the drag flaps open, buying them some time while she engages the reverse thrusters. A curved hunk of metal hull lies in their way, but before she has to execute a complicated evasive maneuver, a well-placed shot from Ginka blasts the metal out of their path. They zoom through the dust, *Bluebird*'s belly almost scraping the rough edge of the hull. Speed's not dropping fast enough…

The reverse thrusters flare to life just in time.

Bluebird lurches violently, and Rig's slammed forward into her seat.

A quick twist of the steering yoke sends her ship spinning through the wreckage below, just deep enough to send them soaring through the gaping cavern of a hollowed-out dreadnaught. Then she shuts the drag flaps, engages the stabilizers, and picks a good bit of ship-gut to land on.

With a screech of metal, *Bluebird* skids to a stop on the ground, coming to a halt only a few meters before what would have been a very painful crash against the interior wall of the dreadnaught.

Ginka sighs. "Thank Ossuary."

Ossuary had nothing to do with it. "We're not out of the black yet."

She turns off all the screaming alarms – warnings that the shields are low on power, panicked reminders of the low level electrical interference Hanera gives off, proximity alerts caused by the dreadnaught they're holed up in. All of that doesn't really matter right now. She checks the radar for anyone on their trail. It's unlikely that Pyrite followed them through that stupidly risky jump, but if they were able to follow them to the Dead Zone, it's not impossible.

Apparently they're in the clear, at least for now. No ships with live engines nearby. Although she's not sure how much she can trust even the most basic radar here, given the planet's interference.

"Come on," she says, powering down *Bluebird*'s main systems and then getting to her unsteady feet. "Let's get going. We can't postpone our job here just because Pyrite's getting on our ass. Daara doesn't have that kind of time."

Ginka's on her heels as they stumble off the bridge. "Will... will *Bluebird* be safe? If they were tracking the ship, then they might simply destroy it while we're gone."

Horror churns Rig's stomach as she imagines the sight

of her ship in pieces, her home turned into nothing more than a smoldering wreckage to lie forever dead amongst the thousands of other ships that cover Hanera. She'd no longer be able to soar through the stars on wings no one could ever take from her. She'd be grounded. Dead. Same thing, really. Every inch of *Bluebird* belongs to her in a way that few other things have – she's touched every part of the engines, modified every system, slept in her bunk and on the sofa and on the bridge. If she were blindfolded, she could still walk from bow to stern without stumbling.

Whatever else might happen while they're on Hanera, she cannot allow her ship to be so much as scratched.

"Cactus," she says. "Let's get Chickadee."

The two of them get her bike out of the engine room and haul it down *Bluebird*'s gangplank with only minimal complications. Despite Ginka likely still shaking off the helltech sickness – and just generally being in poor shape – she's physically stronger than Rig, and capable of both carrying the bike out and then going back for a bag of supplies while Rig considers her bike.

A cursory attempt to terraform Hanera had been made before the planet became a complete wreck of a warzone, and as a result there's normal gravity and breathable – if gross – air. She tilts her head up, scanning the hull far above them to see if there are any noticeable cracks. There aren't. Fortunate, as she doesn't fancy any toxic rain falling on her ship and scouring the metal.

Ginka shoves the bag into the storage compartment on the back of the bike. "We should be alright for a few days out here, although if it takes longer to locate the necessary transponder, we'll have to double back to *Bluebird* and try a different part of the planet."

"We'll do it in *a* day. We haven't got *days* plural," she replies, bending down to open up Chickadee's chassis.

"…What are you doing?"

"Hiding *Bluebird*."

Rough wires scrape her hands as she pulls out the stealth field generators. There's two of them cozied up next to each other – she only needs one for a bike her size, but she'd made a backup just in case.

A few adjustments to the generators extend the size of the stealth field – at the cost of battery life.

She tosses one to Ginka. "Put this on the starboard side."

They separate, and she heads over to fix the generator to the port side hull. They're not designed for this, not really, but it'll work well enough for a day or so, and it's not as though she'll attempt to fly *Bluebird* with the generators clinging to her ship.

Ginka's done with her side when they meet up back at Chickadee. Rig pulls up the holo screen on her link and makes a final tweak to the settings.

"Three," she counts off, waiting for the calibration to finish. "Two. One."

With a shimmer and a shine, the stealth field flickers up, consuming *Bluebird* until it's completely invisible.

Can't get much more hidden than that.

"I'm impressed," Ginka concedes. "How long will they last?"

"Hopefully long enough."

Usually the generators could last upwards of a week, however a spaceship is a far bigger power drain than just a bike. It's hard to tell. She'll simply have to keep an eye on things from her link and hope that they find the transponder quickly enough to get back before the generators run down.

Without *Bluebird*, she's suddenly far more aware of just how tiny they are here. Ants squatting in this dreadnaught's shell. And there are ships beyond counting on this massive world. Given a thousand years and infinite supplies, she still wouldn't be able to map all of Hanera.

Ginka must catch her gaping and staring. She gestures to the ship they're hiding in and says in a dead flat tone, "Welcome to the Throttle of Hanera. Enjoy your stay."

INTERLUDE
The Second Fall

Rain drizzles outside, drops clinging to the single window of the tiny hotel room located on the five hundredth floor of the massive skyscraper. The dreary, perpetually damp city of Rydn is a landscape of towering grey buildings, rocky cliffs, and a vague metallic smell from the many mines that the city is built upon. The only interesting thing about the place is that Pyrite Governor Tai'alani is arriving to make a speech, shake hands, and kiss babies. A perfect window of opportunity to take him hostage and end the Pyrite occupation of this star system.

Spirit X-74 stares out the window, her thick, long gloves protecting her arms from the freezing cold air.

She flexes her hands, the bulky wireframe of her helltech manipulators moving smoothly. She's properly kitted out – knife hidden in her boot, link attached behind her ear, mask tucked into her belt. Over and over again, her hands run over her gear, double and triple checking until her tools are laid out in her mind's eye even when she's no longer looking at them.

On the other side of the cramped room, she can see Seven doing the same. His things are spread out neatly on the bed as he carefully and meticulously assembles his rifle. There's a tension to his movements, not unusual before a mission, only now it seems amplified to the extreme.

"This is our last chance," she asks quietly, "isn't it?"

He nods, a short, sharp jerk of his head. "I received the

transmission from our Controller this morning. One more sloppy job and we'll be split up and reassigned."

Coldness sinks into her, and this time it isn't from the frigid weather.

It's only practical, really. They've botched even more missions this past year, and there are apparently only so many times that they can be relegated to clean-up duty. Taking care of other team's messes isn't what partnered pairs are supposed to be used for, and if they can't function as supposed to, then they're nothing. Just one more failed partnership and a waste of resources.

"I don't understand what keeps going wrong," she admits.

"We need to figure this out. If we succeed here, I can put in a request for extended leave to train, but we'll have to justify it somehow, and show some sort of results before we return to the field."

Months of training can't fix this. Frankly, she's not sure what can fix this.

Broken bones are fixed with a stint in a medbay. Sore muscles are fixed with careful stretching. Every problem that she's encountered in her career so far has been anticipated; she had been told that they would occur, and she knows the steps to take in response. But this is hardly a problem she's had before – she can barely identify what the problem *is*, and she has no idea where to even begin addressing it.

Years and years ago, they'd sat her down and made her learn how different emotions felt, made her go through all the ones that she might encounter in the field.

This is what it feels like when someone is planning to betray you, X-74.

This is aggression.

This is bloodlust.

This is revenge.

No one ever taught her more than that. It isn't as though she's touched anyone else with her bare hands since then, and she already knows what she's feeling, even if she can't name it, can't place it into those neat little boxes of things she needs to watch out for. This, she thinks, should have been included in those warnings. It's making her falter.

She knows fear and anger and panic, and *yet*... This isn't that. How is this *not* that?

It's *better*. It's a better feeling, but it's just as lethal.

"Maybe we *should* split up," she murmurs, her breath fogging up the window. Whatever she's feeling mustn't spread to Seven. If it's lethal, she must keep it from him at all costs, surely. "If our Controller thinks it's for the best, how can I argue with him? And I refuse to drag you down with me."

His lips silently part in confusion. "I... I don't understand. You're not *dragging me down*. Our Controller is *wrong*."

"I'm distracted, we both can see it. *You* distract me, and I don't know if that's something that can be fixed with training, and I don't know how to get rid of this stupid problem, and I think that the only way to prevent this from tripping both of us up is to... to stop working together."

It's clear that he's trying to keep still, trying to think through what he's saying. Hopefully he does not guess her shameful truth. "I'm distracting you?" he clarifies. "Have I done something wrong?"

"No! No, not at all; this is my fault and my fault alone."

"So then..."

The betrayed sadness in his eyes breaks her heart, and she can put a name to the feeling gnawing at her insides.

"I... I care about you," she admits, and once she says those first few words, the words come unhindered and without her consciously thinking them. "More than I should. I'm sorry. I never intended... I know it's not allowed and that these things have been the downfall of other partnered teams, and that's why I need to leave. My emotions can sink myself for all I care, but I won't burden you."

Guilty silence stretches between them.

And then, to her shock, he lets out a sigh of relief.

"Oh, thank Ossuary." He runs a hand through his hair, pushing it away from his face. "I thought you were going to say something horrible."

"This is... I've just admitted a transgression. This isn't allowed, you should report me, at the very least – aren't you disgusted? By me?"

"No, that's... that's not what I'm saying at all. I'm... Oh, I'm no good at this. Could you take off your gloves?"

She flinches. It feels as though her gloves constrict around her palms like shackles. If she is lucky, they will cut off her circulation until she loses all senses in her hands. It's a more monumental request than he probably realizes. But she trusts him more than she's trusted anyone before, trusts him enough to know that if he asked, he must have a very good reason.

Her teeth bite down on her lower lip. First off are her heavy vambraces, the helltech generators that are strapped to her arms like clunky plate armor. Then the protective padding and the tubes plugged into the veinports in the crook of her arms. Finally, her gloves. Thin black fabric that covers her from fingertip to elbow. After so many years of wearing them near constantly, she cannot help but feel as though she is removing part of herself. And she knows, deep down, that Seven is the only person in the galaxy who she would remove them for.

When she peels her gloves off and her damned Zazra hands are finally bare, she hesitantly holds them out to him.

The backs of her hands are safe to touch, the skin blackened to the same dark tone as the tips of her pointed ears and the facial markings that stripe her cheeks and forehead. The danger rests solely in her palms. Even the cool air brushing against them is enough to make her hair stand on end after so long keeping them covered.

Seven offers her his hand, adding, "You don't have to if you don't want to."

She does want to. That's part of the problem.

Only her fingertips brushing his skin at first, just the slightest contact, and then she slowly slides her hand down to wrap around his wrist, her palm against the beat of his pulse.

Sights and sounds and feelings rush through her mind in a crashing wave.

Heat of his blush, music as they dance on the roof... Watching her stretch out in the sunshine after training, sitting next to her like everything's right in the galaxy and this is where he's meant to be... A laugh trapped in his lungs, remembering a joke she'd made, trying not to lose composure during a briefing...

She feels the smell of her hair when they sit close together, and hears the weight of her on his shoulders when she leans against him.

"Oh."

Her eyes flutter open – when did she shut them? She can barely breathe. Her lungs don't seem to understand that she's in her body and not someone else's. It's like staring into the sun after being in a dark room for years, overwhelming and inescapable, and she doesn't know if she can break the connection at all. She doesn't think she wants to.

Deep green of her eyes, pupils dark and wide, the most beautiful color he's ever seen, not even Ossuary themself had eyes like...

He nods. "It's not just you."

"But that's... How did you even *know*? That you felt that way? I didn't until now, it's... it's not something we're trained to know?" If she could have figured this out earlier, perhaps they wouldn't have failed so many damn missions.

He coughs, somewhat awkwardly. "I have been known, on occasion, to read a romance novel or two."

She can't help it, she bursts out laughing.

"Is that *really* necessary? I know we're not supposed to read fiction, but some of it is quite good, you know."

"No, no. It's just–" She giggles between the words. "Do you actually go looking for paper copies or do you download everything to your link? I'm imagining you opening it up on your targeting screen during stakeouts and I need to know if that's true."

"Paper, obviously. Easier to burn the evidence." His fingers twitch against her palms and she gets another flash of *care and worry – going too fast?* "Are you sure you're... alright with everything? You don't have to remain my partner if you don't want to. I don't want to lose you, but I would never force you to stay."

"I know. I never want to leave you either."

"Oh. Good."

Then he's getting closer and she's leaning in...

It's impossible for her to tell if she kisses him or if he kisses her first, and with her hand still touching him, she feels it twice over. The physical sensation of his lips against hers is almost entirely buried by the emotional feedback loop that sinks into every corner of her body. How do his books describe kissing? Next time, she'll have to read them and see if they have any advice.

"Well then," he says when they finally pull apart. "Now that we've figured out what our issue was, I suppose there's only one other question left."

"Oh?"

"Do you want to go kidnap and torture a Pyrite governor?"

She snickers. "I thought you'd never ask."

CHAPTER FIFTEEN
Throttle of Hanera

A good smack and a shake can fix nearly all technological problems. To Rig's great consternation, her scanner is proving to be the exception.

She's standing on the top of a *Maru*-class fighter that's buried in another ship, nose down and stern in the air, providing a nice resting place for two tired women and their dutiful bike, letting them survey the great Throttle that stretches before them. Cold, clammy air creeps across her skin, leaving an oddly sour taste clinging to the roof of her mouth and coating her lungs. Just because the atmosphere on Hanera isn't as bad as the rest of the planets in the Dead Zone doesn't mean it's *good*, either.

Perhaps the damp has gotten to her scanner. It's been leading them steadily northeast for about two hours now, but it's started to freak out and tell them that it's getting signals from every direction. It's hard for her to say what part of it got busted up. If she knew what exactly was wrong with it, she'd have a better idea of how to fix it, and without knowing what to do, she's hesitant to open it up and expose it to the wet air.

With any luck, it'll start working soon. Night is approaching faster than she'd prefer.

"This thing is impossible," she mutters. "Maybe if I try smacking it *and* shaking it at the same time..."

Ginka says nothing. Once more, she's completely conked

out, curled up into a tiny ball of black clothing and messy hair on top of the fighter ship, her nose occasionally twitching and her eyelids shifting as she presumably dreams.

"Hmm." Rig may as well talk to herself if Ginka's dead to the world. "Maybe there's a calibration issue. Ah damn, if that's what's wrong then I'll have to crack open the back and dig around in its guts. On the other hand, maybe it's a signal problem... Hm... Or the wiring?"

Ginka kicks her and grumbles, "You talk too loud."

"You sleep too much."

"Maybe I wouldn't need to sleep as often if I could get some *uninterrupted* sleep."

"Are you intending to sass me this whole time?"

"Are you intending to wake me up again?"

"...We are on a *mission*, Cactus. I don't know how you can pass out at the drop of a meteor, but this really isn't the time. Besides, we've got a problem that I need fixing."

Ginka pushes herself up and holds out her hand. "Give it. Let me see if my eyes are sharp enough to spot the problem."

"Sure," she replies, tossing it over – maybe tossing it will give it the right shake? "Knock yourself out."

Ginka makes an annoyed sleepy noise as she turns the scanner over. "It's not broken."

"I suppose the issue could be with the display–"

"We're on top of it."

Rig blinks. "On top of what?"

"On top of the transponder." Ginka tosses her back the scanner and then gestures to the ship they're standing on. "It doesn't seem to be broken – the dial can't stop spinning because we're standing right above the transponder. A Pyrite stealth ship must be buried beneath this *Maru*-class fighter."

A plague on all flat display screens.

"Why didn't I figure that out?"

Ginka shrugs as she properly gets up and kicks Chickadee to life, revving the engine. "You were too focused on *how* it worked. I just assumed it *did* work. Are you coming?" she demands, waiting on the backseat of the bike.

"Right, yeah." The scanner is in her pocket now, and they have a stealth ship to find.

She slides onto Chickadee's seat, fingers digging into the handle, and steers them off the *Maru*'s edge. They descend slowly, dropping into the hull of a cruiser and then through to an open pit, bigger than the dreadnought they'd parked *Bluebird* in and lined with twisted and torn up ship guts.

It's not long before Chickadee's headlights fall on the flaming gear of Pyrite, emblazoned on the shimmering carapace of a stealth ship. The design is relatively familiar, too, probably three years old or less.

"There!" She points at the treasure below. "We've struck platinum, Cactus."

There seems to be a scale to the severity of Ginka's silence. Certain silences are angry silences, whereas she could spend a whole chunk of time in peaceful, companionable silence during a long trip in luminalspace. The silence while Rig lowers her bike down onto the Pyrite ship is a tense one, charged like a whip pulled taut, prepared to snap out at any moment and lash those in its path. She imagines Ginka is preparing a colorful assortment of cutting insults.

She hops off the bike as soon as it lands, grabbing her roll of tools from the storage compartment and hurrying in the most casual manner possible to open the ship's emergency hatch.

Beneath the hatch is a beautiful chaos of wires and panels and gadgets, and hidden in the middle of it all is the transponder. A small, cylindrical device nestled inside like an egg in a bird's nest.

"Ah-hah. Perfect."

"Get to work," Ginka grumbles. "I'll stand watch."

Rig places her heavy cloth toolkit next to the opened-up section of ship-guts. Metal shimmers like an oil-slick in the summertime as she unrolls the toolkit to reveal her selection of toys. Wire cutters first. Best to do this slowly and carefully. As the name implies, every ship that rests in the Throttle is dead; however, that doesn't mean there won't be booby traps lying in wait for her. Dented and damaged booby traps, perhaps, but booby traps nonetheless.

The only booby trap she's interested in is June's.

"Shouldn't be more than a hot minute," she says as she begins to clear away the wires, exposing the core where the transponder rests. "Then we'll be in the clear to go kick down PI's front door and get Daara the fuck out of there. Gods, I hope Janus hasn't done anything to her that we can't... can't *fix*."

When no response is forthcoming, she prods, gently...

"Cactus?"

The silence breaks.

"I apologize," Ginka says stiffly, each word more enunciated than Rig thinks they should be. "I shouldn't have implied that you didn't know June's mind."

Well that's some emotional whiplash. Rig hadn't expected her to be the first of them to admit fault. It had seemed way more likely that Rig would have to spend a good long while psyching herself up to be the mature one – not a role she takes well to – and eventually have to just pull her big girl pants up and smooth things over.

Rig gives her a weak smile. "Thanks, Cactus. Listen, I *do* get it. You're an empath and even if you didn't touch June with your magic empath hands, there's probably some other cues or whatever that you picked up on, and I get wanting to tell me that. It's just that I'm *always* going to listen to what she *says* first."

"I understand. Truly, I do."

"You know..." Rig adds, even though part of her brain warns her that it might not be the best thing to say. "It's kinda funny that you were saying June should leave with me. Given that it'd mean deserting her library. Never thought *you'd* advocate for someone becoming ex-factioned."

"What, no that's not–" Ginka sputters, "I'm not saying *that*… You can leave and still… still not be ex-factioned."

"Seems very much the same thing to me. I mean, fuck, Daara's going to end up ex-factioned once we've saved her ass, but it's a better life. Better than being stuck under the boot of some faction that's just going to work you till you're dead and then strip your corpse for raw materials they'll use as building blocks for their next city. No thank *you*. I'd rather take my family and get the fuck out of there, and if Daara hates me for it, then… then at least she'll be safe. I think I'm okay with that trade."

It's a trade she should have made when she left Pyrite three years ago.

Silence – far less seething this time – stretches between them again as Rig begins to pry and wiggle and sweet-talk the transponder out. Wet dirt and goo has begun to weld things together, fed heavily by the damp and stale air that permeates all of Hanera, particularly potent in the lower and older levels of the Throttle. Gunk – possibly toxic, although she hopes not – covers the metal in patches, a sort of slime that's worked its way into the joints.

Of course that all ends when Ginka asks, "May I ask what it's like?"

"Gonna need a tad more specificity there."

"Loving someone so much that you'd rather they abandon their faction than lose them."

The first thing that comes to her mind is that she doesn't give a shit about factions anyway, but that's not going to be helpful to Ginka at all. "I… don't really know, Cactus. I think if I cared more about being loyal to a faction, then maybe I'd understand where you're coming from. To me, I guess the way I see it is that *people* are a home, not a planet or a house or a faction. And having people to come home to is more important than loyalty. I'd never think any less of June if she's a loyal Ascetic to the end of her days or if she left and never went back; but if she decided to leave *me*... That'd... that'd hurt."

Daara'd chosen that, and Rig doesn't know if she'll ever forgive herself for not being a better home than Pyrite.

Another bout of silence.

Pressurized air hisses and metal scrapes against itself as Rig finally rips the transponder free. It's a lot lighter than she imagined it would be. She places it down on the hull and wipes her hands off on a corner of her cloth toolkit before packing everything up and ensuring that she won't leave anything of import behind.

She wipes her greasy hands on her pants. "The question for you, I suppose, is if you've already made up your mind there."

"What?"

"You're staying away from your Handler. You chose that you'd rather they remain all loyal and shit than reach out and have them by your side."

"That's... It's different." Ginka stares at the floor like the secrets of the galaxy are written on it. "People like me are built to be kicked in the ass by the passage of time. I haven't seen him in three years. He might not..."

"I haven't seen Daara in three years," she points out.

"And you're still tracking her down. Even though she told you not to..."

"If you care about someone, there's not usually a time limit. Besides, what other choice do I have? I'm not going to let anyone else die because of my stupid pride and my stupid mistakes."

Ginka chews on her lower lip as though chewing over a particularly difficult question.

Lights flood the cavern in that second of indecision.

Bright, painfully white lights, sweeping over every crevice with the attentiveness of flies cleaning every last speck of meat from a bone. And as the lights slide over them, their creators are revealed.

Skiffs. A half dozen vessels, hovering high above Rig and Ginka.

Pyrite skiffs.

How the fuck did they get found out? If the tracker was on *Bluebird*, then PI should have showed up at the ship, not here. More pressingly, how the fuck are they going to get out of this? Although it's distant, she can see figures perched in the vehicles, light catching on long gun barrels – snipers. PI isn't here to fuck around. Are they sending assassins after her? No longer content to wait for her to make a decision or to slip up and reveal the location of the plans, are they?

Ginka tenses up. "Hide."

In a blinding flash, each and every one of the skiff's lights turn and converge upon the two of them.

Rig shoves the transponder into her vest pocket and then reaches for Pizzazz before realizing that it's stupid to try to take this fight. They're surrounded, they have no real defenses, and they're immobile.

Every muscle in her body tenses up. "Run. *Now*."

A skiff descends right behind Chickadee.

Beside the handful of soldiers that are aiming guns at them inside the open-top skiff is a familiar silhouette. The skiff comes to a stop behind her bike, the door opens, and the smarmy, smirking figure of Special Agent Janus steps out.

"If it isn't Double Trouble," he drawls, shifting his weight to one foot and casually resting his hand over the gun holstered to his thigh. "Pleasure to see you both again."

"If it isn't… I don't have a good nickname for you yet; but I *will*, and it'll be devastating, cause you're an *asshole*," Rig snaps back.

"Charming. It's quite the mystery, how someone with such a crass mouth had the intelligence necessary to craft such a cunning and subtle nanomite weapon."

"Get to the point. Why are you here? My week isn't up; I still have time."

"*Yes*, but after you – admittedly, with Windshadow's help – caused such a scene on Tides, I thought it would be best to keep an eye on things myself. And I thought I might give you a little tidbit of important information."

"Hit me then."

He gestures with a sweeping arm to Ginka. "Your friend here is a Windshadow agent, as well. She's been sent to recover the weapon schematics. Did you really think you were safe with her? That you could–"

"Yeah, I know all that already."

The stunned surprise that widens his eyes is beautiful. Rig savors it.

A frown twitches across Ginka's brow. "How do *you* know who I am? How did you know I would be at Governess Moor's party? Because you didn't know *Rig* would be there, just *me*."

That smirk of his returns. "I have my ways. The real question, Traxi–"

"For fucks sake, it's *Rig*."

"Rig, then. The real question is: are you here, in this godsforsaken part of the galaxy, because you've hidden part of the weapon schematics in the Throttle, or are you here as part of a greater plan to double cross me? I gave you *such* a nice deal, you know. It would be a shame if you reneged on it, for Daara's sake."

"So what are you going to do? Traipse around after me as I retrieve the plans from the Throttle?"

"Precisely. Or, if you've double crossed me, I give the order for dear Daara to start having her extremities removed."

She punches him.

It's not even something she's consciously aware of doing. She only realizes what's she done when her knuckles crack against his cheekbone. Pain stings her hand, but then the anger and the fear kick in. That white hot fire burns away any pain she feels and fills her mind with a single thought:

Fuck. Him.

Everything goes to shit.

Noise shatters the air as a few of the PI agents open fire, Janus too close to Rig for a proper shootout; but Ginka is farther back, and she must be getting fired at. There's a burst of gold light, and out of the corner of her eye, she can see Ginka twirling a shield made out of golden helltech. The shield spins like a discus in her hand, turning the bullets that collide against it into pellets of formless hard light, sputtering and flying off in a shower of sparks.

Janus jerks back from Rig's punch, looking almost as shocked as she is by her actions.

Before she can blink, his hand snakes up to catch her wrist. He yanks her arm behind her back, bending her elbow in a way it should *not* be bent. But she's still too furious for it to hurt. She bends her head forward then snaps back.

There's a *crunch* as her skull smashes into his nose and he lets her go, staggering backwards, and in that moment of distraction she pulls her hand back to gut punch him – his fist is suddenly filling her vision way too fast...

She drops to one knee to avoid getting the daylights smacked out of her head.

Then she's having to leap back real quick to dodge the kick that he sends towards her and – huh, that's weird... That kick looked exactly the same as when Ginka kicked down doors in Moor's palace.

"Down!" Ginka screams.

Rig flattens herself to the ground and the golden helltech shield whizzes over her head with a high keen of cutting energy.

It collides with a skiff.

The shield slices a solid two meters into the skiff's interior before the entire thing blows up like a dying star in a truly pants-wettingly majestic explosion. The PI soldiers unfortunate enough to have been standing in it don't even get a chance to scream before they're consumed by fire and chunks of metal.

Rig just has time to scramble to her feet and see a squad of enemies converge upon Ginka before she has to quickly avoid getting smacked by Janus.

Her boots skid on the slimy surface of the metal, forcing her to widen her stance and steady herself. Janus deflects her next punch with laughable ease, and she almost doesn't catch the sneaky stomp to her instep that he tries to follow up with. Their feet dance around each other, maneuvering for position as she struggles to block his sharp jabs and retaliate with cheap shots.

To her extreme disappointment, she utterly fails at kneeing him in the groin, and instead almost loses her footing when he moves out of the way.

Damn it.

Then he's stepping way too close for comfort, fist pulled back, and she knows, she just *knows* that he's about to try and slug her in the solar plexus because she's seen Ginka do the *exact same thing*.

She sidesteps the blow, grabbing his wrist with one hand and turning; puts her back against his chest, his arm gripped firmly; leans forward, *Yanks*…

It's a move also ripped out of Ginka's playbook, but it works, and she throws Janus over her shoulder like a sack of bricks. He hits the ground *hard*, a silent gasp of air punched out of his chest.

Holy shit.

She can't believe that actually worked… Oh *shit*–

His fingers are gripping her ankle and he delivers a painful heave, bringing her down with him.

In an undignified whirlwind of cursing, she topples on top of him, all knees and elbows and flailing, and then the two of them are tussling on the ground like teenagers in a schoolyard brawl. She does finally get in that cheap shot to the groin – disappointing, because he barely so much as grunts before flipping them over so that she's pinned under him, and the retaliatory punch that connects with her forearm is going to bruise like a *bitch* tomorrow.

The heel of her palm smacks into his nose – already trickling blood from when she'd headbutted him before – and his head jerks back. She takes advantage of his distraction, does something weird with her hips, and twists them around so that she's on top again.

She scrambles to her feet, getting off of him, fingers fumbling for one of her guns because she can see that he's pushing himself to his knees, and the other two squads are converging on Ginka so she's not going to be able to buy much more time…

Janus's hair falls over his shoulder as he's kneeled over, and on the back of his neck, peeking out from under his shirt collar, is black ink.

Fifty. No numerals. Just the spelled out, clear-as-day lettering:

FIFTY.

It looks exactly the same as D-39's tattoo. In exactly the same place. And Janus had been reporting to *Umbra*, not a PI higher up…

She stares at him as he gets back up, and her face must be doing something really peculiar because he doesn't try to hit her again, giving her a perplexed look. The furrow in his brow puckers the odd scarring on the right side of his face. Exactly where Thrush-Eleven's fancy, fused-to-her-head, horrible-to-remove-or-deactivate, Handler link had been.

"Nice scar," her mouth blabbers.

He simmers, lips pulling back from his teeth in a furious snarl. "Don't you dare taunt me, you filthy little–"

Whatever he's about to say gets cut off by him grabbing her arm and *wrenching* her down. It feels almost like he dislocates her shoulder, her chest smacking into the metal ground and her free hand scrambling to get purchase on something, *anything*.

There's a tug on her belt and she *laughs*.

Janus is trying to take her guns from her.

"Nice try, asshole," she grunts.

"What the–"

In his moment of surprise, she twists around and kicks him off her. "You can't take my guns off me, you dumbass. They're locked, and only my DNA can release them." She grabs Panache and aims it at him. "Want me to demonstrate?"

He's about to rush her–

Something gold, glowing, and made of helltech zips past his head.

The skiff behind him explodes.

"Let's *go*!" Ginka yells, standing protectively in front of Chickadee and forming another shield in her palms.

Rig scrambles away from Janus and kicks Chickadee to life, holstering Panache as she does so. The seconds it takes for the bike to wake up stretch into eternity, and then it's up – it's running.

"Get on!"

A bullet whizzes over her head. She hops onto the seat and kicks the brakes off as soon as she feels the machine sink with the addition of Ginka's weight.

"Go," Ginka orders, voice carrying through the crack of guns and the hiss of bullets against the helltech shield. "I'll watch your back."

Rig slams her foot down.

"*GET THEM*!" Janus screams but it's too late, they're flying.

Putrid air streaks past her face as they hurtle away from the stealth ship, bullets flying, her engine roaring.

She puts her bike through the paces. Twisting and spinning to avoid getting hit, recklessly falling only to soar upwards – open space is fraught with peril for a small bike like hers, and she has to be tricksy until she's in some place more cramped.

"Two-eighty degrees!" Ginka calls out. "Straight down!"

She lets the bike plummet without double checking to make sure that Ginka's call out is good.

They speed towards a dark hole, a crack between two fallen ships. Big enough for her bike, too small for a skiff. There's a cracking sound and the gold light at her shoulders vanishes – Ginka must have dropped the helltech shield and let it shatter.

Before any bullets can touch them, Rig drops down into the tunnel.

Her hand flicks the bike's headlights on. It's pitch black, the light beams dancing across the ships pressing in on them as they whizz past, illuminating leaning hunks of metal and wires stretched across the gap, poised to snare them. She weaves between obstacles at full speed.

Turns and roadblocks present themselves and she veers right, then left, circling around the center of a massive *Asceticai*-Bolt power core, and then shooting off towards a speck of light in the distance.

PI couldn't have followed her through here, and she hopes that her detour will have thrown off whatever tracking method they've managed to implement.

They burst out of the tunnel and into the dim light of Hanera's setting sun.

"How," she says as soon as they're speeding through open – and somewhat safer – space again, "did they manage to find us? We ditched *Bluebird*, even if by some miracle they *were* tracking the ship... Are they tracking Chickadee?"

Ginka shakes her head. "No, they couldn't be. They never had the chance to plant a bug."

How certain is she that the chip Pyrite put in her stomach all those years ago is gone? Could there be another, buried deeper inside her, perhaps more than two, perhaps three or four, contingency after contingency, a thousand layers to Pyrite's control over her...

The roar of skiff engines cuts through the heavy air.

"Shit!" She glances over her shoulder to see her pursuers have returned. "We can–"

Her eyes stare across the space, locking on to the shine of light off a sniper's scope. Time slows down even as she tries to send her bike spinning to the side.

A gunshot cracks.

Rig's head slams into the grip. There's a squelching *thunk* of the bullet piercing meat. A weight falls against her back.

She pushes herself up an inch, turns, and finds herself almost unseating Ginka.

Ginka, who's lying against her. Ginka, who's stretched out as though she'd tried to push her out of the way. Ginka, who's got a dark red patch on her shirt slowly spreading like a star until the red is staining almost all of her torso.

"*Cactus!*"

No, no, no, this isn't happening. She abandons the steering and presses her hands to Ginka's stomach in the hopes that she can somehow stymie the flow of blood.

Another gunshot goes off.

This time the bullet smashes into Chickadee's engine. Something explodes, fire blooms next to her, and she's suddenly plummeting, gravity sinking its fingers into her.

Impact after impact jars Rig's body as they crash through layer after layer of sheet metal, the bike too heavy to be stopped, and their momentum carrying them deeper into the Throttle with every passing second.

All Rig can do is hold on as they fall.

CHAPTER SIXTEEN
Dare and Shen

Rig blearily cracks her eyes open.

Or *an* eye, that is. Something warm and sticky is sealing her left eye shut, and when she brings a woozy hand up to her face she can feel gunky blood crusting on her forehead. She must have gotten dinged by a rock or something when they fell.

Her fingers prod at her pocket, feeling out the shape of Daara's pin. Still there. Still in one piece. Thank the gods. She didn't lose the one thing of Daara's she has.

Her nails are ragged and her palms a hot mess of scrapes as she fumbles at the ground.

"Cactus?"

She pushes herself up, spitting out a mouthful of foul air and dust, smoke burning her throat as she coughs. Next to her lies the crumpled remnants of Chickadee, the once beautiful machine barely recognizable. Twisted casing, a warped frame – the bright pink racing stripe has been scraped back to a few flecks of dirty paint. The storage compartment must have been cracked open, and now the contents are spilled out across the dimly lit hole she's in.

Only the faintest beam of cold evening light streams in from above. Dust motes dance in the column, drifting through the air and onto her hands as she pushes hunks of her bike aside in her quest to shift the rubble and find–

She draws in a sharp breath.

Ginka's lying in the middle of the floor, curled in on herself in the defensive manner of all wounded animals. Blood, now thick with dirt, still drips from her stomach in a viscous, sticky flow. The only thing to give Rig hope is the uneven rise and fall of her chest.

Aches and pains shoot through her limbs as she crawls to Ginka's side.

Blood – she needs to stop the bleeding. That's the first thing to do. Memories of first aid crash courses come to mind, and she recalls that she has to put pressure on the wound. Wrap it tightly with whatever she has – but she doesn't have any bandages. They packed rations and such on the bike. Not a medkit.

Her hands run over the thin fabric of Ginka's clothes – nothing long enough. Nothing that would work. She goes to her own shirt before realizing that it wouldn't work either. Her breath hitches and her hands stop.

They ghost over her headscarf.

Weird, violent, stupidly sneaky Ginka. Ginka and her sarcasm and her vices. Ginka and her abomination coffee. Rig can't do this without her. Not because she needs an asskicker around, or someone who's familiar with this shadowy world of spy versus spy, or even simply an extra pair of hands. She can't do this alone. She can't *be* alone while she does this.

She unwinds her headscarf.

Damp air brushes against her bald and exposed head, but she tries not to pay it any attention, focusing instead on the checklist of first aid.

Clean the wound as best she can. Dump water on the injury, wash out dirt. Remove Ginka's shirt so that the cloth doesn't get in her guts and cause sepsis.

She can do this.

Her knife is still on her, it hadn't been lost in the fall, and her blood-slick fingers slide over the handle before she can get a solid grip on it. Carefully, so, *so* carefully with her trembling hands and Ginka's uneven breathing, she places the tip of her knife at the high collar of Ginka's shirt and slices all the way down. She tosses the knife aside once she's done and pushes the ruined shirt out of the way...

"Oh merciful *gods.*"

The silver metal of Ginka's gauntlets runs not only all the way up her arms, but up her shoulders as well. Up, up, up until it sort of stops around her collarbones. It's hard to tell *where* it stops, exactly. It's not the smooth edge of nanomesh or metal armor. It's... Rig doesn't know what word she'd use here, really, too disgusted and horrified by what's been done to Ginka.

Where the metal meets skin are scarred, jagged lines knotting Ginka's flesh, twisted white dents around metal screws that are... that are *in* her body, sinking the gauntlets into her, evidence of ripping and tearing and *invasion*. Her skin has almost grown around the metal, filling into the flexible joints where steel meets skin, settling around the edges of the... not gauntlets...

Prosthetics.

No wonder Ginka never uses her empathic abilities. She *can't.*

She doesn't have hands with which to use them.

Holy fucking... Okay. Okay. Rig takes deep breathes. Just makes things worse, really, because now she's forcing herself not to gag on the rotten air. She can do this. She *has* to do this. She refuses to let someone else die because they got involved with her, her mess, and her weapons.

She turns her mind towards getting the length of her headscarf wrapped around Ginka's stomach. Her fingers fumble to do up bloody, wet knots and she has to shove a corner of the material between her teeth in order to pull the makeshift bandage tight.

"Cactus?" she tries again. "Can you hear my voice? It's me. I'm here, I'm going to help."

Ginka's eyelids flutter. Her hand moves an inch. "R-Rig?"

She sighs in relief. "I think we got Janus off our trail. He must think we're dead, or at the very least injured enough to be out of the game for a while." Which, they are, really. She presses a hand to her vest for a moment, just to make sure that the transponder is still there. "I need to get you back to *Bluebird*, okay? We have meds on the ship and you're – you're not in great shape."

"My... my bag." Ginka coughs and tries to point a finger. "I need..."

She reaches into the bag and her fingers find sharp edges and something wet.

All she manages to retrieve is the syringe, filled with five mils and cushioned by a jacket. The glass vial was not so lucky.

"Cactus..." she whispers, picking up the shards of glass. "I... I'm so sorry. There's just the syringe. The vial, it's... There's nothing else left."

It's hard to tell if Ginka understands her, and she has no choice but to give Ginka the final dose of Grace.

The needle goes clear through the fabric of Ginka's pants into her thigh, and then she presses her thumb down on the plunger and lets the drug enter her presumably struggling bloodstream.

She gets to her knees and slides an arm around Ginka's waist. Sticky warmth soaks into her sleeve and then smears onto her leather vest as she pulls her up and lets her lean her weight against Rig's side. Ginka can stand – *barely*, but it's enough to let Rig put one foot in front of the other and move them slowly forward.

One step at a time. There's nothing else she can do.

"Come on," she says, stumbling towards a collapsed tunnel at the end of the hole they've fallen into. "I've got you."

"Rig?"

"Yep, that's me. The one and only. I'm still here."

She uses her one free hand to push a collapsed sheet of metal out of the way and then continues through the tunnel into the darkness. No light lives down here, only the rarest and faintest of flickers, and she finds that she can't take more than two steps before she's forced to activate the flashlight on her link. A white glow begins to emanate from the device. The light drapes itself over the perilous tunnel, leading her hopefully outwards.

Noises scurry around in the dark. Vermin squeaks and reptilian hisses, always originating from a direction that's just out of Rig's sight and vanishing before she can turn her head around to look.

Images of the scars on Ginka's shoulders fill Rig's mind despite her best efforts to push them down. She can never unsee that. She probably *shouldn't* have seen that. If Ginka had wanted her to know, she'd have said something; and despite the necessity of it, guilt still rankles at her. Even though she didn't have a choice, it leaves a sour taste in her mouth to have violated Ginka's privacy.

Talking helps drown that all out. "We came northeast to get here, so we need to go southwest to get back to *Bluebird*. We'll just keep going, okay? We keep going and… and we get there. Sound good, Cactus?"

Blood trickles from Ginka's split lip as she mutters, "Don't…"

"Nope, we gotta keep going," she says, barreling ahead because she can't stop talking now that she's started, and talking is one of the few things she's sometimes good at. "I know you want to stop; I know it hurts, but you have to keep moving."

"No, not–" A hacking cough sends another burst of panic through Rig's heart. "Don't slow down… for me. I'm not… not worth it. Sorry I can't… can't help you save Daara anymore."

She sets her jaw into a hard line. "Shut up. You're worth it. Just about everyone is."

"I'm supposed… to die." Those words sound more mantra than thought, and the idea of Ginka reciting her death is infuriating. "For… glory of Ossuary."

"Ossuary can fuck right off."

Ginka's response is lost in another cough.

"Listen to me," Rig implores her. "I owe you my life and I sure as fuck am not going to drop you like trash because you can't keep up. You took a bullet for me. Not for Ossuary. For *me*. You don't have to die for a faction that doesn't give a damn about you just 'cause you're supposed to or you've been told you have to, okay? *You* made a choice. And you didn't choose what they'd told you to do. Do you know how much that matters?"

"A choice... that killed me. You're not... proving a good point."

"You're not gonna die. I refuse. I am... I am *done* letting Pyrite take people because of me."

Ginka's cough sounds more like a bitter laugh, but before Rig can address it, she finds herself turning a corner and staring at a blocked door.

Decay has sealed the edges, crumbling what must have once been a keypad into a hole in the wall. If she could only go a different way... No, this looks like the straightest route to *Bluebird* that she's seen so far. Nothing in the Throttle is a given, especially in the lower levels that they've tumbled into, and a simple blocked door is hardly the worst threat she could be facing here.

"Alright." She lets Ginka lean against a wall and dusts her hands off. "Give me a sec to get through." The metal is brittle. She shoves her gloved fist through the hole left by the keypad. A few rough edges scrape her skin, drawing tiny beads of blood – nigh invisible against the dirt from the fall and the stains left by holding on to Ginka. She gropes blindly behind the door, accidentally putting her thumb in something slimy, and finds an emergency release handle. It puts up only a token protest and then...

With a screech and a groan, the handle falls off and the door is released, sliding back into the hull of whatever ship they're squatting in.

Although the light from her link pierces only so far into the depths, she thinks she can see the tunnel beginning to widen up ahead. Far less promising is the slight downward slope of the path, leading not towards the higher levels where *Bluebird* sits and waits, but instead deeper into the dangers of the Throttle.

She squares her shoulders. Can't go back. "Onward again?"

No reply is forthcoming.

"Cactus?"

Rig turns around just in time to catch Ginka before the woman smacks into the ground.

Shit. Okay, think... Ginka's still breathing, although when Rig presses her ear to Ginka's chest, it sounds shallow and labored. Still alive. Doesn't seem as though she's lost a ton more blood, given the relative size of the red stain. Why couldn't Rig be a medic, or a librarian – June is such a fountain of knowledge that she's certain June would have some idea of what to do here. Anything would be better than Rig's shitty guesswork.

Damn it. *Damn it*! Why does she have to be so fucking *useless*?

Something blurs her vision as she tries to pull Ginka to her feet. Only when hot tears start to roll down her cheeks does she realize she's crying.

Ginka is so heavy, and Rig is so much weaker than she thought.

She draws in a shuddering, gasping breath and stops herself from retching at the foul air that enters her lungs. Her face is a mess of tears and snot and dirt, and when she tries to wipe it with her sleeve she just smears everything.

"Come on," she says again, to herself as much as Ginka. Her throat is raw and scratchy. "Keep moving."

Ginka's eyes crack open to reveal a sliver of fever-mad and unfocused green. "...Crane?"

Is that another Windshadow rank? The Handlers? They'd all had bird names. "No birds here, Cactus. Just us."

As long as she can keep shuffling along, she can worry

about Ginka's fever later. Delirious and alive is better than fully aware and dead. Keep Ginka awake and walking. One slow, painful step at a time.

Years and years ago, when she'd been very young, she'd fallen ill with neotoma flu. Fever, shakes, vomiting – it'd been horrible. Her mother hadn't been able to risk taking time off work to take care of her. So instead, Daara had been charged with the task, although she'd taken to the role of babysitter with more than a bit of reluctance. They'd drifted apart by then, and so she'd simply sat stiffly by Rig's bed, handing over water and blankets as necessary. And then, when the fever had peaked, Rig had needed something to hold onto, so she'd asked:

Tell me a story?

"Hey, do you want to know about *Bluebird*? Listen to me, Cactus, okay? Just focus on my voice." Perhaps it's her imagination, but she swears that Ginka's next shuffling step is a bit easier. "That statuette I have, the one of Dare of the Spire and his lover, Shen. There's a story behind that."

She pushes a door to the side and begins.

"Dare started out as an indentured, just like I did, in the slums of Kashraa during the initial Pyrite Invasion, five thousand years ago. But he was clever and sly, and he ended up tricking his master into revealing the location of his servitude contract – the secret room where his master kept *hundreds* of contracts. Then he burned down the entire place, stole a ship, and blasted off into the wilds of Kashraa. That was when he named himself."

And when Rig had flown away from Pyrite, she'd chased away her fear and her loss with the story. With the idea of someone standing against Pyrite, wreathed in broken chains and fire, and deciding to name themselves after something that mattered.

"There are hundreds of myths about Dare," she continues. "The most famous is that of Agaraan Spire. He was famous by then, and the one thing standing between him and Kashrini freedom was the Pyrite base of operations – Agaraan Spire. But no one could break into it. He made them think that he was giving up, that he was unarmed, and they just let him in through the front doors. He burned the place down from the inside out. He tricked masters, out-flew Pyrite fleets, and snuck Kashrini rebels into vaults to recover the long-stolen treasures of our people. People like to say that there's a myth for every contract he burned up. One for each person he saved. He and Shen formed a crew of rebels and thieves, librarians and soldiers, inventors and arsonists."

"Are you... an arsonist?"

"Yeah. I am. See, that ship that Dare flew in, the ship that shot through the sky and told every damn Pyrite looking at it that they could never catch him, that ship was known as the *Night Bird*."

Those last two words echo throughout the tunnels.

Eventually the echoes fade into the beat of Rig's determined footsteps and the rasps of Ginka's labored breathing. An old strength sits in Rig's bones, the history in her body waiting to be awoken. Even when she didn't know the tales, they were there. And the first time she heard them, it was as though she saw a version of herself that she wanted to be, and knew the first step on the path towards that Rig. She walked with legs that understood the ground beneath her and saw with eyes that could name every star.

Ginka's head shifts where it leans against Rig's shoulder. "Night... bird. So that's... why they call themselves that."

"White wings and a bird painted on the nose. When I got my ship, the first thing I did was paint a bird on her prow. I painted it blue, exactly the same color as my skin."

"I've always... liked birds."

"Me too. I needed to... needed to *become* the story. I'd done so many horrible things under Pyrite, and when I realized that I couldn't carry on as I had been, I had no other metric by which to measure myself. Dare was a mold. When I was lost, I'd ask myself what he would do. What would someone brave and honorable and cunning do."

It says quite a lot about how far she had fallen when she realizes that after three years, she's still asking the same questions. Only this time she's doing so while staring at the crystal statuette of Dare and Shen.

Is she trying to save Daara because she truly loves her sister?

Or is she doing it because it's what Dare, the hero of every Kashrini story, would do?

At the end of the day, does it matter?

Ginka makes a noise that she likely intended to be a hum but instead gurgles and cracks, and then mutters, "Names…"

"He named himself. I did the same. Traxi stumbled, she made mistakes, she was… flawed. Rig could put that behind her. Rig could be new, a fresh start. I could be who I wanted to be. Not what Pyrite told me to be, not what the circumstances of my birth forced me to be. Just me."

She had left Traxi behind when she burned down her old spire, abandoned her old self to the flames. A phoenicae, from the old legends – a creature with the face of a person and the wings of a bird, bursting into fire only to rise as a newborn from the ashes. Only she's not a phoenicae, not completely. Feathers on her wings are left over from her old body, weighing her down and dragging her backwards. Until Daara is saved, she cannot be completely free.

All she wants is to rip all those old feathers off.

With one hand she shifts a piece of rubble out of the way, and with the other she adjusts Ginka's weight against her. There's a flight of stairs in front of them, winding around a central pillar of some kind. At least the stairs seem to be going in the right direction.

"Tell me a story," she says, giving Ginka a gentle tap on the shoulder. "Come on. Keep talking. You gotta stay awake somehow."

"I... I don't have any stories."

Tell me about your arms. No, that's not... She changes her question. "Tell me about *your* bird. Tell me about Crane."

Getting up the stairs is its own challenge. She has to take each step first and then practically haul Ginka up after her, trying her best not to strain Ginka's injuries in the process while also making sure that Ginka doesn't have to carry too much of her own weight – again, injuries and strain thereof.

"Crane..." The first word is nothing more than a soft exhale before Ginka properly finds her voice. It's a scratchy and broken voice, but it's there, nonetheless. "Crane was my Handler. My Raven. My transgression."

"Because you cared about him?"

"Because I *married* him."

Oh. That makes a *lot* of sense, now that Rig thinks about it. Also, it's pretty fucked up that getting married got her kicked out of Windshadow, but not *that* fucked up compared to the fact that she's pretty sure Ginka didn't get these prosthetics after losing her arms in some accident. Having prosthetics is such a *neat* solution to the whole 'having to carry around a helltech generator' problem; and that neatness, above all else, reeks of faction amorality.

"You must've loved him a lot to risk that."

"Operatives... We're disposable." Blood dribbles down her lips as she talks, a thin line of red painting the corner of her mouth and dragging down her chin until it drips onto the grimy steps. "Cheaper. Lesser than. Crane looked at me like... like I was *worth* something. Worth *everything*. I stumbled into loving him. Didn't even know what it *was* 'til it happened to me. But him... He *chose* to love me. Loved me *on purpose*."

"Sounds like he had his head screwed on straight. Despite all that rubbish Windshadow propagates. You know," she offers, "you could change the favor you want from me. I don't know if I'll have any luck getting you Grace, but I'm good at smuggling people across the galaxy. I could get you to him."

Ginka coughs roughly as she replies, "N-No. If I go back… I *can't* go back. Not yet. I have to figure out… what to do."

"Don't you miss him, though? June's said before that it hurts her when I stay away for too long. Sometimes I can't help it, but I try to be back whenever I can and call when it's safe to send a message. I get why you're choosing to stay away; only don't you think maybe it hurts Crane, too? I'm sure I could get you back to him without that bastard Umbra knowing. You don't have to play by the rules of his damn unicorn hunt."

As much as Ginka's a zealous loyalist, there's got to be a breaking point for her. *Everyone* has a breaking point, even the ones that desperately don't want to admit it.

"Think about it, Cactus," she says as she pulls them up the last two steps. "You can change your favor. What do you *really* want?"

She can feel Ginka growing colder against her. Is that just the chilly air?

Ginka's voice is nearly silent, cracked sob. "I want to go home."

Rig swallows painfully. She makes an aborted movement to June's handkerchief, still tucked safely into her breast pocket, before realizing that she'd just get it irreparably dirty. She can't do that. If she closes her eyes, she imagines that she can smell June's perfume. She wants to go home, desperately wants it, but the image in her mind is incomplete. Home is *Bluebird*. Home is also June. Selfishly, she wants both – *needs* both with a desperate desire that she can't quite repress.

"Okay. I promise." The words reverberate through the collapsed ruin they're standing in. "We'll be back on *Bluebird* in no time, I'll patch you up, and then once we've saved Daara, I'll get you home, you hear me? I *will*."

Silence.

"Cactus?"

She swirls her head around fast enough to crack her neck. Ginka's eyes are shut and sunken into dark sockets, her face sickly pale and sweat-slick. A vein twitches in her forehead. That, and the barely noticeable rise and fall of her chest, are the only signs of life. Rig hastily presses a hand to her forehead, fingers slipping on the sweat, and tries to guess Ginka's temperature.

Cold. Way too cold.

No. No this *isn't* going to happen. Ginka's not going to die. Rig can do this.

She looks forward, into the darkness ahead. The stairs have come out into another hollowed out ship hull, and the thick metal walls have blocked out all chance of moonlight.

And yet in the dark ahead of them, firelight flickers.

INTERLUDE
Names and Numbers

There are very few places in the heart of Ossuary space where true privacy exists. Spirit X-74, as a member of Windshadow, knows better than any civilian just how impossible it is to find a restaurant or park or even a deafeningly loud publica where one can speak with full certainty that what they say will actually remain secret. That rule changes a little when a Handler is involved. Mechanical eyes and ears are still present nearly everywhere, but there is no better way to circumvent a system than to be part of that system. A Handler knows exactly what sections of each planet have no surveillance.

Currently, X-74 is lying down on the back of an open-air skiff, legs crossed and hands tucked behind her head, with complete certainty that no all-seeing eye is watching her.

A canopy of gold hangs overhead, amber-colored leaves glowing with sunlight, the white bark of the trees turning yellow in the light. A summer breeze drifts through the forest that she and Thrush-Seven are resting in, lazily warming her skin and tugging at her hair – No, wait, that's Seven.

She cracks her eyes properly open. "Are you playing with my hair?"

"You *were* falling asleep. I didn't think you'd mind."

"I don't. And there's nothing wrong with me falling asleep. We aren't on mission and it's nice to take the day off for... What are we taking this day off for?"

"Technically, it's for training in forested environments," he cheerfully reminds her.

"Ah, yes. Anyway, I'd rather sleep out *here* than in the Operative barracks. I understand that so many of them work together frequently, and that I've worked with so few of them, and that presumably their stupid pranks are all in good faith – stress relief, that sort of thing – but my fellows can be so... so *rude*."

Seven smiles and shakes his head in sympathy. "The Handler in the barrack next to mine got her keypad combination changed to a string of zeros. She almost broke down her own door before the perpetrators told her."

Even the dumb shit Handlers do is on a different level than the dumb shit Operatives do. "It's such bullshit to deal with. I miss being on a ship. I miss being able to sleep with you instead of being five buildings away."

"About that. I... I wanted to... There's something I wanted to discuss with you. We have been together a year now. Doing... whatever this is."

"Doing it rather well, in my opinion." She recalls the adrenaline-filled, heated aftermath of their last mission. "Unless you're not happy with something? I thought, since our mission performance improved drastically... Am I doing something wrong?"

"No, no, of course not. This isn't related to that." He takes a deep breath. "I want you to know who I am. All of who I am. Not just... I want you to know my name."

Oh.

Oh.

That's... She doesn't know how to respond to that. He's a Handler; him knowing his name isn't forbidden. Surely he can tell whoever he wants, right? Surely he won't mind that she can't give him her name in return?

"However," Seven continues, "I realized that if I told you my name and you had nothing to tell me in return, it wouldn't be… even. I don't want there to be that imbalance between us. So I snuck a look at your file."

Her eyes are wide open now. "You–" Her jaw isn't quite working properly. "You stole it."

He stole her name. *Hers*. What would that even be like? Part of her – most of her, on days when she's with Seven – knows that she's a person, that she's not just the weapon Windshadow made her into. That knowledge has always felt sort of secret, something that is just between Seven and her, and having a name – her name – feels like it would solidify that, somehow.

Indisputable proof that she's an *actual person*.

"I didn't *steal* it – I'm good, but that's not my specialty. I was only able to catch a quick peek. And I was going to let you choose," he continues hastily. "If you wanted to know your name or not. I know that it's… a risk, and I wasn't going to force that choice on you, but–" He looks away from her, staring morosely at a patch of forest. "You don't have a name. It seems as though you were either brought into Windshadow before your birth parents could give you a name, or it was never added to your file."

"Oh."

She hates herself for the disappointment she feels. It was foolish of her to have gotten her hopes up in the first place. Of course *she* doesn't have a name – her, the *Zazra*, not a human like Seven, not important enough for a name.

"But," here he perks up, "I figured that's no reason for you not to have a name. If you want one. I brought a number of books with me today. Some are novels with interestingly named characters, some discussing Zazra naming conventions, and a few are historical in case you wanted to name yourself after someone important."

"Seven…" She tries to block out the memories from that horrible clean-up mission. "If you do this, we can't undo it. How do we not end up like… like Erian and Wei did?"

"They screwed up a mission. Our performance in the field

has been flawless for a year now. There's no reason for any Controller to come after us if we continue to excel."

True. "May I ask your name first?"

"Crane." He laughs and explains, "Since our caretakers knew that we were being raised to become Handlers, bird names were considered auspicious. You have no idea how many friends I had named Hawke or Robin."

She hums, considering the tune of it. "Crane. It suits you."

"Thank you." He tucks a strand of dark hair behind his ear and smiles with a touch of nervousness. "I'd hoped that it would still fit me, after everything."

Crane. She rolls the name around in her mind and finds that it's an easy name to smile to, the *a* tugging naturally at her lips, the *c* sounding like the start of a kiss.

What does she want to name herself?

Because she *does* want a name. She wants to have what he has, she wants to stand on equal footing next to him, she wants to be able to give him all of herself in return. The idea of naming herself after someone else, be it a character or a historical figure, doesn't really appeal to her. It might be selfish, but she doesn't want to share. A Zazra name, then? Perhaps, but she doesn't know anything about being a Zazra, not really. She wasn't raised as a Zazra, and all she knows about being one is what she can do with her hands, and that is something she has only recently begun to explore.

She wants to name herself after a feeling. After the warmth on her skin and Seven – *Crane* at her side.

A star-shaped leaf flutters down from the trees above to land gently on her chest. Absently, her fingers pick it up, turning it over, the light beaming through the golden leaf, illuminating each and every vein that runs inside it. Ephemeral, yet no less beautiful for it.

A single, perfect ginka leaf.

CHAPTER SEVENTEEN
A Night Bird

Rig stumbles toward the firelight with renewed desperation, increasingly aware of just how cold Ginka is getting. Ginka is in her arms now, no longer responding, no longer able to take even the smallest of steps. Even though she can count Ginka's ribs by feel, it's shocking how heavy the Zazra is, Rig's back bowing beneath the weight.

As she gets closer, the firelight solidifies into a campfire, and the warm orange glow it casts pulls shapes out of the darkness. A large frigate is squatting by the fire, gangplank down and engines cycling through a low power sequence, judging by the sound. Figures sit around the campfire. Some small enough to be children, some tall as grown adults.

Another few steps closer and the fire reveals that the people are all wearing headscarves.

They're all Kashrini.

All the air seems to sink out of her in one great exhale. She's barely aware of putting one foot in front of the other. One moment she's staring at the campfire in the distance, and then next she's almost falling to her knees in front of her fellows.

Her head tilts up to face a man standing in front of her.

The man is easily a foot taller than her, skin a shade more purple toned than hers, and a scar running across his cheek. His hands brush over the grip of a sawed-off shotgun strapped to his thigh. A few of the others behind him reach for weapons, as well – she imagines that the grimy nature of her and Ginka's appearance doesn't exactly endear them.

"*Who*," he demands, "are *you*?"

"I'm Rig." Her hands tighten around Ginka's body. "My friend's named Ginka. Please, we need help."

None of them stand down. "Everyone running around the Throttle needs help. Half of them would sell us out for a single kydis."

Even Ginka's injuries don't prevent them from being potential threats. It's not as though any faction is above damaging their own people to get a leg up on the competition.

"*Please*," she begs, tears stinging her eyes.

She sticks out her bloodied and bruised left forearm.

The man's eyes slowly widen, and she can see him reevaluating her, taking in the absence of Rig's headscarf, the Zazra stripes on Ginka's cheeks. He grabs Rig's elbow, locking her arm into place as he pulls her glove out of the way. Under the layer of grime is her tattoo, still visible, peeking out through flecks of dirt and red smears. The white ink shimmers in the firelight.

"Nightbird, huh?" He gestures over his shoulders to one of his fellows. "Aazi, help me get them to the medbay."

Rig's body slumps. "Gods, thank you, *thank you*–"

"You can thank me once we've stabilized your friend."

He turns on his heels and ushers them up the frigate's gangplank. The woman he'd gestured to before follows. As soon as they're onboard, a susurrus of chatter spreads through the group behind them. Whatever. It stings to have her own people question her, but it's understandable. She'll put up with a lot worse if it means saving Ginka.

Aazi rushes in front of them and leads them through the ship's halls until they stop in front of white medbay doors. The woman punches in a keycode and the doors open, the sterilized smell of chemicals seeping out.

"Put her down on the table," Aazi says in a flat, no-nonsense tone. "Tell me what hit her."

"Pyrite slug. Sniper."

Rig does as she's told, laying Ginka carefully down on the starched surgical table. The man that brought them here lingers at the doorway while Aazi takes point, snapping a pair of white plastic gloves on and donning a polished veneer of professionalism. A neat sweep of her hands lays out a gleaming array of surgical tools, and then it seems as though she's ready to get to work.

"Pyrite, huh?" Aazi comments as she picks up a pair of scissors. "This looks like a nasty stomach wound – frankly, I'm shocked she's not dead."

So is Rig. "I… I tried my best to keep her alive."

"Not a bad bandage job. Hm. I'll have to scan the area and dig the bullet out. It's likely that the hard light is still in one piece, so it should be a clean removal." She frowns at Ginka's arms and touches the metal with the tip of her finger. "Hope all this won't interfere with scans. Do you have much experience with this sort of thing? If you think you're going to be sick, you should leave."

"I used to be indentured under Pyrite," she says, unconsciously bringing a hand up to rest over the scar on her stomach. "Cut my tracker out with a knife and a swallow of booze."

"Ah, I suppose you have quite the constitution, then."

The last of Ginka's shirt falls away. Aazi takes a washcloth and methodically wipes the blood off, pushing the ruined fabric off Ginka's torso. She grabs a scanner, quickly running it over her. There's a beep, and then, a moment later, a second beep.

"Found the slug. She indentured, too?"

"No… Why?"

"She's got a chip."

Names may change, but all factions are the same.

This, at least, does not really surprise Rig. She presses her eyes tightly shut for a moment, and when she opens them, she knows that she'll have an easier time cutting out Ginka's tracker than she did cutting out her own. And this time they even have a medic. Score.

"Once she wakes up, let's ask her if she wants it out."

Aazi looks at the scanner again. "Unless you're a medical genius, we can't get that out. It's in her damn brain."

Perhaps her earlier assessment was wrong. Although their methods are similar, it seems as though Ossuary's claws dig deeper than Pyrite's. In Ginka's brain... Hm. Rig wonders if that's connected to how she controls her helltech. Must be... there doesn't seem to be a manual activation that she's noticed.

"I'll have to ignore it for now." Aazi puts the scanner down and holds out a gloved hand to the stoic man. "Ditra, pass me the forceps."

It turns out that Rig's earlier assessment was wrong.

She has no squeamishness issues with gross blood and guts. She'd managed to get her own tracker out just fine after all, and she'd been panicked, but not puking her guts out, while dragging Ginka through the Throttle.

What she *does* apparently have a problem with is *sterile* blood and guts.

As soon as Aazi starts methodically opening Ginka up to get at the hard light bullet, Rig finds herself snapping straight back to her Pyrite days. To the corpses they'd asked her to look at, to see where her inventions could be better at killing, better at sheer *destruction*. The smell of latex and the cleanliness of the metal tools is far too close to neat Pyrite labs. She's nearly sick on the pristine medbay floor.

She wimps out in half a second and faces the wall while Aazi works. It's totally a fascinating wall. A funny spot on it looks like a dancing kajik fish.

There's a *squelch*. Ginka moans in pain.

Focus on the fish, Rig.

She kinda dissociates for a bit.

Sometime later – she's not sure when – she's drawn back to reality by Ditra shoving something in her face.

"Here," he says in a gruff tone. He gives the object a shake. "For you."

It's a headscarf. A deep purple scarf that's not all too different from the one she had been wearing previously – albeit dirtier and rougher around the edges. She hastens to wrap it around her head. The moment the fabric settles against her skin, comfort sinks into her like a cloud of warmth.

"Thanks. Nice to meet you, by the way."

"Hm." Is that an agreeing grunt or a disgruntled grunt? "Nightbird, huh?"

"Yeah. Any of you lot are?"

He sticks out his left forearm and tugs his sleeve back to reveal an identical tattoo.

"So, uh," she asks, "where you running from?"

Ditra gives her a long, hard look. "...Pyrite. Trying to head to the border of Ascetic and Ossuary from here. Strip of spacedocks and moons. No one looks too close there. You know how it is."

"Do I ever," she dryly remarks. "If you ever need help, I work with a guy named Mohsin. We run jobs in a section of space from the Dead Zone all the way up the Pyrite-Ascetic border."

"Maybe."

"I'm just saying. Mention my name to him and he can help you out. That's all."

"Hm."

Wow. She's never met anyone more loquacious. But she greatly appreciates the distraction.

There's a clatter of tools and she turns in time to see Aazi put down the last of her sharp-looking instruments. Ginka's still lying on the bed, breathing finally steady.

"She's stable," Aazi declares. "I've sealed the wound and given her enough of a uni-blood transfer for her to no longer be in the danger zone. She'll have some aches and bruises, but nothing more. Should wake up in a few minutes – I had to administer something to block out the pain and keep her woozy, but there's some weird drug in her system that's burning through everything I've been giving her."

"Can I wait here for her to wake up?"

"Sure. I'm gonna go grab some dinner. Yell if you need anything. Ditra?"

He shrugs. "Suppose I could eat."

They troop out and Rig wanders over to the side of the medical bed, pulling over the single metal chair in the room and carefully perching on the seat.

Now that Ginka's no longer quite as covered in blood, and the initial shock of her gruesome prosthetics has worn off, Rig can take a moment to actually *look* at Ginka. White bandages cover most of her torso, red staining underneath them, but not nearly as bad as it was before. A medley of scars pattern what little of Ginka's skin she can see, from thin lines on her collarbone to a pale, bullet-sized circle on her lower belly.

Through all this, Rig finds her eyes being drawn to the string around Ginka's neck. Just a simple cord of leather from which a tiny glass jar hangs. Inside the jar is a red flower, the color of a pure ruby, its petals dried and pressed. Perfectly preserved.

Pristine, next to the gnarled flesh where her prosthetics attach.

On Tides, the Windshadow Operatives had been using helltech, too, but not like this. A sword, a baton – all connected to the blood stream through a power generator. They were *weapons*. *External* weapons. Not parts of the body.

Which means that Ginka didn't only have her arms chopped off for no good reason, oh no, although that alone would be enough to make Rig pissed off as all get out. No, what's making her truly simmer inside is that someone chose. Someone looked at Ginka, a Zazra, and decided to cut off her arms. They thought about her empathic abilities, about her ability to *feel*, and they decided that Ginka was better off without it.

Rig's hands curl into trembling fists.

A muffled groan emanates from Ginka's form.

"You're awake!" Rig instantly tones down the volume as Ginka winces. "How do you feel?"

Ginka pushes herself up with a grimace. "Shockingly, I feel as though someone shot me."

"I can't fathom why that might be."

"Hah hah," she mutters, but Rig swears that her eye roll is more fond than annoyed.

Rig sort of pats Ginka on the foot – the nearest part of Ginka bit that she can easily reach. "Don't almost die again, okay? I didn't know what to do, and... and *please* don't take anymore bullets for me. I mean, obviously I'm thrilled that I'm alive, but I don't want you to get hurt because of me."

"I will attempt to keep that in mind, should you be shot at in the future."

"Good, given that being shot at seems likely."

"Rig..." Ginka hesitates, hands tightening around fistfuls of sheet. "Thank you. For saving my life."

"You're very welcome."

"And about my... you saw my... Before you get any misconceptions, you should know that despite what you might think about my prosthetic arms, they are highly effective weapons that enhance my combat performance far better than my previous external helltech manipulators did. They're useful and they make me a better weapon, and they aren't–"

"I'm not going to judge you for what Windshadow did to you, but you have *got* to stop trying to justify their bullshit. You're seriously telling me you're *happy* they chopped your arms off?"

Ginka gets very quiet and then changes the subject with less subtlety than a person yelling 'let's change the subject.' "It doesn't matter. We need to move as soon as we can. Who knows when Janus will find us again."

"About that... I think he's Windshadow. Or a former one. Like the ones we met on Tides." She gestures to her neck. "When we fought, I caught a glimpse of his tattoo. But it wasn't like D-39's, it was only the number fifty, spelled out in letters, not numerals. And then there's that scar of his – right where Thrush-Eleven had her fancy link."

"Only Handlers have unlettered numbers," Ginka confirms. "He must have… he must have done something *terrible* for them to remove his link permanently instead of simply deactivating it. I don't want to imagine what that must have been like…" She presses the back of her hand against her mouth, eyes wide with horror.

Wonder what Janus did that was so bad. If Ginka got kicked out for getting married, maybe Janus had a bunch of kids or something. No, on second thought, there's no possible way a guy like that had kids. Or if he did, he'd be that shit dad that packs his bags and heads for open space on day one.

"He's on this unicorn hunt for me." Rig sinks into the uncomfortable chair. "Fucking *spectacular*."

"He must have infiltrated PI after being forced out so that he could utilize their resources, adding them to what he learned as a Handler."

Only he must have still been using Windshadow's resources, too. Because he was talking with Umbra, *getting* something from Umbra. He had some way of finding the other unicorn hunt agents and getting them to Tides, but there was something else that Umbra mentioned giving him…

"When Janus was talking to Umbra," Rig says, working through the puzzle of it aloud, "he mentioned getting something. Something, something… tracking codes for someone called X-74. And the other agents, I think. He must have summoned them to Tides, eliminating his competition. Actually, I think that he's still in league with Umbra, or maybe he's just the guy's favorite horse in the race."

Ginka slumps. "*Shit*."

"Yeah, it fucking sucks–"

"Not that. I know how he's been finding us," she admits. "Lord Umbra sent him *my* tracking code."

"For... for the chip? In your brain?"

"I haven't got more than one."

How would *she* know if she did... the severity of what Ginka's saying suddenly washes over her like cold winter rain. "Oh. Shit."

"He hasn't been tracking you. He's been tracking *me*."

In her three years on the run from Pyrite, she'd never once slipped up, or so she'd thought. She'd thought that she *must* have fucked up somehow to allow PI to finally pin her down, but no. They never found *her*. If she hadn't happened to be in the same place as Ginka at the same time...

"He didn't track you to Red Dock. He was tracking *me*, and I happened to end up on the same spacestation as you. Same thing happened on the Ascetic homeworld." She presses her eyes tightly shut. "I'm sorry. If it hadn't been for me, none of this would have happened to you."

If Ginka had shuffled off to some other corner of the galaxy, then Rig would still be undiscovered, free to... free to keep running. Free to let them hold onto Daara as their rainy-day hostage. What kind of freedom is that, really?

"They'd still have Daara," she says quietly. "Even if I'd never met you, they'd *still* have Daara and they'd *still* have found a way to use her to get me and the schematics."

"It might be prudent," Ginka begins, "for you to leave me here and–"

"Shut up, I'm not doing that. Give me a few hours and I might be able to cobble together something to block the signal from that chip in your brain. We must be safe here because we fell so far down into the Dead Zone that all signals in this area are scrambled by the bullshit radiation on this planet." Hopefully. "Bet Janus is waiting for us to rear our heads instead of going into this mess to catch us."

"That's a risk you can't–"

"I told you to shush. I don't know how you did things under Windshadow, but I don't leave people behind to die just because they might be a liability. There," she says before Ginka can respond, "that's settled. Do you feel okay to stand up? How are you feeling, by the way?"

"Sore, but little else. I don't normally trust these sorts of medics, but Aazi did an acceptable job. So long as I don't attempt to use my abdominal muscles overmuch, I should be fine."

"Good. Let's go outside and get you some dinner. Aazi and Ditra mentioned food."

The rumbles and gurgles emanating from Ginka's stomach are loud enough for Rig to hear them. "Dinner would be nice," Ginka sheepishly admits.

CHAPTER EIGHTEEN
Campfire Stories

The Kashrini group – plus Ginka – are all eating, sitting around the fire, the susurrus of low chatter filling the air.

Rig feels oddly disconnected from it all. Stuck in that slump, the low after having a ton of adrenaline leave her, yet not quite at the point where the next wave of panic starts the process all over again.

The transponder is still in her vest pocket and her hands turn over Daara's pin. A bit of red is smeared over the plastic. Her thumb rubs at it until it's gone and then keeps rubbing, worrying at it like an infected tooth. All she's holding onto are pieces. A pin. A transponder. Her guns and the schematics within them.

It feels like she's sitting at her workbench, staring out at the parts in front of her, knowing what goes where, but once the parts are in her hands she finds that they don't slot together in the way she'd thought they would. Rough edges scratching at each other and cutting into her fingers when she tries to make it all fit. Only if she gets this puzzle wrong, it won't just be herself getting hurt. If she fails to save Daara then she'll have let her sister die *and* dropped the schematics into PI's hands – even if they don't know what form they've taken.

She tucks the pin away and retrieves her link to type out a message to June.

'*I'm alive*', she writes, and '*I love you.*'

Signal in the Dead Zone ranges from tricky to nonexistent, and there's obviously very little way to connect to the netspace here; but if Rig queues up the message now, then it'll automatically send whenever there's even the slightest blip of a signal.

"I think that's enough," Aazi tells Ginka. She yanks the plate of food out of Ginka's hands and passes it to one of the other Kashrini – an older woman who scrapes the meat onto a young child's plate. "Graftgel can only do so much, and if you eat much more you're going to strain all those newly healed bits of stomach."

Rig tilts her head up from her link and tries to smile. "She's got a point, Cactus. Don't want to pop open like a sausage."

"That," Ginka pointedly remarks, "is a disgusting image."

"I'm glad to know I haven't lost my touch for poeticism."

Rig clips her link back to her wrist and picks up her now-busted scanner. It hadn't done well in the crash, and it's mostly a ruined hunk of parts. Which is exactly what she needs right now. A series of odds and ends and tools sit by her feet, helpfully provided by Ditra. She leans back against the warped piece of junk metal that's serving as a bench for some of the younger kids and starts to salvage what she can from the scanner.

There's got to be something here that she can use to block the signal from Ginka's transmitter chip. Does she have enough for a signal dampener or maybe a counter frequency? It'll be difficult to do anything too wide scale, but it'll keep them from being hunted down.

Diagrams and wire patterns flit through her thoughts as she sorts through what she's got. A necklace design of some kind, perhaps? That could keep a dampener close to the chip in Ginka's head.

Footsteps scuff on the metal next to her. Ditra has decided to stand at her side, arms crossed and eyes staring out at the group of refugees.

"Can I help you?" she asks tentatively.

"Pyrite sent snipers after you."

"Yes, I was there."

"Don't normally do that. Only if their target's real important. What'd they want from you?"

The meager amount of dinner she'd eaten turns into a brick in her stomach. They want the lives of every single Kashrini sitting around her. Not specifically. Her own life, Daara's life – those they quantify. Everyone else is just a casual bonus. They're at a buffet where a few dishes have gone off and so they sweep the whole affair into the garbage.

"I stole something, and they want it back," she ends up saying. Simple. Not too much information. Not knowledge that would endanger him. "Pyrite in a nutshell, isn't it? We'll be heading back to my ship as soon as there's light, so don't worry about them coming here."

"We can give you a ride."

"You don't have to do that."

"Your friend is still weak. Shouldn't be walking as far as you'd need to walk."

"...Suppose you're right. Thank you, really. I know you have troubles of your own."

"Doesn't everyone?"

"True."

Ditra eventually goes away after a child tries to treat his leg like a climbing pole, leaving Rig in relative peace to continue work on her signal-blocker-dampener-counter-signal device. Hm, she thinks she'll call it... Sparkle.

Sparkle is coming along swimmingly as the fire starts to die down, the cluster of people thins out a bit as some go into the ship to sleep, and some of the children fail at smothering yawns. There are only a handful of tweaks left before she can sync it up with her link and begin the reprogramming process.

In the soft quiet, she can easily hear it when a young boy asks, "Mamazhi, tell us another story?"

Someone laughs at the boy's insistence. Ginka tilts her head up.

Sitting in a place of honor near the fire is an old woman dressed in midnight blue. Lines crinkle around her eyes in the written memory of a thousand smiles, and a pair of spindly glasses is perched precariously on her nose. Two children bounce at her feet with exited expectation.

"Ah," the Mamazhi says. Her voice is the wind through twisted ship beams, creaking and smooth at the same time. Mamazhi is not a name. It's a title. Rig supposes the closest translation would be 'grandmother,' but being a Mamazhi has nothing to do with family relation to anyone. It's being everyone's grandmother, all the time. "Since we have guests, why don't you ask them if they would care to receive a tale or two?"

The boy who initially asked turns to Rig. "Wanna story?"

She gives the boy a thumbs up. Anything to distract herself from the million problems looming over her head. "I'd love one."

"Then I ask for your attention." Mamazhi straightens up in her seat, making her short frame tower over all of them. "I give you this story so that you may see the galaxy as no faction wants you to see it.

"Ten thousand years ago, a star fell into our galaxy. On this star were three old beings and with them they brought humanity. They had torn the star apart in a never-ending battle between the three, and by the time the star tumbled here it had been burnt out almost entirely, clinging onto the last scraps of life. Once it crashed into our galaxy, the three groups of humans broke their star up into pieces and spread out from world to world. The pieces of the star were kept as trophies, and eventually they were worn down over the millennia until nothing of them remained."

"That's not true," Ginka protests, "Ossuary still has a shard. We *do*. It's still around."

Mamazhi simply stares at Ginka.

Eventually silence reins once more, and she continues as though there had been no interruption at all, "Those three factions brought war and domination to our galaxy. For their banners and sigils, they named themselves after their dead gods and honored them in worship.

"Pyrite, the burning machinator. Ascetic, the merciless thorn. Ossuary, the soul swallower.

"While it's not known why the three originally warred on their dying star, it *is* known why their war continued once the star burnt out. You see, to the humans, only one of their apparent gods survived the collapse, and only one of them went on to have children that are supposedly destined to rule over all things. However, none of them could decide which of those gods lived and which of them died. They argued and fought and eventually started a war which they declared would only end once a true god had been declared.

"And that is why we live under a sky filled with warships, my children, that is why our planets are steeped with poison."

"But which of them was *right*?" the young boy asks.

Mamazhi leans forward in her seat. Her eyes twinkle and shimmer in the firelight.

"And that," she tells him, "is their greatest trap."

Embers snap and crackle in the dying blaze as the pile of trash they've been using as fuel shrinks. Rig can see three sigils in the twisting fire – the flaming gear of Pyrite, the jewel and laurel of Ascetic, and the all-seeing eye of Ossuary.

Ginka gets to her feet, her shoulders trembling. "You're wrong. That's not how it happened; that's the *wrong* version. Ascetic and Pyrite want to wipe us out because they want our shard of the star for themselves, because they're jealous–"

"And you know that because…?"

"Because *I* was told the *right* version, and Ossuary has a fragment of the star, that's our proof–"

"Has Ossuary always had it?"

"Of, of course!"

"Were you there ten thousand years ago?"

Whatever question Ginka was about to ask next is lost, her jaw snapping shut and her pupils narrowing into angry slits. Rig braces for the series of accusations that she worries might be coming, and then, to her surprise, Ginka drops the argument.

Instead she storms off into the night.

"Damn it," Rig mutters, and then to the Mamazhi, she adds, "I'm sorry. Please excuse me."

She tucks a mostly finished Sparkle into her pocket and sprints to catch up to Ginka.

By the time she gets to Ginka's side, the two of them are a good bit away from the group, the frigate's form blocking most of the golden campfire glow. Earlier blood loss has left Ginka's face looking pale, the dark color of her hair and her facial markings blending into the night and leaving behind a cutout of her brown skin. Bit eerie, in Rig's opinion – probably par for course with assassins, or Operatives, or whatever.

"You didn't need to be rude," she says gently.

Ginka glares at her. "She was *wrong*. Ossuary survived, Ossuary is the true ruler of this galaxy, Ossuary was *right*."

"And you're sure about that?"

"*Yes*. And maybe I wasn't there ten thousand years ago to see it with my own eyes, fine. But neither was she and neither were you, so how do you know any better?"

Maybe they don't. The version they just heard is the version that Rig's known for years now. The version that she believes to be true. Still, she knows that all the stories have holes in them, given how old they are and how many people have told them over the years. It's almost impossible that information wasn't lost.

"Fine," she agrees. She spreads her palms out and shrugs. "I'll buy that. Maybe we don't know any better. Does it matter?"

Ginka gapes. "Does it… Of course it matters!"

"Why? It was ten thousand years ago. Whoever theoretically *did* survive the star's crash is long dead now. They're not exactly going to be resurrected. Who knows if any of it was real? I don't think it matters. Whoever lived or died, their followers are killing people. That matters more than any bullshit destiny excuse they might try to justify their actions with."

"But, but we have proof! Our war is just! We have a shard of the star. We have our immortal King Tenus, blessed with long life–"

A bitter laugh sneaks out of Rig's throat even though she tries to smother it. "Tenus isn't blessed with some miraculous longevity. It's a bunch of different guys that they swap out each time the current guy starts to get older looking. It's the same schtick as the other factions. Ascetic's shamans are just two people who make stuff up and pretend they heard it from Ascetic themself. Pyrite's Council are hardly direct descendants of Pyrite themselves; if you actually look at the bloodlines, none of the current Council are related to *any* of the Council from ten thousand years ago – fuck, not even related to the guys *one* thousand years ago."

"No," she insists, almost desperately, "No, if... if King Tenus was being replaced, we would have noticed. Windshadow notices everything."

"Do you?" 'Cause that doesn't sound physically possible, and she thinks that Ginka knows that, although she might not want to admit it. "Or do you only notice the things that you're told to notice?"

"That's not the point and you know it! I am not going to be like you – like the rest of them! I am *not* ex-factioned, I am *loyal*. I'm not a traitor to my faction like *you*. Why do you... why do *all of you* choose to leave your factions? Pyrite wasn't right, obviously, but they're better than living on the fringes of society, squatting in ruins and running from everything."

Is that what Rig's doing? Fringes of society. She doesn't really think about it like that. Sure, she does sort of live in the grey areas of the galaxy, but there's often more society and culture in the middle ground than there is in the center of factioned star systems. What's left of Kashrini culture can't thrive on the Pyrite homeworld; they've taken to the in-between zones to survive. Places like Red Dock, or the collection of less strict systems, or even the damn Dead Zone.

Hadn't Ginka just *seen* that? *Heard* that? Stories like that can't be told in factioned star systems.

Rig forces herself not to get pissed. She can't cause another argument here. She needs Ginka to save Daara and she needs Ginka to fucking *understand*. "Indulge me for a couple of questions, okay? Do you think that Pyrite and Ascetic are right?"

"Of course not! Ossuary is the only one with the true right to rule."

"So Pyrite and Ascetic are totally wrong heathens."

"Yes."

"So *I'm* a totally wrong heathen because I'm not under Ossuary rule."

"That's not... well, *yes*."

"So," she continues pointedly, "by that logic, I'm just as wrong about this as Pyrite and Ascetic, right?"

"Yes."

"So then why is my way of living *worse* than if I were under Pyrite's heel?"

"I–" Ginka snaps her mouth closed. "Well... I suppose..."

"See, here's what I think, Cactus. You know that according to those rules, *logically* I'm exactly as incorrect as Pyrite and Ascetic. Everyone who rejects Ossuary as the one true ruler of everything should be just as wrong, just as unlawful, just as despicable. But the real reason why you think I'm worse than the other two factions is because no matter how theoretically wrong they are, they're still part of the same system. They play by the same rules. And I don't."

In the span of seconds, Ginka goes from slack-jawed

confusion, to tense fury, and to a pained wince when she draws too deep a breath and presumably strains her sore muscles.

Rig shoves her hands into her pockets. "That's why Nightbirds are hated by *everyone*. We're outside it all. And I think it scares you, because you'd rather it be black and white. Factions good, outsiders bad."

"I…" Ginka's mouth twists into a series of squiggly lines as she stares at the fire. "I don't *want* things to be otherwise," she says quietly, "I wish… I wish I was *blind*."

Rig sighs. "Cactus… Whatever you want to believe, you can't ignore the fact that people all over the galaxy are getting seriously hurt because of this petty squabble over something that, honestly, is totally meaningless in the long run."

"I can't just get up and walk away from my faction because I believe something different than what they believe. I have a life there, I have… I have someone there who I… I can't abandon that. I can't make that meaningless. That's true regardless of what else I think."

If only things were that simple. Rig had a life under Pyrite, too. She had a home that was relatively safe and a sister that she loved, and that's a good life, isn't it? That checks the boxes on a list. It's just that to her, what she *believes* is more important than some list. Standing with conquerors and killers because she happened to be born under their banner and live under their rule for so many years isn't a choice she was willing to keep making. It'd hadn't felt like much of a choice at all to her, not really.

Rig inhales a long, dragging breath. Then she lets it go. "If that's your choice."

"Thank you." Ginka sighs, shoulders sagging as the anger seeps out of her. "I know we're different but I… I do respect you. I hope you know that."

A frozen little shard inside Rig's chest melts. Her entire body sags. She didn't even know that she needed to hear that until Ginka said it. Like not knowing that she's hungry until she smells food. A tiny part of her soul, a part of her that she suddenly realizes is *starving*, whispers at her: *Daara never said that.*

She has no idea how to reply, and instead pulls out Sparkle. "Here. I cobbled something together for you."

Ginka takes it as though it's a live bomb. "And this is...?"

Sparkle, in its almost finished glory, is an approximately choker-length necklace. It's a circle of wires with a massive mechanical clasp at the back that emits a signal-dampening field. Slapdash work, but it'll hold.

"That's your newest accessory," she says, pointing out how the clasp works so that Ginka can put it on properly. "It's going to stop Janus from tracking your signal, but it's temporary. If my theory is right, and the chip in your brain is also what lets you connect with and manipulate your helltech, then this may interfere with that. Fair warning. Either way, you'll only need to wear it while we make our way to the PI headquarters. After we arrive, you should be in the clear to take it off."

Ginka's lips press into a thin line. "It'll do."

There's only a handful of people in the galaxy who could pull off something like Sparkle using the time and parts Rig managed with. Ginka's not a techie though, so she'll accept the lack of fawning and bootlicking.

She pats her vest over the pocket that contains the transponder. "We've got everything we need now. Ditra says they can give us a ride back to *Bluebird*, and once we're there we'll be heading to wherever PI has decided to stash their headquarters. Then we sneak in, jailbreak Daara, and get out before they can stop us."

Then she will finally be free of Pyrite for good.

Starter blocks are being added to the fire when Rig returns, Ginka following her like a morose shadow. A few of the younger kids are passed out, sleeping on parents' laps or just sprawled out in front of the fire.

"Back?" Ditra asks, crossing his arms. "Good."

"You guys okay to fly us?"

"Better sooner than later." He jerks a thumb towards the ship and it's a struggle to keep pace with his long strides up the gangplank. "No signal here – group should be safe while we give you a lift."

Ditra and Aazi fire up the frigate's engines and cart Rig and Ginka across the Throttle to *Bluebird* with the practiced efficiency that only comes from having been here a thousand times before. They must make a lot of runs through here. Not surprising. There's a lot Nightbirds can do near the front lines to fuck shit up.

It's a short flight, for which Rig is eternally grateful. As much as she loves being around her people again, she misses her ship. She misses being able to talk to June. She misses Daara.

Or she misses the idea of Daara. The concept of her sister.

Landing in front of *Bluebird* adds a good ten years to Rig's life, or at least that's how she's choosing to interpret the soaring sensation in her chest. The other option is that it's some weird lung problem caused by inhaling the foul air here, and she doesn't really want to think about that.

"Thank you so much for all you've done," she says to Aazi and Ditra as they stand on the frigate's gangplank. Ginka's a bit behind them, taking some initiative and removing the shield generators from *Bluebird*'s hull. "Really. You didn't have to."

Aazi dismissively flaps hand. "Oh please. We're all on the same side. No need for groveling."

To Rig's surprise, Ginka bows deeply from the waist, hands at her sides and back ramrod straight. "Then please allow me to offer *my* gratitude. Thank you, Doctor Aazi, for saving my life. I am in your debt."

"Damn." Aazi reels backwards. "You're an uptight one, aren't you? But you're welcome."

Rig waves goodbye to the two.

She heads across the metal ground and up to *Bluebird*'s entry hatch, placing her bare left hand on the lock and letting the ship scan her print. When the door slides open, it's a welcome home from the one place that's truly hers. She does not look back as she enters.

"Let's get into orbit and then set course," she says.

Ginka vanishes into her room for a moment while Rig heads to the bridge.

Chill has sunken into her ship while she's been gone, and she winces at the kiss of cold leather on her ass when she sits down in the pilot's seat. She draws her hand over the terminal, powering everything up, basking in the familiarity of her home. Lights awaken and wink at her, warmth slowly begins to circulate throughout the ship, and the engines buzz with life. From a compartment underneath the terminal, she retrieves the mess of wires and the bastardized link that Triton made for her before he…

She clears her throat with a rough cough and plugs the link into the terminal, letting the coordinates transfer to *Bluebird*'s systems. Shouldn't take too long. Just enough time for them to get out of atmo.

On the terminal sits the crystal statuette of Dare and Shen. The ship's lights hit it from below, making it sparkle in the darkness of the Throttle. Red shines in the firestone the two crystal figures hold, and in the gloom it's indistinguishable from a live flame.

"About to have a family reunion, and then I'll see you soon, June," she whispers, kissing her fingertips and then resting the kiss atop the crystal sphere. "I promise."

"You will."

"*Damn it*, Cactus, I will make good on that bell idea, so help me."

Ginka just leans against the doorway and ignores her. "Where does Triton's link tell us to go?"

"I don't know," she says, giving the terminal a tap and pulling up a holo screen. "It's sending the coordinates directly to the ship's nav systems; I could muck around with it, but I don't really understand what Triton did, and I don't want the link to think we're attempting to access multiple versions of the coordinates. That might cause a shutdown. We'll find out when we get there, it seems."

"Walking in blind, then?"

Yes, but Rig refuses to think of it like that. If she accepts how hilariously outgunned they are, she'll lose the battle before it's begun. "Not *blind*. We know we're going to them. We know we have the transponder, so they won't shoot us out of the sky or blow up our ship or anything. We know Daara's there. That's a lot of guarantees."

In a roar of power and freedom, Rig takes the helm and steers *Bluebird* up into the sky, away from the Throttle, from Hanera, from the Dead Zone, and towards her sister.

I'm coming for you, Daara, she thinks. *Just hold on a little longer.*

INTERLUDE
Ring of Roses

Sunsets on Kadan-Nine are strangely beautiful.

The planet itself is sort of a dump, but the capital, K-3, is a sleazy, extravagant, gilded explosion of a city, covered from head to toe in sex, drugs, and whatever musty smell chronic gamblers always have lingering on their lapels. When the sun begins to dip low the horizon, it goes down with a symphony of golds and oranges and reds, turning the towering skyscrapers into sharp purplish shadows dotted with glitzy lights from holographic advertisements and flashing signs.

Ginka – who is still getting used to having a proper name – is finding herself oddly fond of the place.

Of course, the view is probably a lot worse from one of the many street levels of the city. But she's lucky enough to have recently broken into a top-floor penthouse suite in order to conduct surveillance. She and Crane have to spend the entire night ensuring that the penthouse remains undisturbed while keeping all eyes on the city block beneath them. Which is basically the most romantic possible mission they could have been assigned. She'd like to thank their Controller, except that would, of course, give them away.

She sits on the balcony railing, surrounded by pots filled to the brim with exotic flowers, petals occasionally drifting to the ground, sweet scents floating through the air. She checks the city square below, waiting for their target to show up.

A pair of binoculars is set up on a tripod in front of her, pointed down at the square. They're hooked up to Windshadow's systems, and it'll pick up the faces passing below better than normal eyes can, run those faces through the database, and tell them if it spots their target – or someone else of import. There are a number of potential enemies on a planet like this and it wouldn't do to miss any.

"Why do you think they're so against all of us factions, anyway?" she idly muses.

"Who?" Crane asks, messing with a weapons crate.

"The Nightbirds."

"The Kashrini object to Pyrite indenturing most of them, right? I've not really read up on their ideology, but I think they don't like being chipped or having to fight in the war or not being allowed to have a say in things."

"That's silly. None of *us* object to that and *we're* fine."

Crane's back is turned to her so she can't see his expression, but she can hear his long silent pause that usually means he's thinking of at least twenty different things to say and stuck on which one to actually voice. "I… guess," he finally decides. "Either way, our target is just a sympathizer selling them information, so none of this is really relevant to our job, is it?"

She shrugs. "True. Odd that we're inadvertently helping Pyrite, though."

"The target is selling *our* information as well. Besides… I've heard rumors from a few of the other Handlers – we're looking to buy something from Pyrite. I don't know what, but it's got to be important if Lord Umbra agreed."

"Or he's playing Pyrite like a fiddle."

Crane laughs without any amusement. "Yeah, that's probably it."

There's another bit of silence and she's not sure exactly what she said that's made him uneasy.

She clears her throat and remarks, "This place has really grown on me."

There's a shift as Crane moves to stand next to her, leaning his back against the railing and giving the city a slightly less than impressed look. The evening breeze gently tugs on his hair, ruffling the dark feather now hanging from the turquoise bead hairpin she gave him so long ago.

A Raven's feather.

She glances over at the weapon crate back inside the penthouse, her mind going to the helltech generators and conductors within.

They've gotten a notice about a weapon's upgrade for her, now that she's a Phantom. Her old models need improvement, apparently, and her mission record has been solid platinum the past two years, a glowing enough record to get her considered for some truly high-end upgrades – although the details have been a bit vague, so far.

Whatever the upgrades are, she's looking forward to them. They're bound to be spectacular.

"It's not as bad as I thought it'd be," Crane eventually decides. "And I appreciate the slower paced mission."

"What will it be like, do you think? Now that you're a Raven and I'm a Phantom. Do we get more decision-making power? I'd love to take missions like this again."

"I'd certainly like to have some say in our jobs – and be able to take more time off after they're done."

"Now you're being unrealistic. Showered in silks and kydis? Easy," she snickers, "But *time off*?"

"We'll find a way to make it work. I can always inflate travel times by a day or so. Spending a bit longer in luminalspace never hurt anyone, so long as we can commandeer transport just for the two of us. Is there something in particular you're worried about?"

"No."

He plucks one of the flowers from the pot next to him, picking the delicate crimson bloom up and winding it into a circle. After a minute of watching him twist it around his finger, she realizes that she was lying.

"Okay," she admits, "I *am* a bit worried. I feel like everything is going *so* well for us. Maybe *too* well. Every mission we take goes more smoothly than the last. We've gotten promoted to the highest ranks we can reach. And I love you more and more each day."

He chuckles. "You've been at my novel stash, haven't you?"

"...Guilty." Some of those books are just too damn good, and she has so many problems with naming emotions and the books are fantastic at explaining that sort of thing. She leans over to briefly peer through the binoculars and glances at the buildings they're supposed to be watching. "I *did* have a point. I'm not used to everything going right. It feels like I'm waiting for the other shoe to drop. And this promotion... I'm glad to give my life and my body for Ossuary's glory, but if I do that... what's left for me to give you?"

"Ginka, paranoia can get you killed. We've been cautious, we've been excelling, we haven't even received a single reprimand in the past two years."

She smiles into the sunset. "True."

"And you don't need to *give* me anything. Just knowing you, loving you..." He lays one of his hands over hers, out of habit making sure that his hand never crosses in front of the netspace-linked binocular lens. "It's enough."

"You flatter me too much." She takes another peek at the city below and laughs. "Looks like another couple of people are entering that tiny, intsa-wedding bethel. Is our target supposed to be heading there as well? Because I'm pretty certain that she was hanging off the arms of a number of very tall and very attractive young women earlier."

"Our Controller certainly thinks so, or else we wouldn't have been posted here."

"Shame she has to be dealt with, er..." she corrects, "Not that I think we're in the wrong here. I don't know... I think it's romantic."

"Spontaneous weddings?"

"Cutting a piece of yourself off and promising it to someone else, instead of to your faction; that level of commitment – maybe I *have* been reading too many of your novels," she adds with a laugh.

He brings their entwined hands up to his lips and presses a kiss to her knuckles. "Who knew you'd be such a romantic. And I get it. That desire to be something other than just what our faction made us. Ossuary may know everything about us, from a clinical point of view, but you know more about me than they ever will."

"I never want to lose this no matter what Ossuary wants," she admits. "I never want to lose you. Is that horrible?"

"I don't think so." He hums and plucks one of the flowers again, a red higan blossom. He circles the stem around his finger and then ties it around the base of the flower, transforming it into a ring. "Funny," he says, holding out his hand to look at the ring, "it's just like that, really. Circular. No matter what happens, I'll keep coming back to you."

"When did you become a poet?" she says with a smile.

"Presumably shortly after I met you and realized that I needed some way to sweep you off your feet." He holds the ring out to her. "For you."

She laughs. "Is that a proposal?"

"Yes."

"What?"

"Marry me."

She carefully sits up so that she can face him properly. She should think about this – marriage is for nobles, for Ossuary's chosen, not for *them* – but there's really only one answer she wants to give, and so long spent with Crane has blurred the moral lines she used to revere. "Yes."

"I'm sure we can leave the room unattended for twenty minutes," he says, grinning and holding out the flower ring. "And besides, we'll have a much better view of the square below from that small bethel. So *technically* we'd still be working."

"Technically."

"We've never been caught on a single lie before."

Before she met him, she'd never have guessed that she'd delight in running circles around her Controller. "What's one more?"

She enthusiastically hops off the railing and turns her hand around so that her palm is flush against her skin, and there's that moment, that contented and all-consuming humming that rolls through him as it rolls through her and as it rolls through the ringing electro-bells of the bethel down beneath them.

In her haste, she forgets about the binoculars pointed at the city square below.

CHAPTER NINETEEN
The Prison

Indistinct colors streak past the viewport.

Rig's laying across the terminal, one finger idly drawing lines on the crystal globe of Dare and Shen, and the other pressed into a flatcake from having her head rest on it for hours. A dry rawness has settled into her eyes from lack of decent sleep, but every time she tries to drift off all she sees is Daara's dead body, floating through the vacuum of space, abandoned and alone, forever waiting for a sister that couldn't get there in time.

There's a *clink*; her vision is suddenly consumed by the large mug that's just been placed in front of her.

"You look like shit," Ginka says.

"You look like you just woke up and are still half asleep," Rig half-heartedly retorts. Her nose twitches in the direction of the mug. "Is that coffee?"

"You need it."

"Did you bastardize it?"

"I made yours plain, if that's what you're asking. It's nothing but coffee. I made a second mug for myself."

A pathetic series of noises escapes her as she pushes herself up and pitifully sniffs the coffee. It doesn't look like Ginka's ruined it, and when she glances over she can see that, sure enough, a second cup is in Ginka's hands.

Rig curls around the coffee, leeching the heat from it, and starts slurping up piping hot sips. "I owe you my life."

"Don't be dramatic."

"Hi Pot, nice to meet you. My name's Kettle."

Quiet, coffee-drinking sounds stretch between the two of them – apparently Ginka has no good response to Rig's excellent point.

Ginka eventually shifts so that she's leaning her hip against the terminal instead of the door. "It's been a long time since you've slept. I know I've been mostly unconscious lately, but you haven't gotten *any* rest, have you?"

"You going somewhere with this or just spouting off facts?"

"I'm asking if you are in a fit state to handle weapons."

"Of course. I'm *fine*. I can do this – and so help me, if you try to call me out on fighting while not in perfect shape, I will kick your ass for being the galaxy's greatest hypocrite, Miss I-Fight-With-Poison-Arms."

"You should rest. Aren't you tired?"

"Of *course* I'm tired," she snaps. "Maybe you can sleep away the days, but not me, alright? I'll rest once I've stopped Pyrite."

Ginka tilts her head to the side. "With regards to Daara or in general?"

"...Both."

"Then you'll never sleep again."

"Better than letting myself fade away, accepting the shit they do to me without even a peep of protest." She sets her empty mug down on the terminal, much more firmly than she'd intended to. "If being tired is what it takes to reclaim everything they've taken, then that's a small price to pay."

Before she can say another word, there's the telltale lurch of her ship dropping out of luminalspace.

She snatches up the statuette and stores it safely in a compartment by her knee, then grabs the controls with one hand and points Ginka to the seat below with the other. "Strap in, Cactus, we're arriving at..."

Outside the viewport floats a small spacestation. There are no noticeable markings on it and there are clear spaces on its hull where weapons systems have been removed. Innocuous and nondescript, it seems to blend into the blackness of space – or it would have if not for the scene behind it.

For the spacestation hovers in front of a mottled green planet and a standing fleet of heavily armed ships guarding the world below.

"*What* are they doing above the *Ascetic homeworld*?"

Ginka's eyes are wide as dinner plates as she stares out at the spacestation. "I... I don't know."

"They haven't fired." Rig's brain is whirling as she runs through everything that might be important. "So the transponder works. Do they think Triton died before we were able to get a location from him?"

"It's possible..."

"And," she continues, babbling out her stream of thought, "we know that they've gained permission from the Ascetic government to have operations on the homeworld before. If they hadn't, they would have been attacked by the Military Police when they chased us down earlier, and their spacestation would currently be blown to pieces. So they're here legitimately."

"I don't think the why matters," Ginka remarks. "PI and Windshadow together could come up with any number of reasons that would persuade Ascetic to turn a blind eye for a brief while. Rare though it might be, it *has* happened before. Better to know where your enemy is than to lose sight of them completely."

"But why *here*, of *all* places?"

"Why don't we go find a PI agent and beat the answer out of them?"

"Good plan. Violent and simple. I could use a bit of violent and simple right now."

Either it's because of the amazingness of her transponder plan, or it's because of a trap, but they're allowed to dock at one of the spacestation airlocks without any trouble.

She'd half been expecting mooring cables to snap out and dig into *Bluebird,* frying their systems and preventing them from leaving until PI agents swarm her ship and take them captive – or do worse. Pyrite always has more tortures hidden up their sleeve. After so long working for them, she knows better than to assume there is a limit to their depravity.

Traps or no traps, she places *Bluebird* on the most secure lockdown she can manage before leaving the ship.

She steps out into the airlock first, Panache and Pizzazz raised and prepared to open fire on any potential threats. Which is basically everyone on board the station, save Daara and themselves. So. No need to be picky about where her bullets end up.

Metal panels clang with each footstep as she and Ginka slowly advance through the airlock. All that's here are empty crates, loose cables, and assorted cargo detritus. No guards with guns, no alarms going off, not even a single person here to greet them.

Which is not how a secret spacestation should be. Every nerve in her body is tensed, poised to spring into action.

A simple tap of the keypad at the end of the airlock opens the door.

She checks right, then left, then steps into the hallway. "Clear."

"This is definitely a trap," Ginka says as she slinks in behind her. "Janus isn't stupid enough for it *not* to be."

Gods, if Daara is already–

"Trap or no trap, it doesn't matter. Daara's here and I'm not leaving till I've got her. Let's get to a computer terminal," she says instead, firmly marching towards a junction up ahead. "We need to know where their cells would be located, and we need to know which one she's in."

More unnerving silence greets them at the junction. Five different corridors branch out from here, each one as deserted as the last.

Rig checks all over before locating a terminal built into the wall. A small tool from her belt will do the job just fine. She cracks open a panel and gets to work. It's not that hard to bypass PI's systems. She's done it before, after all. Although never for stakes this high, and her fingers slip and fumble now, despite normally being steady as an asteroid. It looks like the system is designed to guard most stringently against outside attacks from the netspace – makes sense – and as a result their internal protections are somewhat lacking.

"Okay, Cactus," she mutters, cracking her knuckles and tossing her tool back into its proper place. "Let's see where everyone is."

First things first: security feeds. Can't save Daara if she's about to get shot in the back by guards.

She flips through each holo imaging file – so many security recorders here – until she finally sees something that yields results. And by results, she means people. A group of Pyrite soldiers are on the spacestation's bridge, diligently standing at their posts, and there *are* guards patrolling the bridge entrance, the main engine access points, and a storage room that she'd bet contains weapons.

"Not abandoned. Just short staffed?"

Ginka scoffs. "Pyrite Intelligence isn't stupid enough to have a short-staffed spacestation orbiting around the Ascetic homeworld – even considering the fact that they're allowed to be here."

So then the missing agents are somewhere nearby. "Hiding maybe?"

"Hm. Are you certain Janus didn't know we were coming?"

"He couldn't have. If he knew we were going to walk straight into his trap, he sure as shit would not have sent a bunch of his forces away. He'd be prepping his torture instruments and licking his chops. And probably popping champagne bottles with Umbra or whatever fucked up celebratory shit your organization does."

"Stop rambling and focus. We need your eyes sharp. See if you can pull up any logs. We might be able to find out where he went."

"If you don't mind, I'm going to look for my sister. You know, the person we came here *to rescue*?"

If the missing agents aren't on board the spacestation, Rig isn't going to worry about them just yet. She's got to prioritize. She ignores the majority of the mess of files in their system and zeroes in on a list of prisoner records. There's only one name – her heart leaps in her throat at seeing Daara's name typed out clear as day. A cell number is listed right next to it.

"Cell three." She pulls up a map, memorizes it, and then shuts down the terminal. "I know how to get there. Let's go."

Her usual caution is abandoned as she practically runs through the spacestation. The maps had shown cells five floors beneath where they are now, and from the holographic footage, that area is only guarded by two people. Not a problem.

Spacestations don't have staircases, and the elevators are kill boxes, so Rig gets creative.

"I did this once for a job on Adura," she remarks, babbling nervously while she attempts to pry open the tightly shut elevator. "Had to dead-lift one of my fellow Nightbirds out of some bullshit, booby-trapped hotel. Give me two seconds to get this thing open–"

"Let me."

"You sure? How's your stomach?"

"Perfectly manageable."

Without further ado, Ginka steps forward and slams her metal fingers into the crack between the two doors. The doors twist and bend until she can simply grab both of them and *yank*.

Sparks fly and the metal yields like it's paper.

"I've done this three times," Ginka flatly replies, "Once for intel recovery and twice for assassination."

That's probably better experience, anyway. When Rig did

this, she used a harness and safety lines. Now she's relying solely on her own strength.

She grabs onto the thick steel cables that run through the elevator shaft. The cables are freezing cold and the rough twisted pattern of them digs into her palms. For the first and perhaps only time, she wishes she had Ginka's prosthetics – a thought that promptly dies less than half a second after it's conceived. Below her is the dark, sheer drop of the elevator, her toes hanging off the edge. She takes a deep breath, trusts in her body, and jumps.

Her hands slip on the metal for an instant before her legs are wrapping around the cables, as well, boots locking around it and slowing her temporary slide downwards.

The first jump was the hardest, but not the most nerve-wracking. Her nerves get more and more wracked as she descends closer and closer to where Daara is being held.

Once she's begun to slowly inch downwards, bit by bit like a shimmying insect, it becomes far more a matter of endurance than audacity. Her arms and thighs are used to this sort of strain, although her fingers feel raw and chafed within minutes. Ginka jumps on after she's out of the way and the cable tremors slightly with the impact.

Rig mouths the floor numbers as she passes them.

Seven…

Six…

"Slow down," Ginka cautions, "You'll slip and break your neck."

She doesn't have time to slow down. "That's a me problem, not a you problem."

Four…

Three…

"This is it," she says.

She shifts around so that she can reach Panache and then shoots the control panel near the elevator doors. Something crackles and a faint smell of burnt something-or-other drifts up into her nostrils.

The doors slide open.

She wiggles back to get a good bit of momentum and then swings herself off the cable and out the doors. Her boots hit the ground with a soft thump. Another near-silent thump later and Ginka's landing next to her.

According to the map, the cells should be... "Left."

"I'll go first," Ginka whispers, taking point and hugging the wall as they turn left. "If the guards see us before we can get the drop on them, better they shoot me in the arm than you."

"Can your arms even be injured?"

"By normal hard light bullets? No."

Handy.

She sneaks along behind Ginka, still holding Panache at the ready, just in case the two guards that are supposedly still down here decide to flank around or something. Or in case the security feeds were sabotaged and on a loop, and there are secretly way more PI agents around here, lurking, patiently waiting for her or Ginka to slip up.

The two guards are standing outside of the cell block entrance, guns safely holstered, no visible tricks – exactly where they're supposed to be.

"Ready? We can take them by surprise if we cause a distraction," Rig whispers, raising her guns and–

Ginka completely ignores her.

She dashes towards the guardswoman with a burst of speed, slamming an elbow into her throat and making her drop to the ground with a heavy *thud*. A spinning kick to the skull takes out the second guard. His eyes roll back in his head before he falls. She winces slightly as she lowers her leg, but apart from that, her injury doesn't seem to have slowed her down any.

"Okay. That works too."

"And now," Ginka mutters as she pulls a key card from the guard's pocket, "we get your sister."

A green light flashes and the wall-mounted scanner gives a friendly beep when Ginka slides the card through it. There's a series of *ckkk-chunk*s as the door unlocks and opens up.

Darkness bathes the cells within, cold white lights flickering on, only casting the smallest of beams inside each cell. Translucent containment fields section off the stark cells, shimmering in the dim lighting, shifting as the hard light energy cycles through the fields. Nothing out of place.

Only there's no one here.

The cells are all empty.

Oh gods the cells are empty... Is Daara even still alive, or... What if she tried to make an escape attempt on her own and Pyrite... No, Daara wouldn't have.

Rig runs down the aisle, rushing from cell to cell as though they'll open up and reveal her sister if she can only look at them from the right angle – an optical illusion that she just needs to flip around because there's no way her sister isn't here.

"Calm down." Ginka's voice cuts through the panicked haze like a knife. "Listen to me. She is *not* dead. Pyrite wouldn't dare kill such a valuable piece unless they were certain that she meant nothing to you or that she was too great a liability. She may be with the missing PI agents or closer to Janus."

"Great!" she snaps, stopping her frantic pacing to glare at Ginka, "Even better, she's surrounded by trigger happy Pyrites that–"

Whirrrrrr.

Her neck cracks as she whirls around to face the noise.

A hologram forms in the center of the room, flickering into existence and solidifying until it takes the shape of–

"Janus, you *bastard*," she snarls. "Where's my sister?"

"Tunnel vision, as per usual, I see," he remarks. "Thanks for showing up. I knew you'd be here eventually, once I realized that you were that pretty Madime on Tides – stealing my link so that Triton could track the station? How simple. Although I will admit you did a lovely job in blocking your associate's tracking chip. A nice touch."

If she could only reach through the hologram and beat the shit out of him with her bare hands...

"Shut your smug mouth and tell me what the fuck is going on!"

"It's simple, really. I'm sitting in a wonderfully comfortable office right now," he drawls, gesturing to the surroundings around him that aren't visible through the hologram. "Libraries are so *cozy* – a fact I'm sure you know very well."

A library.

He's in a *library*... and this station's above the *Ascetic homeworld*...

Everything goes cold. She can't speak. Her lips move and no sound comes out and, *oh gods he's in June's library.*

She finally manages to demand, "How. How did you find her?"

"We have an accord with Ascetic and her friend in their Military Police told us everything after a bit of prodding. I must say, your librarian is *so* accommodating," he remarks, every one of his words like a screw boring into her bones. A slow, grinding pain that she can't stop from sinking into her. "It would be a real shame if we had to do something unpleasant to her, you understand."

"If you touch a hair on her head I will rip you limb from limb!"

"Now, now. No need for that. Bring the plans and that dear Phantom of yours and all will go back to normal for you in due time." He gives her a mocking bow. "See you soon."

The hologram shuts down.

If June dies because of her... she honestly doesn't know what she'll do. Part of her brain sort of has an idea about what will happen if Daara dies, a vague picture of what the galaxy will look like. It would be a different galaxy, filled with sharp edges and missing important details, but it would still be there.

Should June die, there will be no galaxy left at all.

Vaguely, through the fog that's seeped into her head, she

can see Ginka remove Sparkle from her neck and shove the device into her pocket. Ginka says something, something that sounds a bit comforting but is entirely indistinct – Rig's brain can't manage to pay attention right now to something as unimportant as empty platitudes.

"Ever killed an ex-Handler before?" she asks through gritted teeth. "Cause if you're not okay with that, you had better get over it real fast."

"I've done worse."

"Good choice." She spins on the balls of her feet and heads back towards the elevator and the airlock where they left *Bluebird*. "Janus is going to fucking *suffer* for this."

The climb back up is electric and cold, and it's up to Ginka to check the halls for guards while Rig opens up the airlock and deactivates *Bluebird*'s security. Her limbs are bursting with a rush of adrenaline, lightning coursing through her veins and turning every step into a panicked run.

Ginka shuts *Bluebird*'s entryway behind them, covering their exit to make sure PI isn't on their tail. Rig would appreciate the help more if her brain were in a place to appreciate anything at all right now.

"I thought they wouldn't dare break into a library," Ginka remarks.

"I did, too." She swears under her breath. "I really thought… She's supposed to be *safe* there. That's… that's the whole *point*."

"It's a mistake we'll make them regret."

Taking things one step at a time to get to June seems an impossibility. Somehow, Rig manages. Moving on autopilot, her hands find the ship's controls, flicking the right switches and pressing the right buttons. Get the shields up, move away from the airlock, plot course to the planet below. Step by step. While her heart ricochets up and down in her chest, her hands are there to pick up the slack and get them moving.

They pull away from the PI spacestation.

She pushes *Bluebird* into a probably-ill-advised full burn as soon as they're clear. Blood, pounding and panicked, rushes through Rig's ears and drowns out the overworked roar of the engines.

In a matter of seconds, there's the fiery burst of breaking through atmo.

Wind buffets *Bluebird* from all sides, tossing the ship around with cruel fervor. They're falling too fast, too steep, Rig unwilling to change their course and lose precious time. She shakes in her chair, partly from the way her ship is being batted to and fro, and partly from the fear – she could be too late. Janus might have decided not to wait for her. What if he doesn't care about the schematics anymore and figures that it'd be better to just…

"Do we have a plan?" Ginka asks.

"Yes." Her hands have a death grip on the steering, trembling as the ship begins to streak towards the capital city.

Ginka, sitting in the weapon's chair below her, nods. "Good. What is your plan?"

"Kill Janus."

"…Detailed. I like it."

Skyscrapers appear in the viewport, cutting through the thin clouds and blocking her path through the city. Like she'd let something that simple get in her way – she twists *Bluebird* around them, weaving between the buildings and keeping the engines on full burn. For a moment she almost turns to land at the spaceport, but if PI is already here, they don't have time for that. Better to ask forgiveness than permission, as the saying goes.

Ginka is staring at something being projected from her link. "There's no security at the Historical Center. I used a Windshadow frequency to access their channels, and all security there has been told to withdraw."

Shit. But if there's no security at least getting there will be easier.

Buildings practically jump out of her way as she throws the

throttle as far forward as it can go, clearing a path straight to the Historical Center.

Rig's guts are a twisted mess by the time the sparkling crystal gardens and tumbling waterfalls of the Historical Center are beneath her. From what she can see through the viewport, the place is deserted. Not a guard in sight, but not a single librarian milling around, either.

She finds a patch of space in front of the library gates.

Yeah, that's big enough. Barely.

Bluebird crushes the marble tiles and dents the smooth concrete, the landing gears winning the contest of brute force, and she can feel the shudder of the gangplank crunching the ground beneath it with the ease of teeth breaking through a potato chip.

The moment the controls are safe to release is the moment she's out of her seat and throwing herself out of her ship.

No guards at the main gates, and the gates themselves are *down*, they've been deactivated. They're *never* deactivated, not *ever*.

Ginka rolls her shoulders. "Be careful–"

"Would you? If it were Crane in June's place?"

"...Probably not."

That's what she thought.

She bolts straight past the gates and runs full speed towards June's library.

The area is deserted. Not a librarian in sight or a single guard, or even some wandering custodian. Just emptiness. Except–

Armed guards are waiting for them in front of June's library.

Five in total, marked with the blue grey uniform of Pyrite Intelligence.

One guard takes point as she and Ginka approach, aiming a gun at them. "Halt! In the name of Pyrite, I command–"

Rig shoots them in the knee.

They go down with a scream and a *bang* from their misfired weapon – the shot goes wild and pings into the concrete.

She can feel the edges of her consciousness going red from fear and anger, her finger tightening around the triggers of her guns, her shoulders rolling back in preparation for the recoil. This isn't any different from fights she's been in before – she *has* to pull herself together. She can't help June or Daara if she dies here.

The soldiers completely ignore their fallen comrade and two of them raise up something that's big and heavy and looks like a mini-cannon.

What the fuck is *that*?

It fires.

Chains of hard light fly out of the cannon, widening and expanding like a spiderweb, and they're not aiming it at Rig, they're aiming it at Ginka.

The fully formed net of solid hard light collides with Ginka.

She's thrown backwards.

She cries out in shock, fighting the snare, the coils wrapping around her limbs like snakes, and Rig can see the wide-eyed panic as she struggles to free herself. To no avail. With every motion she makes to break out of the net, the hard light chains only ensnare her further; and with the lingering soreness from her injury, she's lacking some of her usual litheness.

Shit. Rig turns to help–

A heavy rifle swings at her, forcing her to twist out of the way or else get a skull-splitting concussion. The guard spins his weapon around to shoot her and, on instinct, she puts a bullet through his shoulder before he can pull the trigger.

Stupid! She should have aimed somewhere fatal – pain isn't a killer. With one heavy shove, he slams the butt of the rifle into her gut, sending her staggering, clutching her stomach.

Gold lights up her vision as a hundred helltech knives cleave through the air.

They crack into the library walls, the ground.

Sliding into the guards like a hot knife through butter, shredding them into a gory mess.

Her head cracks around to see Ginka rising to her feet, lines of gold running down her prosthetics. The remnants of the net are shattered around her, disintegrating into nothingness as though her mere presence is tearing them to shreds. Fury burns in her eyes and her chest heaves from the effort – an effort that must have cut through her life as quickly and as precisely as it cut through her enemies.

"Fuck–" Rig trips over her own two feet as she straightens up. "You… okay?"

Ginka flicks her wrist, crackles of light shaking off it in white hot sparks. She winces, pressing a hand to her stomach before straightening up. "Fine. The toxin won't kill me instantly."

Rig's brain shoves that into the 'not urgent' category and proceeds to ignore it.

Then she's stumbling through the library doors, one hand clutching her aching side where she was punched and the other still shakily grasping one of her guns.

Stillness has sunk into the library.

Not the usual muffled quiet and dusty, undisturbed nature of a library, no, this is a forced emptiness, unthinkable and unnatural. There are no overturned shelves or smashed cases to suggest the wrongness of it all, but there are scuff marks on the soft carpet and the stench of gunpowder. When she passes through the main chamber, the glass-ceilinged sanctum, she sees sticky blood splattered on the walls. A shoe, a librarian's silk slipper, lies discarded near a display plinth.

Bile rises to burn her throat and she has to bite it back.

They raised their hands against librarians. They desecrated this place, a sacred library, as though it was just some publica in the middle of nowhere. She's not simply sick to her stomach, her very soul feels stained by being party to it all. This didn't just happen. Janus – he only did this because of *her*.

June's office door has been torn from its hinges.

The slab of old oaken wood has a bullet hole splintering the center of it like a rot. Panicked, fluttering coals lie in Rig's stomach. The ruined door consumes her vision and the coals burst into an inferno.

Something inside her snarls and it's that feeling that allows her to draw herself up and steel her expression before she's stepping into June's office and trying not to scream.

There must have been a fight; thousand-year-old treasures and precious documents thrown about like trash, the refrigerator that Rig gave June lying on its side, door open and a can of soda leaking onto the carpet. The fizzing pink liquid has soaked into an essayon Ascetic clay working techniques – even from a distance, she knows the shape of that document. June had spent six months agonizing over it before she felt it was thorough enough to send to her boss.

June is sitting in her chair, hunched over. Heavy cuffs bind her wrists together behind her back, a rough gag is shoved between her teeth. A muffled cry breaks free when her gaze locks with Rig's.

She's bleeding.

A thin stream of blood trickles down her nose, one of her nostrils a sickening purplish red. A dark, nearly black bruise is painted across her right cheek like a sweep of blush.

And Janus himself is standing behind her, casually spinning a pistol around in his hand. There's that smug grin, worse now that Rig's seeing it in person again.

He hurt June. He *hurt June*...

She's gonna kill him.

"Hey there," he drawls. "Let's talk like adults, shall we?"

CHAPTER TWENTY
Change of Plans

"No guards in here?" Rig practically growls as she takes a slow and careful step towards Janus and June. Anger is burning up her fear, twitching in her limbs, ready to lash out and gut him. "Bet that you realized we know you're former Windshadow, and your PI buddies wouldn't take too kindly to us revealing that piece of information."

"Not at all. Pyrite knows who and what I am."

"And Ascetic?"

"When presented with the golden opportunity to stand back and aid in the elimination of an organization that's decided to become the unruly and uncivil fourth enemy in this war," Janus says cheerfully, "Ascetic decided that the loss of one more minor library was well worth the trade. I *did* want to have this conversation without another tagalong, but it seems that my Pyrite associates didn't have what it took to stop her."

"You *know* that if it comes down to a fight, Ginka and I can kick your ass."

Janus keeps smiling. "Oh, I know. I'm not here to fight. Like I said, I want to talk."

"Then let June go, you piece of shit."

He nudges the back of June's head with the gun's muzzle and it's such a struggle to keep from punching him in the face – she might get the hit in, only she wouldn't be fast enough to stop him from shooting, and then it wouldn't matter, would it?

"She's just a security measure. I need you to actually listen instead of resorting to your usual crass methods."

"Like when I beat you up in the Dead Zone?"

"You and I remember that incident very differently." He nods at Ginka. "Didn't I kill you?"

Ginka glares at him. "I've had worse."

For once in Rig's life, trash talking just makes her feel worse because June is *right there*. Her heart aches to run to June, but she knows it'll just cause her more pain. She has to think about this; she can't simply act and damn the consequences. "I don't care about semantics right now. Talk. *Fast.*"

Another tap of the muzzle, this time poking at the bruise on half of June's face, making her wince and making Rig boil. She's gonna kill him. She's gonna rip his arms off and beat him to death with them. "So hasty," he drawls. "Now I went to a good deal of trouble to ensure that you'd sit down and listen, so why don't we all talk about this like reasonable adults?"

"You have ten seconds to blurt it out before you let June go. Longer than that, and I won't listen to a damn thing you say."

"Fine." Janus's smug grin falters for a brief second. "The truth is... I don't have Daara anymore. Kill me, and you'll never know where she is."

Then he unlocks June's handcuffs and lets her go.

What does he mean *he doesn't have Daara...*

June rubs her hands together, soothing the angry red marks that have dug into her wrists. She staggers to her feet, ripping the gag out from between her teeth and spitting it onto the desk. Her hands are braced on the desk as she leans forward, drawing in a deep breath.

"Now," Janus says, "let's discuss–"

June slams her head backwards.

There's a pained scream from Janus and blood flecks in June's curls as she whirls around. Blood leaks from Janus's nose where her skull had smacked into it. Not hard enough to kill him, just enough to shock him.

He raises a hand to prod at the injury and he's gapes at the red smear on his fingers.

With a quick twist of motion, June grabs the slide of Janus's gun, yanks it off the rest of the pistol so it can't shoot, and then plants her knee firmly in his stomach. She drops the slide, grabs something from her pocket, and jams a taser into Janus's side.

He crumples with a gasp.

Rig's eyes blow wide. "Babe, what the fuck?"

"I've studied self-defense manuals." June pushes her hair back, her hands shaking ever so slightly. A curl remains plastered to her face, stuck there by a drop of sweat. She sags and takes a few uneven steps away from Janus. "Our archived tutorials are seriously underutilized tools."

"…Tutorials."

"How hard could it be?"

"Clearly pretty damn easy for you. Are you…?"

"Alright? That's not important right now."

It *is*, in her opinion. Now's not the time to argue though.

She hops over the desk to June, pulling June's pink handkerchief out of her pocket and using it to dab at her bloody nose. "Try not to swallow any blood. It'll make you sick."

June presses the pink harder against her nose and winces. "Thank you."

"Right. Let's get him trussed up so that he'll spill the beans as soon as he's awake. I need to know what in the fuck he meant by not having my sister anymore, and we need to be in control of this little interrogation. No fucking chance he gets to call the shots anymore."

Ginka moves the desk aside and picks up the chair. She sets it in the center of the room, pulling Janus into it and cuffing his hands behind it with practiced motions. Not her first torture and interrogation, then. Disturbing, in general. Very helpful, currently.

"Hand me that taser?" June passes it over and Ginka examines it. She gives it an approving nod. "Nice model. Good voltage. He should wake up soon. Soon*er*, if we hit him a bit."

Spec-fucking-*tacular*.

Rig punches him in the face.

He draws in a sharp gulp of air, eyes snapping wide open, head cracking backwards as he flops and strains against his bonds.

"Wakey wakey, motherfucker."

He sputters. "You… you and your damn little librarian son of a–"

She punches him again.

"Much appreciated," June says, the words a bit unclear as she's still holding the handkerchief to her nose.

"Any time." She turns back to Janus. "Now start singing like a godsdamned bird. Where's Daara and what did you do with her? You better not have killed her, or else you're gonna start losing a lot of blood real fast from the shit ton of bullet holes that I'll put in your chest."

Janus coughs and spits a bit of blood onto the carpet, his – hopefully broken – nose still leaking. "She's not dead. That's all I can safely say, at least. She's worth more to Umbra alive than dead."

Yeah, of *course* she is, they already knew *that*; what the fuck does that have to do with *where* she is?

Ginka blows out a long puff of air that ends in a shocked little laugh. "You damn *idiot*. You thought I was dead and you jumped the gun, didn't you?"

What's *that* supposed to mean?

It must mean something to Janus, based on the way a vein in his forehead twitches. He ignores Ginka and keeps his focus on Rig. "I'm sure your friend has told you all about the little unicorn hunt some of us have been sent on, and yes, I was one of those unlucky few. When I couldn't get the plans from you in the Dead Zone, I… I gave Daara to Umbra," he admits.

"You did *what*?" To Rig, Windshadow is a thousand times worse than PI – unimaginably worse. Literally. PI is horrible, but she understands them, she knows how they work, how they think, what they're likely to do. Windshadow is such an unknown, a void in her info bank, and that shadowy reputation and lack of knowledge creeps up her spine. "Umbra's using her to get to me, right? Will he keep her unharmed while waiting for me to show? Will he torture her just... just *because*? What's he going to *do*?"

Janus shrugs, the cuffs on his wrists pulling his shoulders back down before he can move them more than a centimeter. "How should I know?"

"The more damaged she is," Ginka says in a calm and detached voice, "the less valuable she is. Any torture would be conducted where you can see it. That would be far greater motivation for you."

At least there's *that*. "Why give her to Umbra? You've clearly screwed yourself over in some way. If everything was fine and dandy for you, you'd be sitting back in Ossuary and not bothering me."

She can see his jaw grinding as he deliberates his words. "You wouldn't understand. I need my link back. Two and a half years I've been chasing you, and now that I finally got *somewhere*... I *needed* it back; I had to *try,* and I thought that your sister would be enough for Umbra. It would be proof enough for him that I deserved to have my link again–"

"You damn fool." There's no gloating in Ginka's voice. Instead she simply sounds tired. Tired and sad. "Nothing short of the utmost perfection is good enough for Lord Umbra."

He shoots her a dirty look. "I'm well aware of that *now*, thank you."

"So what do you want from me?" Rig asks, crossing her arms. "We're not friends, I don't give a shit if you don't have your precious link, and now that I know that Umbra has Daara, Ginka and I can probably figure out some way of getting to her."

"I came here bearing a proposal of cooperation."

"...You're joking, right?"

"Regrettably, no." He sighs, and explains, "Listen, we both know you don't care about the schematics falling into Umbra's hands."

She looks at June in confusion. June looks right back at her with identical – if slightly bruised – confusion.

"We know what now?"

"You've clearly thrown your lot in with X-74 and are helping *her* get back into Windshadow. You only want your sister back. I understand. And I can help you. Work with me *and* X-74. You'll get your sister with my help and both of us will get back into Windshadow. As a result of your cooperation, I have no doubt that Lord Umbra will keep you both safe once he and PI release the anti-Kashrini nanomites."

That's a lot of incorrect assumptions.

So he thinks that she's picked a side in Umbra's fucked up unicorn hunt? She's on her *own* side.

He leans back in the chair and that grin starts to return. "I can offer you safe passage to Ossuary space. X-74 isn't allowed in and neither am I, but I've hacked into a number of their communications and I have clearance codes to get us past the border checkpoints, through to the homeworld, and straight up to a landing pad in the Windshadow headquarters. And once you've gotten your sister back, having a Raven – *me* – inside the organization to ensure that you stay safe will be quite handy, won't it?"

"Yeah…" she slowly drawls, "see, there's one problem with all that. I'm *not* giving the schematics to Umbra."

He jerks his head back in surprise. "Are you *crazy*? No one crosses Umbra. *No one.* Besides, if you try to get your sister without my help, he *will* catch you and he'll just *take* them from you by force."

"I'd like to see him try. No one can get them from me without me handing them over, and even if someone *could*, they still couldn't access them without me. So tough shit for Umbra." Something curious shifts in Janus's features, but it's gone before Rig can pin what emotion it was. "If Umbra has my sister," she decides, "then I'll take the fight to him."

He barks out a laugh. "You're a lunatic."

"Maybe so, but I'm gonna do it anyway."

What other choice does she have, in the end? Give up and let Daara die a slow, probably painful death at Umbra's hands? Or let June and every single Nightbird be murdered by her own ill-conceived nanomites?

In her mind, there's no way that wiping out one pesky organization of Nightbirds can be worth slaughtering an entire species. Would it even end there? Or would Umbra take the base research and corrupt it? Find a way to twist the designs, make them work on other species, adjusting them for each new enemy that stands in his way? She'd say it's impossible, because she knows the intricacies of her own designs, but she has no idea what scientists he has under his command. Certainly people clever enough to figure out a work-around to helltech – albeit a shitty one.

"You can stand in my way, if you want," she continues. "Or you can choose to work with me. You're right, you *would* be helpful to have along; and since I can't trust you enough to let you go, your options are really either help me take out Umbra and free my sister, or I shoot you here and now. I know you Windshadow people are devoted to Umbra and everything, so I get that you might prefer the bullet–"

"No need." He interrupts her with a full-on, proper grin. Stupid, smug piece of shit. "I have no issues with killing Umbra."

She very nearly glances at Ginka to catch her reaction. That's not what she'd been expecting, not from someone who seems to have been kept at least partially in Umbra's favor – or at least been the man's favorite horse in the race. "Seriously?"

"He took my link from me," Janus coolly replies. "All I want from him is my link back and, well, if he won't give it to me willingly then my only option is to take it. One way or another. You're a Nightbird – I'm sure you understand. Your little band takes whatever you want from factions without care or concern."

Yeah, but there's no need for him to say it like it's a bad thing or in any way, shape, or form comparable to what *he's* doing. Pyrite took whatever it wanted from her, after all, and he seems to have no problem with *that*.

"O...kay. Let's be clear about a few things, then. Making sure Umbra, PI, or Windshadow in general don't get the plans is the number one priority. If you compromise that, I shoot you. Getting Daara back safe is the second priority. If you compromise that, I shoot you. Rigging things so that no one comes back to harm June is the third priority. If you compromise that–"

"Let me guess, you'll shoot me?"

"You're learning."

"Then we have an accord. I'd seal the deal but..." He wiggles his arms and the cuffs rattle. "Care to shake on it?"

June picks the slide off the ground and fixes the gun, holding it unsteadily at him. She nods. "I can shoot if necessary."

Somewhat reluctantly, she steps behind Janus and uncuffs him; it *is* necessary for him to be able to move and stuff if they're going to work together to get Daara back from Umbra, but at the same time every instinct she has is telling her that he's going to put up a fight as soon as he's free. He's been her enemy too long for her to think anything else, really.

"Any funny business," she warns, tossing the cuffs away, "and you've got three people armed and ready to end you."

He rubs at his wrists with uncalled for elegancy, as though merely adjusting cufflinks. "We're on the same side now and I have no reason to compromise that. I'll play nice."

"Sure you will," she replies tersely. She doesn't trust him one little bit. "Now, about getting to the Ossuary homeworld–"

"Rig," Ginka interrupts. "I need to speak with you."

Is now *really* the time for... Rig pauses when she turns

around. Ginka looks as though she's turned to stone, cold and frozen and really kinda scary.

"Uh. Sure, Cactus. June, you okay to hold down the asshole while we talk?"

June keeps the gun pointed at a smarmy, confident Janus. "I'll manage."

Ginka's out the door like a shot, marching into the hall and shutting the door tightly behind them as soon as Rig has scurried out after her.

The library's silence is a creeping thing now that the fear and rush of earlier has faded. It crawls up her spine and unnerves her. Horrible thought it may be to think, it's a good reminder. Janus can sing his song about helping them, and she's going to use everything he can give her, but at the end of the day, he still did this. He still destroyed this sacred place. And he's not going to get away with that. He may help them faithfully and they may succeed, but when the dice fall, she will not allow him to live.

How easily she becomes a murderer again.

"I don't know if I can do this," Ginka blurts out after a tense moment of wringing her hands. "I can't just go against Lord Umbra."

"Why not? He certainly has no issues with killing *you*."

"Excuse me?"

She gestures to Ginka's arms. "He cut you off and left you to die, and you can say whatever you want about needing to get the schematics from me to 'prove your loyalty' or some bullshit like that, but it doesn't change what he did. Why be loyal to someone who doesn't give a shit about you? Why be loyal when–" She lets her hands fall and chews on her lower lip. "Why be loyal when you're already dying?"

That last sentence lingers in the deathly silent hall.

Ginka slowly flexes the fingers on her right hand, watching them curl and uncurl as though they contain great secrets of the galaxy. "I am, aren't I? I suppose I've been heading that way for a while now... Even if I hadn't just used helltech, what little Grace I had was never enough. Not really."

"Exactly! But if we get to the Ossuary homeworld in time, if we get rid of Umbra in time... You'd have their supply of Grace right there, free for the taking. You could save yourself. Why not take that chance?"

"It is my solemn duty to die for the glory of Ossuary–"

"Enough with that crap, Cactus! Don't you hate what they did to you?" she demands, pointing at her helltech arms. "Don't you *resent* them for it?"

Ginka wraps her metal arms around her torso, head fallen, her hair covering her features, and goes completely silent.

Perhaps not the best thing to say. Quieter this time, she adds, "Don't you want to see Crane again?"

It's a manipulative card to play and she knows it. If someone said that to her about June, she'd probably abandon the last of her moral compass in a second. But she needs the help, and she can't do this with Janus alone and... and she honest-to-gods thinks that it's the right thing for Ginka to do *anyway*.

At the end of the day, she can't force Ginka to be the person she thinks she should be.

Ginka's hair still shrouds her face in shadow, and all she can see is the way her fingers dig into her arms, unyielding metal against unyielding metal. Unyielding loyalty against unyielding love – a battle where Rig would pick a side in an instant.

With a lonely sigh, Ginka admits, "...More than anything."

"Then you know what you have to do. Come with me. For what it's worth, I think you have a good chance at making it. It's probably, what, a day to the Ossuary homeworld? It took you a couple hours to get real sick after that party on Tides. Twenty-four hours doesn't sound like more of a long shot than anything else that's happened over the past week."

Not that she would know, really. It's only a guess. A guess and, shamefully, a twist of manipulation.

"It's... possible," Ginka agrees, in a quiet and sad tone that makes it clear she doesn't believe a word she's saying. "But I would be of no use to you once we arrived."

"I don't need you to be useful, don't you get it? I don't *want* you to die because you're… you're my *friend*. And I can't do this with just Janus. He's a two-headed viper, and we both know it. It's not as though June can come with me to watch my back, even though I want… even if she–" She chokes on the words. "I need a friend."

She holds out her hand. She's shaken the hand of one enemy today; surely, she can breach the gap with Ginka.

"Please let me do as I promised, Cactus. Let me take you home."

Ginka's upper lip wobbles slightly, her attention still fixed firmly on the ground. Her hair curtains her face, but between the strands, her eyes are big and glassy, redness beginning to puff up in the corners. One of her hands moves to rest around her neck. Her fingers toy with something hidden under her shirt – the tiny glass bottle she wears as a necklace, the one containing a single preserved red flower.

Slowly, deliberately, she reaches out with her other arm and shakes Rig's hand.

"I place myself under your command," Ginka murmurs.

The smooth metal of her arms is cold and dense and so much heavier than Rig had been anticipating. They must hurt.

"You're not under anyone's command, let alone mine, Cactus. Please don't think that you're trading in Umbra's control for mine, cause I sure as hell won't leave you to die like he did, I swear."

Ginka pulls away after a moment, nervously hunching back in on herself. It's okay though. She still reached out. That's enough. "I'll do my best to believe that."

"Good, 'cause I wasn't lying. Now, let's go deal with the asshole back in there."

She strides back, head held high because there's no way in the galaxy that she'll let Janus see her flinch any more than he already has. This time, she's in charge, and she's not going to let him forget it. If they're going to get Daara back, if this uneasy alliance is going to work, then she needs to make sure he understands that he can't fuck with her.

When she gets back inside the office, June is still holding the gun to Janus's head. He's sitting comfortable as a king, one leg crossed over the other, hands casually folded on his lap.

"Come to a consensus?" he asks. "I would so hate for there to be discord amongst our little group."

"Okay, first of all," she snaps, "you're not part of our group. Second of all, shut up."

He mimes zipping his lips and flicks the invisible key at her.

"Asshole." She places her hands on her hips. "You said you had clearance codes to get us into Ossuary space. We'll be taking my ship – mess with my ship and I'll shoot you, by the way. This is going to be a stealth mission, first and foremost, so you're going to keep a low profile if we get stopped for an inspection. You won't be armed until we're on the Ossuary homeworld, and even then not until you absolutely need a weapon. Try to steal one of my guns again and I'll just laugh at you as you fail and *then* shoot you."

He smirks. "Crystal clear. You know, you say a lot more than you intend to when you're angry."

"Stop insulting her," June replies sharply, kicking his knee with her slippered foot. "You've done your fair share of talking as well, so you're hardly in any position to make such remarks."

That's not wrong, but something about the way he'd phrased it makes Rig think he meant something different. Has she given anything away?

"Fine, fine. Shall we get on with it then?" Janus gets to his feet and is about to saunter out the door without any supervision before Rig grabs the scruff of his shirt.

"Not so fast," she grumbles. "Ginka? Take him to *Bluebird*."

He dramatically rolls his eyes but doesn't put up a fight when Ginka hauls him out of the office.

The sound of him sassing at her fades down the hallway, and then it's just Rig and June left in the office.

In the span of a heartbeat, June's in her arms. She clings to her, and it all merges into one sensation; the warmth of her, soft curly hair tickling her nose, hands clutching at her vest – it all becomes the single feeling of *June*.

Something wet stains her shoulder. June's crying.

"Oh love," she murmurs, hugging June like her life depends on it. "It's okay. I've... I've got you."

As horrifying as the destruction wrecked upon this library is for her, it must be a thousand times worse for June. This is her home. Her sanctuary. All she's known for most of her life. And every day she must remain here, stuck seeing all of this, even after Ascetic rebuilds the place, because this library is all she will ever know for the *rest* of her life.

Telling her that everything's going to be okay is a meaningless platitude at this point, and she's not going to insult June by thoughtlessly blabbing out that line. Maybe it will be okay in the end, maybe it won't be – right now it sure as fuck is looking bleak. All Rig can do is make sure that it's gonna get better. She *will* make it better. That's what Nightbirds do. That's what Dare would have done.

"I'm sorry," Rig whispers again. Her voice breaks. Her throat swells up. "I'm so sorry," she says again, and this time it's a sob. "I should have been here, I should have protected you better, this is all my fault."

June shakes her head, rubbing her face into the crook of Rig's neck, and it must hurt with her nose and her bruise, but she does it anyway. Loving her even though it's painful. "I thought I was safe, I really thought that here was *safe* – I was so *stupid* to think that Pyrite wouldn't come this far. I was stupid to think that Ascetic wouldn't... wouldn't *abandon* me."

"No, no, don't say that. It's not your fault. You couldn't have seen this coming. No one else would dare touch a library. If it had been anyone other than Janus... I'm so sorry that my stupid actions from three years ago keep hurting people I care about. And I'm so sorry that I can never... Just when I think that maybe I'm free of my shit past and that, just maybe, the future where I can stay here with you approaches, everything falls down again."

"What's the point of any of it if here isn't safe?"

There's no time for her to answer that because June's dragging her down for a desperate kiss. She can taste salt on her lips. Salt and iron.

She doesn't know what to do. There's nothing she can say that'll make this alright. So she just holds on. Her love. Who she very nearly just lost.

Gods, she almost lost June.

There had been a gun to June's head and Janus could have easily just...

It feels like her stomach is kicked out from underneath her, along with her legs and then the very planet she's standing on. She buries her hands in June's curly hair and digs her nails into the soft cotton of her surcoat and does her very best to *breathe,* because hyperventilating right now isn't going to help anything.

"If I asked you to stay," June whispers, so very nearly silent and buried in the fabric of Rig's headscarf, "would you?"

Stay. Stay and leave Daara and the Nightbirds and–

June shakes her head. "Never mind. I wouldn't ask. I'm sorry."

"I'll... I'll come back." She'd thought, before, that maybe it'd be fine if just Daara made it out of all this, if maybe she herself doesn't... That seems like a fair trade. Making those weapons was her mistake. On her head be it. Only she'd felt like she was going to break into pieces when she'd thought June might die; and how could she make June feel the same thing? How is that fair? "I promise I'll come back."

"You don't *have* to go," June sniffles. "You aren't obligated to save someone that turned their back on you. And I know that she's your sister, but why..."

"Because it's all my fault to begin with," she admits, quietly, because maybe if she mumbles it, it'll make it better. "If I hadn't decided to invent the nanomites. If I hadn't decided to *keep* them…"

Panache and Pizzazz and her *pride*. She can feel the weight of them resting on her belt, the brightest jewels in the treasure box of her inventions and the rotten apples that spoiled the bunch. It was so foolish of her to keep them. They were the first thing she'd made after she left Pyrite, and at the time, she'd thought herself *so clever* for coming up with such a tricksy place to hide the schematics.

Well done, her. What a fantastic idea that ended up being.

She should have destroyed the schematics entirely, committed them to the same fires that burnt her former spire to the ground. But they… they showed just how smart she really was. How smart she always knew she was and struggled for years to prove to everyone else. Growing up as nobody at all, and then she'd *made* it; she got into the best innovative spire on the Pyrite homeworld, she was top of her class and then the best on her team and then they told her she was the best of the Kashrini and she…

She was The One Kashrini That Made It.

Swallowed up all their stories. Hook, line, and they sunk her.

"I'm just making up for my mistakes."

And unlike, say, *Ginka*, her mistakes were severe. They got people hurt. They're *still* getting Daara hurt. They weren't something as light as merely getting married. Being that dream couple that gets married against all odds – that ignores the practical and the rules and decides that it's all worth it, that the risk is negligible. Is Rig *jealous*? She knows that June needs to stay safe. She knows that and she understands it, and she would never in a million years hold that against her. But maybe, just maybe, she's too fond of risks.

"Rig, love…" June trails off.

"I'll fix it." She pulls back but doesn't let go, holding onto June's hand like a lifeline. "Come on. Come with me to the gates."

Come with me as far as you can go.

June allows her to lead her out of the library, slow, quiet steps past her ruined home. A home that Ascetic decided was an acceptable casualty.

Bluebird rests just outside the gates, exactly where she left it, untouched.

Inside the ship are the silhouettes of Ginka and Janus, the former with her back turned to the latter, likely ignoring whatever venomous bullshit he's spouting off.

June halts on the last step of the Historical Center, toes an inch from the boundary line, puffy eyes gazing up at *Bluebird*. "I've never seen her before," she admits quietly. "You've told me, but I've never..."

"She's even more beautiful on the inside," Rig says before she can think about it, about how tempting it sounds, the implicit suggestion of it. "Will you be safe? Here? While I'm gone?"

"No... Perhaps. There are more librarians here than just..." June face twists in sorrow. "I can find the rest of us, pull out some of the deeper security measures here on the off chance that Pyrite comes back. I... I doubt they will. What they want," she says, resting a hand over Rig's heart, "will already be gone."

Rig tucks a stray strand of hair behind June's ear. "Stay safe, please."

"For you? Always."

Regrettably, inevitably, she pulls away. She steps back and her boots land on the hard concrete of the street. June steps forward and her slippers perch on the edge of the last step of the library.

"Love you," she whispers.

June repeats it silently, her lips soundlessly forming the shape of the words, her hand moving ever so slightly as Rig takes another step back, as though to reach out and stop her. But she doesn't. Another step and then Rig has to turn her back and walk onto her ship with her tentative friend and her allied enemy.

She promised she'd come back. Hopefully the galaxy won't make a liar of her.

INTERLUDE
The One Thing

Ginka has never once resented her helltech weapons. Grace dependence has never irritated her in the way it seems to ever-so-slightly annoy Crane on her behalf. Maintenance isn't much of an issue, considering how advanced they are. They are, on occasion, bulky enough or heavy enough to be in the way, but that is the extent of their problems. Every detail of them is designed for maximum efficiency. Peak field performance. Unrivaled lethality.

So when she'd been informed that she needed to undergo surgery to get her Phantom-level upgrades, she'd assumed that they needed to update the chip in the back of her head so that it would properly sync up and control her new weapons.

She wakes up in a medcenter bed, staring at a white ceiling, alone and cold.

Her head doesn't hurt.

That's strange, is all she's able to think before she floats out of consciousness again. Cotton seems to be stuffed into her ears and she manages a few moments here and there of alertness in between periods of blackness.

When she next opens her eyes, the white ceiling is somewhat obscured.

She blinks.

The black shape blocking her view comes into focus.

A black feather and a blue bead dangle near her chest,

hanging from silky hair on a bowed head. Crane. He's sitting next to her, his hands awkwardly on his lap, his eyes lidded as though he's struggling to keep awake. Was he here for long? How long was she out, exactly? It isn't as though there's a clock in this room, and the lights do not change to show the passage of time.

She means to say 'Crane,' but all that comes out is a fuzzy, "Mmmf?"

Probably for the best, when she thinks about it. She shouldn't be saying his name aloud here. There may be someone watching.

At her incoherent noise, his snaps alert and sighs in relief, checking over her prone form as if to make sure that nothing's changed between now and when she was asleep. His hands twitch but he doesn't reach out for her. Why? Did something go wrong?

"X-74," he says, soft and gentle, and she can hear her name hidden underneath his tongue. "Are you... How do you feel?"

She can't move and her limbs are as heavy as metal. "Mm... 'm tired."

"You slept for twenty-one hours," he informs her, as though he's read her mind. He glances at one of the machines near her bed. "They still have you on a lot of drugs – Careful," he warns when she tries to turn her head. "The IV is placed here."

The tip of his finger brushes against something at the crook of her neck. She feels the pressure, the shift of the needle that must be there, and, despite her curiosity, she doesn't turn her neck to look.

"Why... Why there?" she asks. When she's had surgery in the past, the needles have been in the back of her hands or her forearms. "Did som'thing... go wrong?"

Silence. His hands tighten into fists on his lap and his jaw clenches. He can't meet her gaze.

"Cr... Seven," she repeats. She licks her lips and the tiny bit of fear twinging in her chest steadiest her words. "Did it go wrong?"

He finally shakes his head and says with unexpectedly vehement bitterness, "No. Everything went exactly as they planned."

"What do you mean?"

"I... I'm sorry. I should have stopped them, I should have figured out what they were going to do, I should have done more digging, I shouldn't have trusted them – I'm so, *so* sorry."

She reaches to gently brush his cheek.

Her arm doesn't move more than an inch before searing pain shoots through her veins like fire and ice.

It *hurts* – why does it hurt? Is it the drugs she's on, or maybe just that she's really stiff from lying down, or... And why does the tiny motion of her fingers make Crane's shoulders tense up?

Push past the pain. It's a skill she's been forced to learn for missions. Think past it, make her body move despite it.

It's the slow agony of a lava flow as she moves, but she manages it.

She raises her hand up...

It's metal.

Metal covers her skin, covers every inch of her hand and her wrist and her forearm and... Further up, up, up it goes, consuming her arm entirely, she can *feel* it now, feel it hurt all the way up to her shoulders, can feel the heaviness and the coldness and the *wrongness*. This is not her body, this is not her flesh and blood, this is... This isn't a covering, this is...

She whimpers and raises her other hand and it's the *same*, it's all gone; she's lost *both*, she can't feel...

"Don't move too much," Crane says, gently taking hold of her hands and lowering them down onto the bed. "The grafts where... where they *attach* are still healing. If you strain them, it'll only make things worse."

Right, of course, yes, the sensible thing – oh, *Ossuary help her*.

Crane's hands are intertwined with hers. Their fingers laced.

His thumb stroking the back of her hand. Her palms resting against his.

Nothing.

She feels *nothing*.

Heat stings her eyes and she can't breathe, her lungs heave without properly drawing breath, tears well up and blur her vision, she's desperately sobbing and gasping for air–

"It's okay, it's okay," Crane hastily reassures her, but she knows he's only saying that because she's hyperventilating, because it's not okay, it's *not*... And dear gods, merciful gods, please let this be a dream... "I'm here," he says, leaning down so that he can whisper in her ear so the all-seeing eyes of Ossuary will not hear. "Ginka, I'm here, I love you. Please, just take slow breaths for me; I need you to do that, okay?"

He loves her? Does he? She doesn't *know* anymore, she doesn't know anything, and she can't doubt him, she loves him, but how does she know that he loves her if she can't...

Hatred burns inside some hidden part of her heart.

When she married him, she swore to herself that she would never betray him, never hurt him intentionally, never *doubt* him. For one brief and eternal moment she doubts her husband and that... *that*...

That she can never forgive.

CHAPTER TWENTY-ONE
A Triple-Cross

Rig stares aimlessly out *Bluebird*'s viewport, her feet up on the controls next to the statuette of Dare and Shen. Underneath the crystal is the sole photograph she has of Daara, removed from its place of honor on the wall, edges worn down to a velvety softness from excessive fiddling.

"We're going to have to pull out of luminalspace soon," Janus remarks.

He's standing in the bridge doorway like an obtrusive and particularly repugnant coatrack. The one small blessing is that he's been pretty quiet the past few hours since leaving the Ascetic homeworld, mostly sitting on the couch and having very one-sided staring contests with a haunted-looking Ginka until she'd been too sick to stand and retreated to her room to sleep.

Rig hums, taking another look at the terminal. "Right. We're approaching the border between Ossuary and Ascetic space. You've got codes that'll get us in?"

"Don't worry, my blue friend." Oh, she *really* wants to smack him. "We'll have to stop to get a security check designation from the border patrol. Without it, we'll be found out the moment any ship stumbles across us between the border and the homeworld. With it, we can pass well enough to get us to where we need to go."

Were Daara's life not at stake, Rig wouldn't go into Ossuary space without at least a month's worth of notice to prep, to make sure her papers are in order and her story straight.

Ossuary isn't like the other two factions. Ascetic and Pyrite may keep their people and their star systems under tight control, but Ossuary... Ossuary whips even the slightest of mistakes into shape, perfectly straight bars guarding every system under their sigil. Pyrite hides behind talk of industrial revolution and innovative freedom, Ascetic behind their love of nature and beauty. Ossuary does not hide. Ossuary tells you straight from the start and without any pretense that they see you, they know you, and they will not hesitate to wipe all traces of you from the galaxy.

"You seem deep in thought. Care to share with this motley crew?"

"You're not my crew and you can stuff it."

"So tetchy. No need for the claws, Miss Madime."

"I have a name; you know what it is, so you had better learn to use it." She glances back down at the statuette and asks, "Why don't you share *your* thoughts, huh? What did you do to get kicked out of Windshadow and get sent on this unicorn hunt? Ginka said it must have been bad if it got your link ripped off."

All traces of his usual smug calm vanish, consumed by something hot and angry. "None of your damn business." And then the smugness rears its ugly face again. "Besides, if you want a story, you should be more interested in all the stuff I did while under Windshadow. The gory details will astound and amaze. I'd be happy to entertain you while we wait to clear border patrol."

"Ugh, never mind. Sicko." She pushes the statuette and the photo into a corner of the terminal, getting to her feet and shoving her way past Janus. "I'm going to see how Ginka's doing. Keep your mouth shut, your feet off my terminal, and your hands to yourself."

"Or, let me guess, you'll shoot me?" he taunts. "Do try and come up with more creative threats."

"Gods you're an ass."

"If you were interested in my ass, you could have just *said*."

She picks up a wrench lying on the table and throws it at his stomach as she leaves. The muffled curse he makes is immensely satisfying.

There's no noise coming from the spare bedroom. When Rig peeks inside she can see Ginka curled up on the cot, tangled in the sheets and with a sheen of sweat on her forehead. Must be fever. At least they've gotten past the stage where Ginka staggers around as though drunk and pukes her guts out.

Rig sits down carefully at the edge of the bed. "Heya."

"Is Janus with you?" Ginka murmurs, wriggling herself into an upright-ish position. Sparkle sparkles on her neck. If they have to sneak into Ossuary space, at least Windshadow won't know she's here.

"Nope."

"Thank Ossuary."

"He's getting on your nerves too, huh?" Especially given that while Janus seems to enjoy pissing her off in any number of ways, he prefers to simply give Ginka weird looks that make the Zazra scurry out of the room – usually towards the toilet, but that, for once, has nothing to do with Janus.

"He's not *on* my nerves." She casts a look out the door as though the bastard in question is about to appear there. "He *unnerves* me."

"Oh?"

"If... if Crane had been sent out on the unicorn hunt instead of me, would he have become like Janus? They're so different, but both were Ravens, both transgressed – I just was the one who got *caught* and was deemed... expendable. I can't stop thinking about what Janus might have been like before he got his link taken."

"Probably still a dick."

"Hm. Probably."

"He was trying to creep me out just now. I think the guy's main source of joy is making other people miserable."

Ginka buries her head further into the pillow and mumbles, "Maybe it gives him evil serotonin. How are *you* doing?"

Twitching every two seconds, unable to sleep, and constantly on edge. "Fine. Want me to get you anything before we hit the border? Food, water, a fluffy blanket?"

Ginka gives her an odd look and pushes her somewhat-damp hair back out of her eyes. "You keep trying to do everything. 'I'm going to save Daara' and 'I'm going to save June' and 'I'm going to help this stranger that I only barely know.' If you keep trying to do everything, you're going to spread yourself too thin and start losing pieces of yourself. There's a reason no Windshadow agent works alone, you know."

"If I *do* spread myself too thin and get bits of me cut off, then that's that, I suppose. As long as it means Daara's safe, right?"

"Daara's lucky to have a sister like you. I've seen a lot of people over the course of my job. A lot of self-serving assholes."

"Your old job sucked," she blurts out.

Ginka's lips quirk like she wants to make herself laugh but can't quite do it. "It was all I was ever told to want to do. I'm certain your sister was told the same – that serving Pyrite was all she should ever want to do."

That's what they told everyone. Only, Rig's over-inflated head was busy thinking she was above all that. "Yeah. I wasn't there to tell her otherwise."

"Oh, because you were so enlightened?" Ginka doesn't say it like an insult, merely as a sincere question.

"No. I wasn't anything like that. I wasn't some magic, propaganda-resisting wonder-child. I was just a smartass who loved doing all the things I was told not to do and learning all the things they told me not to learn."

"Hm."

Ginka's earlier wooziness seems to return in full force, and a moment later she's falling over the side of the bed and hurling into the bucket there. Guess the puking stage isn't quite as done with as Rig had been hoping. She awkwardly pats Ginka's back until it passes.

"Gods, my stomach…" Ginka moans, clutching at her gut as she drags herself upright again. "Sorry."

"Nothing to apologize for."

The entire ship suddenly lurches.

Ginka doesn't so much brighten up as look slightly less peaky. "Border patrol. Why did you stop?"

That was definitely the feeling of them leaving the luminalspace tunnel and slowing down to normal speeds, but… Rig holds up her link and checks the timers she has running. One counting since they left the Ascetic homeworld, one counting down until when they're supposed to be on the Ossuary homeworld, and one ticking away towards when they're *supposed* to be out of luminalspace at the border.

They're running thirty minutes ahead of schedule.

"No, it can't be – it's too early."

Which means… She scrambles towards the door. How could she have been so stupid as to not fully lock down the ship's controls when she left to speak with Ginka? Shit shit *shit* – what a *moronic fucking mistake* for her to make!

She skids onto the bridge with a hand on her guns.

Janus is lounging in her seat, fingers flying over the terminal as he types something out. A yellow light flashes on the screen – he's sent a message. He's fucking *sold them out*.

"Hey there," he says with a grin.

She draws Panache and levels the sight between his eyes, fingers painfully tight around the grip. "Step away from the controls."

Grin unfaltering, he raises his hands and shows her his opened palms. His gaze drops to Panache and his grin widens. "Thought so," he triumphantly murmurs, and before she can figure out what that means, he's saying, "Let's calm down a bit, shall we? There's no reason to get all up in arms here."

"Tell me what you did, you triple-crossing, egotistical, slimy son of a bitch!" she demands, heartbeat pounding in her veins.

There's a thud of Ginka stumbling out of her room.

She has to grab onto the wall to stand up in the bridge doorway and her eyes are unfocused – still on the verge of unconsciousness and being vertical clearly isn't doing anything to help.

"What's going on?" she asks, coughing up a mouthful of phlegm. "Why have we stopped early?"

"Because this triple-crossing, egotistical, slimy son of a bitch pulled us out of luminalspace and is sending our location straight to whatever bastard he works for – PI, Umbra, who the fuck knows at this point."

Janus turns his grin on Ginka. "I did you a favor just now. Think carefully about how you want to repay that."

"Yeah, at this point, I doubt you've ever helped anyone who wasn't yourself." Rig aggressively flicks her gun at him. "Get the fuck out of my chair and stay right where I can see you, hands up, no movements."

The moment his ass leaves the seat, she's taking his place, tossing Panache back into its holster so she can type with both hands.

Ginka wraps a hand around Janus's forearm, holding him in place as she peers down at the terminal screens. "That's... that's a Windshadow frequency."

Well, *shit*.

If she can scramble his message... Damn it, she's too late; it's already sent. She's screwed in that department. She quickly pulls up their previous course, the numbers flashing across the screen as fast as she can type. If she can get them back into luminalspace, then Umbra or whoever Janus has signaled will arrive to see nothing but a patch of empty space–

Crrrrkkk-Boom!

Bluebird is jerked back and forth as something *smashes* into the ship from behind.

Something shatters and crashes and Rig's slammed into the terminal, impact punching her lungs.

The statuette rattles and tips over.

A cry is ripped painfully out the back of her throat. She drops, fingers scrambling across the floor to try and find where it fell. All she can feel are crystal shards. The beautiful statuette is shattered. Gone. She grabs a handful of the crystal, shoving it into her pocket before turning to make sure that Ginka's alright – she is, although she's fallen to the floor and is trying to cough up a lung.

Warning lights bathe the bridge in red before the engines suddenly go out and the holographic screens show only scrambled code.

They're dead in the black.

"Mooring cables," she snarls, slamming a fist on the terminal.

Ginka pushes herself to one knee and sways, back thudding against the wall. "They've got us. Umbra has us. They never let go, they never miss a shot, not on a captured target–" She cuts herself off to retch up another dry heave. "Standard procedure. Two missiles. Directly to our engines. If the explosion doesn't kill us, vacuum will."

Rig grabs Ginka and hauls her up. "They haven't started shooting yet, and I'm not giving in until I'm actually dead. Besides, they need me alive and they need the plans."

"The plans–" Ginka's brow furrows. Her green eyes stare into Rig's and her pupils widen in realization. "Are they on the ship…?"

Shit, she shouldn't have phrased it like that.

Janus cracks his knuckles and brushes his jacket off. "Calm down. All I did was tell them you're here, X-74."

"You… you told them I'm in Ossuary space. You bastard." Gold light weakly crackles around Ginka's fingertips, and even that small effort visibly shaves hours off her life. "I can… I can fight… I'll fight them… Fight you–"

"No you will *not*," Rig tells her sternly.

She grabs Ginka's arm and rushes her to her room, practically dragging her as she stumbles and trips over her own feet.

"You need to stay here," she instructs, helping Ginka fall onto the bed and pulling the blankets up around her. "Stay quiet, don't try to fight. If I can draw their attention away from you then you'll have a chance. Got it?"

Ginka doesn't respond, her eyes wavering shut, sliding in and out of consciousness.

"Cactus, for once in your life, *don't fall asleep–*"

Another collision smashes into the ship.

That's the airlock being forced. They're about to be boarded.

"Hide," she repeats, and then forces the door shut.

She dashes back to the main room just in time to hear the hiss of compressed air as the entry hatch is cracked open, the pained wrenching of the ship's hull. *Bluebird* putting up its last fight and loosing.

"Honestly, don't worry," Janus tells her, straightening up and clasping his hands neatly behind his back. "I told you this was a favor, didn't I?"

The door opens.

She makes a split-second decision and raises her hands in the universal symbol of surrender.

A half dozen Windshadow agents march onto her ship the moment the door has been fully forced open. They're dressed from head to toe in black, faces uncovered. Uncovered? She knew the Tides group showed their faces, but she'd thought that was due to the unicorn hunt thing. Wouldn't normal agents be masked?

The Operatives spread out, blocking her from the bridge, from the hallway, from the exit. Trapping her in more thoroughly than a bird in a cage.

"I won't put up a fight. I surrender," she declares, gaze darting from Operative to Operative, trying to figure a way out of this even as she recognizes just how screwed she is. How screwed she and Ginka are. A man steps through the entryway. He's human and not wearing a mask either, and she can see an unusual link curled around his ear, turning a streak of hair there white. Exactly the same as Thrush-Eleven from Tides. That and the black feather she notices a moment later tells her everything she needs to know. A Raven.

She swallows a painful lump in her throat.

He stalks forward, his black greatcoat dragging menacingly behind him, terrifyingly reminiscent of the bird that is his appellation.

"Misha, Hanami, Dune – search the ship," he orders. "Secure the area and neutralize whatever traps are set up."

Half the Operatives dash off to do his bidding and the other half remain here, circling around the room, like an honor guard. Wait...

Did he just... use their *names*?

"Raven-Fifty," the Raven says, ignoring her completely, focusing only on Janus. A gun is in his hand, sights aimed at Janus. "Or whatever you're calling yourself now – I don't care. I know you're a liar, but your trap was sadistic enough that I had to spring it, if only to kill you for your sheer damn *audacity*."

Janus rolls his eyes towards the ceiling. "Re*lax*."

"I don't scare easy," Rig warns the Raven, staring up at him and trying to project as much confidence as she can manage. "If you really wanted us dead, you would have shot my ship full of holes from the moment you stuck us with mooring cables. You're just like the rest of your organization. You want what I have and for that you need me alive. So if you want to threaten me with guns and assassins, go right ahead. I'll call your bluff."

He blinks at her in utter confusion. "Threaten *you*? Not unless you're on his side in all this. I don't even *know* you."

"Sir!" One of the agents calls out from the hall where Ginka's room is. "It wasn't a lie – we've found her!"

No no no–

"Stay away from her!" Rig screams. "Don't hurt her!"

She throws herself toward the room and then gets smacked in the stomach when an Operative reaches out an arm and catches her around the waist. She chokes on her own throat, loses her footing, and practically bends in half around the Operative's elbow.

"Please," she begs, "she didn't do anything!"

She tries to reach for her guns, to do something, anything to stop the Raven who's…

Who's full-on *running* down the hall?

"*Ginka*!"

CHAPTER TWENTY-TWO
Measure of Grace

The screamed name didn't come from Rig.

It didn't even come from Janus.

It came from the *Raven*.

Rig flails and kicks the Operative holding her in the shin. There's a second where he flinches. The only chance she needs. She shoves past him, bolting after the Raven. One of the Operatives shouts at her to stop – as if she'd listen.

She flings herself through the door and then stops dead in her tracks.

The Raven is kneeling at Ginka's bedside. With unexpected tenderness, his hands cup her pale cheeks, thumb brushing a stray hair to the side. He presses two fingers to her neck and checks her pulse.

"Medic!" he calls out. He's on his feet again the next moment. "We have to get her to the ship, get her to a medic!"

What in the actual fuck? Do they need information from her? Need her awake and not dying so they can torture her to find out something? That seems sinister enough for Windshadow, but the pieces Rig's trying to put together just don't fit.

He picks Ginka up, her boney body hanging limp in his arms.

"Hold the fuck up. She's not going anywhere with you–" Rig tries to say.

Two of the Operatives pull her out of the way as the Raven barrels out of the room and back towards the main entry hatch.

"Hey, wait, I have questions!"

Once he's exited the ship, the Operatives let her go and she's after him like a shot, her toes scraping the ground and tripping her up as she shoves past the Operatives on her way out the main entry hatch, leaving Janus to jauntily traipse along behind her.

She freezes as soon as she's through the hatch and onto the Windshadow ship.

Whatever she'd been expecting from a Windshadow ship – skull decor, Ossuary sigil plastered everywhere, ominous spider webs – this isn't it. It's surprisingly sterile. The interior hull is sharp white, black accents and neatly laid out corridors. Actually, that's probably exactly what she should have expected, when she thinks about it. Something so nondescript that there's no way for someone unfamiliar with the ship to navigate it. If she were imprisoned here, escape would be difficult at best. And if she didn't know this was a Windshadow ship going in, she'd never be able to guess from the interior.

The Raven turns a corner, flanked by an unmasked Operative – a young Undarian man, a humanoid species with long, limber tails. There's another weird thing about the Operatives, she notices. None of them are sporting helltech generators. They must *have* them, right? But why wouldn't they *wear* them all the time like Ginka does?

"Contact Asher," she can hear the Raven ordering. "I need their help. Stay with Fifty."

"Hold on!" she yells, resuming her mad dash after him.

He doesn't slow down, and she barely manages to slide between two rapidly closing doors in her haste to keep up.

She finds herself having tumbled into a medbay.

It's barely different from the rest of the sterile white ship. What distinguishes it are counters filled with surgical tools, cabinets stocked with more medicine bottles than she's ever seen in her life, and a medical bed sitting in the middle of the room. Ginka's limp body has been placed there, a medic dressed in white hovering, cutting a slit in her shirt collar and placing an IV needle into a vein on her neck.

"Grace," the Raven commands.

The medic – Asher? – nods, replying, "Triple dose?"

"How long has it been since she took her last dose?" the Raven asks, and it takes Rig a minute to realize that he's talking to her.

"Oh, uh… about a day and a half. But she's used helltech since then and she was shot. Don't imagine that helped."

"Triple dose it is."

A bottle is tossed across the room like a toy ball. In quick, familiar motions, the Raven snatches a syringe and draws a large dose of the shimmering clear liquid, tapping it once to remove any air bubbles in exactly the same way Ginka does. He pulls the cap off with his teeth and stabs the needle into her thigh.

Asher starts rifling through the contents of a cabinet, pulling out bottles and needles and all sorts of terrifying looking instruments. "Scan her."

One of those unusual hard light panels is projected from the Raven's link, hovering in front of his right eye. "The adrenomycin toxin has spread to her heart and lungs," he reports, and Rig is not imagining the way his voice cracks on those words. "Her vitals are failing–" He clears his throat. "It says to administer adrenaline. We need her awake and her blood pumping for the Grace to start working properly."

"I always trust someone with the entire netspace in their head," they dryly remark as they prep another syringe.

Rig is suddenly nearly sick on the clean white floor as the medic slices Ginka's shirt open and raises a really *really* long needle over her bare chest.

She turns to face a wall just before the tiny, sickening sound of the needle going straight into Ginka's heart. Maybe it would have been best if she waited outside or something – she's pretty sure that the Raven has almost completely forgotten she's here anyway, so clearly focused on helping Ginka that it's real unlikely he's going to be telling her what's going on anytime soon.

She forces herself to tune out the chaos of whatever the Raven and Asher are doing to Ginka, given that she's confident enough they aren't trying to kill her and that she knows her ability to determine what medical stuff, specifically, they're doing is just a hair above nonexistent. She puts her back to them and tells herself that her boots are really very interesting, and if she just keeps staring at them this will all be over soon. It's crazy that this is the second time she's had to do this in two days.

It's impossible for her to say how long she quietly stands there before Asher startles her out of her thoughts by resting their hand on her shoulder.

"She's stable," they inform her, in a way that she thinks might be an attempt at kindness. "There isn't anything further I can do for her other than let the Grace do its job. For what it's worth, she should be waking up shortly."

"Oh." Her mouth ends up giving a surprised, "Thank you?"

They step out, shutting the door behind them with a soft click of a privacy lock sliding into place. A hush falls upon the room as Asher's disappearance leaves only the soft sounds of beeping machines connected to Ginka and the steady dripping of something that might be Grace into the IV bag.

The Raven leans over her, and as Rig watches, he picks up the bottle she wears around her neck and turns it over, and there's that gentleness again...

The realization suddenly dawns on her. "You're Crane."

"She... she mentioned me?"

There's such a wistful sadness to the question that she feels obligated to reassure him. "Of course she did, she's rather obviously in love with you. *Still* in love with you, might I add, even after three years, which is rather more than I can say for a lot of people in this galaxy. I mean, she mentioned you even when she was trying not to let me know too much about herself – although she didn't use your name until just recently."

"Three years..." He presses his eyes tightly shut for a moment, like he's trying to block out the truth. "I thought she was dead. They told me she was dead, and still I–" His eyes open a crack, looking down at Ginka through long eyelashes. "I don't know if you know this, but one year on limited Grace supply is considered the extent of what Operatives are able to handle."

She tries to imagine being in the same position. Having June just vanish one day and waiting, hoping desperately for even the slightest of signs. Between them, Ginka's chest rises and falls with slow, steady breaths. She can imagine the sheer relief. The miracle this must seem like.

"I'm sorry." She gives Crane a slight smile. "I'm glad that you found her again. That you found her in time."

He tucks a strand of Ginka's hair behind her ear and sighs. "So am I. If I'd arrived even a few hours later..."

"You didn't. That's what matters."

"I..." He hesitates before finishing, "I'm sorry about how we met."

That isn't a grudge she's going to die holding. "Eh. I can understand not trusting Janus – or me, since I was standing next to him. He's an absolute shit-nugget."

He laughs. It's short and almost more of an undignified snort, but it's a laugh; and now that the terrifying Raven has faded into a person, she's beginning to see the shape of who Ginka fell in love with. Without the attacking-her-ship detail, she actually thinks she approves. Not that Ginka needs her approval or anything.

"Yeah," he agrees, "he is. I only met him once, about a month before he was sent off, but he was... not the best person to work with. My associates are keeping an eye on him right now. Who knows what he could get up to."

"Can I ask... the Operatives you've got with you. Why aren't they wearing masks, and why do you use their names? I thought all that stuff was bad, given that you've all got numbers instead, and Ginka had to pick her own name, in the end. Umbra doesn't seem like the type of guy to be all thrilled about people getting names."

"He isn't. After Ginka left, I started... well, I wasn't making a lot of smart decisions. I got sent out with a lot of different Operatives on missions, and then I began to get to know them and found that I was bumping into people like us, people that had picked their own names or wanted to know what name they were born with. I started stealing looks at classified files and giving out names whenever I could."

She gapes. "You started a little rebellion." Wait... she almost wants to laugh. "Hold up, did Ginka marry a *bad boy*?"

Crane makes a flat, unimpressed face that is practically identical to Ginka's flat, unimpressed face.

Whatever comment he's about to make is cut short by a tiny, breathy noise from Ginka.

She's awake.

It's like Crane's been electrocuted. "Ginka?" he asks, leaning forward and activating that link of his for a second, presumably to double check that she's not getting worse. "Ginka, can you hear me?"

Rig's stomach has leapt to her throat as well, only in her case she can't speak at all. She doesn't even know what she'd say. 'Welcome back to the world of the living and by the way you know how we were being attacked when you passed out well that was actually your long lost husband' somehow just doesn't strike any good tone.

Ginka's eyes crack open.

"C-Crane?" Her voice stutters like a worn-down engine, breaking on her words. Green wavers beneath her thin eyelashes, her pupils dilated, trying to focus and seemingly failing. "Am... am I... dead?"

Tears shine in his eyes as he shakes his head. He rests a trembling hand on her cheek, and Rig can imagine that need to tangibly feel that the one he loves is alive and here and real – something Windshadow took away from Ginka forever.

"No," he tells her. "No, you're not dead, love. You are very much alive."

"But…" Ginka's brow furrows as she haltingly turns her head to look at him. "You're here."

"I am. I can only beg your forgiveness for taking so long to find you."

Ginka's eyes redden, and tears, fat and blubbery tears, start to fall down her cheeks.

"I'm… gonna go see what Janus is up to." Rig quietly turns around and slips out of the room, leaving Crane and Ginka behind as she reaches up to embrace her husband with unsteady arms.

That moment is for them, and Rig isn't going to encroach on it.

It was an excuse, yes, but she should actually go make sure Janus isn't starting shit. These unusual – *rebellious* – Windshadow agents might not stop him from doing something if he does it real sneaky.

Janus is, fortunately – or perhaps suspiciously innocuously – exactly where she left him, casually leaning against a wall, a few of the unmasked Operatives subtly lingering in the background, far enough for the illusion of distance and privacy, close enough to pin him to the floor if he so much as twitches wrong.

"See?" he says as she approaches. "I *told* you I was doing X-74 a favor."

"Her name is Ginka, and you know it," she corrects automatically. "And alright, fine, I suppose it was… not *un*helpful. But a bit of warning would have gone a long way. I was a hair away from blowing your brains out." She pokes him in the chest. "If you actually want to do this whole 'working together to save my sister' thing, then you have to spit it out when you've got some plan to send out magic Handler codes and get a missing husband to show up."

"I doubt something so specific will be happening again; so certainly, I have no issues agreeing to that."

"That easy? Seriously?"

"I'm *always* serious. Can't you tell?" He gestures to his smarmy smirk. "This is my serious face."

Gods, it's like looking into a screwed-up mirror version of herself – all the swagger she tries to project on the usual, but with a heaping tablespoon of dickishness thrown into the mix. If she ever starts acting like him, she hopes to any god that might exist that June puts her out of her fucking misery.

Janus shifts his weight from one foot to the other and it somehow smoothly takes him from reclining against the wall far away from her to right up in her personal space in a second flat. "In all seriousness," he says, "I think we need to have a chat. Now that it seems we're a larger team. Plans need to be adjusted. Unless you want it to be just you and me going up against Umbra…"

Does he want it to be just the two of them? Presumably she presents an easier target without a Windshadow assassin-person-friend-buddy – whatever Ginka is – hanging around. And yet he'd called Crane over, anyway, seriously increasing the Windshadow assassin-people-friends buddies. If he really wanted to make it just the two of them, that's a pretty big risk. Or does he want Crane's assistance in all this? Did he know about Crane's friends? Gods, trying to figure out what Janus is thinking is a damn nightmare.

"I guess," she eventually replies, "it would be best to talk about what we're going to do. I'm sure Ginka and Crane will have loads of ideas about how to save Daara, now that we have all these new resources."

His expression doesn't change at all. She's tempted to grab him by the scruff of his shirt and demand he tell her what his game is. "Is she awake?" he asks.

"Awake and singing. Not that I imagine you care."

"Shall we go have a chat?"

With that, he strides off towards the medbay, the unmasked Operatives trailing him from a distance.

They do stay out of the medbay when Janus and Rig enter, though. It's interesting how well-run Crane's little organization is. Almost reminds her of the Nightbirds, but with a clear power structure and chain of command and faction trappings.

Crane stands in the doorway for a moment as they enter, giving Janus a long, stern stare before stepping aside. "Come in," he says. "We need to discuss our next move."

Ginka is sitting upright in the bed, her legs curled up beneath her and her hands resting in her lap. There's more life on her face than Rig's seen from her in the entire time they've known one another. Crane drifts back to Ginka's side, twining his hand in with hers.

He glances at Rig. "I understand you're the inventor everyone's been searching for."

"That's right." She crosses her arms and prepares to stare him down if necessary. "Got a problem with that? No offense, but if you're planning on handing me over to Umbra in exchange for Ginka getting off scot free, then I have some bad news for you about the schematics that everyone wants, namely in relation to *me* and to *not a chance, buddy.*"

With a sharp shake of his head, he waves her off. "No, that's not what I'm thinking, at all. I've been told that the three of you were planning to take on Umbra directly."

"Eyup. Got a problem with that, either?"

"Not even a little."

Oh yeah, Ginka *totally* married a rebellious bad boy. Honestly, not quite what Rig had been expecting. She'd been thinking someone a little more by the book, given how tenaciously Ginka's held onto her loyalty after all this time. Not that she's complaining. Ginka needs that bit of bad to shake up the stupid faction bullshit she clings to.

Rig cracks her knuckles and starts going through her mental rundown. "Alright then. Basic plan is this: we save Daara, my twin sister. Umbra has her, he's going to use her to get the schematics from me, and I'm pretty sure that now he knows we're coming. Ginka's got a fancy do-dad that hides her chip's signal, but I didn't see anything like that on your friends. Umbra's probably picked up on you lot changing course to join with us."

"So we've lost the element of surprise," Ginka agrees. "I suppose that's the end of our original stealth plan. Something more direct, perhaps?"

"We still can't just bust in, guns blazing. People will get caught in the crossfire. People that *we* care about. Remember: Daara. Comes. *First*."

Janus shrugs. "If you really want Umbra gone, prioritizing your sister is a waste of time–"

"Shut *up*!" She slices her hand through the air, wishing it could zip his mouth. "You have done nothing but ruin shit since the moment you showed up in my life. From now on you are not allowed to say anything that's not helpful. Got it?"

There's still that glib amusement quirking his lips, but he raises his hands and takes a performative step back, nonetheless.

"Right." She takes a deep breath. "So we can't do surprise. Can we do infiltration? Crane, how many of your friends do you have?"

"There are twenty-four of the Named," he reports – and sweet name for an underground organization, by the way. "I can have all of them return to headquarters asap. We'll need numbers no matter what tactic we end up taking. Fortunately for us, at any given time, approximately half of Windshadow's forces are deployed in the field. We'd only need to deal with the half that remain in headquarters."

Ginka shakes her head. "That's still too many. And our lord... And *Umbra* will notice."

"Not if he's distracted." Rig's great at loud and irritating distractions.

"Fine, if we can theoretically distract Umbra, *even then* we just don't have the numbers to launch any kind of attack."

"Ahem."

The three of them glare at Janus.

"Just a slight hiccup to add to the pile," he explains cheerfully. "I believe you are all forgetting about the Controllers. There are ten total, and while they're not trained for combat, they have some basic self-defense skills. None of them are field agents, and as such, each and every one of them will be home when we come knocking."

Gods, this is frustrating. If only banging her head against a wall would actually help. "Okay. So we somehow distract Umbra. We somehow use twenty-four people to deal with all the Controllers – not quite sure who they are, but I get the gist. We need to get Daara out of whatever prison cell Umbra has her in. And we need to deal with the fact that Umbra knows me, Crane, probably Ginka, and also probably Janus, are coming for him. Not going to lie, I'm drawing a blank on any plans here."

"I'll bet the Named can persuade the others," Crane says with a thoughtful frown. "Not the Controllers, obviously, but some of the Operatives and Handlers might stand aside if they see what's going on."

"Awesome. Control the chaos on that end. Sweet. I mean, we might want chaos, but we want chaos that we're starting, not chaos other people are starting."

"You're rambling."

"I'm aware, Cactus."

Distraction, distraction... Umbra knows they're coming... Daara's hidden...

The story she told Ginka in the Throttle.

Thousands of years ago, Dare of the Spire beat Pyrite by pretending to surrender. They let him into the heart of Agaraan Spire, their fortress, because they were proud at having beat him and wanted to execute him themselves. And then he burned the place down from the inside out.

"Okay," she decides, the words flowing unhindered as she realizes what needs to be done. "If Umbra knows the four of us are coming, then we give him what he wants. We surrender."

Ginka's jaw falls open. "Are you crazy? We'd be taken straight to Umbra."

"Actually, that might just work," Crane says slowly, a slight buzz about him, as though he's figured out her idea as well and is thinking it through just as fast as she is. "It'd eliminate the need to locate your sister. He'd bring her straight into his throne room to... well, to *use* her to make you reveal the schematics' locations. Umbra has patience; but after three years, I imagine that patience is running thin."

"So the four of us are a distraction," she continues. "While we're busy, our people take out the Controllers and make sure that the agents who *aren't* part of your Named friends don't do anything to complicate the whole thing."

Ginka frowns. "I thought we went over this. We don't have enough people."

"No, you don't. But I have the Nightbirds."

Part of her hates the idea of asking her fellows to help with factioned business. Even though it's toppling Windshadow, they'd still be fighting alongside die-hard factioned loyalists. And that, on the surface, is the antithesis of what they stand for. And yet... she has this gut feeling that at least a few will show up if she explains, if they can understand the Named, if they get the stakes that are on the line, if they know what Umbra is doing and what he wants. Maybe it's not a gut feeling. Maybe it's just a hope.

"That's not an organized group," Ginka points out. "I mean no offense, but you're merely a nomadic bunch of..."

"Ragtag law-breakers? Rebels, thieves, librarians, and arsonists?"

"I was going to be more polite about it, but yes."

"Those aren't insults, Cactus. I give my friend Mohsin a call and he can have all the Nightbirds in the area coming to help us in three hours flat. With luck."

If they listen.

Crane shrugs. "I'm alright with that. Honestly, they're not all that different from us, are they?"

"From the Named? Not... not all that different, no." She does a quick bit of mental logistics. "Okay, here's how this goes. The four of us stay in Crane's ship and approach the headquarters that way. Once my Nightbirds arrive, they'll cram into *Bluebird* and use my ship to approach. See," she brags, "I recently stumbled across this nifty Pyrite stealth ship transponder that'll let my ship sneak in under the radar."

Crane smiles at Ginka for a brief second. "And here I thought *I* was the one with a knack for picking friends."

"Thanks for the compliment, I think? Our people take the Controllers out, we secure Daara, we take Umbra out. Ginka, you can overpower his guards, right? Crane, no offense for not including you in that, but I have no idea if you're a fighter or only an info guy. Janus, *full* offense, we're still not giving you a weapon."

Another bit of amusement from Crane. "I'm competent enough."

"I can get security codes to allow your Nightbirds inside," Janus offers, to her great surprise.

"Finally, something useful from you." She nods. "Do it, then."

Crane taps his chin. "That's everything dealt with. Except... do you actually *have* the schematics? We may need to show Umbra proof to stop him from simply killing Daara, should he get *truly* impatient."

"Yeah," she admits quietly. "I've got them. It's not as though it matters – he'll never get them. So," she claps her hands together and changes the subject with the utter lack of subtlety that she'd normally associate with Ginka, "I'm going to call my people; Crane and Ginka, go call your people; Janus, do whatever you need to do. And then we're going to go steal my sister back from Umbra."

"Good luck," Ginka says with a smile. "With Ossuary's blessing, we might just get through this."

She flinches. If they *are* to get through this, Ossuary needs to stay as far away from them as possible. None of the faction gods are on their side. They're on their own side and there are no gods watching over them.

INTERLUDE
No Goodbyes

Ginka wakes in the middle of the night to the sound of a fist pounding on her door.

It's probably one of the assholes in the Operative dorms. She rolls out of bed and shakes off the last dregs of sleep within seconds. Though she's returned to Windshadow headquarters after her last mission ended four days ago, she never leaves the mission mindset – always be ready to fight. Attackers could come at any second.

Her metal fingers – only a year old now, still unfamiliar, and too heavy – brush over the door panel, unlocking her room, and allowing whoever's causing a ruckus to enter.

It's not one of her fellow Operatives.

It's a Controller, nameless and faceless, their features covered with a white nanomesh mask. Answerable only to Lord Umbra himself, she dares not lift so much as a finger against them.

Not even when the Controller grabs her by the arms and drags her from her room.

"Sir?"

She struggles to keep up as they pull her through the halls of the Operative dorms and towards the center of their headquarters. It's about two in the morning, and no one but the night watch will be awake – although, actually, she doesn't see the night watch *at all*. There should be guards patrolling the halls and standing by the entrance to the main audience chamber that the Controller yanks her through.

"Sir," she tries again, "What's happening?"

"Shut up."

The Controller pushes her into the center of the audience chamber, shoves her to her knees, and then leaves.

The *bang-clack* of the doors locking behind her echoes through the room.

She shivers on the cold marble floors. Her eyes dart to each dark corner, trying to pick out the shapes of whoever is hiding there. Someone must be here, someone must be watching her. In the heart of their headquarters, someone is *always* watching. Dead silence sits heavy in the room, like a shroud in the air.

"X-74."

She whirls around.

The throne carved at the head of the chamber is now occupied.

Lord Umbra himself rests there, his legs crossed and his fingertips pressed together as he gazes dispassionately down at her. Unlike her first – and last – meeting with him, he sneers at her as though she's worse than the dirt beneath his shoes. There's something so penetrative about his gaze. It strips her bare, peeling her skin off and picking out her bones one by one.

"My lord," she says, bowing deeply enough to press her forehead to the ground. "I didn't... Please forgive my unruly appearance. I was not anticipating your summons–"

He holds up his hand and silences her more thoroughly than a gag shoved between her teeth. "I did not bring you here to listen to your pitiful apologies. I have brought you here, *X-74*, because you are a traitor."

He knows.

"What? My lord, I assure you, I have never–"

"*Silence*," he hisses, and the chamber itself falls still. "I also did not bring you here to listen to your lies and excuses. Did you really think that your transgressions would go unnoticed?

I see everything that occurs under my roof, I know *all* that my agents do."

"That's not–"

"One more unwanted word from you and I will take your head here and now."

Her jaw snaps shut.

"That's better," he says when she offers no further protest. "I have every reason to execute you for what you've done. You're a threat to our organization, it's only a matter of time before you blow up in our faces. It is fortunate for you then, that I am *merciful*. I will give you one chance to redeem yourself and prove that you can still serve our organization. Doesn't that sound far better than execution?"

When she manages to speak, her words are directed to the ground. "You are more merciful than I deserve, my lord."

"Yes. I *am*."

"My lord, Seven–"

"Your Handler? He will remain close to home. Consider it… motivation, for you to neither fail, nor return. You have ten minutes to gather your belongings and then you will leave."

But then, "My lord, if I may ask a question?"

"If you must."

"If this is to be a long-term mission… I only have two bottles of Grace in my room, if I could–"

"Then," he says, "you had best not dawdle. There is an item of great importance, you see, one that has gone missing. I need someone with your level of competence to retrieve it quickly and quietly. You'll have competition. A number of our other… more *disobedient* agents will be sent to retrieve it in due time. Prove that you can still serve – that you can serve *better* than they – and you will be able to return."

"I won't fail you, my lord. What am I to retrieve?"

"A most unique weapon from Pyrite that they have apparently just lost." A thin smirk slices across Umbra's features. "Oh, and X-74? A final word of warning before you go. If you *do* attempt to return before you've completed your task, the moment you take a single step into Ossuary space, you'll be placing Raven-Seven's neck on the guillotine before your own."

Her heart is being ripped out of her chest and Umbra's nails dig into it as he smiles.

CHAPTER TWENTY-THREE
Eye of Ossuary

The first thing Mohsin says to Rig is, "You're a crazy maniac, you know that?"

Ah, good to see him again. She lets him clap her on the shoulder in greeting. "Yeah, but I'm *your* crazy maniac."

A series of associated frigates, schooners, and sloops are taking turns with the Windshadow ship's airlock, unloading maybe one or two people per ship. Fortunately for her, a couple of the ships the Nightbirds are bringing are *actual* stealth ships with some pretty impressive scavenged tech on them, so *Bluebird* won't have to be filled to a truly ludicrous capacity. Her ship is still going to be in the precarious position of taking point, though. Mohsin had better be as good a pilot as he claims.

Most of the Nightbirds are Kashrini, but maybe two percent of the people milling about and getting organized are other species – a Da'vade woman over there, marked by her luminescent eyes, and the knobs running down her spine that pick up sound vibrations and allow her to hear. Another four-armed Trant lingers, carrying a nasty-looking traditional seven-pronged staff. Two Oriate siblings down the hall, polishing the spikes on their skin-like weapons. It's not only the Kashrini that've been given the short end of the galactic stick.

Mohsin laughs a deep, belly-rumbling laugh. "Good to see you again. I've got a good gang together. Couple friends of mine from back in the old days. Don't know if you ever figured it out," he says, rolling his sleeve up to show a wicked tattoo of a red and blue axe on his shoulder, "but I'm former Crimson Butchers."

"I did, actually – sorry to steal your thunder. But nice tattoo! And hey, you've got former soldier friends. That'll be a real help."

"Yeah, most of the others just know their way around a gun with no real formal training. You know how it is. People like you, really."

"Excuse you, I manage fine."

"Oh and uh," he jerks his thumb towards the ship currently docking, "these guys say they know you."

A bulky, drab figure steps out of the airlock and gives her a stoic nod. There's a sawed-off shotgun at his thigh, and behind him is a smaller figure, walking at a quick trot to keep up with her companion's longer strides.

"Ditra! Aazi!" Rig spreads her arms out in welcome. Gods, it's good to see more familiar faces. "Glad to see you're here."

Aazi smiles and waves. "Hello again. When we got Mohsin's call, we dropped off our refugees at the nearest safe port and headed over as fast as we could. Something this big and bold, we couldn't miss it. How's your Zazra friend? Injury healed well?"

"Good as can be, thanks for asking." She points them down the hall. "There's a couple of really intimidating people in all black that'll tell you where to go. Good luck, alright?"

"Hey," Ditra says with a grunt, "that's our line. We've got the easy bit."

True. Although not particularly comforting.

They hurry off down the neat and orderly ship corridor, leaving her and Mohsin to get nearly mowed down by the tall Kashrini woman that's leaving the next ship.

"Seriously though, good luck," he says, and it only just now occurs to her that he's a lot older than her, got a lot more wrinkles on his face; and if he's former Crimson Butchers, surely he's seen a lot of fights go bad real fast. Maybe this is going to be one of them, and maybe he's only taking *this* fight as a favor to her. "You're gonna need it. And I'm looking forward to meeting your sister when this is all done."

Her hand slides into her pocket to wrap around the headscarf pin resting there next to the shards of crystal from the broken statuette. "I hope you two would get along. Take care of my ship out there, okay? I'm trusting you to make sure not even a single scratch gets on the hull."

"No need to worry about *me*," he grumbles.

"*Bluebird* is the real important thing here, and we both know it."

"Yeah, yeah, get going and stop giving me grief."

"And Mohsin?"

"Yes?"

"If I die and you don't, please bring *Bluebird* back to June."

He pauses, eyes locking onto hers. He nods with the solemnity that her request deserves. "You have my word."

She gives him a very tight handshake and heads off towards the Windshadow ship's bridge where Ginka and Crane – and regrettably Janus – are waiting.

After twelve planning and panic-filled hours, she's gotten the hang of navigating the ship. Or at least she's better at it than she was eleven hours previously, which, now that she thinks about it, isn't really much of a brag.

The bridge here is a plaza compared to the tiny cubicle of *Bluebird*'s bridge. There's a helmsman's seat, two pilot seats, gunner controls – the works. Whole thing is a sparkling wonder of smooth white computer terminals and pristine order. She prefers her ship, of course, but this one is damn beautiful once she gets past the intimidating blankness of it. There's a sole empty chair in the middle of the bridge, and as she passes she swears she can see the ghostly image of Daara sitting there, bright eyes staring accusingly back at her.

Ginka is standing in front of the massive, floor-to-ceiling viewport, her metal hands clasped behind her back in a perfect picture of rigidity. An image that is totally ruined by the way her shoulder leans slightly against Crane's as he stands next to her.

Rig's quick steps slow down as she approaches them, drawn to a halt by the celestial spectacle outside.

"Is that…?"

Ginka hums in agreement. "The Ossuary homeworld."

Five moons orbit the planet below, covered in the black shadows of metropolis and the yellow lights of cities, each surrounded by tiny specks that she knows must be defensive fleets of ships. Only two are currently illuminated by the single sun of the Ossuary Prime System, the other three draped in darkness.

Beautiful as they are, they're but the corona that surrounds the homeworld itself. The planet appears as though it's carved from marble, smooth waves of white sky and inky swirls of black mountains, golden lines of glowing cities winding through as they follow curves in the continents like the fine tip of a paintbrush trailing over a canvas. Stunning and regal and magnificent in the most terrifying sense of the word.

"We'll be landing shortly," Crane says. He gives Ginka a quick peck on the cheek. "I'm going to go speak with Heron, make sure he has everything ready to go."

It gets significantly less awkward for Rig after he heads off to double check everything – she likes him as a person, but it's weird to be third-wheeling. Her fingers are nervously twitching against her thighs as she takes a step forward so that she's slightly closer to Ginka, who's still staring out the viewport.

"You okay?" Rig asks, because it's a fuck load easier to ask someone else that than to try and ask *herself* that.

"Are you?"

"Eh." Doesn't matter, does it? "What if–"

"Don't second guess this. No plan survives contact with the

enemy. The key thing is being adaptable. Being able to change strategies once the original plan begins to go downhill."

She swallows a lump in her throat. "Great for you and all, but I don't know how to do that. My 'strategy' once everything goes to shit is to *run*. Things go wrong, I get out. I *can't* here – I can't just run off if it goes bad, there's too much on the line. I can't leave my friends, my people, my *sister*."

"Umbra is... not a threat one can dodge." Ginka glances at the door Crane vanished behind. "I've gotten everything back and now I have to fight to keep it, and honestly if I had it my way, I might just disappear off into the corners of Ossuary space, hide and hope that Umbra never finds us. But you've proven that such a tactic doesn't work. Not forever. And I... I *want* a forever."

"A forever sounds pretty nice. You're really that scared of Umbra?"

"*Terrified.*"

"...Good to know we're on the same page then."

They stand in silence, staring at the rapidly approaching planet, until a door on the bridge opens and an unfamiliar man steps in.

He's tall and blond and objectively, from a purely aesthetic point of view, drop dead gorgeous. A Handler link curls around his ear.

"We're ready," the man says. He gives Rig the same weird formal bow that Ginka did when they first met. "I'm Heron, by the way. Come on."

Rig and Ginka troop after him off the bridge and down the ship levels towards the main exit hatch. The halls are more empty now. In order for this to go right, the Nightbirds can't be seen landing next to this ship, and so all of them have left by now, zooming off on their own with their various bits of cloaking tech.

The Named are the only ones remaining onboard, and they, too, are hurrying into place as the ship begins its final descent.

Crane and Janus are waiting by the exit, pointedly ignoring one another.

"Alright," Heron explains, handing out four sets of handcuffs. "We've fixed these up to be dummies. All you need to do is press the green button near your thumb, and they'll unlock. If this is to work, we need to put up a convincing appearance of having taken you lot into custody for treason, and these are the best option we've got. Any questions? No? Good."

So as long as she doesn't bump anything or accidentally touch them or let anyone else mess with them, she'll be fine. That, too, gets added to the list of things she needs to mostly ignore in order for her to not lose her nerve.

Cuffs are distributed.

Crane and Ginka assist each other while Rig tries to figure out the best way to put them on herself – she doesn't trust Janus.

"Need help?" Crane asks.

"Yeah. I'm dexterous, but not *this* dexterous."

He holds the cuffs in place while she snaps them shut around her wrists.

Heron did a good job. Even with them locked she's able to drop her hands and twist her wrists without disturbing them. Without really noticing, she brushes her fingertips against the outside of her pants pocket. Tiny bumps are raised in the fabric, pointy edges and soft curves from the crystal shards of the statuette that she'd grabbed onto before. How did Dare manage to do this?

"Thanks. Shall we?"

"I hope we have Ossuary's favor in this," Crane says, and *damn* she's really starting to get annoyed by that.

"Stop saying that. Ossuary needs to fuck right off."

"Ah, well... perhaps. For what it's worth, Ossuary isn't Umbra. Condemning one doesn't have to condemn the other."

"No need to try and convert me."

He sheepishly rubs the back of his head. "Sorry. Habit, I suppose."

There's a jostle, smoother than anything *Bluebird*'s capable of, the kind of smoothness that only comes with brand new, top of the line, factioned tech.

The ship has landed.

"Alright," Heron says, taking his place in front of them and tapping out commands into a control panel on the door. A couple of fake guards are starting to flock behind them. He turns, deferring to Crane. "Mission start?"

"Mission start," Crane confirms.

"And eyes open," Ginka finishes.

The door opens.

The four of them are marched out through the white-walled hatch, down a gangplank, and then into the cold air of Ossuary's homeworld.

Snowflakes settle on Rig's eyelashes.

Somber black and white stretches out before her in a reflection of the ship. It's reforged into craggy mountains blanketed with snow, a landing pad the color of pure obsidian beneath her feet, a cloud-mottled grey sky above her head, and snowdrifts swept to the side to allow skiffs to fly swiftly past. Darkest of all is the towering complex that looms above her. It's not tall on its own, its height mostly gained by virtue of being a multitude of large structures built into the mountainside, like the black and white scattered boxes of a chess board, just as neatly organized and just as austere.

Chilly wind curls around her ankles and snow crunches beneath her feet with each step she's forced to take. The air is lighter here, thin and winding, icing her nose with each inhale.

No one she's ever spoken to before could say for certain what the Ossuary homeworld is like. She'd assumed another city world to match the clockwork spires of Pyrite and the glittering towers of Ascetic. Surely the rest of the planet can't be like this. Surely there must be sprawling cities, entire continents devoted to the metropolitan complexes that mark the other homeworlds, or massive spaceports that float just above the clouds.

But here, at the heart of Ossuary's all-seeing eye, the galaxy is quiet and still.

Eventually their honor guard of Named bring them to the main entrance and out of the cold. A handful of snowflakes sneak in after her before the doors slam shut.

Another series of white halls awaits her inside, like a stone mausoleum.

"Everyone in position?" Crane whispers.

Rig's link is tucked away into the hidden pocket of her headscarf and so she can hear the series of affirmative responses from the Nightbirds and the Named.

Janus's lips peel back from his teeth into a confident grin. "This should be fun."

CHAPTER TWENTY-FOUR
Daara, At Last

Rig and her band of three are forced to halt in front of a towering set of double doors.

Two silent guards stand watch, neither of them allies and both of them carrying intimidating rifles. One of the Named guarding her hands over a key card. A guard nods, and then both of them stand aside to allow entry.

"Is–" Her jaw hangs open as she stumbles through into a massive room. "Is this place supposed to be Umbra's office?"

"Yes," Ginka says tersely, "It's subtle."

An office? Yeah right.

This is a throne room.

The heart of this so-called headquarters is more palatial than she would ever have imagined, in a way that clashes so obscenely with the blank ship and the building's stark exterior that she wonders if it's all to throw visitors – or prisoners – off guard; if the marble floors are just for a show of richness and power; the maze of columns around her designed to distract and confuse more than serve any structural purpose. The ceiling, so high and so dark that she cannot make out any details of it, must be for intimidation's sake alone...

No lights illuminate the edges of the room, giving the impression that it simply fades into shadow and nothingness. As she tentatively creeps closer to the center, she gets the feeling that a thousand eyes are watching her, peering out of the blackness and stripping her bare before their gaze.

There is one light in the chamber.

It's impossible for her to say if the white light is projected up from the floor or down from the ceiling – it's simply white light. There.

In an aura around a tall, carved chair.

"Yeah, this is a throne room," she mutters under her breath.

Gods, even though she hopes to end this day still in possession of her life and not having gone up in flames, part of her wishes that she were truly in Dare's shoes, facing down Pyrite, instead of Ossuary. There is no possible way that the Pyrite Council of old could project even a fraction of the sheer terror that drifts through this room.

Eyes are forming out of the dark.

In silent unison, six Windshadow Operatives form out of the shadows and take up guard positions around her. Each puts their back to a pillar less than twenty feet from her in any direction, standing straight as a board, armed with a menagerie of helltech weapons – some prosthetic, some not. Faces covered, eyes blank.

"Heya," she says, turning around to wiggle her fingers at the Operatives around her. And she has once again reached the nervous blabbing stage. Lovely. "Nice weather outside, yeah? How's it going? Hope you're well? Where the fuck is Umbra?"

"Right here."

Out of the corner of her eye, she can see Ginka and Crane stiffen. Janus's grin only spreads.

Slowly, her heart stuttering, she turns around to face the voice.

A man steps out from behind the throne.

A man who can only be Umbra.

It's not simply that he spoke to her, but everything about his demeanor suggests an individuality that has been stripped from the rest of his agents. He's a tall human, long, dark hair braided back and threaded with a few strands of silver that match the hint of wrinkles around his eyes. It's impossible for her to say how old he is – she could guess anywhere between thirty and seventy. More ageless than Ossuary's supposed immortal king.

Although he wears the black uniform of Windshadow, a white fur cape is thrown over one shoulder, trailing on the ground as he elegantly settles into his throne. He crosses his legs and rests his hands on the armrest. A finger taps against the stone, as though counting the heartbeats she has left.

Her feet are made of lead. She couldn't approach him even if she wanted to.

"I'd say I'm surprised," he drawls, "but we all know I'm not." Another tap of his finger. "My agents. Three great failures that only succeed when they don't intend to. I suppose I must thank you for bringing me Traxi."

It's Rig, she longs to say, but fear pinches her tongue between Umbra's tapping fingers.

She squares her shoulders. "You want my schematics, right? If you want 'em, you know what I want in return. Where's. My. *Sister*."

Without taking his eyes off the four of them, he idly reaches out and snaps his fingers at someone hiding in the shadows.

They must have been waiting for this demand, because within moments there's vague shifting in the dark, shapes forming into distinct figures, and she can hear the soft thuds of footfalls and the labored breathing of someone scared and exhausted.

Shadows coalesce into two Operatives and a woman dragged between them.

Daara.

Daara.

Her sister is a shadow of her former self. Even though, objectively, she hasn't worsened since that call on the Ascetic homeworld, seeing her in person exaggerates every horrible detail. The paleness of Daara's skin from lack of sunlight makes her ghostly, the slight tightness of her skin makes her emaciated, the dark circles under her eyes sink into massive bruises that swallow up her face.

A black prison uniform hangs off her body and her hands are cuffed in front of her, and when she tilts her head up her eyes blow wide enough for Rig to see the red veins in her sclera.

"T-Traxi? You came, you actually *came for me*–" She takes a fumbling half step closer before one of the Operatives yanks her back. "No...Get away from here! They'll *kill* you, they want to *hurt* you. *Run*–"

"Daara!–"

An Operative claps their hand over her mouth, muffling her cries.

Umbra languidly shifts in his throne, perching his chin on one hand. "Satisfied?"

"What have you done to her?" Rig demands, her entire body shaking. "If you've hurt her in any way, I swear I'll destroy the schematics right here and now and you'll *never* get what you want."

"I've not hurt her since she was dropped on my doorstep. She is of little personal interest to me. However, make no mistake – I *will* do all manner of things to her if you do not surrender the weapon plans. Now do go on. Hand them over. I know you've brought them with you. You'd be an idiot to leave behind your only bargaining chip."

Rig's peripherally aware of the fact that her feet are quaking in her boots. "Let Daara go and *then* I'll give you the schematics."

A corner of his lips quirk up. "And give away *my* bargaining chip? No. Your three traitor friends will stay right where they are. My Operatives will send your sister to them. You will walk to me, you will hand me the plans, and then you will remain while your friends leave with your sister. Deviate from that and not a single one of you will leave here alive."

"What guarantee do I have that you won't shoot Daara the moment the plans are handed over?"

"None at all. You'll simply have to–"

"As if I would *ever* take you at your word."

His jaw tightens. "You," he declares, each word clipped and sharp, "are *not* to interrupt me again."

If it were possible to swallow her tongue she would.

"Good." He straightens up in his seat, the smallest of shifts that makes her shrink even more. "It seems you have a choice to make. Either abide by the rules I've set forth or…"

"Or what?"

"Or I'll take my leniency off the table. Your friends will die, your sister will eventually die, and then so will you. We're going to get the schematics out of you first, but we'll kill you in the end. I suppose it's only polite to ask your opinion before your mind is completely broken. Would you prefer if I put your sister before a firing squad? Evisceration? The slow death of being thrown out a ship into vacuum? I imagine that for someone who relies so thoroughly on a single run-down ship, that last option must be quite the recurring nightmare for you, isn't it? Care to see if your sister has the same fears?"

That tosses her right back to her first few months in space. Running from Pyrite to a dozen different worlds, staying on each for only a day or so before the need to flee nipped at her heels again. Each ship was new and untrustworthy, and yes, he's right. That had been her unending nightmare, images of Pyrite ships appearing out of luminalspace and firing upon whatever frigate or cruiser she'd hitched a ride with that week.

Her link buzzes, the vibration drilling into her skull from her jawbone to her temples. Mohsin's near-silent voice comes through, *"We've taken out two of the Controllers. Couple of the Named are locking down the Operative barracks. Heron's group is taking the south right now, we're going west."*

They'd all been shown a map before landing, a map that's currently running through her head as she plots out where Mohsin and his group must be at this moment. Damn, she'd hoped they'd have gotten further by now. She can only stall for so long, and her sister is *right there*, could be shot any minute, entirely at Umbra's mercy.

She forces herself to keep her gaze firmly on Umbra instead of Daara. It would be stupid beyond belief for her to ignore the greatest threat in the room just because she desperately wants to hug her sister and tell her that everything's going to be alright.

Ginka turns her face ever so slightly so that Rig can see her lips move and Umbra cannot. She mouths one word – *stall*.

Yeah, no shit she needs to stall.

"Alright, alright *fine*," Rig tells Umbra, gritting her teeth. She can't think of anything else to do that won't endanger Daara's life. "I'll give you the schematics. As long as you don't hurt my sister, I'll give you whatever you want."

She takes a step towards his throne.

The Operatives holding Daara push her a step forward.

"Don't do it!" Daara yells as soon as her mouth is no longer covered. "He's not even Pyrite – he's Ossuary scum! Don't give him *shit*!"

Ignoring her sister's pleas is one of the hardest things in the galaxy, and she has to force herself to keep her head straight. There's no way she'll actually give up the schematics, but if she can buy a few moments of Umbra thinking he's won, then she'll have succeeded.

A clock ticks away in her mind. That's all she needs. A bit of time.

Another step closer.

Umbra drags his eyes over her form in a way that makes her certain every single flaw of hers is being pulled to the surface to be picked apart by him. Her pace is even and measured and it's all she can do to focus on that, to keep her mind from spiraling into fear and panic, to push down the bone deep instinct to run away and never look back, to hide on whatever distant wasteland of a moon will shelter her.

Her feet stop in front of his throne.

There's an odd object leaning against the side of the chair, she notices, now that she's close enough to get a proper look. It's some kind of long baton made of metal. Dark, thin tubes run along its grip in harsh, symmetrical patterns, something black running inside – or perhaps dark red? Curious. If he wanted to keep something close, a weapon would make more sense.

He crooks a single finger at her. "Hand them over."

"Of course."

She raises her cuffed hands to her vest.

Heron's voice crackles in her ear, *"We need more time–"* There's the sound of a fist hitting flesh in the background. *"One of the Controllers is putting up a fight – we've nearly got her but it's drawing attention!"*

Daara's footsteps cease.

"It's alright," she can hear Ginka say, "We've got you."

Safe. Thank fuck.

She reaches into her vest pocket with a good deal of difficulty – these cuffs are not designed for mobility – and retrieves a thumbdrive. It's about the size of two of her fingers, plain grey metal, and completely, utterly, mockingly *blank*. Void of any data whatsoever.

Every good plan needs a dummy, and she's not in the mood to play that role.

"Here." She presents the thumbdrive to Umbra. "I hope it's everything you wanted."

Elegantly and languidly, he plucks it from her palm and spins it around between his fingers as though luxuriating in his prize.

"Now," she says carefully, "my sister and my friends are going to leave. As promised, I'll stay until they've gone and then–"

"Then you'll join up with whatever other friends you have hiding out?"

She makes her face go blank. "Friends? What friends?"

"Don't insult me. When Raven-Seven diverted from his planned course to meet up with your ship, I knew that at least one of the agents working underneath him must have assistedNo one, not even a Handler, could fly a ship that size all by themselves. I imagine that irrespective of what your friends might think they've accomplished here today, they'll find that things aren't going according to your plans. They'll soon discover that their getaway ship has been... ah, *impounded*."

Ship *singular*. Umbra's only found one of the Nightbird groups.

"Yeah, okay." She shrugs. "So you knew we were a diversion."

"Of course–"

"But someone who's been on the run for as long as I have learnt not to put all their kydis in the same safebox."

"*What* did I say about interrupting me?"

"Ossuary themself could stand before me and I'd still interrupt them. You're not special. What you *are* is a bastard."

Umbra bristles, opening his mouth–

"Sir!" An Operative in the background presses a finger to their ear and calls out, "None of the Controllers are responding! Sparrow-Thirty-Two is reporting that a group of rogue agents and unidentified Kashrini have taken the Operative barracks."

Something else comes through her link.

Behind them, Crane cheerfully adds, "I believe Thirty-Two just surrendered. Half the Operatives and Handlers involved in this were either already ours or have joined up, and the other half are too confused to figure out if they should be attacking or helping, and as a result are mostly just sitting out entirely."

"And you were only able to take *one* of our ships," Ginka says, echoing Rig's earlier realization. "We've got far more than that ready and waiting."

Umbra's fingers keep spinning the fake thumbdrive.

"You made a *big* mistake, Umbra," Rig says, the lead in her feet that pins her to the ground disappearing.

He raises an eyebrow. "Did I?"

"Actually, you made more than one. You thought that you could get away with treating your agents like *things* instead of *people*? You thought that none of them would break free of that and come back to make sure you couldn't do it do anyone else again? You thought that it would really just be Ginka and Crane and *maybe* one or two others?"

There's a faint sharp intake of breath from Daara. "Traxi... I don't understand. What's going on?"

"What's going on is us tearing down everything he's built! You're going to be safe, Daara, safe forever, I promise, and so is *everyone else*." She locks eyes with Umbra once again, buzzing with success and adrenaline. "See, that was your *second* mistake. You assumed that I'd be willing to exchange one life for millions of Kashrini lives. I don't play by your rules. I'm not picking. I'm going to save *everyone*."

He leans back in his throne. "Are you going to tell me what my third mistake was?"

"Yeah. Your third mistake was assuming that since we were handcuffed, we didn't need to be stripped of weapons."

Wings of victory soar inside Rig's chest. Her thumb presses the button on the cuffs, letting the heavy metal drop to the floor, and then she's grabbing Pizzazz from her belt and aiming it straight at Umbra.

Clack-clack-clack–

The sound of Ginka, Crane, and Janus similarly stripping themselves of their bonds.

The cuffs hitting the ground, the hum of Ginka's helltech weapons powering up, the slide of Crane drawing a gun, all a thousand times louder in the rush. Rig draws Panache and lobs it like a handball over her shoulder to Daara, who catches the gun in uncertain and still bound hands. It's okay. She'll be okay. She's the only other person in the galaxy who's able to use that weapon. Nowhere better for it to be.

"We're outnumbered," Rig admits to Umbra triumphantly,

baring her teeth in a snarling grin, "but we're not outgunned."

"Eliminate them," he orders.

Everything goes to shit very quickly as the Operatives around the room attack.

But not all of them.

Two dive towards Ginka with flashes of gold helltech light. Another group peels off to lunge towards Crane and Janus, weapons raised.

One of the Operatives tears her mask off to reveal dark skin and blonde hair. A helltech spear whirls around in her hands, gold blade igniting, flashing through the air; she plunges it into her comrade's back.

Blood stains the white marble.

The man screams, dropping to his knees, his deactivated helltech weapon tumbling from his hands. The woman pulls her spear out with a sickening sound and a splatter of red on her black uniform. A second later she's ripping out the cords connecting the man's helltech generators to his weapon, and then turns to one of the Operatives who had previously been guarding Daara.

The Operative nods and removes their mask, baring grey Oriate skin and spikes.

An enemy swings at Daara–

Rig turns and shoots without even thinking about it, not sure if her sister will be able to fight well enough, and even though it's stupid to turn her back to Umbra, she does it anyway, because there's no way she's gotten this far only to lose Daara to some random Operative. The body hits the ground and she's not sure if she killed them or just downed them, so she shoots again to make sure. No pulled punches.

Crane puts a bullet through someone's eye and Ginka forms a blade, carving it through someone's neck with a single, powerful swing.

The last Operative falls to a shot from Pizzazz.

In an instant, the tables have turned in their favor.

Rig breathes in, anger filling her lungs and her lungs filling her ribcage. Slowly, deliberately, she turns her gun back towards Umbra, putting the sight in the center of his forehead.

She cocks her head to the side and tightens her finger around the trigger. "You were saying?"

The throne room holds its breath.

Umbra leans back, features unreadable. The fabric of his cloak shifts and rustles. He holds up the thumbdrive, drops it from his fingers into his palm, and then...

He crushes it.

What... But *why* would he *do* that?

When he opens up his hand, the drive is cracked in two, wiring and circuitry exposed. "Don't insult my intelligence. I made *no* mistakes."

He drops the ruined thumbdrive.

His free hand taps twice on the throne's surface. A hard light panel pops up, and before Rig, or *anyone* can move, he presses a button on the panel.

Ginka and Crane fall screaming, and the two rebellious Operatives drop as well a second later.

"What did you do?" Rig screams, "Stop it! Stop hurting them!"

Ginka is collapsed on the floor, curled into a ball, her metal hands scraping and clutching at the back of her neck. Crane's gun is discarded and useless and he merely whimpers as he struggles against whatever Umbra's doing, hands pressed to his link.

A memory floats through Rig's mind – Ginka's chip was in the base of her skull. And if Crane has something similar where his link is implanted, then that has to be what Umbra is using to hurt them. Some kind of frequency – a built in control feature. It's got to be transmitting something... Damn it, why can't she do anything more than just spitball ideas?

She has no idea how to *stop* him.

"Only a mild shock," Umbra dispassionately explains. "I'll do worse to them later."

They stop twitching, but they still aren't moving, still aren't getting up or reaching for weapons or anything over than suffering through the aftershocks.

Daara stumbles backwards, holding up Panache in both hands, her knees knocking together and her shoulders trembling. The gun wavers. "You got what you want from Traxi, just let us *go*. I'm tired of this – I'm so *tired* of all you people and your damn games. Let me *out*!"

"I've not got what I want quite yet."

Umbra taps another command into the hard light panel. Part of the armrest slides back, revealing a hidden compartment. A compartment that spits out a single, shiny pistol.

He throws it.

Rig can do nothing more than watch as the gun sails past her shoulder and through the air and straight into Janus's raised hand.

He grins a toothy, leonine grin. "Thanks."

He twirls the gun around in his hand, flipping it and tossing it and doing all the damn tricks that she does when she's showing off, and he's got that *fucking smug look*. That traitorous, triple-crossing bastard. She didn't trust him, but she thought that she knew his motivations well enough to... She was wrong, she was so wrong, and now he's got a *gun pointed at Daara*.

She jerks Pizzazz closer to Umbra's face, hand shaking. "One more move and I kill you! Let them *go*!"

"Ah yes," Umbra drawls. "That brings us to my so called third mistake. Letting you bring your weapons into my throne room was never an oversight. I have *who* I want and *what* I want exactly *where* I want."

His hand falls to the side of his throne and his fingers wrap around the odd metal stick resting there.

It's almost as though he's moving in slow motion, her brain freezing time as every fiber of her body screams that something's wrong, even as she's too slow to do anything in response.

Her trigger finger tenses.

Gold light bursts to life and sweeps across her vision.

The stick in his hand isn't a stick at all, it's a *hilt*.

A glowing, double-bladed axe head blooms at the top and the dark tubes running along the metal are filled with blood. Helltech, but *sustainable* – her theories were right; it *is* possible to run helltech without connecting it to a body. A bloodstream alone will work, and of course Umbra is the only one to get the non-corrosive version of the tech. But still, she was *right*–

Her eyes blur.

Refocus.

Umbra swung his axe past her. And he *didn't miss.*

A *thud* and a *squish* as something hits the floor.

Her wrist ends. It just ends, and at the end is a lot of red and a lot of blood and *oh*, that was her hand that hit the floor; he *cut her hand off*–

The pain kicks in.

A scream claws its way out of her throat like sandpaper as red-hot tongues of flame course through her veins, burning her nerves to ash, cutting through her mind until all she can see is fire so hot it's white and black spots dance in her vision and she can't stop *screaming*.

Her knees smack into the floor and she curls up around her arm, because maybe if she hides it, protects it, maybe then it'll all be okay and it'll not have happened. Tears stream down her cheeks, and they're like blistering ice against the inferno of the pain. Every movement of her lungs makes it hurt worse but she can't stop sobbing, her chest heaving as she struggles to breathe through it all.

Distantly, she can hear Daara cry out. The words vanish in the roar of blood in her ears, the drum of her rapid pulse.

Umbra's shiny leather boot flashes out and kicks Rig in the head.

The world spins again. She falls back, sprawled out on the cold marble. Her head bends over the edge of one of the thin stairs and she can see the throne room upside down, can see through the blackness of her vision; can see Daara staggering back from Janus, Ginka and Crane trying in vain to get up, the Named Operatives still unconscious; can see her own blood ooze down the step.

There's a quiet shift as Umbra bends, and she can hear him picking up her gun and... and her hand.

Nausea mixes with unbearable dizziness at the sheer wrongness of seeing her own detached hand. Every bone in her body strains. She tries desperately to push herself to her feet, but she can't move and she *hurts so much–*

"Thank you," Umbra says, gloating voice slithering in her ears, echoing in the whirlwind that's spinning in her skull, "for your DNA and your gun. They'll be of great use in allowing my technicians full access to your schematics."

How did he...?

"You say more than you mean when you're in a tizzy." The grin in Janus's voice grates at her. He pitches his voice into a high, mocking imitation of herself, "'You can't take my guns from me, Janus. They're locked and only my DNA can release them.' 'No one can get the schematics from me without me handing them over, Janus, and even if someone *could* take them from me, they still couldn't *access* them without me.' Oh come *on*, it was obvious once I put two and two together. I sent Umbra a message when I was calling Crane. And you thought I was helping X-74 – I've only ever helped myself."

Another choked scream scrapes in the back of her throat, and yet she can't draw breath to give it life.

The hem of Umbra's cloak drags past Rig's legs as he moves to loom over her. "Former Raven-Fifty, you've done quite well. As for the sister... keep her. They are identical, after all. Her DNA could act as a substitute for Traxi's, should we need fresh samples in the future."

"With *pleasure*."

Janus sweeps his leg out and kicks Daara's unsteady feet out from under her, sending her tumbling down, Panache *clacking* onto the marble as she drops it. It feels like Rig's body goes up in flames as she watches the inverted scene unfold, pain and rage fueling the same fire.

"Good." Umbra takes another step closer until his feet are next to her shoulders, right on the edge of the stair where her head limply hangs. If she only had a hand with which to grab his foot and trip him. "Raven-Fifty, I leave you to claim the prize you lured in."

Prize? But the only thing Janus wants is…

Janus puts his knee onto Crane's chest before he can get up, shoving him back down with a painful smack of his back hitting stone. There's a knife holstered in Crane's boot. Janus draws it in one smooth motion.

The metal glistens in the white light.

Janus raises the blade. The tip hovers above Crane's panicked eyes and then shifts to the right. Janus carefully slides the blade towards the link that's attached to Crane's head. He lines up the edge where the link meets skin. Preparing for a neat cut.

"Finally," Janus murmurs.

His shoulder tenses to pry the link off.

Ginka screams.

Gold burns.

Time stretches into an infinity as a glowing shard of helltech shatters through the air and pierces the side of Janus's skull.

Blood bursts from the entry wound as if in slow motion, each tiny drop of crimson crystal clear, every vein in his shocked eyes sharper than if they were drawn there by a pen. Janus exhales a near silent, breathless '*oh*' just before the blade smashes out through the other side of his head. Gore splatters the floor. The flecks of blood misting the air, the sound of bone cracking, the way the exit wound looks like a gnarled, twisting spider lily blossoming from his temples – every single detail is seared into Rig's mind.

He topples backwards and hits the ground with the softest of *thuds*.

With his head bent unnaturally back, he is perfectly upright in Rig's upside-down world. Surprise is painted on his face, the last expression he will ever make, eyes staring out at nothing as though he had never even comprehended that he could lose.

Umbra curses. "No matter. The lot of you have been quite the thorn in my side but it's time to end this now. Traxi will die first. The rest of you will have slower ends."

The golden axe he wields towers above Rig as he raises it into the air. Perfectly angled to fall straight down and cleave her in half.

"*Traxi!*" Daara yells.

There's the grating hiss of metal against stone as Daara throws Panache.

The gun slides across the marble.

It hits the base of the short stair.

With her aching but functional left hand, Rig makes a grab for the gun and raises her arm, pointing the barrel up at Umbra.

"My name," she snarls between gritted teeth, "is *Rig*."

She squeezes the trigger.

The gunshot booms in her ears and she sees the flare of light as the shot goes off.

Bullet under the jaw. Straight up through the brain. Up and out the top of Umbra's skull. Had he not been so determined to look down upon her, she never would have had the right angle to put the bullet in his head.

Umbra's corpse falls.

The golden axe slices into the marble, wavers for a moment, and then the helltech shatters.

Her weak fingers can't hold on to Panache for long, and once it's done, all the adrenaline leaves her body in a rush. Things go fuzzy. She can't hear what Ginka and Crane say to one another, even though she can see their lips move.

Black stars burst in front of her eyes, and the next thing she knows, Daara's kneeling behind her, resting her head in her lap, and Daara's *real*, she's *solid*, she's *here*.

Rig can't move much. Her useless fingers fumble for her vest pocket and retrieve the headscarf pin.

Hot tears splash onto her cheeks.

Daara's crying.

She reaches up and tucks the pin behind Daara's ear, the stones a beautiful compliment to her sister's skin and dazzling purple eyes. Her fingertips linger on her sister's cheek, unwilling to let go.

A smile floats onto her face. "Heya..."

She's vaguely aware of Daara yelling something before darkness swallows up her vision.

INTERLUDE
Here and Now

"Thank you," Ginka whispers, "for taking me home."

Not that Rig can hear her.

A dozen or more tubes are connected to veinports all over Rig's body, various machines humming, bags of fluids dripping into IVs, a clear mask covering half her face, fogging up as she breathes. Underneath all the apparatus, it's difficult to make out the shape of her – her *friend*, Ginka supposes. Rig is visible mostly by the slices of her blue skin against the white of the medical bed and the bandages and the monitors.

That ragged headscarf of hers remains. Aazi, who's bullied her way onto Rig's medical team, insisted that it stay. Ginka doesn't quite understand, although perhaps she doesn't have to.

Speaking of, Aazi opens the door and raps her knuckles against the wall. "Knock knock. We're about to start her surgery. Best if you head on out while we prep her."

Ginka rises to her feet and bows. Her neck twinges slightly, protesting the movement. Whatever shock Umbra had given her has left a less than pleasant aftereffect. According to Crane, it's psychosomatic and will go away with time, but for now it lingers. "I didn't mean to intrude. Please take good care of her. Are you going to...?"

She trails off as they both glance down at the third person in the room.

Daara is slumped in a chair at Rig's bedside, fast asleep.

"I'll wake her," Aazi says. "Don't worry about it."

Ginka bows again and leaves, making way for the handful of medical personnel that push their way into the room after her.

The headquarter halls are, for the first time she can remember, filled with idle chatter.

After Umbra was cold, the Kashrini Nightbirds and Crane's Named finished securing the area, ensuring that everyone was either merged into their ranks or detained. Or, in the case of all the Controllers, neutralized. It's what the Controllers taught them to do, after all. Contain what cannot be assimilated. Kill what cannot be contained.

She makes her way to a large briefing room that has now been turned into a sort of office space.

"Hello, Crane." She nods to the room's second occupant. "Heron. How'd the operation go on your end?"

He grins and flashes her a thumbs up. "Pretty good. That guy your friend brought in – Mohsin – he's a monster on the battlefield. Excellent to have in a fight. I knew the Nightbirds were formidable, or else we'd never have been so infuriated by them, but I hadn't expected a former Crimson Butcher in their ranks."

"They're... more than we thought they were," she decides. "I hope I'm not interrupting, by the way. I was kicked out of the medbay."

Crane smiles. "Not at all. Heron, could you get in touch in with Kestrel's operation? I think they're in an info blackout area and haven't heard the news yet."

"Of course."

After Heron's left the room and closed the door behind him, Crane asks, "How's Rig?"

"Alive. About to go into surgery. We'll see what happens after she's awake." She glances at the maps spread out on the table. "Have we heard from our more distant agents? If we can, we need to recall as many as possible. Just while we figure out where to go next."

"I had the exact same idea. I sent out an order calling every field agent back to headquarters and grounding those that are already here, and, honestly, I didn't know if anyone was going to obey... Then King Tenus backed up the order."

"...You're fucking with me."

He laughs, drifting closer to her as she drifts closer to him. "I wasn't expecting it either. I don't know if Umbra was blackmailing him, if they personally didn't get along, or if he just thinks that it's better to have *someone* in charge of Windshadow than no one at all – and we're loyal enough that he doesn't see us being an issue. Guess we'll never really know. But for better or worse, we're... in charge?"

"Us, as in *us*," she gestures to the two of them, "or us, as in the Named?"

"I don't have a clear answer there, either."

"And Pyrite? Ascetic?"

He merely shrugs.

She leans against the table and lets her body sag into it. "I suppose we're going to have to get used to the chaos for some time now, aren't we?"

"Seems likely."

Crane kisses her on the cheek and she doesn't... she doesn't know what to do. Not anymore. It's like her body's forgotten.

She doesn't know what expression she's making, but from the way Crane's face falls, she doesn't think it's anything good.

"I... I would understand, you know," he says softly. "It's been three years. If you've... If you've decided that you'd rather not... I'd never hold that against you. Our relationship put you through three years of isolation and Grace rationing and I completely understand if you... I don't know, if you blame me for that, or don't want to risk it happening again, or–"

"It's not that," she quickly assures him.

It's *not*. She *does* still love him. With all she has. The necklace containing her wedding ring is like a second heart beating over her flesh and blood one. It's that she put *him* through three years of fear and scrutiny, and she doesn't think she's worth it. She wouldn't blame him for thinking that hanging on to her isn't worth the struggle, and she knows that he'd be polite about turning her away, that he'd let her down gently.

"Is there anything I can do to help?" he asks.

"I–" She chews on her lower lip. "I love you. But I don't see why you'd still love me after everything *you* went through, after so long apart, and I can't *tell* just by feeling and I... I've never figured out what to do now that I can't tell."

He hums thoughtfully. "Ah."

With enough tenderness to break her heart a hundred times over, he takes her hand in his, her dead, unfeeling hand.

Sensation is odd to her mechanical limbs, even after all this time, and she feels him as if through a thin curtain. Part of her mind is still waiting, holding its breath, stubbornly insisting that any minute now she'll be able to sense his feelings, to see what he hears and to feel his memories. Any minute now it'll all come back like it was never gone.

He places her hand on his chest, directly over his heart, cupping his hands over hers so that her fingers are splayed out over his shirt.

"Can you feel that?" he asks.

That empathic connection never happens. It never will again.

She shakes her head and hates that part of her is disappointed. It's been years. Why still have hope? Why can't she just get used to being blind? "All I can feel is your heartbeat."

His black eyes are warm and gentle, and he smiles softly at her. "I know. That's for you, Ginka. Only for you."

Oh.

Her heart beats in time with his own.

CHAPTER TWENTY-FIVE
Beating the Game

A white ceiling greets Rig when she blearily opens her eyes.

It's promptly obscured by Daara's face.

"You're awake," her sister states.

She guesses she is awake. Bit of a surprise, that.

Soreness and pain buzzes under her skin, obscured by a cloud of what she's going to assume are some very nice anesthetics. She's sitting in a white medical bed. The whiteness around her is the white of a medcenter, machines beeping and humming around her, all doused in the sterile smell of rubber and alcohol. She gags in the back of her throat and presses her eyes shut for a moment to push down the nausea.

When she manages to open them again, she takes a deep breath and makes herself face what's become of her right hand.

There's a casing of some kind around her wrist that twinges with a sort of hazy, blocked-off pain, and at the end of the casing is smooth metal.

A prosthetic.

She twitches her fingers and watches as the hand moves. It's a silvery, almost black-tinted metal, expertly put together, all the pieces of it perfectly aligned so that even when she flexes her hand in a myriad of ways there are no exposed internal bits, only the polished outer plating. It's almost as seamless as nanomesh. It's sort of beautiful, and if she had gotten it voluntarily, she'd probably be gushing over it.

"I'm awake. I guess," she agrees, sliding her gaze from her hand to her sister. She wishes she could say she's in one piece. "How are you doing?"

"I'm fine. Nothing but bruises. You've been unconscious for five days now."

Daara's not looking her in the eyes. Her hands are fisted into the fabric of her pants, her posture rigid as she sits in her chair. There're no injuries on her though; Rig checks twice to make sure, and then a third time just to make extra sure. Is she... *angry*?

"Daara..."

More tense silence. It's... awkward.

Which makes sense, she guesses. It's been three years since she and Daara were in the same room together, and maybe another two or three years before *that* since they had a long and pleasant conversation. As her work got more intense, she and Daara grew apart. Now that they're together again, she's struggling to figure out what to do or say.

Daara silently glowers at her lap.

"Are you okay?" Rig tentatively asks. "You look a bit... a bit *pissed*."

Daara purses her lips. "You... you ruined my life."

"Excuse me?" Her jaw falls open. What the actual *fuck*. "I hauled ass across half the galaxy and back again to *save* your life!"

"Only *after* you did everything else! I was *happy* under Pyrite, I really was, and then all these PI people came in and dragged me out of my home and... and it was all because *you* had made something special they needed. You never even told me why you needed to leave, you never said what you'd done, you just did that *thing* you do where you make everything suddenly so dramatic–"

"Our lives were in *danger*! I tried to tell you and you–" Rig chokes on the words. "You didn't *listen*."

"Well I ended up in danger *anyways*! I *trusted* Pyrite, I was *loyal*, and it turned out that I was nothing at all to them beyond a thing that could be used to bring you back into the fold. *You.* My special, smart sister," she spits out bitterly. "Now I *know* that I'm nothing. That I'm no one. And now that it's all over I can't even go home anymore."

But you're alive, Rig thinks selfishly. *But you're safe. But I saved you.*

"If I hadn't left," she points out, "you'd probably be dead already."

"I would be *fine*. They'd have had no reason to go after us in the first place. Things would be *fine* and *normal*."

"No reason? When," she demands, "has Pyrite *ever* needed a reason to hurt Kashrini? I can't believe you've never understood that. You want things to go back to normal? Your normal fucking *sucked*. Your normal had you slaving away for Pyrite. Normal means you have a fucking tracker chip in your gut. Normal was our mother dying–"

"Don't act as though you ever cared about our mother–"

"I cared just as much as you did, you damn hypocrite! Normal had us not caring!" She'd been so tired when she woke up, almost too tired to be angry. Now she's too angry to be tired. "I did what I had to do."

What *could* she have done to make Daara leave with her three years ago? If her sister won't listen now, after everything that's happened, what argument could she possibly have come up with back then? Staying on Pyrite wasn't an option, taking Daara with her wasn't a choice her sister had let her take. No matter how many times she plays it out in her head, she simply can't see a scenario in which Daara leaves with her.

"I did what I had to do," she repeats, "and I'd do the same again."

Daara opens her mouth and then is cut off.

The door slides open and Mohsin barrels in.

"I see you're back in the land of the living," he remarks, giving her a rough once-over. "I hope you liked bed rest, cause it's the last you're gonna get right now. Get your lazy ass up, you're needed."

"Fuck you too," she says jovially. "What am I needed for?"

He throws a bundle of clothes at her, a bra smacking her in the face. "Important chit chat. Put some damn pants on."

She puts some damn pants on.

Getting up is hard – sort of. She's not attached to any machines, and, although she's a little woozy, she doesn't do anything embarrassing like trip over her own feet or pass out. The weirdest thing is using her new hand. Her body knows what it's doing, all the instincts are there; it's simply that everything feels a tiny bit off. Like her hand is shit-faced drunk while the rest of her body is sober.

Getting dressed also means she has an excuse not to talk to Daara for a while, and she really appreciates that.

Gods. All that to save her sister and now she can't look her in the eyes.

As soon as she's decent, Mohsin is herding her out the door, letting her stumble into her boots and tug on her vest as she follows him.

"So," she asks. "What have I missed?"

"Most of our friends are still here. There's... stuff that needs to be sorted. The chunk of Windshadow folks that weren't originally on our side have mostly adjusted. It's sort of cute – some of them are all excited about it. Oh, you'll get a kick out of this. I heard Crane shouting at one of your medical team about three days ago."

She sputters, "What?"

"After they put that casing thing on your wrist, one of the Windshadow medics on staff tried to give you some helltech bullshit prosthetic. Crane ripped him a new one and Ginka was doing this *thing* – not *saying* anything, just *lurking*. Fantastic grade A lurking."

Thank fuck for Ginka and Crane. There's no way in the galaxy that Rig would be okay with having one of those death generators strapped to the end of her arm. What happened to her hand is bad enough. Having to deal with a prosthetic determined to slowly destroy the rest of her body as well would be simply too much for her to deal with right now – or *ever*, really.

"Glad to know that I've got two terrifying assassins to be my personal defenders. It's a warm, fuzzy feeling."

Mohsin comes to a stop. "Here we go."

He throws open the doors of Umbra's former office.

The dark throne room is gone. Bright light fixtures illuminate every corner, revealing a high crystal ceiling through which the cold sun shines. The platform where the throne once sat now stands empty. A large table has been set up over it, concealing the platform entirely. Two holograms are hovering over the platform, but at this distance, she can't clearly make them out.

At the head of the table stands Ginka and Crane. Neither looks the worse for wear. Ginka's dressed in a new uniform that oozes formality. The dark coat Crane had been wearing is gone and Umbra's white fur cape is slung over one shoulder, tied in place with a silver chain. Who are they talking to that requires this level of fancy dress? Rig glances down at her ratty pants and her dirty leather vest. Maybe it would be better if she'd dressed up. No. This is her, down to her core, and if someone has a problem with that then they're going to have to deal with it.

The holograms solidify as she approaches.

"–not our problem," Ginka is gruffly saying, staring down the two holograms.

Each is a person, a figure cut off from the waist below. Both utterly unfamiliar and yet dressed in familiar colors.

One is a woman, long, white hair sleek and flat against her skull. A series of tattoos crawl up her neck and across the left side of her face, a pattern of flowers and thorns and creeping vines. The second is a man. He's blankly unremarkable, from his plain brown hair to his plain grey eyes. Unremarkable, save for a thin scar that cuts across his lips. She is wearing the white and green of Ascetic and he wears the blue and red of Pyrite.

The man turns as Rig steps closer, eyes narrowing. "If it isn't our missing weapons developer."

"Rig," Ginka says, emphasizing her name, "Let me introduce you to our guests." She gestures to the woman. "Commander Dwale, of Ascetic's Military Police." A gesture to the man. "Pyrite Intelligence's Director, who refuses to give us more of a name than that."

Quite the crowd.

A pressing feeling of smallness closes in on her. The faceless powers that be behind everything that's happened to her, powers that she never thought she'd meet in person. But she'd met Umbra, hadn't she? And come out on top. Windshadow has always been a terror to the galaxy, a hidden knife in the dark. PI and Ascetic can't compare.

Mohsin stands behind her. Ginka and Crane next to her. She squares her shoulders and finds that she's not so small after all.

"Heya," she says to the two, and then, "You gonna get out of my life now, or what?"

The Director's face puckers like he's just smelled something abhorrent. "You have something that belongs to us. *You* belong to us. You are in no position to argue."

"I beg to differ." Ginka crosses her arms, her terrifying helltech arms. "Rig may not be Ossuary and she is certainly not Windshadow, but she has our protection. I know that Pyrite and Ascetic have always had a healthy respect – no, a healthy *fear* of our organization. I suggest that you remember exactly why neither of you have ever succeeded in infiltrating our ranks or assaulting our homeworld."

"Are you threatening us?" the Director demands.

"Yes."

"Then where is Lord Umbra? Ah, right – he's *dead*. Windshadow is not what it once was, and we all know it. Your organization has just been torn in half by a coup d'état. You have no power to make threats."

Mohsin takes a half step forward. "What about *us*? You – all of you faction bastards – have been trying to get rid of us for years. Wanted us gone so bad you crossed faction lines to try and kill all of us. Nightbirds helped kill Umbra. Don't think you want to take on both us and Windshadow at once."

"And if you want to talk about how strong each of our organizations are," Crane adds, "then I fear we need to break some bad news to you. Pyrite has lost a number of agents, a good deal of resources, and a *superweapon*. What position are *you* in? Ascetic is no better. How do you think it will look when a highly respected librarian reveals that you willingly abandoned a sacred library, allowing it to be attacked and pillaged?" He checks a clock projected on the table. "Information that's about to be released in about five seconds."

They got in touch with June. Rig breathes a sigh of relief. Whatever else, June knows she's safe and alive.

Dwale simmers. "I see."

"What are your demands?" the Director coldly asks.

Simple demands, really. Rig doesn't want much, not in the end. "You all leave me alone. You leave my sister alone. You leave First Assistant Librarian June Rivera alone. You see someone and get even a sniff that they're my friend, you leave them alone. Don't forget what I can do. Don't forget just how desperately you all wanted my weapon. Think of what I could do if you give me reason to get back into that business."

Only she knows it's an empty threat. She's done working in that field, done with it for good, and nothing and no one can make her go back.

"So. Are you lot going to piss off, or not?"

Dwale closes out the hologram call with a terse, "Very well."

"We'll see how long this lasts," the Director grumbles, signing off a moment later.

All the tension *whooshes* out of Rig's body as soon as both of them have vanished. Even given that she was apparently a step ahead of them the whole time, both those bastards are still intimidating as all get out.

"Let me get one thing straight." Mohsin is pinning Ginka and Crane with the sort of intense stare that makes most people quake in their boots. "I said what I said there to get all of 'em to fuck off. Here's how it's actually going to be. We stay out of each other's way. You don't do the type of shit that your predecessor did, you make an effort to get Ossuary to change, you don't interfere when we go after Pyrite and Ascetic."

Rig clears her throat and adds, somewhat sheepishly 'cause she does actually like Ginka and Crane, "One more thing. There's bound to be Kashrini relics in Ossuary space. I know Windshadow might not keep an eye on that specific sort of thing, but if we tell you where one is, I want you to return it to us."

Mohsin nods along. "Yeah. Keep to those terms, and we'll help you out when you need it."

Ginka gives Crane a look out of the corner of her eye and whatever unspoken thing passes between the two of them must give her an answer. "Understood." Her mouth quirks up. "I can see why you and Rig get along so well."

Rig can't help the laugh that bubbles out of her lungs. "I'll take that as a compliment."

"I suppose it was." Ginka tilts her head towards the doors. "Sorry to drag you out of bed like that. Go get some rest. We can iron things out without you."

"You know what? For once, rest sounds fantastic."

She gives the three of them a cheeky, two-fingered salute before sauntering out as best she can. Sauntering isn't all that easy with a still-woozy head and an off-balance hand. But she manages.

The door closes behind her.

Daara is waiting outside.

Her sister finally looks her in the eye and confesses, "I'm *so* angry with you. I can't stop being angry even though I know you gave up a lot to help me. I don't know what you want from me right now, I don't know if you have some dream about the sisterhood we never really had, but I... I can't go with you. I just *can't*."

"Oh."

She should be disappointed, heartbroken even. And she is. Sorta.

Only she's just beaten Pyrite, Ascetic, and Ossuary at their own game. Ensured not only her own safety, but the safety of the Nightbirds and every Kashrini in the galaxy. She's... she's free. For the first time ever, she's honestly, completely *free*.

"Okay. Do you have a plan?"

"I don't know anywhere else to go. I don't know my way around the galaxy. The only time I've ever left the Pyrite homeworld was when PI was dragging me around and dumping me with Windshadow. I have no job, no home, no friends, not a single kydis to my name."

Rather like Rig had been when she fled Pyrite three years ago. Nothing but the clothes on her back.

"I'll help you figure something out," she offers. "If you want."

"Maybe."

Daara's hands are tight fists at her sides, her arms rigid lines, her furrowed brown bitter and angry. She nods – sort of. It might just be an involuntary twitch of her head. She turns sharply on her heel and marches in the opposite direction. Apparently, she has nothing further to say. But Rig... Rig is tired and fed up and has something *she* needs to say.

"Daara." Her sister stops in her tracks. Her throat goes dry. "I tried, you know. Three years ago. We weren't close and we both know it, but I tried to reach out to you, I tried to tell you. I tried and you... you didn't listen. I don't know if I can forgive you for that."

That's it. That's all she has to say.

If Daara listened or not, she can't say. Daara doesn't acknowledge any of it, silently leaving, her back permanently turned.

She lets her sister go.

CHAPTER TWENTY-SIX
From Ashes

"I don't see why you couldn't have done this somewhere else," Ginka remarks, trailing quietly after Rig as they walk.

Snow crunches beneath their feet as they continue steadily upwards.

"This seemed the right place to do it," she explains.

Her lungs begin to protest the thinness of the air up here. It's so beautiful that she barely notices the discomfort. Down below she can see the stark buildings of the Windshadow complex, the orderly geometric forms slowly being consumed by the organic whorls of snow and ice.

The sun set three hours ago, and she has been hiking for two of them. Despite the time, it's not dark. Above the peak of the mountain she's climbing is the largest of the Ossuary homeworld's moons, shining blue light down on her. A sky full of stars glows over her head, two smaller moons hanging in it, pretty pearls floating in the shimmering space. Between it all, ribbons of green and blue light dance through the sky in an ethereal aurora, a road leading them up the mountainside.

No wonder that Ginka wants to remain here. If it weren't a factioned world, Rig could really see the appeal.

Once Rig finally gets to the top of the mountain she has to sink to her knees in the cold snow and catch her breath. Air wisps through her lungs in thin, freezing gasps until she can force her body to get its shit together.

"Can I ask..." Ginka, annoyingly enough, seems completely unaffected by the climb. "I didn't mean to look, but... those tattoos on your legs."

Rig slowly gets her breathing under control. "Do... Do you know how many people you killed working for Ossuary?"

A casual shrug. "It's in my file somewhere, I suppose."

"Pyrite never told me. So I... I decided to mark down how many people I saved from Pyrite. Maybe one day the scales will be even, but either way, this way I ensure that I'll never forget."

"Hm. A bit arrogant, don't you think?"

She laughs, the cold snow scouring her lungs. "Yeah, maybe. You're not the first person to tell me that I've got a bit of pride to get rid of, but I think I'll keep this habit for now. Maybe one day I won't need it anymore."

"Will you add one for Daara?"

"No." She hasn't even really thought about it, but the answer is obvious. "She'd hate it."

"Ah. From what I've seen of her, probably."

"Yeah. Get the fire set up?" she requests.

Ginka sets down the pack that she's been carrying and places the stack of flammable wood chippings onto a somewhat flat rock that's quickly cleared of snow. The chippings aren't going to burn all that well, but they make for good containment. The real fuel is the three blocks of fire starter that Ginka drops into the quickly constructed circle.

A cold lighter is tucked into Rig's heavy jacket. Her metal hand is slow in retrieving it – she's still not totally used to the thing – and then struggles again when she flicks it open and ignites it.

Pale yellow flame wavers in the lighter's hold.

She tosses it onto the blocks of starter and the whole thing goes up in a *whoooooshhh* of bright orange fire.

The flames burn as high as her chest, turning blue in the center from the heat and licking at the snow outside their wooden confines. Such intense heat staves off the cold air in moments, warming Rig's fingers and toes. She can feel the warmth in her prosthetic hand as well, distantly, though, a vague sensation. Fuzzy, compared to the clarity she gets from her flesh-and-blood limbs.

She tugs off her glove and holds her metal hand out towards the fire, turning her wrist around in circles to watch the light catch on the semi-reflective surface.

"I'd like to say you'll get used to it," Ginka murmurs. "In truth, I've yet to completely adjust. It'll be easier for you, though. You only lost the one hand."

"Will I ever get to feel stuff properly with it again?"

A tiny smile crinkles Ginka's eyes. "Yes. It'll be different, but it'll still be there."

Hm. That's something at least. An airy lightness rests in her ribs, and she finds that she's looking forward to learning just what Ginka means by that.

Ginka gestures to the case in Rig's left hand. "Shall we?"

Rig places the case in the snow and cracks the lid open. Inside, nestled in protective fabric as though they're delicate as crystal, rests Panache and Pizzazz.

"Yeah," she says quietly. "It's time."

The guns are cold in her hands from the ice and snow and the night air. That'll change soon. Their fire is burning bright as a star on the mountaintop, flames rising and streams of odorless smoke curl upwards, floating around the two of them and kissing her skin before drifting off into the night air.

The guns are the last vestiges of the pride she'd had under Pyrite, the pride that she'd thought she'd abandoned, the pride that had tenaciously held on in some part of her heart all this time. Her guns. Her finest creations. The last thing to mark her as the One Kashrini Who Made It.

She doesn't need them anymore.

With solemn finality, Rig drops her guns into the fire.

* * *

Two ships sit on the landing pad, both dusted with a faint coating of powder-white snow. One is *Bluebird*. The other is a ship Rig hasn't seen in quite some time, beat up and held together with what she can only assume are bits of tape and string. A beautiful, well-travelled frigate.

She stands on its gangplank, her hand resting on one of the supporting beams that connect the plank to the ship's hull. She lovingly runs her fingers over the surface, tracing every scratch and dent.

Mohsin's trusty frigate.

The ship she named herself after.

And standing in the entry hatch is a young Kashrini woman, hurt and alone and lost and without a home to go back to. The mirror between her and her sister has never been sharper. In her memory she can taste the smell of ash on her tongue. All that's missing is the rain of the Pyrite homeworld pouring down upon her.

"I'll keep an eye on her," Mohsin promises. "Get her set up somewhere. Plenty of places to see in the galaxy."

"Places that aren't going to be trouble? Somewhere safe?"

"She'll be alright."

There's no doubt. Rig turned out alright, after all. In the end. She smiles at Daara. "He's a gruff bastard, but he's a good sort. Take care of each other."

"I'll... see you again," Daara says, still stiff and awkward, the anger fading into something less pronounced. Something a little more uncertain and almost a bit regretful. As though she hadn't truly thought that Rig would keep to her word and let her leave until this moment. No one under Pyrite would have kept their word to her, after all. "I will."

Rig holds out her hand because a hug seems too much and nothing seems too little. Hesitantly, almost nervously, Daara reaches out and shakes her hand.

"Goodbye," Daara says. She stares at where their hands are intertwined. "Perhaps one day I'll get to know Rig instead of Traxi."

"Maybe you'll like Rig better. I do."

Then she lets her sister go and watches as Daara and Mohsin disappear into the ship. She steps backward off the gangplank until her feet hit snow. Then that, too, is hauled up, secured into the ship's hull, the engines beginning to fire up as the frigate prepares to lift off.

She turns to the other two people standing on the landing platform.

Ginka and Crane. Standing together, as they always will be, and happy, as they always should be.

The smile on her lips widens and wobbles a little as she admits, "I'm really gonna miss you, Cactus. You too, Birdy."

"Birdy?" Crane frowns.

"Yeah, not my most inspired nickname, I'll grant you that. In my defense, the pain meds have really gotten to my creativity." She lightly punches him in the shoulder. "I'll do better next time we meet, promise."

He laughs and it sounds like snowfall. "Thank you."

"If there's anything I can do to help, give me a call. I'm not factioned, and I never will be, but you're my friends and that counts for something. And this isn't goodbye, even though I'm leaving – I'll be back to bug you both before you know it. The really hard part is getting rid of me, honestly."

To Rig's surprise, she finds herself being pulled into the tightest and most inelegant hug of her life. Ginka's metal fingers are cold against her back, and she can only return the hug from a sort of weird angle, and it's perfect.

"I'll miss you as well," Ginka murmurs.

She sinks into the embrace. "Thank you, Cactus. For everything."

Eventually though, she has to head back towards her ship, towards *Bluebird*, and towards the rest of the galaxy.

"See ya!" she says, one foot on the gangplank.

"Go home!" Ginka tosses back, laughing.

More than happy to, she thinks as she strides into her beloved ship.

EPILOGUE
A Beginning

The sun shines down on the Ascetic homeworld, warming the lazy breeze and making the polished stone walls around the Historical Center shimmer like silk. Elegantly armored guards have returned, standing around the borders of the Center, presumably grateful to be back now that the MPs are pretending to care about their libraries again. Librarians are some of the most resilient people in the galaxy, and, despite what's happened here, there's no doubt that the Historical Center will be back to its former glory within a week.

Rig idly strolls towards June's library.

She passes the guards at the front gates and keeps going. The guards will not stop her. No one will now. She wanders around the high walls for a good long while, passing side entrances that lead to smaller record departments in the Center or tiny research libraries.

Finally, she stops in front of a far back gate in front of the residential buildings.

She types a number into the control panel on the gate wall, waits for it to buzz with an affirmative and cheery tone, and then fidgets at the base of the stairs. It's not as though she's afraid. At this point, she's rather done with being afraid. She is waiting. Stuck in that gap between being very anxious and, with luck, being very happy. Anticipatory hopefulness, perhaps.

She knows what she wants to say. What she's yet to figure out is how best to say it.

When she shoves her hands in her pockets, she almost cuts her fingers on something sharp.

The shards of the statuette rest in her palm when she pulls the sharp things out. Little bits of crystal are all that remain of Dare and Shen, some in large chunks, some no more than dust.

Something red shines in the silvery crystal.

In its unbroken form, the statuette had Dare and Shen holding the jewel torch above their heads, their hands forming a ring. Their figures might be broken, but their hands remain. Sculpted glass forms a perfect ring, and atop it is the brilliantly cut firestone, shimmering and sparkling red under the sun.

She tosses the ring up. It spins in the air, flipping over and over until the shape of it blurs and all she can see is the stone, wavering until the red turns into fire.

The ring comes down.

The gates are open and June stands in front of her.

"Heya," Rig says. She's pretty sure her grin is the dopey-est thing in the galaxy. "I'm home."

"You're... You're safe." June teeters on the edge of the final stair, the final boundary of the Historical Center. The final line. "I knew, but it's not the same factually knowing it as it is to see it, and I... Is that a ring?"

"Only if you want it to be. I can't... I can't give you more safety than you'd have here," she admits. "I can't give you the comfort of a librarian's position. I can't give you riches, or a house, or stability. All I can give you is myself and a well-traveled spaceship. I can only hope that's enough."

June's eyes are wide and surprised and for one moment Rig thinks that it might not be enough, after all.

Then a beatific grin blossoms on June's lips. She steps forward. Her slippered feet cross that final line, and she lands outside the Historical Center, in Rig's arms, in the sunshine.

ACKNOWLEDGEMENTS

First and foremost I'd like to thank my long-suffering beta reader, Andrea. I'd also like to thank Jon, for Knowing Things About Science. This book never would have gotten written if they hadn't let me rant at them for at least, as Rig would say, five bajillion years. Thanks as well to my mother and step-father for all their support. Massive thanks goes to my fantastic agent, Lauren, who believed in me and this book since day zero. Similar gratitude goes out to my incredible editor Gemma and everyone at Angry Robot who helped get this book onto shelves.

I also must extend an apology to my university professors. Yes, I was writing in the middle of your classes. I promise I was paying attention to your lectures as well (mostly).

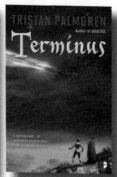
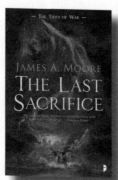
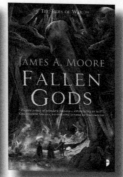
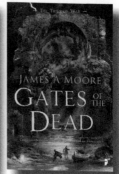

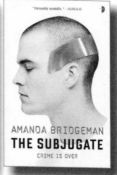

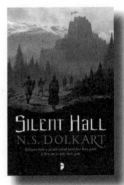

SILENT HALL
N. S. DOLKART

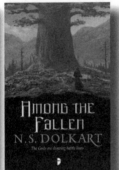

AMONG THE FALLEN
N. S. DOLKART

A BREACH IN THE HEAVENS
N. S. DOLKART

Science Fiction, Fantasy and WTF?!

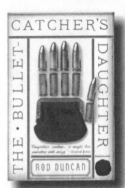

THE BULLET-CATCHER'S DAUGHTER
ROD DUNCAN

UNSEEMLY SCIENCE
ROD DUNCAN

THE CUSTODIAN OF MARVELS
ROD DUNCAN

@angryrobotbooks

PAIGE ORWIN
THE INTERMINABLES

MOONSHINE
JASMINE GOWER

AN OATH OF DOGS
WENDY N WAGNER

We are Angry Robot

angryrobotbooks.com

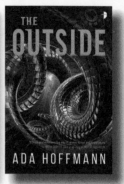

Science Fiction, Fantasy and WTF?!

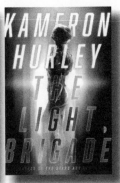

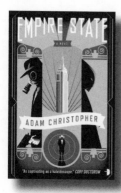

We are Angry Robot

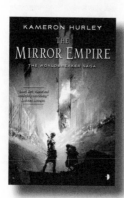

angryrobotbooks.com

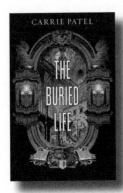

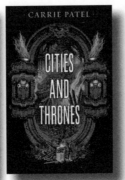

We are Angry Robot

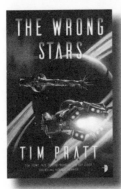

angryrobotbooks.com